A Gift of Love

In the wood and leather-accented library Tom opened the top drawer of the sleek modern desk and brought out a box from Van Cleef and Arpels. His eyes steady on hers, he opened it. A dazzling twelve-carat marquise-cut diamond ring reflected the light.

"Tom, it's—it's magnificent. You read my mind. You knew that tonight you'd have my answer. And you knew it would be yes."

"I've waited a long time for you, Diane." His hand crept onto her knee. "But it'll be worth it, I know it will."

He finished his champagne, took the still-half-filled glass from her and drew her to her feet. She felt unnaturally stiff, tense. He kissed her, gently at first and then with more passion, and walked with her into the dimly lit master bedroom. He drew her into his arms.

"I feel as though I were eighteen and making love for the first time," he said.

She let him undress her, enjoying the tenderness and care with which he removed each article of clothing.

Her arms closed tightly around his shoulders as he lifted her up and carried her over to the bed. At the first touch, she knew he would be a wonderful lover . . .

JULIE ELLIS

RICH IS BEST

ZEBRA BOOKS
KENSINGTON PUBLISHING CORP.

For Esther and Sam Meyers'
much-loved granddaughter, Kerry Meyers.

ACKNOWLEDGMENTS

I would like to express my deep thanks to the staffs of the various divisions of the New York Public Library, the New York Historical Society, the Museum of the City of New York, and the Museum of Broadcasting for their help in my research for the New York segments of this novel.

My thanks, also, to the Reno Chamber of Commerce, the Southampton Library, the Montauk Library, and the Montauk Historical Society for their assistance in research for the Reno, Southampton, and Montauk areas.

Also, special thanks to Claudia and Brad Dickinson—no relation to my heroine, Diane Dickenson!—of Claudia's Carriage Shop in Montauk for sharing their personal reminiscences of Montauk in the 1960s and 1970s.

And thanks, too, to my "personal word processor" —my daughter Susan, who may leave me to the mercies of the word processor now that she is a college graduate and embarking on a career.

Chapter One

The sky was overcast, filled with dark gray clouds which seemed to dampen the ardor of the brightest summer flowers blooming in the Champs de Mars. Today, few nursemaids sat with their charges on the benches lining the paths. Few middle-aged ladies sat reading or knitting.

A long black Cadillac limousine, an unusual sight on Paris streets in this postwar year of 1947, drew to a stop before an early twentieth-century house that had been built to eighteenth-century proportions. The liveried chauffeur—whose jacket concealed a holstered revolver, in keeping with his second role of bodyguard—left the wheel to open the rear door of the limousine and reached a hand toward eight-year-old Diane Dickenson, doll-like in her demure school uniform, her silken near-black hair falling to just above her waist.

Diane's father, born David Seligman, had been browbeaten by his mother-in-law into changing his name legally only months before Diane's birth.

Many years earlier, when Diane's grandmother moved with her husband from San Francisco to New York, she had prevailed upon her bridegroom to change their name from Cohen to Carstairs, in an effort not only to smooth the path for him in a business world where certain areas were closed to Jews, but also to free herself from the social limitations inherent in being a Jew in the early twentieth century. Being the only child of one of San Francisco's richest families had not bought her entry into the highest social circles; she was still a Jewish storekeeper's daughter.

After Diane's kidnapping four years ago—when, drugged on paregoric, she had slept through a shoot-out between captors and police—her mother, currently Princess Olivia Broninski, had taken her to live outside the United States despite the outrage of Mrs. Carstairs, her grandmother. However, at frequent intervals the Princess appeared in New York to attend the theater and ballet, in Palm Beach for the season, and during the summer for a month at Southampton. As soon as World War II was over, Olivia took up residence in Paris.

"It will rain before dinner," Philippe said to Mlle. Jeanne, Diane's governess. In accordance with Princess Broninski's demands, English was spoken in Diane's presence. "A bad storm," he added. "Perhaps by the time the princess leaves for the theater it will be over."

Before becoming Princess Broninski—marrying into a titled family that only a generation earlier had been active in the pogroms of Poland, Olivia had been the Countess de la Cointreau. Diane's father,

her first husband, had been resented by his mother-in-law, not only because he was Jewish but also because he was only mildly wealthy. When Diane was two—and the marriage already shaky—he died one sunny Sunday afternoon when his shiny new Mercedes slammed into a towering oak.

Philippe opened the heavy oak door that led into the elegant, burnished wood foyer. As he and Mademoiselle chatted about the impending storm, Diane's hand tightened on Mademoiselle's, her lustrous violet eyes fearful. Thunder and lightning terrified her. She didn't want to be left alone in her upstairs bedroom for two hours, having what Maman called her beauty sleep. It was a routine she'd always detested, interrupted only on Wednesdays, when Mademoiselle took her to the beauty salon for her facial.

"I'll be downstairs as soon as Diane is prepared for her nap," Mademoiselle told Philippe. Philippe nodded and slipped outside.

Rest time was a universally accepted ritual in the Carstairs household. Mademoiselle would take Diane to her room, help her into a nightgown, and see her into bed before leaving for her hours off, driven by Philippe; and the other servants would retire to their rooms at the top of the house for what Maman called their afternoon siesta.

Sometimes Diane sneaked out of bed to listen from the top of the stairs. Maman never entertained more than one friend at a time, and they were never ladies—always a young gentleman, always handsome . . . and always delighted or so it seemed, with whatever Maman had to say.

11

In a dainty white crêpe nightgown Diane settled herself beneath the light coverlet on her eighteenth-century canopied bed and waited for Mademoiselle to finish tidying up and leave. As soon as she heard the downstairs door close, she got out of the bed and walked over to the window, where she could watch people strolling by in the Champs de Mars. Diane heard the doorbell ring. Maman was going to the door to welcome her guest. Diane listened to the sounds at the door, comforted by the presence of Maman and her friend on the floor below.

Lightning was beginning to brighten the sky, thunder rumbling in the distance. Though the afternoon was warm, she felt a chill of fear. A crack of lightning sliced through the room and she jumped back from the window. She hesitated, trembling. What could she do? She'd never be able to sleep; she was afraid to stand at the window. But she couldn't very well disturb Maman and her guest. She hurried to the door and slipped out into the hall.

She sat down at the head of the stairs, drawing her knees up under her nightgown. Maman's voice, uncharacteristically shrill, floated up the stairs.

"What is the matter with you?" she was saying. "I want to talk to you about your career. Not some stupid girl you think you may want to marry!"

"I'm sorry." The young man's voice—not nearly so self-assured as some of the others. "I thought I ought to tell you."

There was a long pause, and Diane was suddenly aware of the stillness of the house.

"Jacques," Olivia said, "I want to help you, you know that. And you know I have the connections you need—I will be able to arrange for your poems to be published."

"I'm honored, princess."

Olivia laughed. "Nonsense. Every poet has someone to help him. Poetry is such a fragile art, and I'm convinced you have the feeling—"

"Princess, I'm afraid you must excuse me." Diane could not understand why he sounded so frightened. "I must leave."

The door opened and he emerged. Diane hung over the mahogany balustrade to get a look at this strange young man. He was younger than Mademoiselle's brother, another of Maman's regular visitors. Maman was thirty-seven, but she told everybody she was twenty-nine and had sworn Diane to secrecy.

"Jacques—" Olivia said imperiously, "if I can't arrange something with a publisher I will personally see to it that there is a private printing of your poems—"

"Princess—"

"Livvy, please. Only shopkeepers call me princess. Come, let's talk about the poems. You'll read to me."

Slowly, Jacques walked back into Maman's high-ceilinged, panelled sitting room.

"Why, Jacques, you sweet boy," Olivia bubbled, "I believe you're afraid of me."

"In awe, I'll admit. You're so beautiful, so generous—"

"Am I, Jacques?"

A sudden rumble of thunder seemed to shake the house. Diane clutched at the balustrade. *"Maman,"* she whispered, *"Maman, I'm scared."* She darted

13

down the long, wide, carpeted stairs and hurried along the corridor lined with old masters toward the sitting room. The door was still open. She froze.

There, lying across the petit-point sofa was Maman, her eyes closed, her newest Balenciaga frock lifted high above her hips, exposing her black, lace-trimmed garter belt. The handsome young poet lay on top of her, moving slowly up and down. Shocked, Diane stood absolutely still.

"Hurry, Jacques," Livvy said. "More!"

At last Olivia let out a long, high wail. Diane turned and ran back up the stairs to her room. She closed the door and slid into bed, her heart pounding. She pulled the coverlet over her head and tried to erase the ugly image from her mind. Forever.

Two years later, Olivia divorced the prince. Diane gathered, from the servants' whispering, that the divorce had cost her mother one million American dollars. But within six months Olivia was a bride again, dressed in an exquisite white suit, standing beside the Marquis Charles de la Frontaine in a Paris civil ceremony that was followed by a huge cocktail party at Maxim's. Diane was paraded through the glittering knots of people as "my darling little girl," carefully coached to call this stranger the marquis "Uncle Charles."

It was at the party that Diane heard that her mother and Uncle Charles were taking her with them to New York. Apparently, it was the marquis' idea, and Diane wasn't quite sure how she felt about it; on the one hand, the thought of New York—everyone in Paris talked about nothing else—was exciting. But she was nervous about the prospect of returning to this huge city she couldn't even remember. Aunt Claudia—Maman's sister—had visited them from New York every year, and once Grandmother Carstairs had come over. But to Diane it was only a hazy memory. As for Diane's grandmother on her father's side, Diane had never even met her; the families didn't speak.

In New York they were met at the pier by a silver Mercedes limousine and taken to the Carstairs mansion on Fifth Avenue. Her grandmother had just returned from the Newport house. Diane tried to remember she was ten years old when she was ushered into her grandmother's presence; too big to hang on to Maman's hand. She felt like a tiny girl when she stood before the austerely thin, stern-faced old lady in black.

"Diane—" Mrs. Carstairs said. "Come kiss your grandmother."

Slowly, her heart thumping, Diane approached the old lady. So this was Grandmère.

"I hope you're well, Grandmère." The words came out in a whisper.

"Call me grandmother," Mrs. Carstairs snapped. "Thank God, you're home. It's time someone remembered you're an American."

"Mother," Olivia said, "Diane knows she's an American."

"I plan to help her understand what that means. I've done a great deal of thinking while you've

15

been . . . abroad . . . my dear, and I've decided that when Diane is eighteen, she'll inherit the Carstairs estate."

For a moment the room was absolutely still, the only sound the ticking of the grandfather clock. "So," Mrs. Carstairs continued, "Diane will inherit your grandfather's money. I'll keep for myself only my inheritance from my mother's estate. I'm sure it will suffice for my last years. Mr. Lewisohn will handle Diane's inheritance."

"Mother, don't you think it's a bit premature to be talking about an inheritance?" Diane saw the pulse hammering at her mother's left temple.

"Like Claudia, you have your share of your father's estate," Mrs. Carstairs said, clearly relishing every minute of her daughter's shock. "The bulk of the estate, of course, was left to me. I've decided to pass it on to Diane. That's my right. I'll leave some jewelry to you and Claudia."

Shakily, Olivia rose to her feet.

"If you'll excuse me, mother, I'd like to lie down for a while before dinner. The crossing was rough."

"I'm sure." Mrs. Carstairs smiled. "By the way, Claudia will be joining us for dinner. I'm sure you two will have so much to talk about."

Diane watched these two women. What *was* grandmother talking about? Maman and Aunt Claudia—who was twenty-two years older—almost never talked. When they did, they always ended up yelling at each other.

"I assume your current husband will be joining us then?" Grandmother asked.

Livvy's face tightened.

"There's been a problem with our luggage and he stayed behind at the pier. He'll be here shortly."

Shortly after they arrived, Mrs. Carstairs sat down with Diane and told her that she had been enrolled at Miss King's, the exclusive private school Olivia had attended. But Olivia intercepted; Diane would be tutored at home.

One month later, as she struggled with her multiplication tables under Mr. Temple's scrutiny, they were interrupted by the sounds of screams from upstairs. In an instant Diane was out of her seat, running up the stairs toward Grandmother Carstairs' bedroom. Standing in the doorway, ashen, was her grandmother's maid, breakfast tray in hand. And there, lying unconscious on the floor next to the bed, was Mrs. Carstairs. Two days later, she was dead.

It was Mlle. Jeanne who told Diane about her grandmother's death. Her lessons were to be suspended for a week, and she went off with Mademoiselle to Saks to shop for suitable funeral clothes. Diane felt numb as she moved through the next few days. Death was a stranger to her; their only meeting had been when her kitten Buffy had died; all of a sudden he had hunched his back, some liquid had spilled from his nostrils, and he had fallen over.

Then she had cried. Would she cry when she saw her grandmother?

It seemed impossible that this powerful, unyielding woman had been conquered by anything. Every night for the last month she and her grandmother had sat down to dinner together in the huge dining room while Maman and Uncle Charles passed their evenings at the Stork Club, El Morocco, or "21." Sometimes Aunt Claudia, who lived two blocks away, would stop by for dessert.

They were never comfortable evenings. As Diane watched her grandmother push her food around her plate, it occurred to her that she didn't even know this strange, gaunt woman. They had very little to say to each other. Grandmother asked her about her lessons; then she talked about how different the world had been when *she* was a girl. Sometimes it seemed as though grandmother didn't even know she was sitting at the table.

Diane wasn't sure, but she didn't think all grandmothers were like that. Once, back in Paris, she had been allowed to go to her friend Nanette's house for dinner, and *her* grandmother had been small and fat and jolly. She had hugged and kissed Nanette. And when she left, Diane recalled with a small surge of pleasure, Nanette's grandmother kissed her, called her *pauvre petite*, and stuffed her coat pockets with homemade candies.

Late in the afternoon of her grandmother's death Diane sat with her mother and aunt in the large, square, bow-windowed library and tried to concentrate on the old masters that hung on the walls while Mr. Lewisohn, the family attorney, explained Mrs. Carstairs's orders for the funeral. Diane was bewildered by her mother's apparent fury as Mr.

Lewisohn spoke.

"It's impossible to arrange for my mother to be buried tomorrow afternoon!" Olivia turned to Claudia for support.

"But I'm afraid a swift burial is required by the Jewish religion."

Mr. Lewisohn looked just as unhappy about all of this as Maman, Diane thought. *But what did the Jewish religion have to do with her grandmother?* She had never even known anybody who was Jewish—most of the girls in her class in Paris were Catholic. Not that she herself had been to church much, only at Christmas and Easter with Mlle. Jeanne—to Notre Dame in Paris and Saint Patrick's in New York.

"My mother was an Episcopalian for overy sixty years." Olivia's sharp voice snapped Diane back to attention. "This is outrageous."

"She wished to be buried as an Orthodox Jew," Mr. Lewisohn repeated slowly. "I'll handle the arrangements. The services at the funeral chapel will be private. Only the family will be at the graveside." He hesitated. "Plus the required *minyan* men." Diane looked at her mother. *What were* minyan *men?* Why did they have to be at grandmother's funeral? "Mrs. Carstairs requested that she be buried in the faith in which she was born. We can do no less than obey her last wishes." Diane noticed the gentle reproof in his voice. Apparently, it was lost on Olivia.

"You're wrong. I know her! She did this to embarrass us!"

"Olivia, stop it." Claudia, pale but composed,

19

spoke from the corner of the room. "Mother will be buried as she wished. Your society friends won't be there. The obituary in the *Times* will simply say that the funeral is private."

Soon everyone left. First Mr. Lewisohn, quiet and somber. Then Claudia, who lingered a few minutes before returning to her apartment. Olivia went upstairs, calling down that she had to find something to wear for the funeral. Diane found herself sitting alone in the Queen Anne chair in the library.

She was utterly confused. How could Grandmother have been Jewish and never told anyone? Did that mean that *she* was Jewish, too? In school they had talked about World War II and Hitler and the concentration camps. If her grandmother had lived in Germany then, that meant she would have been thrown into one of those awful camps—even if she had turned Episcopalian.

Suddenly Diane wanted to feel closer to this mysterious person, this austere woman who had seemed so forbidding in life. She ran up the stairs toward the huge, square, high-ceilinged Empire bedroom with its walls hung in gray silk and the tall narrow windows draped in blue damask, and pausing in the doorway for one guilty moment, stepped inside closing the door behind her. Her heart pounded at her daring—what if someone discovered her? She didn't even really know why she was here.

Glancing around the room, she heard her grandmother's voice, their last dinner together.

"Everybody of importance in this nation," she had said with pride, "has been a guest in this house. President McKinley, Theodore Roosevelt, even that second Roosevelt to sit in the White House. Justices who sat on the Supreme Court, bankers and financiers who directed the course of this country. Your grandfather was a brilliant and powerful man, Diane; everybody respected him. Don't you ever forget that."

After pressing her ear up against the door to make sure no one was coming, Diane tiptoed across the bedroom toward her grandmother's study—in the room into which only Dora, Grandmother Carstairs's personal maid for over forty years, had ever entered. Holding her breath, she creaked the door open.

Burgundy velvet drapes closed the room off from the view of Central Park, shutting out the early May sunlight. A pair of Louis XV chairs, their frames delicately carved and gilded and upholstered in Beauvais tapestries, faced each other in front of a small marble-faced fireplace. The *parquet de Versailles* floor's brilliant polish was highlighted by a pair of small Chinese rugs. An oriental cabinet lacquered in black and decorated in gold stood before a writing table adorned with finely chiseled ormolu mounts.

Diane walked over to the Coromandel screen that stood like a majestic barricade before a corner of the room. Curious and yet afraid—as though her grandmother would leap from behind the wall— Diane walked through the narrow space.

Instantly and instinctively Diane realized that this was where her grandmother had left her heart. A mahogany kneehole desk, faded and chipped, stood alone in the space, in sharp contrast to the luxurious elegance of the rest of the bedroom. The wall above the desk was covered with fading daguerreotypes, carefully printed names beneath each. *"Mama."* *"Papa." "Uncle Max." "Uncle Louis." "Aunt Sophie."* Cousins of varying ages.

Diane tried to remember something—anything—about her grandmother. She had been an only child, as had Diane's grandfather.

It was strange, Diane thought. Grandmother had been a widow for over thirty years—Maman had been a little girl when her father died. Now as she sat at the desk, in this oddly beautiful little tomb, Diane felt close to her grandmother.

A parade of silver-framed photographs of herself, her mother, and Aunt Claudia stood in one corner on the desk. Diane noticed that there were no photographs of any of the men Maman had married—her grandmother had disapproved of all of them.

Diane had never seen a photograph of her father—all she had been told was that he was killed in a car accident when she was two. She knew nothing about his family.

She looked at the center desk drawer. What secret life lay inside? She hesitated, then quickly opened it. There, lying in a neatly folded square, was a yellowed, tasseled silk scarf, a square inch of linen notepaper pinned to it with what Grandmother had called a beauty pin: *"Ben's* tallis, *which he wore at our wedding."*

Her grandfather's name had been Bertram. Ben must have been a kind of nickname. What was a *tallis?* Diane wondered. It had to be something special, whatever it was, for grandmother to keep it all these years.

Beside the *tallis* lay an ornate ivory-covered book. Diane opened it. The writing was in a language she didn't understand. Even the lettering was unfamiliar —maybe German. Grandmother Carstair's parents had come to America from Germany before she was born; they had lived in San Francisco during the famous Gold Rush. According to Grandmother, that was when they became rich—from her great-grandfather's store.

Inside the ivory-covered book was a dried rose and a scrap of faded pink stationery. *"The prayer book and the rose I carried when I married Ben. June, 1886."*

Fascinated, Diane slowly opened each of the other drawers. Time stood still as she read birth and wedding announcements, death certificates, all dated before she had been born—probably, Diane decided, around the time grandmother had lost touch with her family.

She started at the sound of footsteps in the hall. What would she do if someone found her here? She hesitated a moment, then reached into the center drawer again for the *tallis* and the ivory prayer book. Why not? Maman would only throw them away . . .

The following afternoon Diane sat between her mother and aunt in the limousine that took them to the funeral chapel. After the brief ceremony, they were driven to the cemetery in Westchester County. The sunshine had given way to a winter-gray, and the fresh greenery of the trees lining the highway was the bleak journey's only highlight. In a limousine behind them rode Mr. Lewisohn and his associates from the law firm.

Olivia broke the silence. "That awful pine casket. You'd think we were poor—it's embarrassing."

Claudia turned, her eyes red from crying. "Olivia, you know it's part of the Orthodox requirements."

"I don't care, I don't think mother should have put us through this."

"Shut up, Olivia," Claudia whispered.

Diane squirmed. Why were Maman and Aunt Claudia always at each other so? It all seemed unimportant; *she* was still trying to accept the fact that she would never see grandmother again, and, even more confusing, this business about grandmother being Jewish. Why did having an Orthodox service upset Maman? It wasn't a disgrace to be Jewish; Mr. Lewisohn was Jewish. And now a part of *her* was Jewish, too. Strange . . .

She looked at the back of Philippe's head.

The servants had made no effort to hide their hurt that they had not been asked to attend the funeral. Only Dora had been allowed to come with them to the chapel, in response to grandmother's request.

At last they arrived at the cemetery.

Diane was glad when Aunt Claudia reached for her hand as they walked to the freshly dug grave. The ten men, all strangers whose presence had been arranged by Mr. Lewisohn, gathered around the grave. Cautiously Diane looked around. Now Maman was crying, too. Should *she* cry? She tried, but the tears refused to come. She was more interested in what the rabbi was saying, especially when he fastened small squares of cloth to the dresses of Maman, Aunt Claudia, and herself. What a fascinating ritual! But she didn't dare ask questions; she stood small and silent, her hand in her aunt's.

And the rabbi said, "May God console you together with all those who mourn for Zion and Jerusalem."

For over two hours, Mr. Lewisohn had been closeted in the library of the Carstairs' house with his late client's two daughters and granddaughter. Now he was gone. Olivia lay sprawled on the Louis XVI sofa in a black crêpe dress, her vermilion lips pressed together in rage as she ran red-nailed fingers through her long dark hair.

Eyes red-rimmed, graying hair worn in a nondescript bun, Claudia sat in striking contrast in an Aubusson tapestry upholstered chair, her back schoolgirl-stiff, as though she suspected Grandmother Carstairs to be watching from another world.

Olivia's voice broke the silence.

"I tell you, Claudia, this is outrageous! Mother must have been senile when she drew up her will!" Mother never forgave her for marrying four times, Livvy told herself. She'd never wanted a second child; she'd been embarrassed at being pregnant again at forty-three. But she might have forgiven a son. "Mother had to be out of her mind to leave everything to Diane."

"Except what was left from her mother's estate," said Claudia, always the fair one. "We'll share that."

"Right," Olivia snapped. "A piddling few

25

hundred thousand each. After taxes what'll we see?"

Claudia sighed. "Olivia, I hope you're not considering trying to break the will. We simply can't. How would it look?"

"Like we're greedy bitches." Claudia flinched at the crudity. "Well, I don't give a damn what people think. It's simply not fair."

"Livvy, you heard Mr. Lewisohn—the will *can't* be successfully contested."

"Well, maybe you don't care." Livvy pulled herself upright. "But I counted on that inheritance. Charles is insanely extravagant."

"Why don't you try restraining him?" Claudia said gently.

Olivia pouted.

"When I try, he goes into a rage. And I can't divorce him—he'd demand a fortune."

"Put him on an allowance."

"He married me knowing mother was eighty-one. He knew she was frail." Suddenly, Olivia looked vulnerable. Scared. "He thought you and I would share the estate. Seventy million, wisely invested. Claudia, I'll die if he leaves me—"

Claudia gazed at her sister, bewildered.

"But you just talked about divorce."

"*I don't want a divorce.*" Olivia's voice was shrill. "Charles has a wonderful old title. He has entrée into the finest families in Europe. I like being the Marquise de la Frontaine."

Claudia spoke firmly.

"Olivia, Charles won't leave you. He's nearly sixty, and people aren't that impressed anymore by titles."

"But his title is real." Olivia had always been especially sensitive to the rumors that her third husband had been a self-styled prince. "Besides, he has style. And he's a marvelous lover." Not true. He was too jaded. But she enjoyed embarrassing Claudia, whom she couldn't imagine with *any* man.

"I'm afraid, Livvy, you have no choice. You will control Diane's estate until she's eighteen. Mr. Lewisohn understands Diane is to be raised in the style you've always enjoyed. You'll be able to live well."

"But at eighteen—in ten years—Diane takes over her inheritance." Olivia stood up. "I'm going to bed. This has been a bitch of a day."

Chapter Two

For a moment, Diane lingered in front of the mirror in her leotard and tights. She cherished these two afternoons a week at her dance class, where she could talk to eleven other little girls of her own age, away from the surveillance of her family.

"Remember, you're coming to my birthday party next Saturday afternoon," Millicent Butler said, preening before the mirror. Millicent, not one of Diane's favorites, loved to boast about how all her clothes were custom-made in Paris. "You'll receive an invitation."

"Thank you, Millicent," Diane said politely, wondering if Maman would let her go. She never felt comfortable with the American children.

The atmosphere in the dressing room crackled with tension. Diane wasn't sure, but she suspected it concerned pretty Irene Levy, who was already dressed and apparently in a rush to leave. Irene looked angry and unhappy.

As soon as Irene left the dressing room, Millicent giggled.

"Millicent, why didn't you invite Irene to your birthday party?" Debra Williams asked. "You invited everybody else in the class."

Millicent smiled.

"My mother never invites Jews into her house. She was even mad when she found out Irene was in our class!"

Stunned, Diane instantly forgot her pleasure at being invited to Millicent's party. Her grandmother and grandfather had been Jewish. And, even though mother talked about being Episcopalian and Aunt Claudia always wore that big gold cross, mother and Aunt Claudia were Jewish. *She* was Jewish. So this was why her grandmother had pretended not to be— because of people like Millicent's mother. It wasn't just in Germany that people hated Jews. Slowly, quietly, she dressed in her sky blue cashmere sweater and matching skirt.

Miss Jeanne was outside, waiting to walk her to the Mercedes. The other little girls, too, disappeared into chauffeured cars. On the way home Diane replied respectfully to Miss Jeanne's usual questions about dance class, but she couldn't forget Millicent's words: *"My mother never invites Jews into her house."*

Again she thought about her grandmother's Orthodox Jewish funeral. She was glad she had kept the yellowed ivory prayer book and the silk *tallis*, now hidden in her closet. A week after the funeral, she had sneaked into her grandmother's room again, only to find that everything had disappeared, including the daguerreotypes on the wall behind the Coromandel screen. It was funny, really—she hadn't cried at her grandmother's funeral, but she had cried when she saw the daguerreotypes were gone. Somehow that made grandmother's death all the more final.

The limousine turned down Fifth Avenue. On this wintry afternoon the park, Miss Jeanne said in her usual sentimental fashion, looked like a Currier and Ives Christmas card. Whenever Miss Jeanne had that look in her eyes, Diane knew she was homesick for Paris, and suddenly Diane too wished that she was back in Paris, with classmates like Nanette. In Paris, life somehow had seemed easier, or at least not so terrifying. She felt an overwhelming wave of homesickness.

The car pulled up in front of the house. As they walked into the foyer, Diane heard Aunt Claudia, her voice uncharacteristically shrill, and then her mother's voice in response. In the ten months she had been in New York she had grown especially close to her aunt, who had often taken her side in family arguments; most recently, it had been Claudia who insisted that Diane be allowed to attend a dancing class two afternoons a week rather than have a private dancing master. *"For heaven's sake, Livvy, let the poor child have some companionship with children her own age. It's unnatural to isolate her the way you do."*

Diane's instinct was to run down the hall to her mother's sitting room to greet her aunt, but Miss Jeanne laid a restraining hand on her arm. "Mademoiselle," like "Maman," had been replaced by the English equivalent.

"Later, Diane," Miss Jeanne said in the now-familiar tone signifying that whatever was being

31

discussed was not for her ears. "Go upstairs and start your homework for tomorrow."

Diane went upstairs while Miss Jeanne went to the kitchen to confer with the cook. Even in her room, with the door shut, Diane could hear the angry voices downstairs. She tiptoed to the door, cracking it open an inch.

Claudia was shouting.

"Olivia, you are behaving disgracefully. Sometimes I'm amazed Charles doesn't sue you for divorce. I mean, my God! The constant snide items in Winchell's column . . . the lurid stories in the *News* and *Mirror* . . . always about you and some stupid man young enough to be your son! It's humiliating!"

Then Olivia spoke. Quietly.

"You're exaggerating, Claudia. But then, at your age your mind can't be expected to be sharp."

There was a moment's pause. Diane held her breath. Then Aunt Claudia's voice, ice-cold.

"There is nothing wrong with my mind. But if you don't stop this disgusting behavior, I might have to ask the court to give me custody of Diane. In the state you're in now, you're not a fit mother."

Her ear pressed against the door, Diane went cold with fear.

"How dare you talk to me like that!" Olivia said. "What do you know about raising a child? You're a dried-up old maid! You only want Diane so you can get to her money. Well, I won't let it happen, Claudia. No matter what."

Claudia sounded drained.

"Behave yourself and there'll be no need. But

Diane's my flesh and blood, and I won't allow her to be raised in this environment. It's not safe."

"Get out!" Olivia screamed. "Get out of this house and don't ever come back!"

That night Mr. Lewisohn's black Mercedes pulled up to the house. Diane stood outside the closed library door, straining to hear what was going on inside.

"Olivia, if you wish to avoid an ugly court battle, I suggest you reconcile with Claudia. Please, for your mother's memory. You don't want a repetition of the Vanderbilt custody case, do you?"

"Claudia won't go to court," Olivia said. "She could never bring herself to face that kind of notoriety. My sister is an overwrought old maid. She makes a lot of noise, but she'd never expose the family to scandal." But Diane knew her mother was nervous.

For weeks Diane had worried that her mother and aunt would go to court over her custody. The thought of again being uprooted just when she was growing accustomed to the house on Fifth Avenue had been very upsetting. Then her mother had announced that she would open up the Newport house for the season.

"I don't care what Mr. Lewisohn says about it being a white elephant," she'd told the marquis. "I have such marvelous memories of that house. We'll close up one wing. Mr. Lewisohn can't complain I'm spending too much money on the staff if I hire just a pair of gardeners and another maid for the season."

"Where will you find help?" Charles scoffed. "They're all off working in factories for more money than they ever saw in their lives."

"It's only for eight weeks. If I offer enough, I'll find help."

Charles's smile was condescending.

"Sell that marble railroad station. Those Newport houses are so pretentious they're gauche."

"It can't be sold until Diane's twenty-fifth birthday. Besides, the money would only go into the trust. So let's enjoy the house."

In early July Diane, Olivia, and the marquis went to the Newport house. As they drove up Bellevue Avenue, past the endless parade of marble mansions, Diane decided that she would hate living here.

"There's Marble House," Livvy said. "The Vanderbilts' house. It's modeled on the Grand Trianon at Versailles."

"Louis XIV didn't surround Versailles with prison walls."

The marquis's voice was sharp as he commented on the colonnaded white marble mansions.

"Charles, you have no respect for anything American," Livvy said in exasperation.

"My dear, you are so right," he mocked.

"Only the American dollar," Livvy shot back. "That suits your fancy."

A few minutes later the Mercedes turned into a wide marble ramp and pulled to a stop before a sweep of broad steps leading up to a white marble palace surrounded by flowering blue hydrangea. An ornate American Renaissance mansion, Carstairs Hideaway had won the respect of the other "cottage owners."

Diane hated it.

"My mother hired Richard Morris Hunt to build the cottage," Livvy said to the marquis with pride. "Did you know that he was the architect for the Astors, the Vanderbilts, and the Belmonts?"

"Well, it does have the air of the nouveau riche, my dear."

Livvy ignored the sarcasm. "I grew up adoring Cliff Walk. It has one of the most spectacular views in the world!"

Below the cliffs on which Newport cottages sat was the magnificent Atlantic. In Southampton Diane had loved the ocean. But here she was frightened by the rocky, winding coastline and the wild, pounding surf, and she didn't think she would ever dare stroll along Cliff Walk.

With the politeness ingrained in her by Miss Jeanne, Diane walked along in silence between her mother and her current stepfather.

At last they arrived back at the house, and were met at the door by Josephus, their butler from New York. As they stepped into the foyer, Diane decided this house was like one of those castles near Paris that her class had visited last year. The entrance hall was two stories high, the ceiling a blue and gold painting encircled by sculptured nymphs. The chandelier was a delicate mass of ornate crystal. Diane envisioned it collapsing on her head, like in that play she heard on Lux Radio Theater. She gazed up the circling marble staircase, its balustrade dripping gold, and imagined a beautiful princess in a court train descending to receive her guests. Or maybe Rowena in *Ivanhoe*.

The "cottage" contained twenty-four bedrooms, many of which had been closed off because they weren't needed with the relatively small staff. The formal dining room could seat a hundred. The ballroom could accommodate four hundred. Diane felt overwhelmed by the size of the room.

Diane sighed in relief at the sight of Miss Jeanne hurrying down the wide marble, tapestry-hung corridor. Nothing terrible could happen when Miss Jeanne was nearby.

Several times a week Olivia entertained hordes of people who drove up from New York. It seemed to Diane that all they did was laugh and drink. But most of the time she was allowed to go to her friend Laura Devlin's house to play. Laura was the daughter of a local laundress. Miss Jeanne did not accompany her on these occasions. Instead, Philippe drove her, staying nearby throughout the afternoon. But being with Laura was a wonderful change for Diane. At last she had a friend, another life outside the house.

"Why can't you come here every day?" Laura asked one late July afternoon as they sat outside her modest frame house at the edge of town.

"Next week mother's going to Bar Harbor, and I know Miss Jeanne will let me come over every day then." She loved playing with Laura. With her thick reddish curls and green eyes, she was so pretty and had dozens of tall tales to tell. "I thought I was going to hate it up here until mother said she'd talked to your mother and that I could come over to play sometimes." She didn't repeat her mother's comment that it wouldn't do for Diane to become too close to the daughter of a domestic—which explained why she hadn't been able to come over every day.

"You wear such pretty clothes, Diane." Laura paused. "Mom says you're very rich." There was curiosity but no envy in her voice.

"I wish I wasn't," Diane confessed. "Then I could go to school like other kids."

Laura stared.

"You don't go to school?"

"I'm tutored." All at once Diane was self-conscious. "That was because I was kidnapped when I was four."

"Diane, you weren't!"

"It was in all the newspapers in New York."

Laura looked absolutely thrilled.

"Tell me about it. Tell me *everything*."

That afternoon, Diane and Laura decided they would be best friends forever. When Diane returned to New York, she would write to Laura. It was Diane's first real friendship and she was delighted. If only the summer could go on forever.

On a sultry late August night, as Diane played with her chocolate mousse at the dinner table, she couldn't help noticing that her mother seemed irritated. Usually she was able to blot out most of the seemingly interminable meal by imagining herself as Diane Barbour. She really belonged to "One Man's Family." She had a mother and a father who sat down to breakfast with her every day, and *never* went out in the evenings—well, maybe once in a while.

"Diane, we're going back to New York on Monday," her mother said. "It's still dreadfully hot in town, but the Southampton house is rented this summer."

"Why can't we stay here?" That meant she wouldn't see Laura anymore. "Why do we have to go back to New York?"

"Because I say so," Livvy snapped. With a grunt the marquis rose to his feet and left the room. Livvy's eyes followed him. So, Diane thought, Uncle Charles must have been extravagant again; mother and he were always fighting about how much money he spent.

She pushed her mousse away.

"I don't want any more."

Livvy pushed back her chair. "I have to run. I'll be late for the Allens's musicale."

Diane sat alone at the table, trying to imagine what her life would be like without her friend Laura. It wasn't until Josephus began clearing the table that she finally stood up. Slowly she walked upstairs to her room, and turned on the radio to listen to "The Green Hornet." Miss Jeanne was always scolding her for listening to the radio so much, though she didn't come right out and forbid it. Anyway, there wasn't much else to do in Newport—especially if she wasn't playing with Laura. Mother had said two of the girls from her ballet class were up here for the summer, but she had never even talked to them in class.

It wasn't until "The Green Hornet" was over and she had turned to Fred Allen that Diane became aware that a summer storm was brewing. She hurried around the room, closing the drapes at each of the six windows.

She tried to concentrate on Fred Allen, but the

tumult outside distracted her. One crash of thunder followed another. Lightning shot through the drapes into the room.

This was the first real storm all summer. If Miss Jeanne were home, she could find an excuse to go to her room. But Miss Jeanne had gone out for the evening with a friend who was up from New York for a week's vacation, and the servants had retired for the night to their quarters.

At ten o'clock she was curled up in bed, listening to the waves crashing on the shore beneath the cliffs. It was eerie. Menacing. Her heart thumping, she pulled the blanket over her head.

Diane flinched as she heard a tree split by lightning crash to the ground outside. When she pulled the blanket away the room was totally in darkness. She looked for the narrow ray of light visible from beneath her door. Then, with a burst of thunder, the lights in the hall flickered.

She threw the blanket aside and slid her feet to the floor, her eyes fixed on the light beneath the door. Then a fresh barrage of thunder rocked the house.

She ran into the lighted hallway, breathing fast. For a moment she hesitated, not sure what to do next. Her thoughts flashed back to another storm—in Paris. *Mother and that young man on the sofa.* But Mother wasn't home—she'd gone to the Allens's musicale. It was all right to go downstairs. Now she heard a trickle of music. Somebody was in the library. Diane sighed in relief. Miss Jeanne had come home.

She hurried down the wide curving staircase. The music in the library seemed to fit the mood of the storm. Diane recognized it as one of the Wagnerian

operas she'd listened to during her music lessons.
Not Miss Jeanne's kind of music at all—she preferred
Cole Porter and Jerome Kern.

Diane paused at the entrance to the library. Uncle
Charles was sprawled on the green velvet Louis XV
chaise. Beside him, on a marble-topped marquetry
table, sat a cut-glass decanter, half filled with an
amber liquid. A goblet stood nearby.

"Uncle Charles, may I stay down here with you?"

He started, frowned, and for a moment Diane was
sure he would say no. Then his dark eyes softened.

"Come here, Diane. Does the storm frighten you?"

She walked toward him slowly. "Yes. I was scared
the lights were going out."

"You came down without a robe." It was a gentle
rebuke. "The nights are cool here. Come, sit beside
me. I'll warm you."

Diane slid beside him, grateful for the warmth of
his arm around her shoulders. Already the storm
seemed further away.

"Poor baby. You were really frightened." He
kissed her cheek.

"I thought there was nobody in the house except
me."

He laughed.

"Dear one, there are a houseful of servants."

"But they're so far away."

"I won't let the storm harm you." He put his hand
around her waist. "You're my little girl, and you're
safe." With the other hand he tilted her face to his.
His eyes seemed strangely agitated. "Beautiful little
girl."

He kissed her on the lips, holding her mouth

against his. His breath smelled of whiskey. His hand moved to the slight outline of a nipple protruding beneath the delicate silk of her nightgown.

Bewildered, her heart pounding, she pulled away.

"Don't you like me to kiss you?"

"I—I think I'll go back to my room." Somehow she knew this wasn't right.

"Not yet." He pinned her down. "Open your mouth."

She started to speak, but he pressed his lips against hers again, this time opening his mouth and pushing his tongue inside. His hand reached for hers and brought it to his pants, where she felt a hard lump. As he groped between her thighs, anger surged through her. She remembered the scene in Paris . . .

"No! No!" But the words were trapped in her throat by the coarse, darting tongue that threatened to choke her. His cold fingers probed her body. Fear immobilized her. The humiliation sickened her.

At last he stopped kissing her. He sought to free himself for further exploration.

"Please let me go." She tried to pull her nightgown down. "Please, Uncle Charles, let me go."

"Shut up!" His voice was rough. "If you make any noise, I'll break that beautiful little neck."

She was his prisoner. Even if she tried to scream, none of the servants would hear her. Where was Miss Jeanne?

She kept telling herself this wasn't happening. *It couldn't be.*

"Let me in, you gorgeous little bitch," he whispered. "Let me in!"

"You're hurting me," she whimpered. But then

41

the hardness that threatened to invade her went limp.

"Damn." He stood up. "Damn."

A bit unsteadily, he walked to the bar, forgetting the decanter on the table beside the chaise. The minute his back was turned, Diane darted for the door. She hurried down the long hallway to the foyer, pausing to glance over her shoulder for one instant, then tugged at the heavy front door and stepped out into the ominous darkness of the night.

It was raining. She hadn't the slightest idea where to go, but she knew she would not return to that house. Not ever again. Her cheeks burned as she thought of Uncle Charles's sloppy embrace: the warm, smelly breath in her ear, the old hands, fumbling, hurting her . . .

She hated him. She hated all of them. Somehow she would leave this house. Suddenly the glare of headlights hit her. A car. It was stopping in front of her. Someone emerged.

"Diane—" Miss Jeanne. "What are you doing out in this rain in your nightgown? Come inside—"

"No!" Diane sobbed. "I won't go back there. Not ever. Not ever." She was trembling as Miss Jeanne gathered her into her arms. "Let's go back to New York. I can't stay here."

"We'll go into the car," Miss Jeanne soothed. "Come along, darling."

In the warm, dry comfort of the car Miss Jeanne rocked Diane in her arms until she was quiet.

"Now I want you to tell me what happened."

"I can't. I can't talk about it ever."

"But darling, I have to know, if you want me to help you."

Diane hesitated. *How could she even say the words?*

"It's—Uncle Charles," she gasped. "He—he touched me. He tried to—" She buried her face against Miss Jeanne's breast.

"Oh, my God—"

There was a long pause, as Miss Jeanne stroked Diane's hair. When she spoke, her voice was icy.

"No, my sweet, you won't go back into that house. We'll spend the night in town."

Through the downpour they drove to the modest rooming house where Miss Jeanne's friend Iris was staying. Diane's face remained buried against Miss Jeanne's shoulder. But she didn't sleep. She couldn't.

At the house, they threw pebbles onto the tiny balcony to wake Miss Jeanne's friend. After a few minutes, Iris appeared at the downstairs door. She took one look at them and, without a word, let them in, up the night-dark stairs to her room.

Later, lying in bed in one of Iris's nightgowns, Diane strained to hear the whispers of the two women as they sat in the next room in front of the fireplace.

"She's asleep," Miss Jeanne said. "I can't believe it. That poor baby—"

"Thank God there was no penetration," Iris said. "At least there was no sign of blood when I changed her into a fresh nightgown."

"But the poor child, living through that experience. I tell you, that family has gone too far."

"When will you notify the police?"

"I can't." Jeanne sighed. "How could I put the family through that disgrace? But you can be sure I'm going to tell the princess about it. This way she'll have to let Diane live with her aunt. If she doesn't, I'll have to report this to the police. It's simple. You can be sure she won't want *that*."

"You're right, Jeanne. We can't send that poor little kid back to that house."

"Absolutely not. I'm taking her to New York."

"When?"

"Tomorrow morning. I'll go back to the house before anybody's awake and pack for both of us. I'll take her directly to Miss Carstairs. Her mother won't even realize she's gone until Miss Carstairs phones her."

"You know what, Jeanne?" Iris said softly. "I never thought I'd feel sorry for one of the richest little girls in the country. But I do."

Within three weeks Diane and her aunt had moved into the Carstairs mansion, and Livvy had moved out. The marquis was exiled to the Riviera on an allowance, and Livvy held on to her title, the Marquise de la Frontaine.

Five afternoons a week Diane went for a session with Dr. Felicia Eberhardt, a well-known psychiatrist. With the approval of the psychiatrist Claudia enrolled Diane in Miss Framingham's School for Young Ladies. Once a week she was to go to her mother's apartment for dinner. Since Olivia and Claudia weren't speaking, the dinners were arranged through Miss Jeanne.

44

To Diane's relief, Olivia's active social life often took her to Europe, so the weekly dinners were often cancelled. The dinners were uncomfortable affairs, artificially gay and always tense.

She always managed to avoid going to her mother's apartment on the nights "The Rise of the Goldbergs" was on television. She adored Gertrude Berg, who played Molly, and her latest fantasy was to be Molly Goldberg's daughter and Rosalie's sister. Surreptitiously, she had looked up Passover and Hanukkah in the *World Book Encyclopedia*, and she knew about the new state of Israel.

Once she tried to talk to her aunt about her father and about being Jewish, but Claudia had turned red and abruptly changed the subject. Someday, Diane promised herself, she'd find somebody who had known her father. Maybe she had a whole set of aunts and uncles and cousins. Even grandparents. A *family*.

One rainy afternoon, feeling guilty but defiant, she had looked through the New York telephone directory for other Dickensons. There was one on East Eighty-first Street, one on West Eleventh, one on Fifth Avenue. Maybe someday she would find out if one of them was related to David Dickenson.

Chapter Three

Dressed in a lilac suit by Dior, a string of small, perfectly matched pearls, and a straw sailor hat, Diane sat in Mr. Lewisohn's elegant but somber private office clutching a pair of short white gloves in one hand while he explained the terms of her grandmother's will. In ten days she would be eighteen, and her inheritance, with certain limitations, would be transferred into her hands. In two weeks she would graduate from Miss Framingham's School for Young Ladies.

"Your grandmother had a deep sense of responsibility about the money she was handing down to you, Diane," Mr. Lewisohn said. "At the time she made out her will, she instructed me to give you this letter at the approach of your eighteenth birthday." He handed her an envelope.

Diane paused.

"Shall I read it now?"

"Please, Diane."

Slowly Diane opened the envelope, pulled out the

letter. There were a few moments of silence as she read. In her tightly written script, her grandmother had instructed her to leave all her financial transactions "in the capable and trustworthy hands of Mr. Lewisohn." In fact, the will made this mandatory. At Mr. Lewisohn's death his oldest son, already a partner in the law firm, was to handle her estate. She was not to touch the capital until she was twenty-five, except in the event of an emergency and then only with Mr. Lewisohn's approval.

Diane smiled.

"Nothing much will change. Soon I'll be eighteen." Except that she would insist on traveling around town *without* Philippe and the limo. It had been so embarrassing at school the way he was always in the background, waiting to take her off to ballet class or painting class or riding.

"Diane, I think it would be best to let your aunt continue to handle all the household finances," Mr. Lewisohn said. It was Mr. Lewisohn who had insisted that Olivia vacate the Fifth Avenue house and that conscientious Aunt Claudia move in to supervise her upbringing. "You know Miss Carstairs takes a sincere interest in your welfare."

Diane took a deep breath. Now was her chance.

"Mr. Lewisohn, now that I'm almost eighteen, don't you think it's time I was told about my father's family? I can't ask Aunt Claudia—she just gets upset."

Mr. Lewisohn looked shocked. Obviously collecting his thoughts, he was silent for several moments.

"Diane, your father's brother died in military service during World War II. His sister died several years ago in a tragic accident. Except for several cousins there's only his mother, who is senile and in a nursing home. So you see, I'm afraid there's nothing to pursue."

Diane smiled sweetly. She was not going to let this go so easily.

"Is she in a nursing home here in New York?"

"Diane, she's senile. She wouldn't understand that you're her granddaughter. She doesn't recognize people she's known all her life."

"I understand that, Mr. Lewisohn. But I want to see her."

Mr. Lewisohn hesitated.

"All right. I'll try to find out where she is. As soon as I know something I'll call you."

"Mr. Lewisohn, there's one more thing. You said I have cousins. Is that true?"

Mr. Lewisohn looked uncomfortable.

"Your father's family disassociated themselves from him not long after his marriage to your mother."

"Why? Is it because my mother was Jewish? Mr. Lewisohn, when my grandmother was given a Jewish funeral, I understood that we were Jewish." She paused. "I mean, I knew that I was at least part Jewish."

"All Jewish," he added. "Your father was Jewish, too. His family was upset that he not only abandoned his faith but changed his name as well. At your grandmother's insistence." He smiled. "She was a most persuasive woman."

"What was my father's name before he changed it?"

"David Seligman. When your mother and he were married, he was just out of law school. It has not always been easy for Jews to enter a prestigious law school." Diane couldn't help noticing that Mr. Lewisohn's tone was uncharacteristically icy. Had it been difficult for him? "David was accepted at Harvard Law School under the quota system that prevailed, and graduated with honors. But your grandmother understood that there would be law firms that would not accept a Jewish attorney, even one from Harvard Law School. She was determined that nothing would stand in the way of his career. He changed his name legally from Seligman to Dickenson. So you were born Diane Dickenson."

"Still, there must be people who know. Even my grandmother couldn't keep that a secret."

"Don't be so sure, my girl. Your father came from Albany, New York. Your mother and he eloped. By the time he met her friends, he was David Dickenson from Upstate New York. There may have been encounters with former classmates, but it was a far better kept secret than that of August Belmont many years earlier. Of course, when your grandparents arrived in New York from San Francisco, they immediately established themselves as Episcopalians."

Diane stared.

"The Belmonts are Jewish?"

"Old August Belmont, the first of the line, was Jewish. Though when he died in 1892, he was accorded a Christian burial."

"But not my grandmother."

"Diane, for three generations your family has been

Episcopalian. Don't you think it's better for you to accept that? I gather from your aunt that you'll make your debut this coming winter."

"Yes. At a supper dance at home, as grandmother wished."

He smiled, clearly relieved to be on a safe topic again.

"I'm sure you'll be the loveliest debutante of the year."

"Thank you, Mr. Lewisohn." She stood up, extended her hand. "You've been very kind to answer all my questions." She smiled. Let him *think* she'd dropped the idea of exploring her past. He looked immensely relieved as he took her hand and led her to the door.

She left Mr. Lewisohn's offices and went down to the waiting limousine. Philippe opened the door for her.

"Take me home, please." She couldn't wait to get back into her own room to think about what Mr. Lewisohn had said. If her father had not gone to court to change his name, she would be Diane Seligman. *Would Diane Seligman be making her debut this coming winter?*

In two weeks she and Deirdre had to go through the graduation ceremony at Miss Framingham's. She had been so excited when the psychiatrist had agreed with Aunt Claudia that she should be sent to school instead of being tutored at home. But school hadn't been the joy she had anticipated.

Fat and comically neurotic Deirdre had been her only friend all through her years at Miss Framingham's. Both she and Deirdre felt out of step with the rest of the class. Deirdre, whose fortune was only slightly smaller than hers, had been shunted back and forth between her much-divorced parents' households. There had been luridly publicized custody suits, and Deirdre knew that she was being used as a pawn in her parents' hostilities.

Diane couldn't forget that she was the only Jewish student in the school. Despite her Episcopalian cover she was forever fearful of being unmasked and seen as an intruder. Instinctively she and Deirdre reached out to each other.

Deirdre taught Diane her own survival tactic: *have fun*. She and Deirdre regularly cut classes to race to a Times Square movie palace to see Tyrone Power, Rock Hudson, or Marlon Brando. Afterwards they'd dash into a nearby automat or Child's before racing back via taxi to appear at the steps of the school when their respective chauffeurs appeared to pick them up. They had seen James Dean in *Rebel Without a Cause* four times and William Holden and Jennifer Jones in *Love Is a Many Splendored Thing* three times. Every Monday afternoon they bought the newest issues of *Photoplay* and *Movie Story*.

In her room Diane switched on the radio to "The Make-Believe Ballroom," stretched across the bed, reached for the phone, and dialed Deirdre's private number.

"I saw *A Hatful of Rain* with Don Murray and Eva Marie Saint and somebody new named Anthony Franciosa. God, he's sexy!" Deirdre said, before Diane even had a chance to speak. "I think I had an orgasm."

"Deirdre," Diane clucked, "suppose it had been

your mother calling you?"

"She'd be jealous," Deirdre giggled. "Mother is frigid. At least that's what her last three husbands said. How do you suppose she ever managed to have me?"

"The usual method." Diane paused, suddenly serious. "Deirdre, do you think I'm frigid? Here I am, almost eighteen, and I've never even had a real date."

"That's because you give fellows the cold treatment," Deirdre said. "You act as though you can't stand them."

"I'm just scared. Whenever I'm invited to a party, Aunt Claudia arranges for an escort. Boys act like I'm a freak because of all the money grandmother left me."

Deirdre laughed.

"Well, look at it this way: with me they take one look at the blubber and don't even think about asking. I brush my teeth with Ipana. I use Mum. I wash my face with Lux. And I drown in Chanel No. 5. So what happens? Nothing. But you—you're gorgeous."

"I'm not," Diane rejected. She saw nothing in the mirror that pleased her. "I wish I was tall and sexy like Lauren Bacall."

Deirdre sighed. "Do you suppose I could lose thirty pounds before my debut? I heard mother talking about the new grape diet of Manya Kahn's. Five days, five pounds off. The first two days nothing but grapes. Fives times a day—grapes." She grimaced. "All that gas! I'd take off like a balloon."

"It's going to be awful to have to go to all those parties this winter. It's such a waste of money." Even though it was going to be held at home, the supper dance at which she would be formally introduced to society would cost almost a hundred thousand dollars. And just last week Diane had read in a magazine that the average factory worker earned $82.99 a week. "Mother wanted to have my supper dance at the Iridium Room of the St. Regis, but Aunt Claudia insisted they follow grandmother's instructions."

"I wish we could have our debuts together," Deirdre said.

"For once mother and Aunt Claudia agree on something. No joint debut."

Deirdre nodded.

"My father said the same thing. He was scared people would think he was economizing—it would look bad for his business."

"My grandmother left specific orders. My debut is to be at home, and five hundred guests are to be invited."

"With five hundred crashers. No matter how many detectives you have, they crash."

"It's to be exactly one week before the Debutantes' Cotillion." Diane sighed. "Another of my grandmother's orders."

"My mother nearly died when she thought she couldn't get the Persian Room at the Plaza for my supper dance. Then somebody canceled."

"I'd like to forget the whole deal." Diane swung over on her back. "I'd like to pack up a valise and take a bus somewhere out to the Midwest. Stop in some small town, find a job as a waitress or cashier in a restaurant. Just be *me*."

54

Deirdre giggled.

"Instead of a debut, I wish my folks would give me the money." Deirdre wouldn't control her inheritance until she was thirty. "Or at least they could make it a less expensive debut and give me the difference. The cheapest way is to give a luncheon at your house. The next cheapest is to have your debut at the Cotillion or at the Grosvenor House Ball. For the Grosvenor House Ball all your parents have to pay is one or two thousand, and you can have ten dinner guests. After that you pay by the head—but nobody invites less than fifty. Then comes the *thé dansant*. Then the dinner dance, and at the top the supper dance—which is us. Somebody will have to dance with us. Mother says there're always at least two men to every girl. It's a rule."

Diane looked dubious.

"How do they make sure? I mean, how can they guarantee there'll be so many boys that somebody has to dance with us?"

"Darling, your family and mine have been planning the parties since March. It's the social secretaries' jobs to dig up men. Of course, lots of them are no older than we are. And isn't it silly the way the minute they get into college they start growing those straggly goatees? But at least they're bodies to dance with." She sighed philosophically. "I wonder how many gate crashers we'll have?"

"I don't want to think about our debuts." Diane dismissed it. "Let's talk about the trip to Europe." She and Deirdre were to spend six weeks in Europe this summer with Miss Jeanne as their chaperone. "All I know is Paris—and that'll seem so different now that I'm grown."

"All I care about is Monaco," Deirdre said. "Do you suppose Prince Rainier has a younger brother?"

The actual day of Diane's eighteenth birthday was marked only by a Sacher torte from Demel's in Vienna, ordered by Aunt Claudia, which arrived in a small wooden box exactly on schedule—to be shared, topped with whipped cream, with Claudia and Miss Jeanne over a birthday dinner and a gift from each. Olivia rarely remembered birthdays.

The following morning Mr. Lewisohn called.

"Diane, my girl, I have some news about your paternal grandmother."

Diane gripped the receiver.

"Yes?"

"Well, according to some friends of the Seligmans, she's a patient at the Goldman Nursing Home in Westchester County. Now I've called the nursing home and explained the situation. You'll be allowed to visit her, but remember that she's bedridden. Sometimes—often—she's incoherent. It may upset you when she doesn't recognize you."

"Mr. Lewisohn, I don't care about that. I want to see her," Diane said. "I can't explain it, it's just something I have to do."

Within an hour she was sitting in the back seat of the limousine on her way to the Goldman Nursing Home. Today she would sit beside her father's mother. Tonight, for the first time, she would reach

56

out to the other side of her family. Who had decided to cut her father out of their lives? It must have been his father's decision, she decided.

She caught a glimpse of herself in the driver's mirror. Did she look like her father's side of the family? She looked at her mother and saw no resemblance there. No resemblance to Aunt Claudia or her Carstairs grandmother either, except that the three of them—Aunt Claudia always said—had the Carstairs eyes. The *Cohen* eyes.

Now she remembered Nanette's cousin who had been in a class above theirs; Nanette and Liliane had been almost carbon copies of each other. Did she have cousins walking around who looked just like her?

Golden clouds of forsythia dotted the road. The sky was clear, the sun bright. But Diane couldn't enjoy the scenery. *What would she say to her grandmother?* She knew it was silly; Mr. Lewisohn had said the old lady wouldn't even know her. She might as well be a total stranger stopping by for a visit.

"Philippe—" Diane leaned forward. "Would you please turn off into one of the towns on the way up? I'd like to find a florist shop." So what if her grandmother didn't recognize her? She would bring a bouquet of red roses.

In Tarrytown Philippe stopped at Victor's Flower Shop, where Diane bought a dozen red roses.

She imagined greeting her grandmother: "I'm Diane. I thought you might like some flowers."

How would her grandmother respond?

She shifted nervously in her seat. It seemed silly

having Philippe drive her in the limousine. She was eighteen; she ought to know how to drive herself by now. In the fall she'd take driving lessons. She'd buy herself a car. Girls her age weren't driven around town by chauffeurs.

As they approached their destination she felt a fresh surge of excitement. At last she was taking charge of her own life. She hadn't asked permission to go up to visit her grandmother; she'd made the decision herself. She hadn't even told Deirdre about coming up here. Later she would. Maybe.

Philippe swung into a curving driveway leading up to a sprawling two-storied white brick structure set on a sweep of velvet lawn. Several white clapboard cottages, immaculate and cheerful with spring flowers, stood at either side of the main building.

As Philippe parked, got out of the car, and opened the door for her, she stared at the neat black-lettered sign: The Goldman Nursing Home. In small script it read Strictly Kosher. Did Philippe wonder why she was here? It was impossible to tell. As always, his face was impassive.

Holding the bouquet of roses, Diane walked into the large, casually furnished reception room of the nursing home. In a lounge off to the left patients sat at tables, playing cards or checkers. A woman dressed in a burgundy stain peignoir sat in a wheelchair and stared blankly at the screen of a large television set.

Diane was asked to wait a few minutes before being shown to Mrs. Seligman's private room. How often did her cousins come here, she wondered. Did their grandmother ever recognize them? Did they know about *her* existence?

"Miss Seligman—" A nurse beckoned from the hallway. Mr. Lewisohn had told the staff that Diane was to be called Miss Seligman.

"Thank you." Uncertain, Diane stumbled to her feet.

As she followed the nurse down the hall, she felt suddenly that this was a terrible mistake. What was she doing here? What could she possibly have to say to her grandmother? But it was too late to turn back.

At last, the nurse paused at the open door of a sunlit room at the end of the hall.

"She's having one of her good days, my dear—" she touched Diane's shoulder. "But even so, she probably won't recognize you. Don't let it upset you."

"I understand." But Diane's heart was pounding. She was about to encounter all she would ever know of her father's family. Had he been terribly unhappy at being rejected by them? Had he been sorry he'd married mother? Had he loved *her*?

A small, round, white-haired woman in a pink silk bed-jacket lay against a mount of pillows, staring into space. Diane searched for a sign of family resemblance, but saw only the heavily lined face of a woman who had lost two sons and a daughter to premature deaths. Once she must have been quite pretty, Diane thought.

Had she been devoted to her other grandchildren? Those admittedly Jewish grandchildren whose parents had not changed their names and become Episcopalians? She envisioned these cousins as small children climbing into their grandmother's lap for petting. She imagined them clustered around a

59

family dining table for the Passover seder, gathering together for birthdays and bar mitzvahs and bat mitzvahs and at Hanukkah parties. *Why had her father let her be cheated out of all this?*

"Hannah," the nurse said, her smile cajoling, "you have company today."

Diane didn't think it was appropriate for the nurse to call her elderly grandmother by her given name—it seemed disrespectful.

"I'm Diane," she said because her grandmother seemed bewildered by her appearance. "I've brought you some roses."

Mrs. Seligman's face brightened. Her eyes dwelt lovingly on the flowers.

"Red roses are my favorite flowers."

"I'll put them in a vase for you." The nurse reached to take the flowers from Diane. "Tell your visitor about the concert last night."

"Did we have a concert?" Mrs. Seligman said. "I don't remember. I've always loved red roses." She seemed pleased to remember it. "David loves them, too," she said, and Diane started. David Seligman had been her father. "Where is David? He should be home from school. He's such a sweet boy. And so bright."

"I'm sure he is." Diane managed a smile. Her father had been raised lovingly. He must have hurt his mother very much by denying his own name. His own faith.

"He's studying already for his bar mitzvah," Mrs. Seligman said proudly. Now she frowned. "David didn't have his bar mitzvah yet, did he?"

"No," Diane said gently.

"I was always bright in school, too," the old lady continued. "David takes after me."

Diane sat quietly while Mrs. Seligman relived the days when her children were young. Clearly this reminiscing was part of her grandmother's daily routine. As Diane listened, she felt a poignant closeness to her father, to the uncle and aunt she had never known. The nurse brought the roses back into the room and placed them beside the bed. For a moment, while her eyes rested on the flowers, Mrs. Seligman brightened with pleasure.

In the middle of a long reminiscence about David's first day at school Mrs. Seligman suddenly closed her eyes and stopped talking, and for a moment Diane thought her grandmother had died. But then she noticed the rise and fall of her chest, and rising to her feet she stared for a long moment at the sleeping old lady before leaving the room.

Late in June Diane, Deirdre, and Mlle. Jeanne left for Europe on an overnight flight, Miss Jeanne trying hard to hide her fear of flying. But once they were on French soil, she was ecstatic, chaperoning the girls on vigorous sightseeing expeditions.

Diane wistfully noticed the clusters of young American girls who seemed to be traveling in such freedom—unlike Deirdre and herself—and in such high spirits.

From Paris they went to Nice, then they rented a car and drove to Monaco. The girls giggled at the horse-drawn taxis and the immaculate white linen caps worn by the horses as protection from the sun.

They saw the pink-and-ivory Renaissance palace atop the Rock, the home of Princess Grace and Prince Rainer II, that rose through the spiked cacti—which blossomed in white and pink and flame in the spring—off the Exotic Gardens, almost two hundred feet above the sea on the site of an ancient Saracen citadel.

They sat in chaises on the sand before the Beach Hotel and dined sumptuously on the terrace of the Café de Paris. From the Beach Casino they watched a night of fireworks brighten the sky. They read in the English language International *Herald Tribune* about the death of the Aga Khan. Everybody was shocked when Aly's twenty-year-old son, Karim, was named successor.

"I don't believe it!" Deirdre shrieked. "He's a junior at Harvard!"

Diane smiled.

"Maybe you should have applied for admission to Radcliffe next fall, the way your father wanted."

"With my grades?" Deirdre said.

"Your father could have handled it. With an endowment or something."

"How can anybody think about classes with a debut to endure? Maybe some of the girls are going to Radcliffe or Sarah Lawrence or Barnard. Not me."

For Diane, it was a wonderful trip—as thrilling to see so much of the world as it was to be out of her mother's grasp. She loved the feeling of waking up every morning and for a moment—just a moment—not knowing exactly where she was. But at last it came to an end and on August twentieth they returned to New York. Deirdre left a few days later to visit her maternal grandmother in California—her mother and prospective husband number four had taken off for Bar Harbor. Olivia returned from England, full of talk about the big party of the year in London, hosted by Mike Todd and his new and pregnant wife, Liz Taylor.

"Mike Todd is unbelievable," she said. "He took over the Battersea Festival Gardens—that's London's Coney Island—and chartered five river steamers. He hired sixteen bands to play. *Everybody* was there, darling. Vivien Leigh and Laurence Olivier and Prince Karm Kahn—it was just before his father died. Of course the party went on *all* night. I heard somebody say there were 175 cases of Moët Chandon champagne and 1,000 bottles of liquor and beer. And would you believe it, Mike even invited Liz Taylor's ex, Michael Wilding. And he came!"

The preparations for Diane's debut began. Diane and Olivia went on endless shopping sprees, Olivia orchestrating every purchase, obviously relieving her own debut. Tailored to her specifications, the invitations were in the name of the Marquise de la Frontaine.

"Darling, you really have a marvelous figure." Olivia scrutinized Diane's slender silhouette as she stood before her in another creme-silk gown. "Though less bosom and another three inches in height would be better for clothes."

Diane shifted impatiently. An anxious saleslady stood by, five more gowns under one arm. "You'll need at least eight ball gowns, four or five cocktail dresses, and five suits," Olivia said. "And lots of accessories. And of course Claude absolutely *must* cut your hair in that fabulous new short look. We'll have to do it all by the fifteenth, though—Charlotte and Philippe Germaine are having a party on the sixteenth that I simply must attend."

As far as Diane was concerned, the sixteenth couldn't come soon enough. At last a wardrobe was assembled. Two knee-length cocktail dresses, one salmon-colored silk, the other aqua. Diane was assigned to various charity committees, and knew that as a result her name would soon be appearing regularly on the society pages of the *New York Times*. She was on the committee for the annual Debutantes' Cotillion and for the Christmas Ball, which was to be a benefit for the New York Infirmary.

Deirdre had other concerns. Desperate to lose weight before her appearance in public, she was shipped off to the Maine Chance spa to be pummeled, prodded, and dieted into beauty. Diane, bored and lonely without her friend, left for a week's stay at the Greenbrier at White Sulphur Springs, West Virginia—as always, accompanied by Miss Jeanne.

Standing with Miss Jeanne at the door of their cottage while two bellhops took their luggage indoors, Diane gazed at the lush countryside, bathed in the golden light of autumn.

"I haven't been here in years," Miss Jeanne said. "Not since the hotel was redone by Dorothy Draper. But it is lovely, isn't it?"

Dinner was served by white-gloved Negro waiters dressed in brilliant red and greenbrier green. The food, southern style and superb, was served on rhododendron-painted china. The hotel's maids wore red, white-fichued dresses, gold earrings, and necklaces.

And the setting was magnificent. The main building and the thirty-one cottages were surrounded by seven thousand acres of hotel property.

Diane was determined to leave behind all her worries about her debut, the cotillion, the lunches for charity drives, the ridiculous rehearsing.

"I'll ride every morning and play tennis with you every afternoon," she told Mlle. Jeanne.

On the first morning at Greenbrier, at six A.M. sharp, a switchboard operator awoke Diane as instructed and wished her a pleasant day. Eagerly Diane got up and hurried to a window, where a balmy breeze swept into the room. In the distance, patches of fog hung low over the trees.

Exhilarated by the feeling of being on her own, Dianne dressed and left the cottage to go for a ride before breakfast. *Alone.*

At the stables she was given Becky Sharp, a sleek black beauty of a horse.

"Be careful, miss," the groom cautioned. "Becky Sharp can be real frisky on an early morning canter. Just be sure you let her know who's boss."

"Oh, I will." Diane smiled.

The early morning tried to peek through the fog as Diane and Becky cantered and then slowed to a brisk walk on the trail that meandered through the vast autumn-foliaged acreage. She had been riding almost half an hour when she heard the sound of dogs. This wasn't the hunting season, was it? Surely the hotel would not permit hunting. She hesitated at a fork in the road. Ahead she heard voices amid the barking of the dogs. Deciding the side road was probably hotel property, she turned left.

The air was sweet and fresh. The fog had lifted. Late-blooming roses along the bridle path drenched the morning air with fragrance. Becky Sharp lifted her head, paused, then broke into a gallop.

"Easy, Becky." Diane was scared. "Becky!" She tugged at the reins.

She could hear another horse on a side path, could see the outline of the rider—a dark-haired young man in rumpled clothes. He caught up and fell in step beside her. Despite her fear, Diane noticed that he was what Deirdre would call "distractingly handsome." He wore western boots and his hair was unfashionably—but not, she thought, unattractively—long.

"Are you okay?" He seemed genuinely concerned. "I wasn't sure who was running the show."

"Becky thinks she is," Diane said, slightly out of breath, "but I can manage, thanks."

"Mind if I ride with you?" He smiled, displaying perfect white teeth.

"No, I don't mind." Her heart was thumping. Mlle. Jeanne would not be pleased with this encounter—there was no doubt about that. But what about all those men she would dance with at her debut? At all the parties this winter? She wouldn't know any of them. The only requisite, she thought grimly, was that they owned a set of tails.

"Down a piece there's a right turn that leads to a pond," he said. "It's beautiful this time of morning.

Shall we give it a whirl?"

"Why not?" Diane tried to sound sophisticated.

He smiled. Together they cantered to a pond where the water was so clear that they could see every fish. The ground was covered with red and orange leaves. It was a breathtaking sight.

"It's gorgeous." She looked at him. "It's like a painting by some old master."

"Let's tie up the horses and walk around the pond," he said. "Oh, I'm Chris."

"Hi, Chris." Suddenly a daring idea occurred to her . . . "I'm Diane. Diane Davis."

"Are you a guest at the hotel?"

"I work for a woman who's staying in one of the cottages. I'm her secretary and companion." She couldn't believe how easily the story came to her, how casually she lied. "Are you at the hotel?"

"No, I work on a horse farm nearby. Just for a few weeks. Then I have to go back to California." He smiled again. "I guess that makes me a trespasser. I wanted to ride for an hour before my working day begins, and the hotel bridle paths are great. Do you ride every morning?"

"I plan to." She couldn't believe how brazen she was being!

"How much longer will you be here?"

"A week." She wished she could see Chris every minute of that week. It was ridiculous, but she couldn't fight the feeling. She wondered how they could manage it, with Chris working—and of course there was always Mlle. Jeanne to contend with. She wouldn't understand. And she'd never believe that Chris didn't know who she was. According to mother and Aunt Claudia, every boy who looked at her saw only her money. *But not Chris.* No one would understand how much that meant to her.

"I tell you what," he said. "Let's meet this time every morning. Do you think you can find your way?"

"Sure." She could barely contain herself, visions of romantic mornings, strolling around the pond with Chris, clouding her thoughts. Wait till she told Deirdre about this!

"You know—" Gently he touched her elbow. "When I saw you riding down the path, I told myself I just had to get to know you." His eyes moved down to her red cashmere sweater, stopped, and lingered. She blushed. "Do you ever get out to California?"

"No." She paused. "But I—I might this winter. It depends upon where Miss Jeanne decides to go."

Chris dropped to his haunches.

"See the fish? There's a man who comes here every day at sunset and feeds them. He whistles, like you would to a dog and they come swimming to wherever he is and wait for bread crumbs. I've seen them follow him all around the pond."

Chris and Diane strolled around the pond, then looked for a pair of tree trunks to lean against. He was keeping an eye on his watch because he had to report to work soon. But what a wonderful morning this had turned into!

As the time came for them to leave Greenbrier, Diane tried to convince Miss Jeanne that they stay another week. How would she survive without

Chris? He hadn't even kissed her yet. For three nights she'd dreamed of nothing else. All they had was their one hour together in the mornings. There was no way to see him in the evenings without Miss Jeanne's finding out. And she would be horrified if she found out that Diana had picked up a boy on the bridle path.

At last, Miss Jeanne capitulated.

"All right, Diane. Please—I can't bear to listen to this anymore. Anyway, it is glorious here. I'll call Miss Carstairs; if she agrees, we'll see if the cottage is available for another week."

"Oh, Miss Jeanne, try to make her agree," Diane said. "I know you can."

"But you absolutely *must* be back in New York after that. The cotillion rehearsals, the fittings for your dress for your debut—"

But Diane wasn't listening. All she could think about was another week with Chris . . .

The week passed by quickly. Every morning Diane and Chris met, rode—and still Chris didn't make the slightest move toward her. By the last morning, Diane began to wonder if this was all her imagination, if he really wasn't interested in her at all. And then—

"Diane, I can't let you just walk out of my life." And at last he pulled her into his arms.

Deirdre had talked a lot about what it must be like to kiss boys and do other things. Diane had just listened. Talking about those things made her uncomfortable. She'd never let herself think about being married—not after that day she'd walked in on her mother and the young poet in the drawing room—but Deirdre kept reminding her that the debut was in effect an announcement that you were husband-hunting. But here she was, Chris was kissing her, and she was wishing he'd never stop.

"Will you write to me?" she asked as soon as he pulled away.

"Will you?" Chris said, his eyes serious.

"Of course I will." But she wondered how she'd manage it. Chris could write to her care of Carstairs—she'd say that was where she worked. She'd have the servants bring "Diane Davis" mail to her. They'd gossip among themselves, but they'd never dare say anything to Aunt Claudia or Mlle. Jeanne.

"Diane—" He sounded concerned as he pulled her closer and for a moment she panicked. "I have to be honest with you. I told you I worked with horses back in California. That's not true. I'm a contract player for a Hollywood studio. I'm an actor."

She almost laughed in relief. Nothing he could have said would have been more romantic!

"Chris, how exciting!" Of course, he was handsome enough to be a movie star, but this would never have occurred to her. "But you'll never write to me."

"I'll write to you," he said quickly. "Every night when I get home from the studio. You know, it's such rough work. I'm up at sunup and I don't get home before nine or ten at night. The only reason I'm here is because we're shooting some scenes for the new film—it's called *Ranch Hand*—at the horse farm."

Diane was fascinated.

"What's the picture about? Do you have a big part?" Then it occurred to her—all those gorgeous actresses . . . He'd probably forget her when he was back in Hollywood.

"I have a small, showy part," Chris said. "The studio says they're grooming me for big roles." He grinned. "The studio bio says I'm twenty-one. You know what, Di? I'm twenty-six."

She laughed.

"That's not exactly old." There was a long moment of silence. Diane knew it was time to tell Chris the truth. *I'm Diane Dickenson.* But somehow the words just wouldn't come. "Write me care of Carstairs." She fumbled in the pocket of her jacket for the piece of hotel stationery on which she'd scribbled the address. "Here's the address."

He took it, read it carefully, then raised his eyes to her. "I'll be coming to New York in January for the premiere of the film. Will you go with me?"

"I can't wait, Chris." Why not? She was eighteen years old—nobody could stop her. "If you still want me to go with you then—"

"Honey, I've got plans for us." He looked at her tenderly. "After all those girls in Hollywood, you're something special."

"All those beautiful actresses?" she said slowly.

"All those ambition-consumed, castrating little bitches," he snapped. "All they give a damn about are their precious careers. Not one honest bone in their bodies. You came riding down that path, and I thought about Elaine, the 'lily maid of Astolat.'"

"Oh, Chris—" She took his hands in hers. "I can't believe that two weeks ago I didn't know you existed."

He kissed her gently. Smiled.

"I'll write to you. Every day, I promise. And you'll

71

go with me to the premiere in New York in January."

It seemed like a lifetime away.

"How can I bear not to see you until then?"

She felt a fresh and exciting independence. A rebellious strength. She *would* see Chris. Nobody would stand between them. Today a new Diane Dickenson was born.

Diane played the role of Diane Dickenson, debutante, to perfection. Philippe drove her to endless luncheons at the Stork, "21," the Colony, to committee meetings and cotillion rehearsals, and finally to the first of the rounds of debutante parties that fall. In their cherished private moments together, Diane shared her secret with Deirdre who, back from her stay at the spa, looked wonderful with a new haircut, a less padded figure, a subtly made-up face, and a store of gossip.

"Is it true that all the Hollywood stars fly out to Phoenix to go to Maine Chance between pictures?" Diane asked. She was getting paranoid about Hollywood actresses, Diane scolded herself.

Through it all, Chris was in her thoughts. Every morning she waited impatiently for the postman. When she got a letter from Chris, she answered instantly.

It didn't bother Diane that escorts had to be arranged for those first parties by her aunt. Nothing did. Chris was in love with her; that was all that mattered. Then arranged escorts became unnecessary. Her private phone started ringing regularly. Clearly New York's most eligible young men were interested in Diane Dickenson. But was it the girl or the money? Diane wondered. Chris loved her without knowing about her money.

A week before the Debutantes' Cotillion, Diane, in a white tulle off-the-shoulder gown designed for her by Jacques Fath, stood in the receiving line with her mother and aunt—who spoke to each other only in public—at her long-awaited supper-dance debut. Six thousand dollars' worth of red, white, and yellow roses filled the ballroom of the Carstairs mansion. Moët Chandon champagne flowed. Lester Lanin led the orchestra. At midnight the guests dined on veal marsala, wild rice, and cherries jubilee. At seven A.M. a hearty breakfast—scrambled eggs with Scotch salmon, steaming homemade cornbread—was served, along with the obligatory morning cocktail of champagne and orange juice.

Seven hours after the last guests departed, Diane woke slowly to see the sunlight pouring into her bedroom. She started to pull the covers over her head.

"Darling, no." Her mother's voice. "Don't you want to see the newspapers? Just listen to what Cholly Knickerbocker has to say about you!"

Diane opened her eyes and pulled herself up to a semisitting position. Her mother dropped the morning newspapers, folded to the society pages, across the bed. "No debut so far this season has gotten so much space," Olivia said. "The photographs of you are marvelous. But then, I've always been photogenic." Her eyes sought Diane's dressing-table mirror for reassurance. She frowned. Diane knew why: she hated having a daughter old enough to be a debutante.

She wished her pictures weren't splashed across the newspapers. Suppose Chris saw them? But he wouldn't be reading the New York newspapers—he'd said he had time to read nothing but the trade papers.

The days flew by as Diane went from party to party. Then the big event of the season arrived—the Debutantes' Cotillion and Christmas Ball. Earlier in the evening she attended the *thé dansant* debut of two classmates from Framingham. Deirdre was there, escorted by a cousin bullied into playing the role.

Deirdre looked at her with pride—and a touch of envy.

"Di, you look like a movie star. Everybody's betting you'll be Debutante of the Year. Wouldn't you think that with what she charges, Elizabeth Arden could make me a runner-up?"

Diane radiated happiness and excitement. After eighteen years of near isolation socially, she was overwhelmed by her newly acquired popularity. Some of the men in pursuit were rich in their own right. But she had no use for any of them. She had Chris.

Shortly before ten P.M. Diane and her escort appeared in the Grand Ballroom suite at the Waldorf, where general dancing had begun. The ballroom and adjoining foyers were decorated in a Christmas motif. On the ballroom stage were a huge snowman and his lady. The tiers of boxes were adorned with wreaths of spruce and balsam and elegant silver cloth.

At exactly ten P.M. the ball was officially opened.

One hundred thirty debutantes, many of them making their formal debut tonight, were present. In a flurry of excitement the debutantes, gowned in white and silver, formed a receiving line. After receiving the guests the debutantes and their escorts began the grand march.

A series of special dances were performed to music sung by Lanny Ross. As a finale the one hundred thirty debutantes gathered together to sing Christmas carols with Lanny Ross as their leader.

As they all sang "Silent Night," tears filled Diane's eyes. Where was Chris this minute? Was he thinking of her? What was she doing at this silly ball anyway? She ought to be with Chris.

Diane hated Christmas. This year would be just like all the others. Tomorrow the servants would set up a Christmas tree in the library. They would decorate it. On Christmas Eve she and Aunt Claudia would have dinner on trays before the fireplace. Then the servants would go off-duty until Christmas night. Miss Jeanne was spending the holidays with Iris. Mother would be off to Palm Beach tomorrow.

She should be celebrating Hanukkah, not Christmas. With Chris.

On Christmas morning, Aunt Claudia would serve breakfast—a rich, homemade coffee cake—and later she would phone downstairs and tell the doorman to get them a taxi that would take them to the restaurant where they'd have dinner, baked ham and sweet potatoes.

"Oh little town of Bethlehem . . ."

Diane was drawn back into the present as the

debutantes and Lanny Ross began the poignant strains of the second carol. She leaned toward Deirdre.

"Deirdre," she whispered, "where are you spending the holidays?"

"Silly, you know," Deirdre said. "I'm flying out to my grandmother's." To California. Diane knew this. She just wanted to hear Deirdre say it aloud. She shivered with anticipation. "My mother's been in Bermuda since my supper dance. Daddy's in Paris. All the servants are going on holiday." She giggled. "I have to go to my grandmother's. They don't trust me to stay alone in the house. They're scared I'll have a guy stashed away in every bedroom." She sighed. "I should have such luck."

"Can I go with you to California?" Diane asked. Aunt Claudia wouldn't question a trip with Deirdre if they were going to her grandmother's.

For a minute Deirdre looked surprised, but then she nodded enthusiastically. "Sure. What a great idea!"

Lanny Ross led the debutantes in singing "It Came Upon a Midnight Clear." Diane's lips moved, but no sound emerged. She was three thousand miles away, imagining Chris's face when he opened his apartment door on Christmas Eve—and saw her standing there.

Chapter Four

Laura Devlin emerged from the IRT subway at Astor Place. After three weeks in New York, the subways still made her claustrophobic. But today she had loved mingling with the two-days-before-Christmas shoppers at Bergdorf's, Saks, and Altman's.

Trim shoulders in the inexpensive fake-fur coat hunched against the blustery wind, tawny hair unfashionably long but a striking frame for the perfect oval of her face, Laura walked toward Second Avenue, her long slim legs flattered by high heels and her full bosom attracting the stares of passersby.

Yesterday Laura had moved into a forty-two-dollar-a-month tenement flat on East Fifth Street with Cindy Arlen, née Clara Feinstein, whom she had met at the headquarters of the temporary office employment agency where she had signed up for work when she'd arrived in Manhattan.

"The apartment's cheap, and it's near most of the Off-Broadway playhouses," Cindy explained. Fresh from a Pennsylvania college with a degree in drama, Cindy was eager to break into TV via the Off-Broadway scene, which was a showcase for new talent.

"I chose the name Arlen because I don't think television is ready yet for Clara Feinstein."

Laura wasn't sure just what she was going to do with her life—except that whatever path she took had to lead to money. Lots of it. At eighteen, totally alone in the world, it was scary to face up to a huge impersonal city like New York; but at least she had managed to escape from Newport.

Back home she'd always be poor Kathy Devlin's daughter. She'd hated the damp cold winters in Newport and the four-room frame house that forever smelled of wet clothes and ironing because that was how mom had supported them. But then Laura had made it through high school in three years just so she could go out and support her mother after Kathy Devlin found out she had cancer. Laura hated Newport in the summer, when hordes of the ultra-rich descended upon them, reminding her every day of their poverty. No, summers were bitter, humiliating times for Kathy Devlin and her small family.

The windows of the small shops in St. Marks Place were filled with gay holiday decorations. Laura stopped in front of a tiny, rundown antique store. God, she dreaded this first Christmas. How could she go through it without mom? She wondered if her memory of the night mom died—the night of the Tiffany Ball, held at the nine-million-dollar estate of the Vanderbilts for twelve hundred members of East Coast society—would ever fade. Mom had spent her last few days in a dingy hospital ward because they couldn't even afford the health insurance that would have provided for a semiprivate room. The memory of her mother—gray, lifeless, surrounded by tubes, still haunted her. Laura shuddered.

"Hi, beautiful—" A well-dressed man in his forties, clutching an attaché case, stood beside her.

"Get lost." Laura turned and walked briskly away, handicapped by her high heels. The guy obviously thought she was one of the call girls living in the neighborhood. No man would ever buy Laura Devlin that cheap.

She turned down Second Avenue and headed south. The flat she was sharing wth Cindy was a fourth-floor walk-up. The halls reeked of garlic, cat, and urine. But it was cheap—she couldn't afford that West Seventies girls' club where she'd been living the past three weeks on her salary as a temporary typist at an advertising agency. And so far she liked what she'd seen of this neighborhood, the mixture of poor families—Irish, Jewish, Italian—plus the new invasion of young people from towns and cities across the country. It was an exhilarating blend of old and new, of exuberance and optimism as actors struggled in small playhouse productions, convinced that someday they would make it big. Laura felt as though she belonged here.

At the corner of Fifth Street three girls, clutching valises and complaining about the cold, flagged down a taxi. Obviously, Laura thought with a pang, they're heading home for Christmas. Cindy was leaving this afternoon to spend the holidays with her family in Pittsburgh. Cindy had invited her to come along; but even if she had been so inclined, she couldn't afford the airfare.

"We have a gorgeous Christmas tree on the front lawn and a beautiful menorah over the fireplace," Cindy had said last night, and laughed at Laura's blank stare. She explained that the menorah was as much a part of Jewish tradition as the tree was of Christian ritual. "Dad finally gave in to all our carrying on and let us have a tree when my brother was in the second grade and I was in kindergarten, but he was always glad my grandparents went to Florida every year right after Thanksgiving. For my brother and me the Christmas tree was a signal of good will and hope for peace in the world."

When Laura had first arrived in New York, she had felt so grown-up and confident. Not now. As she approached the drab tenement, she felt like a kid. *I'm alone in the world. I have nobody.*

At times like this, she always wondered whether her father was alive. No one knew. A week after Pearl Harbor, with no job, no means to support his wife and baby, he had enlisted. Mom had said that during the war he'd sent money home every month. After V-E Day, he was sent back to the United States—but he chose not to return to Newport and his wife and daughter. He went back to a woman in Italy. He never came home. The monthly checks stopped.

Laura walked up the three chipped dark-green steps that led into the murky hallway of her building. The couple in the ground-floor rear apartment were yelling at each other about money. On the second floor the wail of an infant blended with a blaring rock 'n' roll station on the radio. The tantalizing aroma of beef stew filled the air on the second floor.

She unlocked her own door and walked into the tiny kitchen. Heat knocked in the ancient radiators. She sighed. At least they worked.

"Laura?" Cindy called from her bedroom. "Is that you?"

Laura put up water to boil for tea.

"What's left of me in this cold." When she'd told Cindy she was from Newport, Cindy had said, "Oh, the place where they have the marvelous jazz festivals. You must have had great fun there."

"Shouldn't you be on your way to the airport by now?" Being on time anywhere was a major hurdle for Cindy.

"Yeah. I have to run like hell." Valise in hand, Cindy emerged from her bedroom. "Look, Ira Ross borrowed our percolator this morning. The little glass thing on his is broken. He'll bring it back later."

"Okay. He can buy one of those little glass gadgets in almost any hardware store."

"Tell Ira," Cindy said, and kissed her. "Merry Christmas and all that. I wouldn't be staying away for ten days if I didn't know absolutely nothing happens in the theater between Christmas and New Year's."

Laura stood in the kitchen and listened to the clatter of Cindy's heels as she hurried down the uncarpeted stairs. With Cindy gone the apartment seemed strangely menacing. She dropped her coat across the back of a tubular dinette chair Cindy had bought at a thrift shop and crossed to touch the radiator, seeking solace in the hissing heat. *What was she going to do with herself all these days until she was working again?*

Tomorrow night would be Christmas Eve. Mom and she had never had much, but at least at Christmas they'd had each other. Her mother had been forty-four when she died. So young! Snapshots of her at eighteen showed that she'd been a beautiful woman; at forty she barely looked a dozen years older. Money made a difference. Money gave you everything: power, comfort, love. *Maybe mom would still be alive if I could have taken her to a specialist in Boston or New York . . .*

Restless, she walked into the living room, hardly as large as the kitchen, and turned on the TV. Only one channel worked, but at least it would make some noise in the empty apartment. She dropped onto the dingy, worn sofa and tried to concentrate on the television program, a noisy comedy.

The doorbell rang. Ira Ross returning the percolator, she thought, as she went to the door. Cindy was friendly with everybody in the building. But *she* was always defensive with strangers. She just wasn't so ready to trust people.

She opened the door to a startingly handsome young man with dark, softly curling hair, dark eyes, and strong features.

"Hi, I'm Ira." He paused. "From downstairs. I'm returning the perc with some spares of hot coffee. Don't touch it," he said as she reached for it. "Let me put it on the stove for you—it's still hot."

"Thanks." Laura opened the door for him to enter. "Would you like to have another cup while you're here?" She didn't really know why she made the offer—it was just that it was so lonely here, the presence of another human being seemed appealing. "I've got a great coffee ring from Rattner's."

"Deal." His warm smile was charismatic. "Throw the cake in the oven for a few minutes," he said. "I'll put a low light under the perc to keep the coffee hot." He reached for a match. "You in the theater, too?"

"I'm not in anything, actually," she said. "I mean, I'm a fairly decent typist. I worked for almost a year in an office back home, and now I'm a temp. But I guess I don't know what I want to do with my life." She laughed. "Except make a lot of money. I have to admit I envy people like Cindy who know what they want."

"Most of them think they know what they want," he said. "Kids like Cindy pour into New York, stay six months or a year, and go back home to lead the same lives their parents lived. A few make it out of the mold. Not many."

"I will."

As her eyes met his, she knew Ira Ross would make it too. "What do you do?"

"Well, right now I work at whatever part-time job keeps me surviving." He slid the coffee ring into the oven. "I'm with an Off-Broadway group in rehearsal now. As stage manager. I want to learn everything I can about the theater. Someday I'm going to have a play on Broadway."

"How long have you been in New York?" She reached up for two plates and mugs. She was glad Ira was here. She felt comfortable with him. She didn't feel comfortable with most men; it seemed like they all looked at her and got the wrong idea.

"I was born in Brooklyn. We moved to Manhattan when I was four and my mother went back to teaching. From Stuyvesant High I went to Columbia. That's my family's version of a trust fund—a degree from a top school. Anyway, I got out a year ago last June with a degree in English Lit.—to please them. They can't understand why I won't go after a job in publishing, or at least go into my father's business. They worry about me constantly." He was being sarcastic, but Laura sensed that he cared about his parents. "My sister went into teaching right out of college. I guess that makes me the family maverick."

Laura laughed.

"I got out of high school a year ago in June. I couldn't have afforded college even if it was free." She studied him. "Playwrights make a lot of money, don't they?"

"The few who have a hit on Broadway. I'm sure Tennessee Williams isn't exactly hurting financially."

Laura listened to Ira talk about the rash of Off-Broadway theaters unfettered by union regulations, the crowded coffeehouses, and the poetry readings scattered all over the East Village. She relished his enthusiasm, envied his conviction that playwrighting was his game. It reminded her again that she was here in New York with no real direction. But, she reminded herself with grim determination, there had to be a pot of gold at the end of the rainbow.

"I talk an awful lot, don't I?" He laughed when they had finished the coffee in the percolator and stuffed themselves on the butter-walnut coffee ring.

"Why not?" Laura said.

"Tell me about yourself." He leaned back, clasped his hands behind his head. "What makes you tick, Laura?"

She hesitated. It was unlike her to speak to a virtual stranger like this. And yet there was something about him that she trusted. His interest seemed genuine.

For the next hour she talked, astonishing herself with her candor. Back home she had kept to herself all through high school. But in spite of her contempt for those multimillionaires who occupied the lavish "cottages" along Bellevue Avenue during the summer, she tried to emulate the way they dressed. Her mother would bring home their discarded magazines, which she devoured. *Someday* had been the magic word that gave her life meaning.

"I thought about modeling for a while," she said. "But I'm not really tall enough for fashion modeling. For magazine modeling I'd have to get all my teeth capped—they photograph lousy. That would cost as much as a Cadillac convertible."

"You're damned attractive, you know. Sexy." He said it dispassionately as his eyes swept over her Marilyn Monroe figure poured into a brilliantly red crewneck sweater, pleated plaid skirt and black tights. "You might make it in films."

"No," she said firmly, not knowing exactly why she rejected it so quickly. "I want to do something where I'm in control of my progress. I don't want to have to sleep my way to the top." Cindy talked about agents who would give a TV walk-on to a would-be actress willing to occupy their beds. She'd vowed no man would use *her* that way. "I figure if I work through the temporaries—in all kinds of offices—I'll eventually hit on something that's right for me."

"Got any plans for dinner?" he asked, gazing out the living room window.

"I—I was planning on digging something out of the refrigerator." She paused. Should she invite him to stay?

"Come down to my place, and I'll make spaghetti for us." He grinned. "It's my sole culinary accomplishment, besides eggs and toast. And I promise not to try to throw you into bed."

His bluntness disarmed her. She laughed.

"In that case, I accept."

No fellow had ever touched her. Except for clumsy kisses and gropings for her breasts when she was in high school. But something told her that Ira Ross was somebody special. If he tried to make love to her, she wasn't so sure she'd turn him away.

Ira's apartment was furnished with contributions from home. He had tried to disguise the condition of the walls with posters and cheap paintings he had picked up in the Village. While he cooked spaghetti, Laura went through his collection of books, most of them plays. She looked at the novel lying open atop the bookcase, the current best-seller. *By Love Possessed*. Nothing would ever possess her. *She* would possess. Money.

"Why don't you put something on the record player?" he called from the kitchen. "Choose whatever you like." The aroma of warming garlic bread and spices filled the apartment.

Laura kicked off her shoes, flipped through the dozen or so albums on the coffee table, and finally selected *Rhapsody in Blue*. She smiled as the music filtered into the warmth of the room. She saw a row of candles set in glass on a shelf above the sofa, reached up and brought a pair down to the coffee table. Ira had suggested they use the coffee table for eating and sit on pillows on the floor. The kitchen table was littered with typewriter, paper, office supplies. She roamed around the room, found some matches, lit the candles, and turned off the one lamp that graced the room.

"Hey, I like that," Ira said as he came into the living room with knives and forks, two wine glasses, and a bottle of Chianti. "I hope you're hungry. I made gallons of spaghetti."

Cindy would call this the routine seduction scene, Laura thought as she helped herself to a heaping portion of spaghetti; but Ira wasn't playing it that way. He was busy talking about the theater—mostly his belief that plays should carry a message to their audiences—and while they dined by candlelight, Gershwin provided them with a sensuous background.

"The trouble with most kids on Off-Broadway," he said, twirling a forkful of spaghetti, "is that they *talk* great theater. They rush here with their degrees from Carnegie Tech or Northwestern or whatever, and they talk up a storm. But when a director hands them a script, they're dead. They hear about all the glamor, the excitement, the money in show business. They envision themselves on TV or in the movies—a few think about the Broadway theater. They're playing games with themselves. They don't realize it's a craft, and any craft requires a hell of a lot of hard work."

Laura limited herself to one glass of Chianti. Whatever happened tonight she was going to be in control. If she decided it was all right to let Ira make love to her, then okay. But it would be *her* decision.

Now Ira was talking about the producer with whom he was working.

"He doesn't pay anybody. Even the Equity members change their names and work for nothing. But this guy has a way of getting agents and directors down to see his productions. About a year ago the juvenile in the play he was doing—the play was a dog but the part was great—was picked up and sent out to Hollywood as a contract player. Christopher Ames. Rumor has it he's going to be the next big star. His first film premieres in New York in January. I have a couple of tickets. Larry—that's our producer—gives me tickets for things in lieu of salary." He hesitated, his eyes on his plate. "Would you like to go with me? Premieres are supposed to be pretty jazzy events."

Laura looked at him in surprise. He sounded almost shy. "Well, sure. It sounds like fun." Why not? Already she felt less alone in this big, impersonal city.

Laura helped Ira to carry the dishes into the kitchen. Right in front of the sink, his plate tilted and fell to the floor, splattering spaghetti and shattering china on the faded floral linoleum.

"I'm sorry, I'm a *klutz*," he said, reaching for a sheaf of an old *New York Times* that sat atop a stepstool by the window. "My motor skills just don't

88

always work right."

But Laura wasn't listening anymore. Her gaze had settled on the front page of the society section of the *Times*. She recognized the face of the girl smiling up at her from the photograph.

"Diane!" Her voice was electric. Ira raised his head as he mopped the linoleum. "Diane Dickenson."

"You know her?" He sounded mildly interested. "They say she's the richest girl in the world. Or at least, in America."

"My mother was the family's summer laundress one season. A long time ago. In Newport." Diane and she had sworn to be best friends forever, but one day Diane had just disappeared. She'd been so hurt—she couldn't believe that Diane would leave without even saying good-bye. And her family never came back. The house was still all boarded up. She'd wanted to write Diane and tell her how hurt she was, but mom said she had no address except for the summer house. "I used to have to dodge around in the kitchen to avoid walking into Diane's fancy silk lingerie," she said.

Ira leaned over to inspect Diane's photograph.

"Interesting-looking face."

"Don't look too hard," Laura said, a bit too quickly. "She's not for the likes of you. Diane Dickenson plays in another ball park."

"Good. Because I like this ball park damn well." His eyes trailed over her. Without her high heels she was several inches shorter than Ira. She felt oddly vulnerable. "Would you be upset," he said slowly, "if I kissed you?"

"Live dangerously." She would *not* let him know

how the very thought terrified her. "Try it."

In an instant, his arms were around her, his warm lips gently against hers, his tongue pressing her mouth open. At school she had played cool and sophisticated, listening in the gym locker room while the other girls giggled and whispered about their love lives. Fellows like to hint about the wild times they had with the girls in school—and she'd been sure that with the way she was built, some of them bragged about making out with her.

But Ira was different. He'd known a lot of girls, both in college and around Off-Broadway. He could probably tell she was inexperienced—and the thought made her tense. Her best asset was her body. She knew that instinctively. Not that she would ever go the call-girl route. But face and figure would help make her way up the ladder to the top—where the real money was. She didn't know just how this was going to happen. But somehow it would—she would make it happen.

"Let's go inside—it's more comfortable in there," Ira said, slightly out of breath when he pulled away.

"Okay." Her docility surprised her. But actually it was more than obeying him—what she was feeling was new and unnerving. Her compulsion to be in charge had taken a back seat to this persistent, inexplicable feeling . . .

Ira flipped off the glaring kitchen light. Hand in hand, they walked into the muted candlelight of the living room. Stopping next to the scuffed coffee table, Ira pulled her into his arms again. When Cindy had told Laura about French kissing, she'd thought she wouldn't like it. But this was a new, delicious sensation.

His hand crept beneath her sweater. Normally this was when she said "Stop." But this time she was silent, trailing one finger along his earlobe. Somebody—was it Cindy?—had told her this made most men passionate. Now she lifted herself slightly to blow into his ear.

His other hand moved under the back of her sweater, searching for and finding the hooks of her bra. She felt a flicker of fresh excitement well up in her throat. His hand made its way beneath the lace to one nipple as his hips pressed against hers.

Everybody said that if a girl was athletic—and from thirteen to sixteen she had thrown herself into backbends and splits and cartwheels—a fellow didn't know if a girl was a virgin or not. She hoped Ira wouldn't find out that she'd never slept with anybody.

"Let's go into the bedroom," he whispered.

"Ira, this is awful fast." A few hours ago she didn't know Ira Ross was alive—and now here she was about to go to bed with him! Was this only happening because she was alone in the city the day before Christmas Eve—and feeling sorry for herself?

"If we both want it, why not?" he said. "Laura, nobody has ever made me feel this way. But if you say no, then we won't."

She debated a moment. Trembling.

"I say yes."

They walked into Ira's bedroom, which had little more in it than an enormous double bed.

"Should we have blown out the candles?" she asked. Ira chuckled.

"I'm saving all my strength for you, baby. Let the candles fend for themselves." He helped her off with her sweater and bra. His hands felt hot on her cool skin. "Don't worry about the candles." He tugged at the zipper of her skirt. "They'll just drip into the glasses."

Ira pulled his shirt over his head, fumbled with the zipper of his slacks. Laura stripped off her black tights and waited.

Ira pulled her down to the edge of the bed.

"Ira, I don't want to get pregnant."

He pulled away.

"That would *not* be a good idea. Wait a minute— I'll be right back."

She lay on the bed, her heart pounding, her thoughts in a whirl. She was eighteen years old. Wasn't it time she learned about making love? At last Ira came back into the room. She liked the way he was built. Broad in the shoulders, slim in the waist and hips. Hair on his chest.

"Let's get this show on the road," he murmured, lifting himself above her.

He thrust heatedly between her thighs. For a moment she was scared. He'd have trouble, she thought in humiliation. But no! Her arms closed in about him as they moved together. Each absorbed in ultimate satisfaction. She didn't have to worry. Ira would never know this was little Laura's initiation.

She stood under the shower spray, remembering

Ira's warning not to turn the water on full blast or the head would collapse into the discolored, chipped tub. Ira was *something*. She was glad he'd been her first. It could have been rotten. Instead it was sensational.

So what if he'd said Diane had an interesting face? She—Laura Devlin—had been great in bed. Not that she would just sleep around with anybody. It would have to be because she liked the guy an awful lot. Or because he could do an awful lot for her.

Chapter Five

The morning was gray and bone-chillingly cold. Snow flurries hit the windshield as Philippe drove Diane and Deirdre toward Idlewild for their flight to Los Angeles. Deirdre huddled delightedly in her new Autumn Haze mink from Maximillian of New York, a gift from her father to make up for the fact that he'd decided to spend the holidays in Paris with his current girlfriend. Diane wore her new Fouke-dyed black Alaska fur seal, because she would feel self-conscious wearing mink at eighteen. And mink might start Chris wondering just *who* Diane Davis was.

Already Diane was feeling guilty about lying to her aunt. But she wasn't exactly lying, she rationalized. She *was* going to California to stay with Deirdre at her grandmother's house. She just hadn't mentioned seeing Chris out there. Or staying with him. If he invited her, that is.

Of course, she was counting on him to do just that. She needed to belong to somebody, to feel that she was the most important thing in the world to someone. Aunt Claudia loved her, but she was caught up in her tight little world of volunteer work and going to church. What did she have? *Nothing.*

She could see now why Aunt Claudia never married. Grandmother had never considered any man good enough—that meant rich enough—to marry a Carstairs heiress. Had there ever been a Chris in Aunt Claudia's life? Someone she had not dared to love?

She'd memorized the lines from Chris's precious letters—they were all she had to see her through these weeks of her debut. Nobody ever guessed how scared she was—except Deirdre, who was scared herself.

Diane knew that she'd disappointed her aunt when she refused to go on to college. But school had been such an ordeal. Why prolong it? Even at Miss Framingham's she and Deirdre had stood apart from the other students because everybody knew that Diane Dickenson and Deirdre Swift were two of the richest girls in America. *Why did everybody think it was so great to be rich?*

Chris was different from the men she'd met at the debutante parties. Chris said he loved her—without knowing who she was.

He'd said in his letters that he couldn't wait until he was in New York next month for the premiere because then he would see her. He wrote that he went to bed every night pretending she was there with him. He couldn't wait to hold her in his arms again. He kept saying he had wonderful plans for them. She told herself he meant when he was established in Hollywood. But she couldn't bear the waiting.

Suddenly she had an idea . . .

"Deirdre. You won't mind if I go to Chris's apartment from the airport, will you?" Why did she have to wait until Christmas Eve to see him? "If I'm in California, it seems silly to wait."

Deirdre pretended to be annoyed. "Okay, I'll tell grandmother you stopped off to see a cousin. She won't think anything of it. All she thinks about are which ribbons to put on her three poodles each day and which collar each should wear. Just make sure you keep in touch."

"Of course." Diane smiled lovingly at her friend. Chris would be pleased to see her. Wouldn't he?

"You look scared," Deirdre said. "If you change your mind when we arrive, you can come right home with me. Maybe you'd rather call Chris first from the house—"

"I'll go straight to Chris," Diane insisted. But it would be awful if she showed up at Chris's door and found he had made other plans for Christmas. *No.* He'd written her that he'd be "holed up alone in the Canyon apartment for Christmas." He had no family except a stepmother whom he detested—and a twelve-year-old half-sister living somewhere in the Midwest. "Deirdre, I can't wait to see him!"

"Just be careful," Deirdre cautioned. "You don't want to trade in your gorgeous wardrobe for the latest from Lane Bryant."

"Do you think he'll be shocked when he opens his door and sees me standing there with my luggage?" Diane said. "He said he would stay home all day Christmas and think about me—"

"Diane, he'll be thrilled. And nothing shocks

97

people in Hollywood. I'm jealous—grandma lives in stuffy Brentwood. It's probably going to be dull as hell. Mother warned me not to wear my bikini in the pool. She said grandmother might have a stroke."

"I don't expect Aunt Claudia to call me out there," Diane said uneasily, "but if she should—"

"I'll brief all the servants on what to say," Deirdre said. "Grandmother never answers the phone herself. Her hearing is bad, and she refuses to wear a hearing aid."

"Deirdre, do you think I'm making a mistake?"

Deirdre laughed.

"Of course not. I just wish it was happening to me."

At last they were aboard the four-propeller plane that was to whisk them to Los Angeles. Diane gazed down at the ice-rimmed marshes as the plane rose into the sky. *She was on her way to the most wonderful Christmas ever.* Only for a few minutes as Philippe brought their luggage out of the car trunk had she felt like calling off the whole thing—but then she'd noticed a poignant family reunion outside the terminal. No, she had spent too many holidays alone with servants or alone with Aunt Claudia to deny herself the joy of being with Chris on Christmas. She wasn't like her mother, she told herself. Mother didn't know about being in love. She was in love with Chris. She would never love anyone *but* him. Someday they would be married.

"While Chris is working at the studio," Deirdre's voice brought her back to the present, "we'll do the tourist scene. We'll have lunch at Perino's—the food is *heavenly*. Even grandmother—the world's pickiest gourmet—says so. Then we'll eat at the Villa Capri—that's Frank Sinatra's place. And we'll shop at Magnin's. Oh, and we have to go for lunch one day at the Brown Derby, though it doesn't look like a derby anymore—it's all covered with vines and new glass and brick additions. But I read in *Holiday* that actors and actresses working at NBC or CBS go there for lunch all the time.''

"I'll call you every morning, I promise," Diane said, trying not to feel self-conscious. She and Chris were in love. It wasn't wrong to sleep with a man when you were in love, was it? It would be glorious . . .

"But remember, Deirdre, to people out here I'm Diane Davis."

When the plane was over Denver, the pilot informed them that the Colorado temperature had climbed to five degrees. They left Colorado, passed over Utah and dipped down into southern Nevada. The Las Vegas Strip at twilight was a ruby and diamond necklace. Diane felt her throat tighten as they approached Los Angeles, the San Bernardino Mountains rising perilously close, or so it seemed.

"Look, Diane, we're almost there," Deirdre said. "See all the lights down there? That's Los Angeles, Hollywood, and Beverly Hills. Beyond the hills is Santa Monica."

In fifteen minutes the plane's wheels touched down at Los Angeles International Airport.

"You'll be glad you wore a light knit suit," Deirdre said, dousing herself with Arpège. "Even this late in the day it's like summer out here. It won't be cool until late in the evening."

Smiling, tanned people in summer clothes waited to greet the arrivals. Diane couldn't get over how healthy everybody looked. And no wonder—the air seemed dry and clear, with no evidence of New York City's smog. They'd left behind a gray, dismal city, probably caught in a heavy snowstorm, for a place where everybody seemed to have just stepped out of a swimming pool.

"There's Frank," Deirdre said, waving at a tall, stooped man in a gray suit. "He'll help us with our luggage and take us to the car."

When they reached the gray Rolls-Royce that, according to Deirdre, had been in the family for eighteen years, she gave Frank instructions to take Diane to Chris's address.

"You sure you want to go straight there, Di?"

Diane wished she felt as sure as she sounded. "Yes."

"Okay—Frank, take us by way of Mulholland Highway." Deirdre used the intercom. "Wait'll you see the view—on one side you look way down on the lights of Hollywood, and on the other down on San Fernando Valley."

Diane laughed.

"Oh, Deirdre, I can see that any time. I just want to see the inside of Chris's apartment!"

Deirdre sighed with mock frustration, and amended her instructions.

"Here I thought I'd have company for the twelve days out here, but I can see now you'll be gallivanting with Chris the entire time."

"No, Deirdre." But she had to admit she loved the idea . . . "Chris will have to go to the studio every day except for Christmas."

Diane waited restlessly while they sat in traffic on the six-lane freeway. Finally the Rolls turned off at an exit, and soon they were cutting through a winding canyon, surrounded by red, white, and pink hibiscus and the scent of eucalyptus.

Deirdre rolled down her window.

"Look at those oleanders." Pink and white, they stood fifteen feet high. "And those camelias and poinsettias and azaleas! You don't see anything like that back in New York!"

Diane suppressed a yawn. It was only 7:30 P.M. California time, but back in New York it was 10:30— and she'd slept little last night in her excitement about her trip.

"Don't fall asleep on his doorstep," Deirdre said.

"I won't." She planned to fall asleep in his arms.

Then the Rolls was pulling up before a cluster of garden apartments built around an Olympic-sized community swimming pool, surrounded by palm trees. Diane's face glowed as she reached to squeeze Deirdre's hand.

"Are you taking all your luggage now?" Deirdre asked, reaching for the door on her side.

"Just the weekender," Diane said hastily. If Chris asked her to stay at his apartment, then she'd bring over the rest of her luggage later.

Over Frank's mild objections, Diane insisted on carrying her weekender up to the apartment herself. She kissed Deirdre and set off for her destination. But which of the apartments belonged to Chris? The lights were on in most of them. *Let Chris be home,* she prayed. *Please God, let him be glad to see me.*

In her plain turquoise knit dress, the seal coat over her arm, Diane walked slowly toward the long, low string of apartments. Suddenly, it seemed all her confidence had vanished. Suppose he'd found someone else? She would die.

Her heart pounding, she set her bag down on the stoop and rang the bell. Light peeked through the venetian blinds. He was home.

A minute passed. Then another. It seemed like forever. Diane held her breath. Maybe he wasn't home. Worse, maybe he was with someone and didn't want to be disturbed. Or—she heard footsteps. Slow.

The door swung open. Dressed in white shorts and a rumpled white terrycloth shirt that set off his tan. Chris towered over her.

"Diane!" His voice was startled but jubilant. "Your boss came out here for Christmas!" he guessed and she nodded.

He pulled her into his arms for a kiss that left no doubt in her mind that she was welcome. "Oh baby, what a marvelous surprise!" He reached for her bag with one hand and pulled her inside the apartment with the other. "How much time do you have off?"

"I'm on my own until New Year's Day—"

"Not another word." He kissed her. "You'll stay with me. God, I can't believe you're here." He took her face in his hands and kissed her again.

The phone rang. "Damn," he said, sighing as he released her and picked up the phone.

"Hello. Oh, hi. Yeah." His voice was sharp. He was frowning. "I'm going out for dinner with a friend from New York." He shifted from one foot to the other. "No, no, nobody you know." He shot

Diane a glance. "No, don't do that. I told you, I'm busy. And I have to be at the studio real early tomorrow—six—for some last-minute shots. Yeah. Okay. No, I'll call you. Uh-huh. 'Bye."

Slowly he replaced the receiver, turned, and walked back to her. His cheek brushed hers as they stood together.

"This is the damnedest business in the world, Di. People out here can be such leeches if they think you can do something for them." He released her and looked her over from head to toe. "Did you bring along something fancier than that?"

"Yes," she said eagerly. "It's in the valise I have with me."

"Then we'll have dinner at Romanoff's on Rodeo Drive." He grinned. "Prince Romanoff has definite ideas about how his patrons should dress. A few weeks ago, a top Hollywood star came to the restaurant in slacks. He wouldn't let her in."

"Romanoff's sounds like fun!"

"Well then, my darling, dig out your dress and change. By the way—" He hesitated. "Is it fancy enough so I can wear my dinner jacket? You never know *who* you'll run into at Romanoff's."

"It's a dinner dress. A present from my boss." She felt a pang of guilt for the lie, but this was not the time to tell him who she really was.

While she opened her valise, Chris walked into the bedroom, leaving the door open behind him. She pulled out her favorite—a short dance dress by Galanos, with a beaded paisley bodice and white organza ballet skirt—then rummaged for the white satin Victorian pumps embroidered in black Schiffli and its matching evening bag.

Suddenly self-conscious, she scooped up her change of clothes and makeup kit and closed herself in the bathroom. Her hands trembled as she took off her knit suit. It didn't seem possible—here she was in California, about to go to Romanoff's for dinner with Chris!

She knew Romanoff's was something special—her mother had talked about it often, because her crowd, which shuttled between New York, Paris, the Riviera, and Beverly Hills, loved being seen wherever movie people went.

Deciding there was no time for a shower, she pulled out her collection of Charles of the Ritz cosmetics from her bag. Carefully, she pulled the Galanos over her head, and then dabbed her throat and behind her earlobes with L'Air du Temps. Deirdre had told her men loved this.

Looking strikingly handsome in his dinner jacket, Chris put down the phone as she emerged from the bathroom.

"I made our reservations," he said, his eyes resting appreciatively on her. "God, Diane, you look beautiful, and in a way that's a million miles from Hollywood." He reached for her coat and held it out for her. "I'm sorry, but we'll have to leave early—I have to be on the set tomorrow morning. I know—why don't you come with me?"

Diane didn't even have to answer—they both knew that they wanted to be together every minute.

They spoke little on the way to Romanoff's in Chris's new white Corvette, which bore his initials on each door. He did talk about his movie, which would premiere in New York in late January, and about the studio's efforts to catapult him into stardom.

"I went to New York straight out of high school," he said as they drove through the soft California night. "I worked in Child's, sold ties at Macy's, did the temporary-office-help bit. I went to acting classes at night and tried out for parts in Off-Broadway plays by day. I made Broadway and TV rounds on my lunch hour. It was rough. It was discouraging. But I wasn't running home, like most of the kids I saw around town. Then I did this play down on Second Avenue about a year ago. It was awful, but I was glad just to have a chance to be seen. Agents and movie scouts come down to Off-Broadway, not as often as most of the kids down there like to believe, but it happens." His hands tightened on the wheel. "It happened to me. I was picked up and shipped out to Hollywood as a contract player. Right away they threw me into a Method acting class with a bunch of other contract players. God, I hated it. By the time I tested for this part, I was ready to cut out. And the rest," he grinned, "as the columnists like to say, is history. I've been featured in half a dozen movie magazines. The studio publicity department is pushing me like crazy. The picture's in the can except for one last scene. The consensus is that I walk away with it." He took one hand off the wheel and reached for hers. "That's what made me Mannie Coleman's new protégé. His new discovery." Bitterness crept into his voice. "But everybody seems to forget the eight years I sweated it out in New York."

Diane squeezed his hand.

"Chris, I can't wait to see the picture."

"You'll see a few minutes of it in the making tomorrow. Mannie had the scene rewritten to highlight my role. That's part of the build-up."

A few minutes later, they walked into Romanoff's. Though it looked like plenty of people to Diane, Chris said the crowd was smaller than usual. Everybody seemed to know him. She noticed how charming and friendly he was to everybody.

Chris ordered for them.

"We'll have the chicken Romanoff, please." He turned to Diane. "Wait'll you try this, Di. It's not like anything you've ever eaten. I never eat beef. Not since that summer I worked in the stockyards."

But for all Diane cared, she could have been eating anything. She barely tasted her food as she listened to Chris tell her about his friends, the movie . . . it was all so glamorous and larger than life. Before she knew it, they'd finished dessert.

They left the restaurant and walked to Chris's car. Conversation came easily. She wasn't scared at all. Why should she be? They were in love.

Back in the apartment, Chris brought a pillow and sheets and dropped them onto the sofa. Diane looked at him in astonishment.

He smiled.

"Tonight you sleep in the bedroom, Di. I'll take the sofa. Tomorrow night will be ours, I promise. But I have to study my lines and get some sleep or my career will be over before it's started." And without another word he kissed her on the cheek, gathered her by the shoulders, and led her toward the bedroom. "Sleep well, my love. I'll be waking you at six."

It happened so fast Diane didn't even have a chance to argue, but she couldn't hide her disappointment. This wasn't exactly how she'd envisioned their first night in California together. But there wasn't much she could do about it, so she got undressed and settled herself in bed—in one of her lovely Saks Fifth Avenue silk nightgowns. Then the phone rang in the living room. She lay back against the pillow and listened. Chris seemed to be trying to placate somebody named Keith. Whoever it was certainly needed a lot of soothing, she thought as she toyed with the edge of the sheet. Chris was so sweet—he couldn't bear to hurt anyone. It was hard to believe he had been living in New York for all those years—and harder still to realize that she might never have met him if she hadn't gone to White Sulphur Springs.

The next morning, Diane felt a warm sense of belonging as she drove with Chris past the studio gates. She sat with him in the makeup department, walked hand-in-hand with him to the set. She watched him perform before the camera for several takes before the director was satisfied.

The set became a frenetic scene of holiday festivity as the cast presented gifts to members of the crew, and a portable bar appeared. Then Diane remembered that she had come all the way out here without a gift for Chris—and Christmas Eve was only hours away! But tonight would be their gift to each other, she told herself.

They went across the lot to the offices of the publicity department, where a party was already under way. As they approached the building, a chauffeur-driven station wagon pulled up and a dumpy woman of uncertain age emerged. As the chauffeur darted forward to open the building door for her, Diane studied her. She looked familiar.

"Chris—" she nudged him. "Is that an actress?"

"That's Louella Parsons," he whispered. "The old bat is here for a drink and to collect her usual loot. With her column she still rules over the Hollywood crowd, though she can't compete with the TV talk shows. Anybody out here would kill to get on Jack Paar's program. Do you realize the coverage an actor gets on TV?"

They followed Louella into the publicity department's large reception room, which was packed with celebrants lined up four-deep before the festive bar and clustered around the ornate Christmas tree.

Chris pushed her inside a small office.

"Stay right here, baby."

Diane watched Chris walk over to one of the deserted desks, pull out a wrapped box from the top drawer, and hurry over to the center of the room, where he pushed his way through the crowd and handed over his gift to Louella with a kiss.

It occurred to Diane that she might be recognized—then she nearly laughed out loud. In glamorous Hollywood who would be interested in a New York debutante?

"Would you like a drink?" It was Chris, his arm around her waist. Diane noticed that people—especially the women—were covertly inspecting her.

"No, I don't think so, Chris. Not so early." In truth, she never drank anything but white wine—and that was only because Aunt Claudia had told her that white wine was the only ladylike drink. Which reminded her . . . "I should make a phone call, Chris. To my boss." Did he notice how nervous she sounded?

"Okay—" he looked around. "Go in here. I don't think anybody's using this office. I'll wait while you call."

She called Deirdre, promised to keep in touch, trying to sound as businesslike as possible. When she hung up, Chris was standing right behind her. Smiling.

Just as they were getting ready to leave, Mannie Coleman, the studio chief, made his grand entrance, and Chris pulled her over immediately to meet him. She was shocked by how nice this important person was to her. Who was Diane Davis to him? But then, she *was* with Chris. She'd heard somebody say that Chris was becoming one of the hottest properties in Hollywood.

At last they left. Chris took her to lunch at the Tail o' the Cock.

"Now I'm warning you," he said in mock seriousness, "the dividing line between Beverly Hills and Los Angeles goes right through the main dining room, so we have to be careful where we sit. Nobody from Beverly Hills dares eat in Los Angeles."

Diane gazed at the wood-paneled-and-brick walls, the open fireplace, while they were led to a table. "It's a beautiful place, Chris."

He looked pleased. "I thought you'd like it. It's the new look out here."

"It has a Christmasy look," she said. "Nothing else

out here looks like Christmas."

After lunch, Chris took her sightseeing. They visited Sunset Boulevard, the San Fernando Valley, and took a barefoot stroll along the beach at Malibu.

As she walked hand in hand with Chris over the warm white sand, beside the electric blue of the Pacific, Diane felt overwhelmed with happiness. This love was unlike anything she had ever experienced. Of course she loved Aunt Claudia and Miss Jeanne, but to her aunt she was an obligation, and Miss Jeanne had become increasingly distant over the years as though to establish her place in the household as an employee. But Chris was different. He loved her for herself alone.

They watched the sun set over the Pacific before heading home.

"You know what we're going to do tonight?" Chris said.

She just looked at him.

"I'm going to cook dinner for you."

Diane laughed. "Good. Believe it or not, I'm hungry again."

While he moved efficiently around the kitchen, she made it obvious that she needed to feel useful.

"All right, set the table and bring out the salad," he said, "I can see you're no good at being waited on. We should have champagne, but . . ." He grinned. "I don't need champagne when you'll be sitting across the table from me."

Diane glowed.

Over coffee and Black Forest cake, they listened to Pat Boone singing "Love Letters in the Sand." Diane was ecstatic. This was the most wonderful Christmas

110

Eve she had ever known. She felt sorry for Deirdre, sharing Christmas Eve with her grandmother—who had little patience for her only grandchild—and three toy poodles. How lucky she was!

Throughout the evening, she was aware that they were going to end up in bed together, and she tried not to worry about it. She tried to convince herself that she wouldn't freeze up and be scared. That nightmare in Newport was over. They loved each other. Wasn't that all they needed?

After they'd washed the dishes and put them away, Chris reached for her hand and pulled her close. As the haunting strains of "Tammy" filled the room, he kissed her, pressing her slim young body against him. She could feel her heart—or was it his?—pounding. *She wasn't scared. It was going to be fine.*

Chris picked her up in his arms, and carried her into the bedroom. *This isn't happening,* she told herself. *This can't be real.*

Chris put her down gently on the bed and slowly began undressing. She lay still, not knowing quite what to do next. She and Deirdre had talked a lot about sex. Deirdre had become a self-proclaimed expert on the subject, having bought a dozen books on "erotica." Diane tried to relax. Dr. Eberhardt had told her that she was normal. That she could enjoy making love. Diane wanted desperately to believe her.

She watched Chris. He was aroused, that much she could tell. He wasn't a boy, she thought with pride. He was a man.

"God, you're lovely." He sat down on the bed. "So different from the actresses out here. You know what

111

I thought the first time I saw you? 'Elaine, the lily maid of Astolat.' I knew you were different from that first moment."

She nodded, afraid to speak. But she knew that now was the time for the truth.

"Chris, I've never made love before." She paused. "I hope I won't disappoint you."

"You won't, Di."

Gently, lovingly, he helped her out of her clothes. She turned hot and cold as he lowered himself above her, his lips teasing her nipple, his hands caressing her creamy white flesh. Only once, and then only for a moment, when she felt the hardness of him against her, did she tense. But it passed. This was Chris, the man she loved.

Her arms tightened about his shoulders as he pressed inside her. *It hurt*—a sharp pain and then a dry, sore feeling. But he paused, giving her time to grow comfortable, until slowly, as if her body had a will of its own, she found herself moving in response to him, making low sounds of passion that blended with his. And to her amazement, she felt herself giving in to her own urgent need . . . "Oh, Chris!" She clung to him as they shuddered together in release. How could she have ever been afraid? "Chris, I love you so much."

Chapter Six

They slept most of Christmas Day. When they did get up in time to cook dinner, Chris said, "You know what, babe? Except for Monday, when I have to be at the studio to pose for some publicity shots, I'm yours. Let's do Hollywood."

Diane beamed at him.

"I'll have lunch Monday with Mrs. Carstairs. I'm sure she'll send a car for me."

Whistling, Chris sauntered off to the shower. As soon as she heard the shower water pounding in full force, Diane called Deirdre.

"Deirdre, he's wonderful," she whispered before Deirdre had a chance to say anything beyond "Hello." "But I'll tell you all about it at lunch."

"Di, have you seen this week's *Life?*"

"No." She tensed. "Why?"

"Darling, there's this gorgeous spread on the Cotillion Ball. And guess who's managed to get herself prime position? Wait a minute, let me quote: 'Diane Dickenson, the number one debutante of the season, who's not only super-rich but super-beautiful.' Di, you're a celebrity!"

Diane went cold with fear.

"I hope Chris doesn't see it." But there wasn't a single magazine in his apartment—only *Hollywood Reporter* and *Variety*. There was no reason to worry.

"Listen, Di, forget about it. The guy loves you! Your money only makes you more lovable! Can you get away on Friday for a lunch party grandma is giving for me at her country club?" Deirdre paused. "But now that I think about it, I don't think you should bring Chris. Sorry. This stuffy old club doesn't allow actors or Jews."

"I'm sorry, I won't be able to make it," she said sharply. "I wouldn't want to go anywhere Chris isn't welcome. But what about you and me having lunch on Monday?"

"Great. Call me Monday morning and tell me what time to pick you up. Oh, will you be there for the next hour? I'll have Frank drive over with the rest of your luggage."

After Diane hung up, she went back to bed, feeling happier than she'd ever remembered feeling. Today, her life seemed perfect—especially Chris's gentle, eager lovemaking. She loved being with him—his friend, lover, confidante.

"Like most producers," he had told her, "Mannie is scared to death of television. But it's so ridiculous. All the top TV shows—'I love Lucy,' 'Dragnet,' 'Four Star Playhouse,' 'Groucho Marx'—are made here in Hollywood. All the big studios—MGM, Warner Brothers, Twentieth-Century Fox—are all into TV."

"Would you like to do television, Chris?" She wondered about his future. *Their* future.

"After I'm established in movies, definitely. I want to go where the money is." He paused in reflection. "But one day I want to go back to the theater. I want to do a really fine play. That's where an actor can really test his skills."

Except for one night when Chris had dinner with his agent, he and Diane ate together at a different restaurant each night: the famed Escoffier Room atop the new Beverly Hilton, Dave Chasen's, Dean Martin's Dino Lodge, the Cocoanut Grove, the Mocambo—Diane loved every one. Chris swore she was going to gain fifty pounds and that he'd still love her. She just laughed.

But not everything Chris taught Diane was new to her—when he explained that Ciro's had closed up late in the past summer, she remembered that this had been a favorite haunt of her mother's. It was hard to imagine her mother in Chris's world.

The Monday that Chris spent at the studio doing publicity stills—the day before New Year's Eve—Diane and Deirdre had a long lunch at Perino's after a morning of shopping in the marble-and-bronze splendor of I. Magnin's on Wilshire Boulevard.

Deirdre speared a chunk of chicken salad.

"What will Chris and you do for New Year's Eve?"

"Chris is taking me to some parties." She tried to sound casual about it, but actually Diane was nervous about meeting all of Chris's friends.

"Oh. Hey, what are you going to do if Chris wants to see you off at the airport when we leave on Thursday?"

Diane frowned. She'd been avoiding thinking about going back to New York, back to that insanity of balls and luncheons and charity affairs. How could she, after everything she'd shared here with Chris?

"It'll be all right." She tried to sound confident. "Chris has to be at the studio that morning for an interview. I told him I'd be picked up by my boss."

Deirdre sighed. "Di, when *are* you going to tell him the truth? If he ever picks up the New York newspapers, he'll find out himself and I don't think he'll be thrilled with your little deception. You're getting more coverage than any debutante of the year!"

"Deirdre, all Chris reads is the *Hollywood Reporter* and *Variety*." She paused. "I tell you what— when he comes to New York for the premiere of *Rendezvous with Life,* I'll tell him then. I promise."

"Okay, pal." Deirdre popped a grape into her mouth. "It's your life."

On New Year's Eve Diane called her aunt to wish her Happy New Year, and phoned Miss Jeanne, who was to spend ten days with her friend Iris, now married to a doctor and the mother of two small boys, before she and Chris started out for the first of a series of parties. They began with Sam Spiegel's—by now a Hollywood ritual—where, upon scanning the room packed with high-powered movie stars, Diane understood for the first time how fast Chris had risen to the top of the business. Now she understood too, why he'd been so thrilled when he'd received the invitation.

"That's Cole Porter over by the piano," he whispered. Diane stiffened. Cole Porter had been a guest of her mother's in Paris. But he wouldn't remember her as the little girl who circulated self-consciously among the guests, clearly at her mother's orders. She squeezed Chris's hand. "I love everything Cole Porter has written."

Too soon he was pushing her toward the entrance hall. They had three other parties to attend before the New Year arrived. The second party, in a magnificent house in Bel Air, was more casual—noisy and friendly, every inch of the enormous California Modern living room packed with bodies. A small orchestra in one corner of the room was playing dance music. Chris and Diane managed to find a tiny space in the corner of the room where they danced close, pressed against the others.

"It's so warm in here," Diane said, giggling. She was on her third glass of champagne and definitely feeling it.

"I'll get you a cool drink," Chris said. "Stay right here. What do you want?"

"Ginger ale," she whispered. "Unless you mean to carry me home."

His eyes held hers.

"My darling, I'd like nothing better." And with that he disappeared into the crowd.

Diane watched as he made his way to the bar. Along the way he stopped and talked to Candace Collins—Diane recognized the New York gossip columnist from the society parties. She smiled. No wonder Chris was so successful—he knew how to play the Hollywood scene.

Indeed he did.

"Hi, Chris." Thanks to plastic surgery and makeup, Candace was attractive enough to compete with the starlets in the room. She reached for his hand.

"You're looking beautiful as always, Candace," he said, knowing she could be helpful when *Rendezvous with Life* premiered in New York. "But we don't see you out here often enough."

"I'm out this trip on a special magazine assignment. Heading back for New York in three days." She looked across the room at Diane then back at him. He smiled; Candace was always on the lookout for fresh gossip. Mannie Coleman was already sore because he'd refused to take Rita Drake—fresh from a Broadway hit and here to do a Menlow film—as his date tonight. As usual, Mannie had Chris's best professional interests at heart; he figured it would be great publicity to link him with another up-and-coming star, and a beautiful one at that. Of course it wouldn't do at all if Chris were seen with an unknown from New York.

"I'll be heading east the end of January," Chris said, trying to sound intrigued by the prospect. He hated New York in January. "For the premiere of *Rendezvous with Life.*" Good. Get that plug in.

But Candace wasn't even listening.

"Tell me something, Chris. Are you serious about Diane Dickenson?"

"You mean Diane Davis." His eyes followed her to

Diane. God, she was beautiful. But she seemed uncomfortable, probably because she was alone. He really should get back . . . He lifted his hand and waved. Diane smiled and waved back.

"No, I mean Diane Dickenson." Candace waved too. "Where *did* you meet the richest debutante in America? And what's with this incognito bit? Is her family opposed to her having a thing with an actor?"

Chris paused, totally at a loss. What was she talking about? Diane Davis . . . Diane Dickenson . . . Good God, could that be . . . *so Diane hadn't been working at the Greenbrier at all—she'd been a guest.* "We're trying to keep it low-key," he said quickly. "Will you excuse me? Diane looks a little nervous at being left alone."

He pushed his way through the crowd again, his heart pounding. God, the publicity he'd get when word got around that he had something going with Diane Dickenson! Candace was only the beginning. And for once he didn't have to act this out. He was crazy about her. She was the first girl he'd ever considered marrying. *But would she marry him?*

"Let's get out of here," he said brusquely, grabbing Diane by the elbow.

Without a word, he led her out to the car. In less than four years he would be thirty. Now was the time for him to make it to superstardom. Right now he was Mannie Coleman's fair-haired boy. A year from now it would be somebody else. But marrying Diane Dickenson would guarantee the success of *Rendez-vous with Life.* Mannie would be ecstatic.

"Diane," he took a deep breath, his hands on the steering wheel. "You've been lying to me! How can I ask Diane Dickenson to marry me?" He chose his words carefully—this was the most important move of his career. "Diane Davis, yes. But the richest debutante in America? No. How could you do this to me? I nearly died when Candace Collins told me who you were."

"Chris, ask me," she whispered. "Ask me to marry you."

Careful, he thought. *Don't ruin it now.*

"How can I? How can I ask you to live my life? Right now I make four hundred dollars a week. You spend that on a dress. Maybe in ten years I'll be able to afford Diane Dickenson." He was giving the performance of his life and he knew it.

"I have enough money for both of us," Diane said, laughing. "For ten of us. What does it matter whose it is, as long as it's there?"

Take it easy, boy. You almost have her. "But why would you want to marry somebody like me? What can I give *you?*"

"Love." Her voice broke. "That's what you gave me when you thought I was Diane Davis. Am I any different now?"

Their eyes clashed. Chris felt a momentary twinge of guilt, but it passed. He was in love with her, that much was true—and he just couldn't gamble on losing her . . . now that he knew who she really was.

"Diane Davis Dickenson," he said softly, "will you marry me?"

"Oh Chris, yes!" She threw herself into his arms. "Yes!"

"Then let's get married right away. I can't bear to see you go back to New York. Let's get married tonight—" All at once they heard laughter and music coming from the house—laughter, singing, whistles. "Wait a minute," he said. "Why wait? Let's get married today—January first, 1958." He knew that if he let her go back to New York her ritzy family would try to keep her from marrying him. Their precious daughter pledging her life to a Hollywood actor? "Diane, let's drive to Vegas and get married right away."

Diane stared at him, shocked, torn between what she wanted and what she'd always been taught, and then he knew by the look on her face that he had won.

"All right, my darling." He felt the trembling of her slender frame as she leaned toward him. "We'll start the new year off married." She hesitated. "Chris, can we take Deirdre along as a witness? She's my closest friend—she'd never forgive me if I got married without her being there."

"The boss lady you had lunch with?" Chris teased.

"Chris, I promise I'll never lie to you again."

He kissed the tip of her nose.

"Of course Deirdre will go with us. I'll take you back to the apartment and you can call her. I have to talk to Mannie Coleman before we leave."

"Why?"

"Baby, he's my boss. My whole career lies in his hands. I report every move to him." He took her face between his hands and kissed her, just like Tyrone Power did in all those movies—it was his most effective move, and it worked like a charm on Diane. He would be a good husband, he promised himself. They'd be the perfect young couple. The fans would love them.

121

Chris left Diane at the apartment and headed for Mannie Coleman's house in Bel Air. Mannie's party was to have been the last they were to attend. Very much in the style of the host, it was sure to be big and splashy and expensive.

Chris arrived at the Coleman house, smiling and charming as always, and made his way through the hordes of guests to Mannie's side.

"Shame on you for not bringing Rita Drake. But as you can see," he scolded, "she's found another escort. So what about you?"

"Mannie, I have to talk to you," Chris said urgently.

"Now?" Mannie looked around warily. "Why?"

"*Please*. It's important."

Mannie took him upstairs to his private office.

"All right, Chris, what the hell's so important you drag me away from my own goddamn party?"

"Mannie, I'm eloping tonight with—"

"You're *what?*" A vein bulged in Mannie's temple. "Like hell you are. You'll wreck your screen image. Aren't there enough starlets in town for you to screw?" He paused. His voice dropped to a cajoling whisper. "Look Chris, any broad you want, I'll get her for you. I know for a fact that Jeannie Somers is just dying to crawl into the sack with you."

"Mannie," Chris said firmly, "I'm eloping tonight. To Vegas. With Diane Dickenson."

There was a long pause.

"The rich debutante? The one who's splashed all over this week's issue of *Life?*"

"I suppose," Chris shrugged. "There's only one Diane Dickenson."

122

"When did you meet her? How did you meet a New York debutante?"

"I met Di when we were shooting those scenes down in White Sulphur Springs," he said. "We've been writing each other ever since. She came out to see me just before Christmas."

"Chris, we gotta do this right." Chris could hear the wheels turning in Mannie's brain. "I'll call Jerry." Jerry Weinstein was head of publicity for Menlow Films. "He'll charter a plane, fly with Diane and you out to Vegas. He'll bring Roger along to take plenty of stills."

"Mannie, we want to get married right away," Chris said desperately. He couldn't gamble on Diane's changing her mind.

Mannie walked toward the phone.

"Where's the bride?"

"At my apartment. We planned on leaving for Vegas in an hour." He was perspiring. "Her girlfriend will be going with us."

"All right, all right," Mannie said impatiently. "Meet Jerry at the airport in one hour. Before breakfast you'll be married and back home. I'll tell him to bring along a makeup man as well as Roger. Your bride's gotta look beautiful enough to grab the hottest new male star in Hollywood. Jerry's downstairs—in the corner near Rita, I think. Find him and send him up to me. Be at the airport in one hour. Oh—" he winked. "And don't worry—the marriage bureau's open twenty-four hours a day."

Deirdre lay on Chris's leopard-covered sofa while

Diane pulled on a dazzling blue silk chemise, another Galanos, and gazed anxiously at her reflection.

"I can't get used to this straight line, Deirdre, even though I know it's in style. What do you think?"

"I think it gives you an air of elegance," Deirdre said. "And that's damn hard to come by at eighteen. Darling, I can't believe this is happening! And I'm part of it."

"I wouldn't have it any other way. Do you think your grandmother will be upset when she wakes up and finds you're not at the house?" Diane kicked off her lavender pumps and slid her feet into a more conservative pair.

"I left a note." Deirdre shrugged. "She went up to bed thirty seconds after midnight. Guess she figured she'd fulfilled her grandmotherly duty of seeing the new year in with me." Deirdre's eyes were uncharacteristically veiled. Like me, Diane thought, Deirdre wishes she had the storybook grandmother—or mother. But maybe it happened only in movies and on television shows.

Moments later, Chris arrived, breathless, full of Mannie's instructions. Diane was unnerved by the elaborate preparations for what she had envisioned as an uncomplicated, private elopement.

"Baby, please, it's important for my career." Chris held her close while Deirdre nodded enthusiastically in the background. "It's playing the movie game. It won't be that bad."

While the three of them walked toward Chris's Corvette, a studio limo pulled up. The driver called out, "Mr. Coleman sent me to drive you to the airport. He says we have to rush. The charter plane is standing by already."

The limousine raced to the airport. There, Roger—the photographer—waited while Claude touched Diane's eyelids with color, brushed more warmth along her high cheekbones. Now, arm-in-arm, she and Chris posed beside the plane for what seemed like an endless montage of photographs. At Diane's insistence Deirdre, to her delight, was included in several shots.

At last they climbed aboard the charter plane and flew off under a near-full moon over towns and highways and vast stretches of desert. Diane sat with one hand in Chris's while Roger and Claude and Jerry argued about the future of the studio. Deirdre listened, fascinated.

The plane touched down at McCarran Airport. Another limousine waited. First they would go to an all-night marriage bureau and then to the suite at the Hotel Sahara, which had been reserved by Jerry. Diane and Chris were to be married by a Nevada judge in the hotel suite.

They drove along a dark and empty road with sagebrush rising on either side from the barren soil and into the Strip, which glowed on both sides with multicolored electric signs and billboards from restaurants, casinos, hotels, motels, and fast-food eating places.

"Ever been here?" Jerry asked the girls cheerfully. Diane couldn't understand his cheerful acceptance of the fact that his New Year's Eve had turned into a night on the job. "Las Vegas is like no other city in the country. Where else can you buy clothes twenty-four hours a day, go to a burger stand or beauty shop any hour of the day or night? There are sixty-four churches and seven wedding chapels in this town, not to mention three hundred hotels, motels, and boardinghouses."

Diane was fascinated by the brash, vulgar beauty of the Strip, the hotels: the Riviera, the Flamingo, the Thunderbird, the Sands, the Sahara, each with its casino, beckoning like a modern-day Circe to eager gamblers.

It didn't take long for them to get their marriage license and temporary wedding bands. Jerry hustled Chris and Diane and their entourage to the Hotel Sahara, which was surrounded by twenty acres of lush lawns and flowers. Inside the hotel Jerry rushed them through the lobby and upstairs to the suite. A hotel employee was still arranging flowers in the sitting room.

"The judge should be here," Jerry barked, reaching for the phone. "Claude, take the girls into the bedroom and do something with Diane's hair. It's a mess. I want some stills before the ceremony. Chris, change ties with me. Yours will photograph like hell."

Struggling to hide her discomfort, Diane told herself all this hoopla was part of marrying a Hollywood actor. It was important to Chris's career. She looked over at Deirdre, who was enjoying every moment of the fuss. Why did she have this urge to grab Chris by the hand and run into the night?

Diane heard what had to be the judge's voice in the sitting room, heard Jerry on the phone asking for a magnum of champagne to be sent up. That reminded her! She'd have to call Aunt Claudia back in New

York before she read about the wedding in the newspapers.

"Diane—" Chris called from behind the door. "The judge is here."

"Okay, I'm coming."

She turned to hug Deirdre, who whispered a teary "Good luck, babe," then walked out of the bedroom into the sitting room. The atmosphere was tense. Electric. And unreal. If Chris hadn't been standing there with one hand extended to her, she might have turned and fled.

Diane stood with Chris before the judge for the brief ceremony that made them man and wife. This is all there is, she thought shakily while Chris reached to kiss her. Those few words and she was married to Chris. It didn't seem possible.

"C'mon, give her another real shmaltzy kiss," Roger ordered. "But first kick off your shoes, Diane."

Chris rolled his eyes.

"For God's sake, Roger, I'm five-ten." But he stood by while Diane took off her pumps.

The judge stayed long enough to toast the bride and groom with Dom Perignon, then took off. A lavish roast duck garnished with white grapes was wheeled into the sitting room by two waiters. For once, Diane barely touched her food, so impatient was she to talk to her aunt before the morning newspapers spread the word. Jerry was already on the phone dictating a news release about the wedding. But she'd have to wait until around six A.M. California time before she could call.

"All right, everybody," Jerry said when he hung up. "Let's head back for the airport. Chris, Mannie wants you at the studio tomorrow. I know it's close, with the premiere set for late in the month, but he's having the writers add another scene, a good one, for you."

Diane just gaped.

"When does Mannie want me there?" Chris said.

"Ten sharp. With luck you'll wrap up the scene in time for dinner."

Deirdre leaned across the table toward Diane.

"I wish you and Chris were flying back to New York with me." She grinned. "But boy, will I be bringing news to the East Coast!"

Diane dozed in Chris's arms on the flight back to Los Angeles. With a brilliant red dawn coloring the sky, the wedding party left the plane and piled into a waiting limo. Diane and Chris were dropped off first at his apartment. Deirdre was next, to be taken to her grandmother's house in Brentwood. The other three would go directly to the studio.

Chris lifted Diane at the threshold and carried her inside. As he kissed his bride, the phone rang.

"Damn!" Reluctantly he released Diane and crossed to answer it. "Diane, why don't you get into bed. I'll be right there."

She was Mrs. Christopher Ames, Diane thought as she prepared to undress. It still didn't seem possible. This was the most wonderful day of her life. But this was *such* a crazy town—who would make a casual phone call at four in the morning?

She heard Chris's angry voice.

"Keith, I'm married. Never mind. We'll talk later."

Diane heard the phone slam down. Then Chris walked into the bedroom.

128

"I left the phone off the hook," he said, reaching for her. "Nobody's going to disturb us between now and nine o'clock."

At six o'clock California time, while Chris lay sleeping, Diane tiptoed from the bedroom, closed the door behind her, and went to the telephone. Aunt Claudia always woke up at eight o'clock. By nine she was dressed and downstairs. It was nine in New York right now.

Her hand trembled as she reached for the phone. How could she say this?

Aunt Claudia picked up on the first ring.

"Diane, darling, what's wrong? It must be awfully early there."

"Aunt Claudia, I have some news." She didn't sound like herself. "I know it's going to be a surprise to you, but—well, I guess there's no way of easing into it. I'm married."

There was a long silence, filled with long-distance crackles.

"What do you mean, you're married?"

"Just what I said." Diane tried to sound calm.

"That's ridiculous. I'm coming out there right away."

"No, Aunt Claudia. Just listen to me for a minute. *Please.*" And then she explained everything—about the elopement, her love for Chris . . .

But Aunt Claudia was unmoved.

"Diane, this is insane. You're only eighteen. I know you think you're in love, but you don't know the first thing about marriage! I'll talk to Mr.

Lewisohn—I'm sure we can have the marriage annulled. You'll thank me later."

"I don't think you understand." Diane said, "I love Chris. This is forever, Aunt Claudia. And there's nothing you can do about it."

"Never mind. When are you coming home?"

"Not until late in the month. We're coming into New York for the premiere of Chris's movie. We'll be in town for a week. Aunt Claudia, please be happy for me."

"Happy! I'm in shock. I tried so hard to bring you up properly. What did I do wrong?"

"Nothing. You did everything right. It's going to be a wonderful marriage."

"We'll have to make arrangements about the house. I suppose I'll have to move into an apartment—"

"No, Aunt Claudia, I want the house to stay open. And I want you to stay there. Nothing's changed. Except that now I'm married to Chris. I can't wait for you to meet him!"

"I'll have Mr. Lewisohn call you. Maybe he can make you understand what—"

"I don't need to talk to Mr. Lewisohn," Diane said firmly. "And there isn't anything for me to understand. I'll see him when Chris and I come into New York the end of the month. Okay?"

Silence. Then a long sigh. Diane knew that, at least for now, she had won. "All right, Diane, but I assume you're not at Deirdre's grandmother's house? At least give me a phone number where you can be reached. There are financial arrangements that must be made if you plan to remain in California. Mr. Lewisohn will take care of that for you."

Diane realized that she hadn't even thought about money, and Chris was already talking about their renting a house in Bel Air or Beverly Hills. They certainly couldn't manage that on *his* salary. He'd been hoping that Mannie Coleman would renegotiate his contract, but he knew that could take months.

Diane gave her aunt Chris's phone number, explaining that they would be there until they rented a house. Chris wanted something in California Modern with lots of open space, she remembered. And a swimming pool, of course.

"Aunt Claudia, would you please ask Mr. Lewisohn to tell mother that I'm married?" She didn't even know where her mother was. But she had forgotten that the marriage of the season's richest debutante to a glittering new Hollywood star would make headlines across the nation. The Marquise de la Frontaine was sure to find out that her daughter was married.

Chapter Seven

Laura clattered down the stairs of the East Fifth Street tenement and tried to prepare herself for the blustery morning outside. She hadn't expected to be sent out on a job on January second, but Mrs. Madison of the agency had called this morning and said it would probably last through next Friday.

Thank God Ira asked her to go with him on a round of East Village parties. She'd been dreading New Year's Eve. They had started off with coffee at the African coffeehouse where a friend of Ira's was reading from his poetry. Last night had been spent with people from the Off-Broadway scene—young, ambitious, and optimistic about the future. Laura felt comfortable with them. It pleased her.

Maybe it would be fun to work in a theatrical office, she thought as she stepped outside. Or maybe for one of the movie companies with East Coast offices in New York. Living in the East Village had given her a sense of being an insider on the theater scene. Just the other day she and Ira had seen Eva

Gabor walking down Second Avenue with a producer from one of the more prestigious Off-Broadway playhouses.

As for her relationship with Ira, they both knew there was nothing serious going with them. But he was fun to be with and great for her morale. Thank God she'd had him over the holidays.

She walked faster. Her legs would be like ice by the time she reached the subway, but she couldn't wear slacks to an office job. She knew her high heels weren't practical, but she loved the way they looked.

At the corner, the front page of the *Daily Mirror* caught her eye. "Di Dickenson Weds Actor." She dug into her change purse for a nickel and reached for a copy. She huddled against the door of the corner delicatessen and turned to the inside page. *Chris Ames*. He was that new actor Menlow Films was pushing. She'd seen his name in Louella Parsons's column and in Winchell's.

Laura kept reading. Chris Ames and Diane were coming east for the premiere of *Rendezvous with Life*. After the premiere, Menlow Films was giving a supper party for Chris in one of the private rooms at the Stork Club.

Ira had already invited her to the premiere. Somehow she'd have to find a way to talk to Diane. Would Diane remember her?

Of course she would. Diane had been the loneliest kid she'd ever met. It was weird the way they just closed up the house one day and disappeared. She'd been sure that Diane would write. But she hadn't. And she'd never come back.

As she made her way up Second Avenue, she was in

high spirits. Climbing up the ladder in the world sure wasn't easy—but who you knew could really make the difference. She was sure that summer with Diane would make the difference. All the difference in the world.

She arrived at the offices of *Paradise* magazine at 9:05, and by 9:15 she knew this assignment was a dog.

When the tall, paunchy boss sent for her to take a letter, she had to be buzzed into his office—he kept the door locked. His eyes brightened at the sight of her in her Scottish plaid skirt and yellow sweater, and he was practically drooling as she sat down opposite him.

"You don't have to rush with the typing," he said. "If you're not finished by the end of the day, I'll send out for dinner for both of us, and you'll finish it later. Just so it's postmarked by midnight."

"Yes, sir." She tried to be polite. After all, she sure could use the cash.

"Maybe you'd be more comfortable sitting on the sofa with me," he said. "Come over here so I can show you where I want you to break up the copy."

She had just cautiously sat down when he dropped a hand across her back and squeezed one breast.

"That's all, buster!" She shoved him aside and stood up. "Get yourself a call girl if you're all that hot."

She walked to the door. One hand on the knob, she turned around and waited for him to buzz her out.

"Crazy little bitch," he muttered, red-faced.

Upset that she had lost at least seven days'

employment and knowing it was unlikely she'd work anywhere else today or tomorrow, Laura left the office and walked to the employment office.

"So that's why nobody stayed at *Paradise*," the interviewer said after hearing her story. "Nobody else ever told me he had hand trouble. I guess they were too embarrassed. But you'll get paid for today. He won't want trouble."

Instead of going back to the apartment, Laura went to Saks. Just to look, she told herself. Or maybe she would try a few things on and pretend she could afford them. All Diane had to do was hand over her charge plate and buy whatever she chose. And now Diane had bought herself a handsome young movie star.

She hadn't let herself get jealous of Diane that summer when they were friends, Laura analyzed. Not until she moved into her teens did she understand the difference between the haves and the have-nots. Then she saw their creepy little house for what it was. Looked at the clothes the other girls wore, ashamed of her own hand-me-downs. Television showed a little typist making fifty dollars a week, and living in a good-looking apartment and wearing gorgeous clothes. Reality had taught Laura otherwise.

She spent almost two hours in Saks, then took the subway down to Eighth Street. Emerging from the subway station she saw Ira walking across Eighth and called out to him.

"You look like you're freezing," he said, chuckling. "Let's go down to Mama's and I'll buy you a cup of coffee." Mama's was the bakery favored by the Off-Broadway crowd.

"Sure. You off work already?" She knew that Ira worked five hours a day in a West Village bookstore.

"Business was rotten. My hours were cut short. So I'll have a little time to hack away at my own work." He shrugged. Right now Ira was outlining a play. "I don't have to be at rehearsals until six." Off-Broadway rehearsals were often scheduled for evenings to allow actors and actresses to earn a living during the day. "Where are you coming from?"

Laura gave him a report on her morning encounter.

"Oh God, I'd kill to be rich," she sighed. "I went through Saks after I left the office and mentally spent about ten thousand on clothes."

Ira chuckled. "Honey, I hate to disillusion you, but the rich have their problems too."

"But they have them in such comfort! I'd change places with Diane Dickenson any day. Hey, that actor you told me about—Chris Ames—he just married Diane. They eloped early New Year's morning. Didn't you see it in the papers?"

"No kidding? Well it won't last long."

"How do you know?"

"Because Chris Ames is AC/DC." He grinned at Laura's blank stare. "Bisexual, my love. One week he flips for girls, the next for boys."

Late Thursday afternoon, California time, Mr. Lewisohn called Diane and wished her happiness. She was just relieved that he didn't push the annulment issue. Instead, he talked about the financial arrangements. He proposed a monthly living allowance of $2,500.

"Mr. Lewisohn, we—I would like to buy a house out here." She wished she could sound more in charge. "I want everything to stay as is in New York," she added quickly. "Aunt Claudia has agreed to remain in the house there and keep everything running as before. But we'll need a house out here. We'll be in California most of the time. Chris's apartment is much too small." And of course once *Rendezvous with Life* made him a star, they couldn't live there.

Mr. Lewisohn suggested Cadman Brothers, a real estate agency. As she listened to him Diane realized with a small thrill that he was treating her like an adult. She was a married woman, capable of handling grown-up responsibilities.

While she waited for Chris to call about their dinner plans, a studio secretary phoned to say that a limousine was on its way over to pick her up for a conference with Mannie Coleman and Chris. She didn't know exactly why, but this made her nervous. She'd wanted to be alone with Chris. Why did such a simple thing seem so difficult? Couldn't they go away somewhere for a quiet few days together before Chris became involved in this new film? And why was *she* being summoned to the studio?

She changed quickly into the olive plaid Traina-Norell suit from Magnin's. If only she and Chris were back at White Sulphur Springs, away from all this craziness . . . But she had to learn to cope with Chris's world, she reminded herself as she combed her hair. She was his wife.

Forty minutes later she was sitting on a black

leather sofa in Mannie Coleman's enormous white-and-black office, and listened—stricken—while Mannie outlined the elaborate wedding he'd planned for them.

"Chris says you're Episcopalian," Mannie said, reaching for a Havana cigar. Where did he get that idea? Diane wondered. Then she remembered that when Chris asked how she'd been baptized, she'd automatically replied Episcopalian. Mannie lit the cigar. "We'll have the church wedding in three weeks, just before the two of you go east for the premiere. That'll be perfect timing. We'll set it up in the biggest Episcopal church in the area. My wife and I will give a reception at the Beverly Hilton. We—"

"Please," Diane said quietly, amazed that she'd been allowed to get a word in at all, "I'm sorry, I—I don't want a church wedding." She was Jewish. How could she get married in a church? She was a stranger to the church her grandmother and mother had adopted as their own. "I hate church weddings," she said self-consciously, trying not to let Mannie's irritated stare unnerve her.

Chris looked at the two of them nervously.

"Mannie, what about having the wedding at the hotel? Or maybe at *your* house?" Diane remembered Chris saying that Mannie was obsessively proud of his home.

Mannie's hairy fist came down on the desk top.

"Chris, you've got it! Because I'm like the father you lost years ago—you asked to be married at my house!"

"In an Ethical Culture ceremony," Diane added. She'd heard that the Ethical Culture Society had been founded by Felix Adler, the son of a man who had been rabbi of Temple Emanu-El in New York. "That will please everybody."

Mannie and Chris turned and looked at her as though she had the tact of an international diplomat and she fought with the urge to tell them that she wanted to be married in the Jewish faith, that she wanted to carry the ivory-covered prayer book that her grandmother had carried seventy-two years ago. But her mother and aunt would be furious. And how did she know how Chris would feel about having a Jewish wife?

"Chris, not only have you picked a wife who is as beautiful as any girl on the screen—even Liz Taylor," he said expansively, "but she has a real *Yiddishe kop.*" He grinned. "A smart Jewish head."

Mannie appointed a committee to handle the wedding details. Six starlets were to be Diane's bridesmaids. Deirdre was to be maid of honor. Half a dozen of Menlow Films top male actors were to be the ushers. Mannie would give the bride away. Chris's friend Keith, a dark and brooding young actor, would be Chris's best man. Diane had met him only once, when he had come over for dinner. She found him distant, but she couldn't imagine why he wouldn't like her.

Ten days before the wedding, Diane and Chris decided on a house of natural wood and native stone in Beverly Hills. Diane loved it because of the privacy it provided. Set on a sweep of lawn that overlooked a wooded ravine, with a Siamese teahouse that overhung the ravine, it had a living room, dining room, den, and four bedrooms, all of which offered a secluded view. There was even a separate cottage, to be used as the servants' quarters.

It took some convincing, but Diane agreed to buy the house completely furnished, which meant they could move in right away. Chris loved the decor; white rugs on dark wood floors, upholstery of beige, white, and a delicate green, with here and there an accent of hot pink. There was an enormous living room with high ceilings, a swimming pool, and a huge outdoor fireplace. It was a spectacular house, and Diane found herself imagining them living very happily there.

But as time went on, she realized she would be spending a lot of time alone in her new home. It seemed Chris was always gone—tied up at the studio with publicity people, his agent, or screenwriters. He promised her that after the wedding and the premiere, things would quiet down.

"We'll leave for New York, two days ahead of schedule, Di. We'll take the Super Chief instead of flying. That way we can make love in every state we cross!"

Diane braced herself for the arrival of her mother, who at first furious, now seemed merely amused by her daughter's hasty nuptials. Three days before the wedding, Olivia settled into a suite at the Beverly Hilton and consulted with Diane by phone three times a day. Determined to blend properly with the wedding party, she had brought along half a dozen designer gowns. Diane's decision to be married in an Ethical Culture ceremony did not thrill her.

"Darling, Episcopalian would have been much more chic, and you know, you must start being more aware of these things. Especially as an important actor's wife."

But Diane didn't dare tell her mother that she really wanted a Jewish wedding. At fourteen she had mingled with the arriving guests at a Manhattan synagogue and had sat entranced during the ceremony. She had lived this lie all her life, and she couldn't bring herself to say to Chris, "I'm Jewish. I want to be married as a Jew." Even in this enlightened year of 1958 there were people who hated Jews. Like California's posh country clubs or some of New York's men's clubs. No, she couldn't risk losing her husband.

With a few mishaps along the way, the wedding plans fell into place. Deirdre, who had arrived the same day as Olivia but on an earlier flight, stayed with Diane and Chris. From the moment she arrived, she was caught up in the prewedding hysteria. Made from measurements submitted hastily to the studio costume department—whose designer would be responsible for all the gowns in the wedding party—Deirdre's gown had to be adjusted to accommodate the few extra pounds she had picked up since flying back to New York.

"All in the waist," she wailed. "I won't eat a bite until after the wedding!"

At last the big day arrived. Diane woke up early that morning. Sunlight poured into the master bedroom, layering ribbons of gold across the king-sized bed. She lay still for a few moments, trying to muster enthusiasm for the day ahead. Chris slept peacefully beside her. She felt like a reluctant actress in a major film production. But she *had* to go through with this elaborate wedding. As Chris's wife, she had no choice.

There were to be a hundred guests at the wedding. Another three hundred were invited to the reception, to be held in the Crystal Room at the Beverly Hills Hotel. From there, she and Chris would board the Super Chief for New York. She couldn't wait to be in their private drawing room, cut off from the rest of the world for three precious days and nights.

The wedding party was to dress in guest bedrooms at Mannie Coleman's house. Diane and Deirdre were the first to arrive. When they heard the laughter and chatter of the arriving bridesmaids, she was relieved to be alone with Deirdre. She didn't even know these women in her bridal party—Mannie had selected them from his stable of up-and-coming starlets.

Diane and Deirdre sprawled across the pair of twin beds in their bras and panties, sipping hot tea sent up to them by Zelda, Mannie's wife, who seemed to be convinced that "a cup of good hot tea" was the answer to all of life's problems. She had fussed over her "bride and maid of honor," as she insisted upon calling them, until Diane finally had to ask her to leave them alone.

"Can you imagine Mrs. Coleman when her two daughters get married?" Diane said, laughing.

"God, she'll be out of her mind," Deirdre said.

"You know, Deirdre, now I kind of wish Aunt Claudia *had* come out. But she's right. This isn't my real wedding." Her gaze settled on the endless yards of white satin and silk illusion net resting on the lilac velvet chaise. "This is like a gigantic costume party or a scene from a movie."

143

"Anyway, Di, your mother's here," Deirdre said.

Diane's expression tightened. "That's not much of a comfort. In fact, I wish she hadn't come. It's just one more stop on her party tour. A wedding shouldn't be like this. There should be warm, loving family all around. A mother who's proud of marrying off her daughter but a little sad at the same time. A father who can't wait to walk down the aisle with his daughter on his arm. It should be one of the most beautiful memories a girl will ever have."

Deirdre leaned over, kissed her on the cheek. "Listen to you! May I remind you that you've nabbed one of the best-looking men in this country, not to mention the fact that he's going to be rich and famous? And when you have your first baby, I'll be the godmother."

Diane laughed.

"You'll be the godmother of all our kids. And their adopted aunt." Chris had no family except a half-sister whom he always referred to as "that little brat."

They both started at the knock on the door.

"Who is it?" Diane asked, reaching for the robe thrown across the foot of her bed.

"It's Zelda, darling. The makeup man from the studio is here. He'll be up as soon as he's had a drink."

"Thank you, Mrs. Coleman."

Diane figured Mrs. Coleman would probably cry during the wedding ceremony, and it pleased her. But her pleasure was tinged with the sad realization that Mrs. Coleman was more "the mother of the bride" than her own mother could ever be.

* * *

The ballroom-sized living room of the Coleman mansion was filled with masses of white roses. A hundred gilt chairs had been set up to accommodate the guests. Zelda Coleman, her ample girdled figure wrapped in turquoise chiffon, waited for a signal that the bridal party was prepared to descend.

At exactly four P.M. the organ music began. A Broadway singing star soon to go before the Menlow cameras sang "I Love You Truly." The bridesmaids in their daffodil yellow gowns, carrying bouquets of tea roses, began the slow procession down the stairs toward the alter. Deirdre followed, dressed in green chiffon, carrying baby orchids. Diane came after, in her white satin gown encrusted with seed pearls and a Juliet cap of matching pearls, its veil yards of silk illusion net, on the arm of Mannie Coleman.

This was worse than her debut, she thought, worse than the Debutantes' Cotillion. She couldn't believe all the reporters and cameras standing in a knot at the back of the room. Out of the corner of her eye she saw her mother clinging to the arm of a handsome young stranger hardly older than Chris. Louella Parsons stood at one side of the room, Hedda Hopper at the other side. Sheilah Graham was in the center.

Her smile froze. *This wasn't real. It was a nightmare.*

Chapter Eight

Dressed in her old flannel bathrobe, Laura sat at the kitchen table and surveyed her makeup collection. Cindy had lit the oven, but the biting January cold filled the tenement flat. No heat made its way to the paint-peeled radiator sitting beneath the drafty window.

Laura squinted into the makeup mirror.

"Cindy, which eyeshadow should I use?"

Cindy came in, holding a tiny box.

"This one. It'll make your eyes look greener."

Laura grimaced.

"My cat eyes. You know, when I was a kid I used to wish they were blue."

"Well, you were an idiot. You've got gorgeous eyes. Millions of people have brown or blue eyes. How many have green? Play it up big."

"Okay, okay. Hey, thanks for lending me the dress," Laura said, dusting the shadow beneath her eyebrow. She'd been relieved that Cindy wasn't upset that Ira was taking her to the premiere. "I don't own a thing that would have been right."

"It's a little short, but with your legs you can get away with it. Anyway, I'm getting a vicarious thrill from all of this. Oh, what about perfume?"

"I've got a bottle of Blue Grass cologne."

"My brother gave me a bottle of Ode by Guerlain. The perfume." Cindy giggled. "It's the purse flacon. More than nine dollars he couldn't swing on his first job out of college."

By the time Ira arrived, Laura was dressed in her fake-fur coat, relishing its warmth. She could tell by his expression when she opened the door that she looked her best. Why not? Here she was in New York City, going to the premiere of a new movie at the Music Hall. And Diane Dickenson would be there. If she had to knock down fifty people, she would talk to Diane. When they emerged into the blustery cold night, Ira decided they would take a cab up to the Music Hall.

"We'll live in style tonight," he said as they walked toward Astor Place.

Ira had told her about the fabulous Music Hall, built twenty-five years ago and now one of the city's biggest tourist attractions. People came from hundreds of miles away every year to see the Christmas show.

"To get into Radio City Music Hall a film has to have something special going for it," Ira said as they settled back in the taxi. "Out of 125 pictures offered to them each year they take only about a dozen. And once the Music Hall books a movie, it's almost sure to be a box-office smash."

The taxi made its way through the heavy midtown

traffic and dropped them off on the side street, off Sixth Avenue. Already people jammed every inch of the sidewalk in front of the movie house. Lights blazed in dizzying brilliance. A man with a microphone in hand stood outside the entrance, interviewing arriving celebrities.

"Anybody I should recognize?" Laura asked as they inched through the jostling crowd.

Ira chuckled. "No stars yet."

With invitation in hand, Ira managed to maneuver them inside to the outer lobby.

"Can we stay here for now?" Laura asked, noticing that most of the guests seemed to be lingering in this area, presumably to watch the new arrivals.

"That seems to be the general decision," Ira said.

Excited voices and girlish shrieks told them that somebody important was arriving.

Ira peered through the crowds.

"It's Jill Jenkins. Looks like she's being interviewed right now."

But Laura was really only interested in the arrival of Diane and Chris Ames.

At the urging of the ushers, those lingering in the lobby were reluctantly moving inside, but she didn't care where she and Ira sat. *She had to see Diane.*

Ira dropped an arm around her waist.

"Please, Ira. Wait just one more minute."

He sighed. "Waiting for the fabulous Diane Dickenson, eh? Well, all right."

Then she heard a loud cry from the crowd outside and she knew that Chris Ames and Diane Dickenson had arrived.

Surrounded by their entourage, Chris, looking

sleek and handsome in a tux, and Diane, wearing white chiffon and a chinchilla cape that reached to her ankles, stepped inside.

"Diane!" Laura called out. "I haven't seen you since Newport!" There was an uncomfortable pause as the members of Chris Ames's party looked her over suspiciously. Diane hesitated, then broke into a smile. "Why, Laura! Laura Devlin—how wonderful!"

Diane introduced both of them all around. Ira was uncharacteristically reserved.

"Chris, Laura was my best friend," Diane said.

"Great!" He turned to Laura, flashed a smile of perfect white teeth. "Why don't you two join us after the screening? Meet us at the Stork Club—this place will be bedlam afterwards. Just ask to be shown to the Menlow Films party."

Diane and Chris were swept inside. Having accomplished her mission, Laura was content to shuffle along with the others. Even Ira was impressed by their after-theater invitation.

Laura studied the inner lobby. Here was the kind of elegance she associated with the Newport "cottages." The Music Hall lobby alone was the height of three mezzanine floors.

"Ira, look at those mirrors!" she whispered. "They must be at least sixty feet tall." Flanked by golden drapes that reached from floor to ceiling, they reflected the explosive beauty of thirty-foot chandeliers hanging from a gold-leaf ceiling.

"I read somewhere that the Music Hall grosses nine million dollars a year," Ira said. "There's not another theater in the world that brings in so many

150

people." But Ira had no interest in writing for the movies. His heart belonged to the New York theater.

Laura barely noticed the film being shown on the Music Hall screen, so caught up was she in her glamorous surroundings. Something told her this was a landmark event in her young life.

The applause at the end of the movie was enthusiastic. Chris Ames was awfully good, Laura had to admit.

"We can walk to the Stork from here," Ira said, grinning. "But I never expected to be invited to such a fancy party. Good thing I wore a suit and tie." Ira's usual attire was a turtleneck and a beat-up suede jacket.

They arrived at the Stork Club, where the famous solid gold chain at the entrance was swept aside when Laura uttered the magic words, "the Menlow Films party." Ira led her past the walk-around bar and spoke to the maitre d', who escorted them past the entrance to the main nightclub, with its ceilings of balloons and mirrored walls—and images of top-hatted storks on display everywhere—to the private room on the second floor, where the Menlow Films supper party was already in full swing.

An elegant buffet and bar were set up at one side of the room.

"Enjoy!" Ira said, reaching for two plates.

"Laura—" It was Diane. "Come sit at our table. I've saved two places for you."

Throughout the elaborate meal of smoked lake sturgeon and venison steak *poivrade,* Laura felt like a modern Cinderella. Chris Ames was making a point of being charming to her, presumably because she was Diane's friend. She could tell Ira was attracted to Diane. She smiled to herself. Sorry pal, you're just a little too late. And I bet Diane Dickenson isn't the type to stray from the range.

But what was with Chris Ames? He looked uncomfortable when Ira mentioned Larry Kaufman, who had given Ira the tickets Chris had sent him.

"Where is old Larry tonight?" he asked guardedly. Laura remembered that it was Larry who had told Ira that Chris was bisexual. Was it true? Impossible. Diane looked too happy.

"Larry's down in Florida trying to raise funds to switch over to Equity for this new play we're involved in," Ira said. "It's tough to get reviewers down unless you have an Equity company. Not a full Equity cast—just enough Equity members to give it Equity Off-Broadway status."

"I came out of one of Larry's non-Equity companies," Chris said. "This year it might not have happened that way."

Slowly the guests began leaving. Diane asked Laura for her phone number.

"Maybe we can have lunch before Chris and I go back to California," she whispered.

"I'd love that," Laura said.

Laura wasn't surprised when Ira suggested she spend the night with him as they walked into the grimy hall of their building. She knew that being around Diane had aroused him. So what? She wasn't in love with him either. But he *was* great in bed. And *she'd* raised his temperature plenty of times.

* * *

Two days later, dressed in a smart beige wool dress bought hastily at Klein's on Union Square, Laura sat across the table from Diane at the lush Venetian Renaissance Baroque on East Fifty-third Street between Madison and Fifth—a restaurant much favored by big-name publishers and editors, according to Ira. Laura guessed that Diane had chosen the Baroque to escape from the theater and film crowd.

Laura scanned the menu. Where were the prices? She folded it, put it down. "You order, Diane. I'm not used to such elegant menus." *But someday she would be.*

Over potage Baroque—a delicious thick concoction of cream of green pea and clear green turtle, pompano air-expressed that morning from New Orleans, and an endive salad, they talked about everything. Laura remembered Miss Jeanne, in whose presence she had been unexpectedly shy that summer in Newport. She had never met Diane's Aunt Claudia, who had fled to Palm Beach before Diane arrived at the New York house with her new husband. By the time they had finished the main course, they had bridged the years between the summer at Newport and the present.

Over dessert—the Baroque's famous chocolate-folded profiteroles—Laura talked about her job. She admitted that she was bored being a receptionist-typist.

Diane picked up the cue immediately.

"Would you like to work at Menlow Films' New York office? I could ask Chris to talk to the people there."

Laura knew she should probably hesitate for a few

minutes at least, but she couldn't stop herself. "Oh, Diane, that would be marvelous!"

A little tipsy, full of affection and high spirits, they parted with promises to keep in touch. In two days Diane and Chris would be on their way back to California, where Chris was to begin work on a new film. Laura suspected that Diane wasn't entirely wild about Hollywood, though she tried to sound enthusiastic about her new life out there. She was wildly in love with her husband, yet uncomfortable with the people who filled that life.

After this lunch, Laura was convinced more than ever that Diane had no suspicions about him. For all her money and fancy upbringing, Diane was really quite naive. Laura thought of Diane's experience back in Newport—all that money hadn't protected Diane from one terrible experience. What was ahead of her now?

When Laura came home from work Friday night, Cindy looked up from filing her nails and said, "Call the personnel office at Menlow Films. Maybe Diane had Chris pull some strings to get you a job there."

"I'll call now." Laura hurried to the telephone and dialed, her hands shaking. Imagine! She had been in New York just two months and already her life seemed on the point of a radical change.

"They're probably gone for the day," Cindy said, but Laura was waving to her to be quiet. Someone had picked up.

Laura made an appointment for an interview with Joanne Thatcher, the personnel director. Apparently a receptionist position was open, and Chris had recommended her for the position.

"Thank you," Laura said. "I'll be there on Monday at ten sharp." She put down the phone and turned to Cindy. "Oh God, Cindy! How will I survive until Monday morning?"

Back in Hollywood, Chris was caught up in the daily business of building his career. It was important, he told Diane, that he follow up—soon—with a second film. He had found a new agent who planned to renegotiate his contract. That was just the beginning. He left the house at 6:30 every morning, sometimes not returning until eight or nine at night. Whoever thought actors didn't really work was crazy, he told Diane. They worked their asses off on every picture. He had no time even to enjoy the magnificent swimming pool that had been the main reason they'd chosen this house.

Chris turned in the Corvette and bought a Dual-Ghia, the sleek Italian car driven by Frank Sinatra, Eddie Fisher, and Peter Lawford. Mannie approved a bank loan for it. When Diane heard about the bank loan, she immediately paid it off. With Chris's encouragement she bought herself a car, a Chevrolet—the car favored by the studio's contract players, who couldn't afford the likes of Dual-Ghias or custom Cadillacs—and arranged for driving lessons. Meanwhile, until she was able to drive herself, the houseman—Mario—would be her chauffeur. Chris had rented a Cadillac limousine.

One morning, during her driving lesson, she saw

155

an old Corvette with Chris's initials on the door shoot past her on a curve. His friend Keith was driving. She was confused—Chris said he'd traded in the Corvette when he bought the Dual-Ghia. He must have sold it to Keith.

She was proud that Chris was widely liked in the industry. Not only was he sensationally good-looking, he was gentle and fine-mannered, he listened to people when they talked. That in itself was a rare quality in Hollywood.

Saturday nights were reserved for socializing, usually at large, noisy parties with other movie people—what Chris humorously called the "second-string clan." The first-string clan clustered around Frank Sinatra, Dean Martin, and Sammy Davis, Jr. Chris's "clan" consisted of a group of young new stars opposed to the middle-aged, Sinatra-led group. Diane had been relieved that Keith wasn't part of that group.

Diane preferred her moments alone or with Chris. She spent most of every week redecorating the house—without a decorator, which upset Zelda Coleman. She visited small, expensive shops on Rodeo Drive, enjoying this creative outlet. Most nights she sat down to dinner alone because Chris would not get home until ten P.M., and then he'd be too exhausted for anything beyond a dinner tray and sleep. All week Diane prepared herself for the Saturday night parties.

She'd hated the debutante parties back in New York, and now realized that she had expected to be more comfortable with Chris's friends. One thing pleased her—so many people in the film business were Jewish. Whenever she thought about it, she found it incomprehensible that her mother and aunt had so easily forgotten that they were Jewish. Of course, even if the Carstairses had all the money in the world, had the powers that be known the truth, she would never have been a debutante.

But here in this new world, Jewish or not, she was an outsider. Everything in Hollywood revolved around movie-making: conversations, parties, the way everyone looked . . . How could she find a place in this world?

By late spring, Chris's second movie was almost "in the can," and he was coming home to sleep alone in one of the guest rooms, apologizing for his tiredness but promising Diane a vacation in Palm Springs.

He said he loved the way she had redecorated the house, but she suspected he barely noticed. How could he? He was barely awake long enough when he was home to notice. Diane had invited Zelda Coleman and her elder daughter for lunch last month, and Zelda had been impressed.

"Diane, you did such a wonderful job. You should have been an interior decorator."

In fact she had for a moment considered taking some courses at UCLA and opening up a shop, but she wasn't sure how Chris would feel about his wife working.

The Coleman daughter had been less impressed.

"With all that money, how could it not look good?"

Early in May, with the picture finally finished, Chris and Diane threw a party for what had become

157

their crowd.

"Let Romanoff's cater," he insisted. "Why kill yourself?"

As at their Saturday night parties, the guests tonight dressed informally. Diane wore a loose white silk top and white pants cut off just above the ankle. Smiling, she moved among their guests while drinks were being served. Later, after their beloved high-spirited word games, a gourmet supper from Romanoff's would be served. As always, the cocktail-time conversation revolved around the business.

"Look, if you can get Swifty Lazar you'll be in clover. He won't even talk to anybody who makes less than a quarter million a picture."

"Sit down and relax, Diane." A young comic, currently on suspension from his studio because of his drug habit, reached for her hand and pulled her down beside him. "You know, for a very rich girl you're really pretty normal. I mean," he laughed, "you're very pretty and very normal."

"Why should money make me not normal?" She pulled her hand away. "It doesn't come with neurosis, you know." Of course she *had* been in therapy, she reminded herself guiltily, but that had nothing to do with her money. A little girl growing up in a slum would need therapy if her stepfather tried to rape her and her mother was a nymphomaniac, wouldn't she?

The comic paused thoughtfully.

"I suppose it's all those stories we've heard about Barbara Hutton and Doris Duke."

"Diane, what's it like?" A thirtyish starlet sat down on the arm of the sofa. "I mean, being one of the

158

richest girls in America. Does it ever get to be a bore?"

Diane sighed. She was so tired of being looked at as though she were a freak because of her money.

"I've seen what it's like to be poor, and I know what it's like to be rich. I'd say definitely rich is best."

To her right, a pair of young male actors were arguing about a certain director. In Hollywood, it seemed to Diane, if you didn't agree with what people said, they thought you didn't like them. Chris kept telling her how warm and generous movie people were, but they were so damn wrapped up in themselves! If you weren't part of the business, it seemed, you'd always be an outsider.

For a couple of hours everyone played Charades. Diane loved the game, even though again movies were the usual theme, but tonight she was too sleepy to enjoy herself. She was relieved when Mario appeared at the entrance to the living room and made the signal that supper was ready.

Over dinner, the talk turned to psychoanalysis. Diane was astonished at the freedom with which the guests discussed their "headshrinkers." Roxbury Drive was known as Couch Canyon.

Psychoanalytic phrases were tossed around as freely as Hollywood producers' names; people were constantly being described as "sick" or "disturbed" or "sexually compulsive." It reminded Diane of her mother.

Over coffee, the conversation swung inevitably back to "the business."

"The only way to make a lot of money today," one of the most successful young male stars said, "is to demand a piece of the profits. You earn much more

159

than in free-lancing—even when you can pull in $200,000 a picture. Why do you think Gable and Grant are doing it?"

Diane knew that Chris was dying to make a lot of money. He didn't like having to depend on hers to keep up their lifestyle. But he'd made it clear from the start that it was important to his career for them to live expensively. Mr. Lewisohn had been shocked when Diane told him that they absolutely needed half a dozen in help plus two part-time gardeners, even though the house was far smaller than the Manhattan house. But the money was there—it wasn't as though she needed to draw on capital.

A week after the party, while she waited for Chris to decide when they could take off for a vacation in Palm Springs, Diane began to feel queasy in the mornings, and she had a feeling she was pregnant. She didn't want to tell Chris until she was sure, but the thought thrilled her. She tried to imagine herself pushing a baby carriage down Rodeo Drive . . .

She phoned Zelda Coleman, who made an appointment the following morning for her with an obstetrician favored by many in the movie colony. Two days later, the test came back positive.

It was a brilliantly sunny afternoon as she drove back to the house, wondering how she was going to tell Chris. She couldn't wait for him to come home from the studio. At six, sounding oddly withdrawn, he called to say he would be home in an hour. Impulsively, Diane decided she would be completely alone with him tonight. She dismissed the servants. There was some cold chicken in the refrigerator, along with salad ingredients and a chocolate mousse.

Humming as she bustled around the kitchen, she uncorked a Beaujolais, set the table for two, and set out the food. The minutes dragged. Unable to contain her excitement, she called Deirdre and told her, swearing her to secrecy. As she hung up, she heard the sound of the car coming up the driveway. She ran to the door.

Chris must have had a rough day—he looked pale and tense.

"You look tired, darling." She lifted her face to his. He kissed her.

"I'm upset. Mannie called me into his office about an hour ago. He was really pissed off. What's this about you going to see an obstetrician today?"

Diane stared.

"Zelda called Mannie and told him that? Nobody was supposed to know until I told you!"

"Mannie has a fortune riding on me. Of course his wife told him. So—*are* you pregnant?"

"Yes." Her voice was a shaky whisper. This was unreal. She had expected Chris to be as pleased as she was. This was supposed to be one of the most beautiful moments in their lives.

His voice was quiet. Firm. "Diane, you can't have a baby. It'll ruin my screen image! I've never seen Mannie so furious."

"Chris, this is what happens when people marry." She fought to keep her voice even. "Even in Hollywood."

He turned away from her. "No! Mannie will cut my throat if you have a baby! Listen—" he turned back, his tone softer, "he knows a doctor with a private sanitarium—a fine doctor, honey. It'll be

161

nothing at all. Later we'll have children, but not now."

"You want me to have an abortion?" she said.

"Darling, it'll be the end of my career if you don't. This is a crazy business, you know that. Everything depends on your image. Moviegoers don't want to see Chris Ames as a father. As the young lover, the young husband, yes. A father, no. Later—when I'm established—then we can have kids. Half a dozen," he promised, drawing her into his arms. "But Diane, don't wreck my career just when it's taking off."

"It seems so awful." Her voice broke.

"It won't be bad," he soothed. "I'll be right there with you. It's not dangerous at all when a good doctor does it."

"But Chris, it's our baby—"

"We'll have other babies." He pressed his cheek against hers. "Di, we can't risk my career. There may never be another time for me. We can't take that chance."

Diane sat in silent anguish while Chris made the necessary phone calls. How could she go through with this? How could she risk losing her husband? She listened to the plans, trying to pretend they had nothing to do with her. The "procedure" would be performed in a sanitarium forty miles north of Hollywood. Chris insisted that she stay overnight to make sure no complications arose, and the doctor agreed.

"I'll be there with you all the time," Chris said. "I won't leave the hospital for a minute. Mannie knows I'm not on call for those two days."

The next morning she visited the doctor's office for

162

a complete physical. He was brisk and businesslike, but sympathetic. He understood the movie business. How many other wives of actors—how many women stars—had he operated on in the posh sanitarium that everybody in the film colony seemed to know about? How many times had her mother and her mother's friends submitted to this? For her this would be the first and last—she couldn't survive this more than once in a lifetime.

Three mornings later Chris drove Diane, pale and silent, to the sprawling white "California Modern" sanitarium. At the entrance she sat in the car, trying to prepare herself. It didn't seem possible that when she stepped out that door again, she wouldn't be carrying Chris's child.

"Honey—" He reached for her hand. "You'll be fine. Dr. Mosley says you won't feel a thing."

She looked at him for a long moment. Did he think she was only worried about the pain? She was letting Dr. Mosley scrape away what would have become their child. Whatever happened with the rest of her life, she knew that somewhere inside she would always mourn for this lost child.

"It'll be all right, Chris." She tried to smile. "People say it's not as bad as having your tonsils taken out."

She was registered under an assumed name. As she waited for the papers to be filled out, Diane thought about the different reasons she'd used a fake name and nearly smiled. Life certainly was full of little ironies . . . A nurse with a reassuring smile led her to a private suite, where she changed into a hospital gown and submitted to the routine prepping. Soon after the nurse gave her an injection, she grew drowsy.

The last thing she remembered clearly was being wheeled up into the operating room. Her head fuzzy, she was vaguely conscious of Chris kissing her. She saw Dr. Mosley and a pair of nurses. She heard voices, hollow in the room.

When she awoke again, she was back in her suite. A bower of heavily scented long-stemmed red roses sat on her bedside table. Chris stood by the window, gazing out into the early afternoon sunlight.

She turned on her side, away from Chris, and very quietly cried. She had let Dr. Mosley kill their baby.

Chapter Nine

Diane was delighted when Chris told her it looked like he would have a break in his schedule in July, which would give them a three-week vacation. She persuaded him to go with her to Southampton—Aunt Claudia's idea—but he was ambivalent until she mentioned that the Gary Coopers had a house only a few minutes away. Chris worshipped "Coop."

Aunt Claudia was at last accepting her marriage, and Diane was surprised at how much that pleased her. Her aunt was the only real family she had—she could hardly count her mother—and she was anxious to bring her and Chris together. And it would be wonderful to be out of the Hollywood madness even for three weeks.

She was determined to stay out of the Southampton party scene, too, though she knew Chris would probably be tempted. This would be her vacation with her husband, *alone*. Mornings they'd get up early to watch the sun rise over the ocean. From the deck of the house they would see magnificent views of the sunset. Diane counted the weeks until they could leave.

In the meantime, Chris was already talking about his next picture, touted to be the most lavish production Menlow Films ever scheduled. He would be playing a dual role—a pair of twins separated at birth and brought together under bizarre circumstances. A topnotch coach was to be brought in to help Chris with the accent required for the role of one of the twins. He was to take fencing and piano lessons. Mannie kept saying it was the kind of role that could win him an Academy Award, and he hoped to release the film before the end of the year so that it would be in the running for that year's awards.

Three days before they were to fly to New York, Chris came home looking unusually somber.

"Honey, I'm sorry as hell about this . . . I know how much you've been counting on it . . . but I can't go with you to Southampton."

"Oh, Chris, you promised!"

"I'm standing by for some plastic surgery that Mannie has set up. The surgeon's booked up for almost a year ahead, but Mannie persuaded him to fit me in somewhere within the next three weeks. I have to stand by for word from his office."

"What kind of plastic surgery?"

"I'm to get just a slight chin build-up." He shrugged. "No big deal, just a hairline, but the cameraman says it'll make a difference for profile shots."

"But—" Diane struggled to assimilate this all at once. "There's nothing wrong with your chin. Why should you have to go through that?"

He smiled, took her hands in his. "Di, it's nothing. It's being done all the time. You go on out to Southampton and relax for three weeks. If there's time after the surgery, I'll come on out, too."

"Chris, no. I can't leave. Not when you're facing surgery."

"I told you, it's nothing. And I'll feel a hell of a lot better if I know you're out in Southampton enjoying yourself. I don't want you hanging around worrying about me." He grinned. "Let Mannie do that. Also, Mannie wants some retakes. We'll try to wrap them up before I go in for the chin job. Even without all this, Di, I'd have had to stay in town for the retakes."

Diane knew she'd lost, and soon she found herself bound for New York alone. On the flight she remembered the long comforting letter Deirdre had written after she'd told her about the baby. They had both cried. The baby was to have been Deirdre's godchild.

Deirdre was bored with the debutante scene, bored with the dull young men who were only interested in her for her money. She wrote: "When they find out I can't touch a cent of my money until I'm thirty, they kind of disappear. How do I find somebody who's crazy about me? Maybe I'll have to follow your example and change my name."

Diane's aunt had gone out two weeks ago to open up the beach house for the summer and Deirdre was to meet her at Idlewild. They'd drive out to Southampton together, where Deirdre would be staying with her rather than with her mother, who was apparently having marital difficulties.

On the ride from Idlewild to Southampton,

Deirdre admitted to a possible romance.

Diane was delighted.

"Deirdre, tell me. Everything."

"Well, his name is Lenny Jackson. He's a sodajerk in a place on Madison Avenue. He's got this sensational body. He works out all the time with barbells." She sounded uncharacteristically self-conscious. "I've been out with him just a few times. He's mad about rock and roll. Especially Chuck Berry. You know what Frank Sinatra said about rock and roll?"

"No." Diane and Chris didn't run with Sinatra and his clan and lately had been too busy to keep up with who was saying what to whom.

"Frankie called it 'a rancid-smelling aphro-disiac,'" Deirdre laughed. "Do you suppose that's what makes Lenny so hot? We drove all the way out to Coney Island last week so he could hear some group playing out there. He comes from Kansas—and seems to think Coney Island is the greatest."

"Is it?" Diane teased. She knew Battersea Gardens in London and Tivoli Gardens in Copenhagen. But she had never seen Coney Island, only forty minutes by car from the Fifth Avenue house. "Did you have fun on the rides?"

"Darling, all I cared about was parking some-where and lying across the back seat of the car with Lenny. He nearly died when he found out I'd never done it before."

"Deirdre—" Diane hesitated. "Does he know who you are?"

Deirdre laughed.

"Lenny's never even heard of Deirdre Swift. All he

reads is the racing form and sometimes *Confidential*. And thank God neither you nor I have made that yet. To Lenny I'm just some hot little number with a Thunderbird. I know my biggest attraction is the Thunderbird, but I don't care. I'm having fun." She sighed. "I'll never lose weight running in for ice cream sodas every day so I can see him. Why couldn't he work at a health food bar?"

"Why don't you go out to Maine Chance?" Diane said. "Last time you cheated, if I recall correctly."

Deirdre smiled. "Maybe I never cared enough about it before. Maybe now I do."

Deirdre agreed with Diane about not getting caught up in the frenetic Southampton social scene. They planned long, lazy days at the beach, quiet dinners with Aunt Claudia. Diane suspected that while her aunt was relieved that Chris had not come out with her, she was a little concerned about the marriage, since Diane had come east alone.

Claudia's life at the beach house changed little from summer to summer. She was involved in local volunteer work, her bird-watching society, and the church. She had a fortune of her own, but except for luxury residences and a chauffeured limousine she might have been an elderly spinster living out a lonely existence. This summer Mlle. Jeanne was in France on a long-delayed sabbatical, so Claudia took on more of the responsibilities of managing the household, which she seemed to enjoy.

Diane sensed a change in Deirdre, and wondered whether she had come to Southampton because she was scared of the new relationship with Lenny. Though she phoned him every day, Deirdre seemed to feel safe with the distance between them. Clearly he was always in her thoughts—she talked of little else. He didn't know about her money. He liked her for herself. Diane refrained from pointing out that the Thunderbird might suggest money to Lenny.

Diane had resolved not to phone Chris, but on her fourth night her resolve broke down. She knew he was busy with retakes, and he'd promised to call before he checked into the hospital, but she needed to hear his voice.

She tried his private line half a dozen times. No answer.

She panicked.

"He's gone into surgery without letting me know, Deirdre, because he doesn't want to worry me."

"Come on, Di, he's working. Or he came home and went straight to sleep. You said he sleeps so soundly he wouldn't even wake up for an earthquake."

"Maybe. I'll buzz him first thing tomorrow morning, California time. Before he leaves for the studio." She tried to sound matter-of-fact, but she was scared. How could she have left him?

In the morning she dialed their private line. Still no response. Frantic, she tried the regular house phone. Mario answered. He reported that Chris had phoned the previous evening to say he would be staying in his dressing room for the night.

"You see?" Deirdre said triumphantly. "Now let's go for a swim."

At close to midnight Chris called to report that he had just checked into the hospital—the sanitarium where she had gone for the abortion. The surgery would be done the following morning.

"And don't worry," Chris said. "It's nothing at all."

"You'll call me as soon afterwards as you can?"

"I'll call you tomorrow night. And if I sound funny, don't be surprised," he chuckled. "Remember, they're working on my chin."

Keith took the phone away from Chris—sprawled on the hospital bed in pajamas and robe—and put it down.

"These last days have been so wonderful," he pouted. "Why does *she* have to come back?"

"Keith, let's take one day at a time." Chris's dark eyes were troubled. It had been stupid to have Keith stay overnight in the dressing room with him, even though everybody except the night watchman had left. You never knew . . . Mannie would be furious if he found out he was seeing Keith again. He'd sworn it was all over.

"I've been miserable these last six months." Keith sighed. "Knowing you were with her. That's why I crashed the Corvette, you know. I was thinking about you with her—"

"Thank God, you walked away from that." Chris smiled. The Corvette had been Keith's consolation present when he married Diane. "And the car looks as good as new since you got it out of the shop." He'd picked up the tab for the repairs.

Keith trailed a hand along Chris's thigh. "I wish we were back at Santa Monica right now. Don't you?"

"C'mon, Keith," Chris pushed his hand away.

171

"You know that wouldn't be bright." Too many gays hung out there now. It had taken a lot to convince Mannie that he was steering clear of that scene. He'd had to sleep with half a dozen actresses before Diane.

"If I don't find a part soon, I'll have to head back for New York," Keith sulked. "Or," he said with a wink, "I can be a towel boy at the steambaths." Chris winced.

"I'll give you some money to tide you over," Chris soothed. "Something will come along soon." Keith was handsome, and he wasn't a bad actor. He should be able to get some work.

"Okay," a nurse stuck her head in the doorway, "visiting hours are over. I'm sorry."

Keith left, promising to come by the next day. Chris accepted the sleeping pill the nurse offered him. He'd never get to sleep tonight without it. He knew he was risking everything by seeing Keith, but he couldn't walk away from it. There were only brief moments when he could convince himself he was happy with a girl.

But more than anything else in this world he wanted enormous success. Here it was, almost within his grasp. He couldn't afford to fuck up. With the climate in Hollywood what it was today he couldn't risk even a hint of scandal. He'd do whatever Mannie demanded of him. Mannie Coleman was his ticket to the top.

Thank God he'd met Diane—she was so sweet and wonderful, so completely different from the conniving would-be starlets he saw every day. He'd been so sure that he was in love with her. That in her arms he could forget Keith and the others. It had worked for a while. He had to make it work again.

Diane stayed around the house the next day, awaiting word from Chris, imagining all sorts of emergencies. Finally at eight o'clock he called.

"Chris, are you all right?"

"Everything went great except my jaw is stiff as hell and the whole lower half of my face is sore. I'm on medication so it isn't too bad. Mannie insists I stay in the hospital for three more days. To keep away from the vultures, as he puts it."

"Then you'll fly out here," Diane said. "I can't wait to see you, Chris."

"I can't, Di. Mannie wants me here for some tests for the film. Costumes and stuff, I think."

"Oh, Chris—"

"Come on, honey, you'll be coming home in a little over two weeks. Enjoy your visit. I'll call you tomorrow night."

On a Wednesday, ten days after they'd first arrived in Southampton, Diane and Deirdre decided to go into New York for a day. Deirdre was anxious to see Lenny, and this was his day off. Diane, lonely for Chris, thought she might do some shopping.

They ate breakfast early and heartily—waffles, bacon, orange juice, and lots of coffee—and left the house at seven-thirty. They arrived in the steamy city just as the Fifth Avenue department stores opened for the day. Deirdre put the car in a midtown garage and headed for the luncheonette-soda fountain where

Lenny worked. They planned to meet again at the garage at four so that they could head back to Southampton before the rush hour. Diane walked into the blissful coolness of Saks to buy Chris a gift.

She chose an elegant dressing gown and had it sent to the Hollywood house. Then she wandered the aisles, a little at a loss as to what to do next. She had hours to fill before they headed back to Southampton. Suddenly she thought of Laura and she went to the ladies' lounge to phone her. In February Laura had written with the news that she was working as a receptionist in the New York office of Menlow Films and thanking Chris for his help.

"I'm just in the city for a few hours," Diane said after Laura had picked up and they had spoken for a few minutes. "Listen, I know this is last-minute, but I was wondering if I could take you to lunch today."

"I'd love it," Laura said. "What time?"

"Whatever is good for you."

"Twelve o'clock all right? That is, I'll leave here at twelve."

"Fine. Meet me at Le Pavillon." Diane remembered Laura's appreciation of luxury restaurants. "Just ask for Diane Ames's table."

Laura arrived slightly breathless, a few minutes after Diane had been seated. She wore a simple black linen that looked as though it might be a designer dress, but probably wasn't. They hugged and Laura settled into her chair, looking around the room.

"Hey—" she nudged Diane, "isn't that Dorothy Kilgallen?"

"Yes." Diane sighed. She should have chosen a restaurant less favored by the columnists. "Now

174

she'll be hinting in tomorrow's 'Voice of Broadway' that our marriage is breaking up because Chris had to stay out on the Coast while I'm here in New York."

Laura laughed. "You worry about Dorothy Kilgallen? That's ridiculous. Besides, any publicity in 'Voice of Broadway' is good. Chris won't be upset. People fight to be mentioned by Kilgallen."

"I'm trying to get used to all the publicity surrounding Chris." Diane knew that in her own right she was as newsworthy in the eyes of the columnists as Chris, but she didn't like it. "Shall I order for us?" she asked.

"Please. I learn from you."

Diane ordered a specialty of the house—Chateaubriand Pavillon with *coeurs de celeri au beurre*, and a bottle of fine Burgundy.

"I'm sorry to be such a drip, Diane, but I have to be back at the reception desk no later than one-thirty. Somebody's already covering me for the extra half-hour. Say—" She cut a generous chunk of chateaubriand, "how do you like living in Hollywood, anyway? Must be quite a change."

"Well, it is exciting," Diane said, remembering guiltily that she had not replied to Laura's letter. "Some of the time it's exciting. But Chris has to spend so much time at the studio—I'm left on my own an awful lot. I've been thinking about taking some painting classes." Chris had kidded her out of the idea of going into interior decorating. How could he object to painting classes?

"That sounds like fun," Laura said. "Ira keeps telling me I need some creative outlet. Besides just chasing after the weekly paycheck."

"Ira's the fellow who was with you at the premiere, right?" He hadn't said much at the premiere party, but she suspected that whatever he had to say would be interesting.

Laura looked surprised.

"That's right. You've got a good memory! We live in the same building. Ira's all wrapped up in Off-Broadway. Right now he's moved up from stage manager to assistant director. He wants to write plays. I think I'm on to my creative outlet. Only I'm thinking in terms of career. I couldn't just play at anything. Whatever I want to do I'll have to do it whole hog."

"What'll that be?" Diane felt oddly defensive.

"The film business." Laura laughed at Diane's startled expression. "Not acting. I want to get into the production end. I've been giving it a lot of thought. One day I'd like to be at the head of a studio. No woman's ever made it big in the business end of pictures. Maybe it'll take me twenty years, but one day I'll be up there, Diane. I'll be somebody."

Diane gazed at her thoughtfully.

"I'm sure you will."

"It's not just the money I'm after, though I'll admit that's damn important to somebody raised as I was. I have to know I've accomplished something on my own in this world."

Laura was too caught up in herself to recognize her friend's frustration. Diane lived on money inherited from a grandfather who had slaved, plotted, and connived to build a great fortune from almost nothing. He'd slaved so that his children and grandchildren could live in idle luxury. What would

176

she ever accomplish on her own?

"And meanwhile," Laura said, "I'm going to do exactly what Ira keeps telling me to do. I'm signing up tonight for a course in film production at the New School. I have to learn everything about this business. I'm not going to let anything stop me."

Watching the clock, they decided not to have dessert.

"So you see," Laura said over coffee, "I have to hang onto this job; it's one step up the ladder for me."

Diane dropped a cube of sugar into her coffee.

"Are you at the same address? I'd like to keep in touch."

"I'm still there," Laura said. "Alone, though. Cindy, my roommate, went back home. She'd had it with the theater and television rat-race. In a year she'll probably be engaged and on her way to becoming a young suburban matron." She made a face. "What a drag."

On the drive back to Southampton Deirdre chattered on about Lenny, while Diane thought about Laura's determination to become a power in the film world. She envied Laura's and Chris's fierce dedication—a dedication that she suspected existed in Laura's friend, Ira, too. It seemed to lend a special meaning to their lives.

Maybe what *she* needed in her life was a creative outlet, something to do during those long, empty hours when Chris was away at the studio. The house required nothing of her. The staff was in full charge.

She had no friends out there. But who were her friends, really? Only Laura that summer in Newport, and of course, Deirdre.

Before her debut she'd had school. Then all that debutante nonsense. Now when she woke up every morning she had to decide what to do with the hours till Chris came home. When she tried to pass away time at Magnin's or the shops on Rodeo Drive, she often ended up fleeing the stares of other shoppers who recognized her. Besides, she needed more out of her life than shopping and waiting for Chris to come home. If only she'd been able to have her baby . . .

"I'm signing up for painting classes when I go back to California," she told Deirdre when they reached Southampton's busy Job's Lane. "If nothing else, it'll be something to do."

"If I recall correctly, you were pretty good when we took painting at school." Deirdre giggled. "As good as a lot of stuff we see at the galleries out here."

Could she have a career as a painter? It was an exciting, terrifying thought.

Chris met Diane at the airport, reporters and photographers right behind him as he rushed forward to greet her. She was thrilled to see him. How could she have stayed away for three whole weeks?

A sleek, dark-haired woman reporter thrust herself at Chris and Diane. "Chris, is there anything to the rumors that Diane and you are considering a trial separation?"

"Does this look like it?" Chris laughed and pulled Diane into his arms for a long, passionate kiss.

With his arm around her waist, Chris submitted to their questions, carefully fielding those directed at Diane. He knew how uncomfortable she was at these press conferences.

She squirmed beside her husband, her smile frozen on her face. This must have been arranged by the studio. How else would they have known what flight she'd be on?

"Look," Chris said, one hand raised. "Diane's had a long trip. Can you guys—and ladies, excuse me— let us go home and do what every young couple does after a three-week separation?" He grinned and kissed her again. This time, Diane realized, for the benefit of the photographers. Flashbulbs were going off like mad.

Mario sat waiting for them in the parking area behind the wheel of a Silver Wraith Rolls-Royce. Diane lifted an eyebrow in surprise.

"It's on loan from the studio," Chris whispered. "Mannie's suggestion."

While they drove from the airport to the house, in the Persian-lamb-carpeted, red-leather-upholstered Rolls, Diane inspected Chris's new chin line.

"I don't see any difference," she pronounced.

"No difference," he said, "except to the cameras."

Immediately after dinner they went to bed, making love with an intensity that surprised them both. Afterwards, content, Diane lay her head on Chris's chest while he slept, trying to convince herself that everything was all right.

Chris was full of enthusiasm for the new picture,

which they were to begin shooting in ten days. Mannie had set up a three-month shooting schedule, which Chris said meant he wouldn't be holed up at the studio for fifteen hours every day. Diane interpreted that to mean he wouldn't be sleeping in the guest room.

Despite hours of coaching every day, Chris managed to be home for dinner. He shared every detail of his day with Diane, which thrilled her. But then the shooting began, and his routine changed. After a late dinner he settled down each evening in the black leather recliner in the den to study his lines for the following day's scenes. Diane sat on the matching sofa and tried to focus on reading. Deirdre had sent her a copy of *Lolita*, which she said everybody in New York was reading.

The Saturday socializing with what Chris called the second-string clan was now forgotten. There was no room in their life for anything but movie-making. He understood the importance of this new film to his career. Diane knew that she was watching the making of a major star.

In an effort to find ways to fill her time, Diane signed up for more driving lessons and arranged to start fall painting classes, registered as Deirdre Davis. She bought a blonde wig and glasses to wear to class, picked up some scruffy jeans and T-shirts in a shop on Sunset Strip.

She was pleased that she was able to pull off the masquerade, especially when the instructor conceded she had some native talent. But Chris seemed irritated when she reported her small successes. She told herself he was upset because the shooting was already running behind schedule, which meant the picture would come in overbudget. But she couldn't be sure.

Zelda Coleman told her that there was a lot of fighting on the set between Chris and his co-star, who was outraged that Chris was to receive top billing. After dinner each night now, Chris closeted himself in a guest room to study his lines. Usually he fell asleep there. On Sundays he slept the day away—too tired even to spend time with Diane in the pool.

Returning from her painting class one early afternoon in October, Diane was told by a maid that Candace Collins had been calling from New York every twenty minutes for the past two hours. The columnist insisted it was urgent she talk with Diane the moment she arrived home.

Diane was hesitant about returning the call. Maybe she'd wait until Chris came home and they would talk to Candace together. He knew so much more about handling these people than she did. But curiosity got the better of her and she decided to phone Candace herself. Why not spare Chris having to be polite and charming after a rough day on the set?

She dialed the number Candace had left. Candance picked up on the first ring.

"Darling," the familiar voice purred, "I'm about to break a sensational story on Chris, and I thought it was only fair to quote his wife's reaction."

Diane tensed, remembering what Chris had told her: "Candace Collins is the worst of the vultures. She'll do anything to push her column."

"What story?"

"About his arrest in Chicago three years ago." She paused. "For propositioning a cop. A male cop."

For an instant Diane was speechless.

"It's not true!"

"He pleaded guilty and paid a fine. It's on the police record. I have a photocopy."

There had to be some logical explanation.

"I mean, it didn't happen the way they said," Diane stammered. *She had to say something. Anything.* "He was framed. He told me all about it." She tried to sound calm. "I'll have him call you as soon as he gets home. Please don't run that story, Candace. Mannie Coleman will be terribly upset." Maybe that would work—Mannie Coleman was a formidable enemy, even to a Candace Collins.

There was a long silence.

"Well, I'll hold it up for now. But make sure Chris calls me no later than nine o'clock California time."

Diane was trembling when she put down the phone. What was she supposed to do now? Sit and wait for Chris? But she had no idea when he'd be coming home. He might not be here by nine. She couldn't sit here with this knowledge until then. She had to talk to someone. *Zelda.* Zelda would know how to handle this.

But Zelda was at one of her committee meetings and the maid wasn't sure when she would be home. Mannie Coleman. That was it. Chris always said that Mannie had to know everything.

The studio switchboard kept her on hold for five minutes before Mannie's secretary—the much-feared but widely courted Marge Mendelsohn—came on the line.

"Mannie's in conference, Diane," Marge said sweetly. "Anything I can do for you?"

"No, I'm afraid I really need Mannie for this one. He has to kill a rotten story Candace Collins is threatening to break. She gave me a deadline—"

"I don't think we should talk about this over the phone," Marge said quietly. "I'll send a studio limo for you."

Forty minutes later Diane sat in Mannie's office repeating what Candace had told her.

"It's a lie, of course," she said.

Mannie gave Marge a look.

"Bring Chris to the office."

While Mannie went to the bar and poured himself a straight shot of scotch, Diane sat quietly. There had to be a logical explanation. It was somebody else named Christopher Ames. That was it. *It was all a mistake.* But Mannie seemed worried. Why?

Pale, uncertain, Chris came into the office. He was surprised to see Diane.

"No calls, Marge." Mannie barked as she left, closing the door behind her. He turned to Chris. "All right, what's this crap about you being arrested in Chicago for soliciting a policeman? And don't deny it, Chris! That bitch Candace Collins managed to get a photostat of the records."

Chris dropped into a chair beside Diane. She saw his knuckles go white as he grasped the arms of the chair. *It wasn't true. It couldn't be true.*

"It was a frame-up, Mannie." Chris's voice was barely audible. "I'd been playing stock near Chicago all summer. I had a night off and came into town and got drunk. A cop—who specialized in entrapment, I

183

found out later—picked me up at a bar. I was lonely. The cop was friendly. I invited him up to my hotel room for a drink. The lawyer the stock company manager called in said it would be best to plead guilty and pay a fine. I had a performance the next night."

Mannie paced.

"Well, how the hell did Candace Collins find out? What asshole tipped her off?"

"It must have been Keith Edwards," Chris said after a moment. "Nobody else out here knows. He went back to New York a week ago. He was mad as hell because I hadn't been able to help him land a part."

"Chris, you're a stupid frigging ass." Mannie's face was flushed, his voice shrill. "You know it'll ruin your career if Candace runs that story! This picture will die at the box office. You'll be finished!"

Chris stared at the carpet, unable to speak.

"Can't you do something to stop her?" Diane said. "You must know somebody—"

Mannie pressed a buzzer on his desk. "Marge, tell the lawyers to get their fat cans over here, pronto. Tell 'em this is a top-level emergency." Now he turned to Chris. "Get back on the set. Do you know what it costs this studio every minute you're away from the cameras? But first put your wife in the studio limo waiting outside."

Chapter Ten

Diane stood by the window in the master bedroom and gazed into the dusk-laden ravine. Usually this scene entranced her with its light and shade, its aura of mystery and other-worldliness. But today she saw nothing.

Why didn't Mannie call and tell her what was happening? Chris would be tied up on the set until the day's shooting was completed—she understood his silence. *But why didn't Mannie call?*

She turned away from the window toward the phone. No. She would not call him. Not yet. He must still be trying to save Chris—and the studio—from this scandal. If the situation had been taken care of, he would have had Marge call and tell her.

Candace had said, *"Make sure Chris calls me no later than nine o'clock California time."* That would be midnight in New York. Candace's story would make the morning papers if Chris couldn't talk her out of it. Obviously Candace was only giving him this chance to clear himself in order to protect herself against a libel suit.

How could anyone believe that Chris would have propositioned a cop? *Keith* must be gay. That was it. He was getting back at Chris for rejecting him. Chris was so sweet and trusting—he'd even made Keith best man at their wedding! She'd felt from the start that Keith hated her. Now she understood why.

The phone rang.

Diane jumped, darted across the room and picked up the receiver.

"Hello—"

"Diane?" A vaguely familiar female voice.

"Yes—"

"Marge. Mannie asked me to call you. Everything's all right. He's talked to the lawyers and to Candace; it's all settled."

The relief made her weak.

"Thank you, Marge."

"My pleasure. Listen, Chris should be home soon. Shooting's over for the day. He's having a short conference with Mannie."

Diane dismissed the servants for the evening. She put two steaks in the broiler, two baked potatoes in the oven, and a bottle of Perrier-Jouet in the refrigerator. Tonight they'd relax. And celebrate.

She hurried to the door when she heard the crunch of the Dual-Ghia's wheels on the black-pebbled driveway. As he walked from the car, she could see his anguish in the moonlight.

"I sent the servants to their cottage," she said after he kissed her. "I'll bring trays to the den."

He held her close.

"Diane, why did Keith do this to me?"

"Because he's a bastard." She hated Keith for hurting Chris this way. "Forget about it. It's all over." She paused. "But Chris, I'm just curious . . . how *did* Mannie handle Candace?"

Chris chuckled.

"It was blackmail. Not against Candace—against her boss. By the time Mannie and the lawyers were through, she was told loud and clear to back off."

Now Chris was back to his grueling schedule, at the studio fifteen hours a day. They even worked on Thanksgiving Day. Mannie was furious that the picture was running so far beyond schedule. But even while he groaned, he gloated over the publicity, thanks to the exorbitant budget: seventy-six sets, with props costing half a million, an orchestra on the set to put the cast in the proper mood . . . it was indeed an extravagant production.

But all was not quiet on the set. Chris was fighting with his co-star and the director, with whom she was sleeping; and even though Mannie regularly interceded on his behalf, it did not make for a pleasant working atmosphere. Chris came home late, ate alone, then closeted himself in a guest room to learn lines for the next day's scenes. He needed absolute privacy; even Diane's presence was a distraction. When the picture was wrapped up, he told her, they would spend a month lying on the beach at Acapulco.

Diane tried to find ways to fill the lonely hours. She talked to Deirdre on the telephone every day. Deirdre reported that her mother had bumped into Olivia at a posh private sanitarium in Geneva.

"Your mother was there for an eyelid lift and a

fanny tuck," she said, "Mine was getting the whole frontal face job."

Diane passed her driving test, but she was nervous about driving on the crowded freeways, and Chris insisted that Mario drive her if she went more than a quarter-mile from the house.

Just when it began to look as though the end of filming—and Chris's absence—was in sight, Mannie scheduled him to begin shooting another movie immediately. That night Chris took a few hours off to have dinner with Diane and explain why the Acapulco trip was off.

"It's important to keep me in the public eye," he said defensively while Diane stared at him in disappointment.

"I know that, Chris, but what about our marriage? I never see you anymore." She couldn't shake the feeling that he seemed happy with this turn of events.

"If Mannie's willing to push me ahead this way, Di," Chris said, "I can't demand time off. I'm getting the kind of treatment every actor dreams about."

Diane knew she had no choice, so she threw herself into her painting. Encouraged by her instructor's approval, she found herself become increasingly confident and daring. It didn't bother her that the others in her class thought her eccentric with her sloppy clothes and bleached blonde wig. One student did ask her if anyone had ever told her she resembled Diane Dickenson.

"You know, that rich debutante who married Christopher Ames."

"A couple of people," she'd said with a shrug.

At the house she set up one room as a studio. She

spent every morning and some afternoons there, painting and then destroying what she'd just painted, never satisfied.

Slowly she became more involved with Mr. Paoletti, her instructor, than with anyone else in her world. With one word of praise or criticism he set the mood for her entire day. Then one morning he told her that in her painting of the ravine behind the house she had used color and depth in a way that reminded him of Constable. Now she waited for Chris to come home, to tell him the good news.

Some weeks ago she had started dismissing the staff every night after she'd been served her dinner. When Chris came home, she served his dinner—kept warm in the oven—on a tray in the den. This was their only time alone together.

She waited impatiently for the sound of the Dual-Ghia coming up the driveway. At last she heard the wheels crunching the pebbles on the driveway and she hurried to the foyer.

"Chris, you have to see the painting I did of the ravine," she said, clinging to his arm as she walked him toward the den. "My instructor was so pleased with it. He—"

"Oh, sure." He grunted. "Poor little rich girl, making like Picasso." Seeing her stricken expression, he said, "Di, I didn't mean that. You know I didn't. I'm just so damn upset about the fighting at the studio I don't know what I'm saying. This was another of those days when nothing went right."

She tried to smile.

"I understand, Chris. Go on into the den. I'll bring in your dinner."

While Chris ate, watching "77 Sunset Strip," Diane went into the master bedroom to change into her four-hundred-dollar chiffon nightgown she had bought on Rodeo Drive. Maybe Chris would relax if they made love. She thought of the last time they'd tried . . . He hadn't been able to do anything. She'd cried inside for his humiliation. Why did men feel that kind of failure was a disgrace? It must happen to every man at some time or other. Chris had said it was because he was exhausted from the long hours on the set.

She paused in the doorway of the den in the black chiffon nightgown. She wore the high-heeled black satin mules that he had bought for her just before their second wedding ceremony.

His eyes were fastened to the TV screen.

"Chris, would you like some more of the casserole?" she asked.

"No." He turned and gazed at her. "I should start studying tomorrow's lines."

"Later?" she said with a wistful smile.

He grinned.

"Later." He walked over and took her in his arms.

His mouth was warm, his hands moved expertly over her body. Couldn't he tell she was dying to make love? When was the last time? A month ago? *Please God, don't let it be like last time.*

He picked her up and carried her to the bedroom. She could feel his tension as he lowered himself over her. She reached her hand down . . . Nothing.

"Chris, I love you," she whispered. She had never slept with anybody but Chris. Maybe a girl who'd been with other men would know what to do to excite him. *Was there something wrong with her?*

Chris swept the nightgown above her hips and prodded limply.

"Damn it, Di," he muttered, "make me hot! You used to be able to."

He thrust himself between her thighs for another few moments, then turned over on his back.

"You know the problem with us?" he said, staring at the ceiling. "You're frigid. Maybe you ought to go to one of those guys on Couch Canyon and see if he can straighten you out."

He got up and walked naked from the room. She heard a door slam down the hall. The guest room. Why couldn't he handle a sexual relationship with her? She wasn't frigid. Lying here alone, empty and passionate; she just knew it.

Diane was relieved when the film company left two days later for two weeks of shooting on location in Mexico. Chris had made it clear he didn't want her to join him. He urged her to invite Deirdre to fly out to visit and to stay for Christmas.

"When I'm on a picture, Di, there's no room in my life for anything else," he said self-consciously.

"I know, Chris. I understand." But she didn't, not really. What about *her* needs? When would there be time in his life for her?

Fortunately Deirdre was in one of her periodic fits to lose weight—Lenny had taken to calling her Tubby—so she agreed to come immediately. Also, she suspected Lenny was seeing a sexy little waitress from the luncheonette, though of course he vowed he wasn't.

Diane and Deirdre passed the time shopping on Rodeo Drive and lunching at whatever restaurants Deirdre felt were "in." Deirdre ate little, though she stared hungrily at the leftovers on her plate.

"I'm going to lose weight, Di," she said, every time Diane tried to talk her into eating. "Remember that fruit diet people were going on last year? Maybe I ought to try that."

"Go to Maine Chance," Diane said. "If you don't cheat, you'll lose weight. And exercise. You should swim with me every morning."

But Deirdre wanted no part of the swimming pool. While Diane swam, she lay on a chaise, covered from throat to toe in one of the half-dozen silk caftans she'd bought after Lenny called her Tubby for the first time. She swore she wouldn't get into a bikini again until she lost forty pounds.

For endless hours each day they dissected Deirdre's affair with Lenny.

"I rented this shitty apartment on West Eighty-second Street," she told Diane. "I could have gone to the lawyers and carried on about having them release money for a really cool apartment, but with mother away most of the time I have her place to myself. The rent's only ninety-six dollars a month. Can you believe it? I piss that away on makeup." Diane noticed that Deirdre was beginning to sound more and more like Lenny. "Did you know that when she was fourteen, Barbara Hutton had her own twenty-six-room duplex?"

Diane laughed.

"I don't think you need a twenty-six-room duplex." She never thought of the twenty-four-room Carstairs mansion as "her" house. It was the family home.

"I rented this el cheapo apartment so Lenny wouldn't get ideas about my money. He thinks I live there. I told him my folks pay the rent and give me enough to eat on to keep me out of their hair. The Thunderbird is supposed to be a consolation prize for testifying in dad's last divorce case so he wouldn't get stuck for alimony. He doesn't know anything about my grandfather's estate, Di. I'm not *that* dumb—or horny."

"Deirdre, go to Maine Chance and lose thirty pounds," Diane said. "If nothing else, it'll give you something else to think about. Anyway, you've got terrific bones—if you'd get rid of some of that weight you could go out and meet other fellows." She knew it wasn't fair, but from what Deirdre had told her, she didn't trust Lenny. He sounded like a creep.

"I'll never know if they're seeing me or the money I'll get my hands on when I'm thirty," Deirdre said. "Even if I looked like you, I'd never be sure."

"Why don't you arrange to go to Maine Chance from here?" Diane tried yet again.

"I have to go back to New York first to see what Lenny's up to. Maybe he's dumped that waitress and he's pining for me. Ha-ha. Oh, I almost forgot, tonight we have to go to my grandmother's for dinner. You don't mind, do you? She'll ask you a million questions about Chris and all the actors he knows. She pretends to have no use for picture people, but she keeps *Photoplay* and *Modern Screen* hidden under her mattress. She's absolutely fas-

193

cinated that my best friend is married to Christopher Ames."

Deirdre's grandmother took them to dinner at her country club. Diane remembered that no picture people or Jews were allowed, but Chris was now listed in the *Social Register* since marrying her, so they were "legal." Nobody knew that Diane Dickenson was really Diane Seligman.

They were just standing up to leave when Diane heard a slightly shrill feminine voice, the phony British accent unmistakably familiar . . .

"Darling, I've been calling and calling you." Olivia came forward, her arms open, dressed in a black faille Dior gown with a dramatically low neckline. "What a coincidence! I'll only be here a few days before I fly down to a houseparty in Mexico City, and I did *so* want to see you."

Before she had a chance to say a word, Diane was swept up in her mother's embrace, then introduced to her young escort, a sleek young Frenchman. Olivia insisted that the five of them go off to Romanoff's for drinks.

"Darling, how are you really?" she whispered as they headed for the limousine. "Chris is so handsome. Of course, I was sure there was nothing to those stories about his being gay."

"We're both fine, mother," Diane said, a bit shaken. Had everyone heard the rumors about Chris? Maybe it was because he was so good-looking. "Chris is off on location for his new film. They're working eighteen hours a day—it didn't make sense for me to go along." She knew she sounded nervous. *Why was she making excuses to her mother?*

Diane was relieved when at last she and Deirdre were alone in the house. She was sorry they'd met her mother at the country club, sorrier still that they'd gone along to Romanoff's. Fortunately, Deirdre's grandmother had assumed that Edmond was the nephew of Livvy's absent husband.

In their nightgowns, Diane and Deirdre sprawled across the king-sized bed.

Deirdre sighed.

"How *does* your mother stay so thin?"

Diane shrugged.

"She starves herself. If the scale goes four pounds over, she phones Maine Chance in a panic."

Diane was silent for a moment, wishing she could talk openly with Deirdre. Deirdre was the closest person in the world to her—even closer than Chris. Why shouldn't she talk about what was bothering her?

Impulsively, she told Deirdre about the near-disaster with Candace Collins.

"Deirdre, do you think Chris is gay?"

"Actually, I never thought about it until your mother made that crack," Deirdre said with her usual candor. "Why? Are you having doubts now?"

"Deirdre, you know better!" She hesitated. "I mean, I can't believe it. I don't want to believe it. But something's wrong with our marriage. We don't make love more than once every three or four weeks— and then it's not right." She couldn't bring herself to elaborate. "It makes me wonder if something's wrong with me."

Deirdre sat up and looked at her sternly.

"Don't be ridiculous. You're nineteen years old

and gorgeous. If anything's wrong, it's with Chris."

Diane smiled, still uncertain.

"Well, I'm going to stop thinking about it then. Let's go out tomorrow and buy ourselves something smashing." But would one more designer dress make her feel less frightened? "Deirdre, is there something special you'd like to do while you're out here?"

"Yes." Deirdre was emphatic. "I'd like to see the inside of a movie studio. And not one of those bus-tour things. Can you swing that?"

"I'm sure I can. We'll go right after breakfast. I'll call Marge, the chief's assistant. I'm sure she'll okay it for us."

At shortly after ten the following morning, Diane and Deirdre drove through the studio gates, Deirdre at the wheel of the Chevrolet. Marge had arranged for a studio employee to show them around the studio. Diane was relieved that no one seemed to recognize her in her blonde wig and dark glasses. Afterwards, she and Deirdre decided to have lunch at the studio cafeteria. The rush was over. Only a handful of office employees remained at the tables.

They carried their trays to a corner table.

Clearly Deirdre had enjoyed the morning's tour.

"God, remember how we used to cut classes to run off to the Capitol and the Paramount, Di? Five years ago I'd have sold my soul to be sitting here."

"I don't know, Deirdre. Picture people work hard—" She stopped, listening to the conversation at the next table.

"It's crazy for Keith Edwards to have come back here," a young woman was saying. "He must know by now that the chief had him blackballed at every studio in town. Coleman won't take any chance of his starting up with Chris Ames again—not when he's safely married to Diane Dickenson."

"How did he ever fool her?" the other girl asked curiously.

"He swings both ways. Like Tyrone Power."

That was why Keith went to Candace Collins. Because he knew Mannie had him blackballed in Hollywood. He wanted to get back at Mannie where it would hurt most: at the box office.

Deirdre looked at her in silent understanding.

"You okay?"

Diane nodded, her throat tight.

She stood up, pushing her chair back. "Let's go over to that new boutique on Rodeo Drive." Later they'd talk. Right now she needed time to think. Without Chris, who was she?

She shopped with an abandon that startled even high-spending Deirdre.

"Deirdre, let's go out for dinner." She couldn't bear going home. "Anyplace, I don't care, as long as there aren't any movie people there."

Deirdre remembered Man Jen Low in New Chinatown. They drove in silence, parked and went inside, upstairs to the Mandarin Room, where they ordered *hop toa har gon pin*—black walnuts, chicken livers, shrimps and oriental mushrooms—and asparagus lobster Mandarin. At last, Diane mustered the courage to ask Deirdre how much she'd heard of the conversation at the other table.

"I heard what she said about Tyrone Power."

Diane looked at her.

"And Chris."

197

"You believe it?"

"Deirdre, how can I not believe it? Everybody in Hollywood seems to know about it." Were they laughing at her? It was a humiliating thought.

Deirdre leaned forward and took her hand.

"Di, you've had some great times with Chris. Don't throw it all away."

"I know I have—that's what hurts the most. But how am I supposed to live with this?"

"Maybe with you he'll be all right," Deirdre said. "I mean, he doesn't have anything going with this Keith character now. Maybe you can take him away from that scene permanently."

"You know what, Deirdre? I might have agreed with you a few months ago. But I don't think I can handle it. No, I'm *sure* I can't handle it. I'm going with you back to New York."

"Would you like to go right away? Like tomorrow?"

"You won't mind?" She didn't want to be here when Chris came back from location. She wasn't ready to face him.

Deirdre shrugged.

"How much of California sunshine and smog can you take without getting bored? The only reason I've stayed is to be with you."

"I'll call the airlines right away. If we can get reservations, let's leave tomorrow."

By four o'clock the following afternoon Diane and Deirdre were bound for New York on Flight 372, Diane silent, staring out the window at the clumps of white clouds. She had told the servants that she was leaving for New York without giving them any indication of when she would return. Their checks would continue to be sent out on schedule by Mr. Lewisohn's office. All the bills were handled by him, too—as though she couldn't handle it herself, she thought with irritation. But he meant only to be helpful.

If Chris called from Mexico, the servants would tell him she had gone to New York with Deirdre. She hadn't even left a letter of explanation. How could she find the words?

But it wouldn't take him long to figure it out. She'd thought their marriage would last forever. Now she nearly laughed at the thought. What chance did it ever have?

When she and Deirdre were fourteen, they'd been convinced they would never marry. Deirdre was miserable about being fat, sure she was the dullest girl in the world. Both of them thought that they'd only be loved for their money. But then Chris came along, and without knowing about her money, seemed to love her. At least for a little while, she had thought she was loved.

She couldn't bring herself to think about divorcing him. Not yet. Her mother moved in and out of marriage as though it were of no more consequence than changing clothes. But she had thought her marriage was forever.

Chris was what held her together. Without him she was nobody. How was she to survive without him?

Chapter Eleven

From Idlewild, huddled in the fur coats that they'd carried on their arms at Los Angeles International, Diane and Deirdre took a taxi into Manhattan. Diane told the driver to drop her off first at the Fifth Avenue house, then to take Deirdre to her apartment in the West Eighties.

"My mother's in Bermuda for a month," Deirdre said as the cab bumped along FDR Drive. "God knows where Daddy is. He comes into New York to deposit dividend checks and to pay bills. You know his signature is getting to be more familiar than his face."

"I should have called Aunt Claudia," Diane said. "She'll wonder why I'm back in New York again." She wasn't ready to talk about her marriage to anyone else yet. "Deirdre, if you decide to go to Maine Chance soon and they have accommodations for both of us, I'll go with you."

Deirdre stared at her. "To lose weight?"

"No. To escape from the world."

"If Lenny calls me Tubby once more," Deirdre said, "we'll go. Stand by."

At the Fifth Avenue house Diane discovered that her aunt had left for Palm Beach.

"The doctor recommended it for her arthritis," Miss Jeanne said with a touch of disapproval. "I wish you would talk to her about spending the winter down there or maybe out in Phoenix or California."

"I will," Diane said. She was no longer at ease with Miss Jeanne. Where was the loving governess who had taken her into her arms and comforted her when she was a scared little girl? Ever since she had come into her inheritance, Miss Jeanne had kept this wall between them. Didn't she know that real wealth had nothing to do with bank balances? Only those in love and able to receive love were truly rich.

Exhausted from the flight, Diane went to her room immediately after dinner, planning to settle in bed and read. When her private phone rang close to midnight, she hesitated a moment before picking up. It had to be Chris. He must have called the California house and discovered she'd flown to New York. Was he furious with her?

"Hello." Though her mind trembled as she held the receiver, her voice was steady.

"Di, we're booked at Maine Chance for two weeks beginning day after tomorrow." It was Deirdre. "You know how lucky we are? It's a miracle to get in on such short notice. Two people canceled because of illness or death or something dramatic—and mother's a regular patron of the salon, so I get preference. Remember, they have only forty guests at a time."

Diane practically laughed out loud in relief.

"Great! So we'll arrive there on Sunday?"

"That's when their week begins. I've already arranged for our flights. You were right," she said, "I should have gone straight to Maine Chance from California."

"Let me guess: you saw Lenny."

"Yep. I went to the luncheonette. He called me Tubby. And you know what? I walked right out. I won't even bother unpacking," Deirdre decided. "My California clothes will be great for Phoenix. And just think—no man is allowed to set foot in the place. Only male staff."

Diane thrashed about in bed most of the night. She had never been to a spa, though her mother was a regular at Maine Chance and at Baden-Baden. She was both relieved and surprised that Chris had not phoned. Had he called the California house and been relieved that he didn't have to talk to her? Or had he just not bothered to call at all?

She slept most of Saturday while Deirdre went on a last-minute shopping spree. At 6:30 P.M. sharp—and at Deirdre's request—they sat down to dinner at the Fifth Avenue house.

Diane was glad to see Deirdre enjoying her food. In California it had seemed to her that Deirdre was literally starving herself. But not tonight. She even managed to choke down a generous portion of Miss Jeanne's specialty—chocolate mousse.

While Diane turned her spoon in her mousse, Deirdre glanced at her watch and excused herself.

"I have to go to the loo, Di. Be back in a flash. Okay if I use the one in your room?"

"Sure." Diane pushed away her mousse. "I'll go into the library and warm up the TV set." She would not think about Chris anymore tonight. Tomorrow night she and Deirdre would be at Maine Chance. Maybe there she could find some peace of mind.

She left the table and went out into the hall, pausing at the entrance to the library. What channel carried that show Deirdre wanted to see? Damn. She couldn't remember. She hurried up the stairs to her room. Opening her bedroom door she heard the sound of violent retching in the bathroom. Was Deirdre sick? And they were leaving for Phoenix in the morning!

She pressed her ear against the bathroom door.

"Deirdre?"

"I'll be okay in a minute."

"Can I get you some ginger ale or something?"

Deirdre leaned weakly against the wash basin and flushed the toilet.

"I'm fine now. I ate that gorgeous dinner, and then I came up here and made myself throw up every bit. So I have all the fun and don't have to suffer when I step on the scale tomorrow!"

Diane stared at her in disbelief.

"Deirdre, that's awful!"

"Why? I mean, I feel rotten for a few minutes, but what's wrong with it? Better than getting even tubbier. Right?"

On Sunday morning Diane and Philippe drove across the park and picked up Deirdre and her new Tosca luggage by Mark Cross.

"Daddy's going to have a fit when he gets the bill," Deirdre said when Diane admired them. "These bags cost $1,200 apiece."

On the flight, Diane battled a new wave of misgivings. Why was she going to a beauty spa now, when her life was in such upheaval?

But Deirdre talked of nothing else as the plane flew westward. She and Diane would be in the main house rather than in one of the cottages; apparently this was quite a coup, but since their mothers were both regulars they rated this preferred treatment.

A limousine met them at the Phoenix airport and took them along with a mink-coated dowager, who volunteered that she'd just had her third face lift, to the spa, a few miles outside of Phoenix.

"There's nothing like Maine Chance," their new companion said as they drove through downtown Phoenix. "It's a way of life for me. But then, your mothers must come here. Or Miss Arden would never have accepted you."

They passed long stretches of desert, adorned only by prickly cactus. Then they passed through a set of elaborate wrought iron gates, and they found themselves in a modern-day Garden of Eden.

Diane looked at the baroque mansion set behind lush lawns and surrounded by rose gardens and tall oleanders. So this was where they would be spending the next two weeks. Those who were not chosen to be in the main house would stay in the elegant whit stucco cottages set amidst blue delphiniums, snapdragons, and sweet peas.

From the minute they stepped out of the car, they were welcomed as though they were visiting royalty.

Two maids led them to their rooms as two young boys walked behind with their luggage.

"I didn't dare suggest we share a room," Deirdre whispered as they separated to enter their respective rooms. "Miss Arden would have been outraged."

Diane's room—one of the most expensive—was exquisitely furnished: a small antique desk stood in front of the bay windows, and a canopied bed was in the center of the room. The Aubusson carpeting picked up the colors in the French water-colors on the walls. The chintz-covered dressing table displayed an impressive array of Elizabeth Arden cosmetics. A bouquet of freshly cut chrysanthemums sat in a vase beside the bed; the maid explained that the buzzer on the night table beside the bed provided twenty-four-hour maid service.

The bed sheets were silk, the pillow slips lace, and the bed daintily dressed in a hand-woven coverlet with organdy ruffles. After the maid left, Diane walked into the bathroom. The floor was covered with a delicate pink shag carpeting. Gold nymphs and crystal cherubs adorned the faucets. Packets of Fluffy Milk Bath and Blue Grass dusting powder lined the tub. From a hook on the bathroom door hung the spa uniform: a white terrycloth robe and a pink tank suit.

Diane decided to throw herself into the regime. Why not? At least that way she'd be too busy to think about Chris. She hoped.

As it turned out, it wasn't so hard for Diane to keep her mind off Chris after all. Every day a dainty hand-painted breakfast tray arrived laden with the morning newspaper, a vase with a single rose, a silver coffee pot, and half a tiny grapefruit set on a Limoges plate. A card listing the day's activities sat beside the plate.

Diane and Deirdre were busy from 8:30 A.M. to 5:00 P.M. They took two or three half-hour exercise classes a day, spent hours in the sauna and Jacuzzi, had massages, and facials whenever they felt like it.

Deirdre, the self-proclaimed expert on the spa, arranged for them to be served lunch every day in her room. All the guests dressed for dinner.

Deirdre outlined every detail of the routine to Diane.

"The butler rings a silver bell. Then everybody forgets they're *Social Register* ladies and rush to the dining room to be first in line because by then everybody's starving."

They decided to eat in a room set off from the main dining room, at a small table covered with a lace-and-organdy cloth and set with a pink candle in a crystal hurricane lmp and a pink rose in an antique silver case. Dinner was served on heirloom china.

"Isn't it awful?" Deirdre sighed as they picked at their Dover sole—grilled without butter—their third night. "All we think about is food."

Diane laughed. "At least the lights go off at ten. When we're sleeping we don't have to think about it." But judging by the shadows beneath her eyes, sleep wasn't coming so easily.

On Wednesday morning, while Diane sipped her morning coffee, her phone rang. Her heart pounding, she set down the Wedgwood cup and saucer and reached for the phone.

"Hello."

"Diane—" It was Chris. "I tried to call you last night, but the operator refused to put me through."

"No calls are allowed after ten o'clock."

"Di, please. I know what you must think of me, but I can change, I *can*. If you come back, I will. I'll—"

"Chris, it's over." She wouldn't think of their happy moments together. They were lies. All lies.

"It doesn't have to be over. I'm going to this terrific shrink on Roxbury Drive. He says he's had sensational results with patients who want to change. That's the key to it, honey. *I want to change*."

"Chris, it's too late." Was it? She was afraid to hope.

"Di, please give me another chance." His voice cracked. "Remember how it was down in White Sulphur Springs? It'll be that way for us again. We'll start a family. That's what we both need more than anything else in the world. I don't give a damn what Mannie says. We'll have a baby. Neither of us ever had a shot at being part of a real family. We can make it together, I know we can. Just give us another chance."

"Chris, I'm scared." But she was losing her resolve. He said they'd have a baby . . .

"I'm scared, too. But together we can make it. Please. Come home."

"Are you back from location?"

"I'll be back in ten days," he said quickly. "We're running a few days behind schedule, but I'll be back at the house in two weeks, even if I have to walk off the set."

Diane hesitated. Maybe he was right, maybe all they needed was time. Dammit, she still loved him.

"All right, Chris. I'll fly back a week from next Sunday."

"Baby, I love you so much," he said huskily. "I swear. Everything's going to be fine from now on."

Deirdre was thrilled when Diane told her.

"The shrink will straighten him out, I guarantee it!" she laughed. "Oh God, by next year this time you may be sticking out to here!" She clasped her hands together a foot beyond her stomach. "Your mother will die. She'll *hate* being a grandmother."

Diane was back in California twenty-four hours before Chris arrived in a chartered plane. His humility, his eagerness to please brought her close to tears. They agreed not to sleep together until the psychiatrist felt he was ready, but for now it felt wonderful just to have Chris hold her in his arms and tell her how important she was to his life.

He lavished her with Christmas gifts. On New Year's Day—their first anniversary—he gave her an original Andrew Wyeth. And his career was flourishing. His new agent had renegotiated his contract, tripling his income.

Three evenings a week Chris left the studio to go to Dr. Everett's office. Sometimes he came home exhilarated, other times moody and uncommunicative. At Dr. Everett's orders he swam every morning. On Sundays he and Diane drove to the mountains and hiked. Diane sensed Chris's efforts to share every side of himself with her in every fashion—except the sexual. He talked about his ugly childhood, his ambitions—not only to achieve towering success but to be a fine actor.

"Nobody takes me seriously about that. Not even Mannie. I'm just a personality that works right on the screen. But I want to be a real actor, Di. Someday I hope I can make it on Broadway in a serious play."

They avoided socializing. Diane resumed her art classes, in addition arranged for three private lessons a week, spent hours every day in her studio. She talked regularly with Deirdre in New York. Their phone bills were outrageously high, but they decided it was less expensive than therapy.

"Di, everybody we know has either been in therapy, is there now, or is thinking about going into it. Lenny should be with a shrink five days a week, but he can't afford it," Deirdre said during one especially long phone call.

"Don't you dare offer to pay for it," Diane said. Lenny might not know about Deirdre's fortune but he certainly seemed to take full advantage of whatever he could get his hands on.

"If you'll remember, darling, I can't. I'm on that allowance until I'm thirty. I'd have to go to court to have it increased, and daddy would fight me."

The next few months passed uneventfully.

By late May Deirdre had lost forty-two pounds.

"Di, you won't believe it! I've had to throw out all my clothes."

"That's an awful lot of weight and awful fast."

Diane was worried—especially after the vomiting incident.

"Darling, it's all right. This new doctor is marvelous. I just stick to the diet he gave me and take these little pills. I don't drink a thing except Perrier. And if I go off the diet, then I just make sure I upchuck afterwards and I don't gain an ounce. I don't dare," she laughed. "I went absolutely berserk in Saks and Bergdorf's and Altman's. Daddy's secretary called up to warn me he was furious at the way I've been spending money. But it's there for me. The dividends and interest, I mean. I'm not into capital. He got drunk when he took me to lunch last month, and spilled the figures. He can't fool me anymore. I could rent a whole floor at the Waldorf and still come in under my annual allowance. And don't tell Lenny. Daddy's got this thing about increasing my real estate holdings by cutting down on my spending. I know I'm worth fifty million. How much more will I ever need?"

"Just make sure Lenny doesn't know about the fifty million." Diane must have warned her about this a thousand times. "And don't lose any more weight. You look great the way you are."

"That's what Lenny keeps telling me. He says he wants some tits and ass to grab." Deirdre giggled. "I get so horny when he's vulgar like that."

"What's with the great Lenny anyway?"

"He's got a job again." For two months Lenny had been out of work, living off Deirdre. Diane found it hard to believe that he was still unaware of her financial situation.

"What about other fellows? You must look marvelous with all that weight off."

"I go out once or twice with somebody, and then I drop him," she said offhandedly. "They're all shmucks, after my grandfather's money."

Deirdre sent Diane a sheaf of snapshots. It was incredible the difference forty-two pounds had made in her appearance. Her fine bone structure was now apparent; her light brown hair was now a flattering blonde.

One snapshot showed Lenny and Deirdre posed on the front seat of the Thunderbird. Deirdre had been amazingly accurate in her description of Lenny. He wasn't conventionally handsome, but even Diane had to admit he had an animal magnetism that some women would find irresistible. To her, it seemed more like arrogance, a contempt for humanity. Diane hoped that with her new look, Deirdre would move on to more suitable companionship.

Diane waited hopefully for word from the psychiatrist that Chris was ready for a normal sexual relationship. But spring turned into summer and still there was no indication that he was ready. In the meantime they saw virtually no one.

Lonely but wary of making friends on her own, Diane started lunching once or twice a week with Zelda Coleman, who missed her own two daughters and seemed happy to play mother to Diane. Occasionally she and Chris went to dinner parties at the Coleman house.

When Diane saw Zelda's expression as she gazed at

the bone-thin models in a fashion-show luncheon they attended, she tried to talk her into going to one of the new spas popping up on the West Cost. But Zelda was not the Maine Chance type.

"I look at all the skinnies, and I wish I was thin like I was at eighteen. But Mannie doesn't mind. He calls me *zaftig* and grabs at me now and then." Her face was tender. "All day he looks at those emaciated actresses. He's glad to come home at night to me." Diane wondered if Zelda knew about Mannie's reputed dalliances . . . but maybe she didn't want to know.

Diane was astonished to discover that Zelda went alone every Friday night to services at the temple in Beverly Hills.

"Mannie's always busy with something at the studio on Friday nights. To tell the truth, I think it's convenient-busy. He goes to temple twice a year, but it's really only to keep me happy. At least I know he won't ever be baptized on his deathbed, like Harry Cohen. We were born Jews and we'll die Jews."

"I'll go with you to Friday evening services," Diane said. "That is, unless Chris starts coming home early." Especially now, she needed to feel as though she belonged.

If the members of the congregation of Zelda's temple were puzzled at the presence of Diane Dickenson Ames at Friday evening services, they didn't say so. As she walked into the temple with Zelda Coleman, Diane felt a special closeness to her two grandmothers.

One afternoon, shopping at Magnin's, she paused at the jewelry counter, her eye caught by a diamond-encrusted gold star of David on a gold chain. Suddenly, she thought of her Seligman grandmother . . . even in her mental state, she would recognize the Jewish star, wouldn't she? It was a little impetuous, she knew, but somehow it seemed right. She told the saleswoman to wrap it and send it to Mrs. Hannah Seligman at the Goldman Nursing Home. Hesitating before signing the small enclosure card, she wrote, "With love from David," knowing her father—David—was still the center of Mrs. Seligman's life. A gift in his name would bring special pleasure to her shadowy existence.

Early in July, Zelda Coleman called Diane. "Let's meet Mannie for lunch today, okay, Diane? One o'clock. And wear something fancy. I'll pick you up in the car."

Diane was puzzled.

"Is something wrong?"

"He'll explain at lunch. Now, get going! I'll be by to pick you up in half an hour."

They arrived at the restaurant ahead of Mannie—a smart, low-keyed spot that was close to the studio but not favored by film people. Diane was sure this meeting had something to do with Chris, and as they waited she became increasingly nervous. Had Chris met another Keith?

"Here he comes," Zelda said, waving.

In a Sy Devore seersucker suit, Mannie came toward them, a tight smile on his face. They ordered immediately, Diane choosing a mushroom omelet and a glass of Chablis.

"Diane, we have a serious problem," Mannie said after the waiter had taken their orders. "You know I have some crazy connections around town. Well, word's out that Chris is about to be picked up on rape charges."

Diane turned chalk-white.

"Now, don't panic," Mannie cautioned. "I hustled him off to my house in the mountains till we clear this up."

"I—I don't believe it!" She turned to Zelda. "Who would make a false charge like that?"

Zelda shrugged. "Some publicity-crazy would-be starlet who's hungry for newspaper space."

"Well, who is she? Did Chris ever even meet her?"

Mannie wouldn't look at her. "He met her at some party."

"But Chris and I haven't been to a party in months!"

"Diane—" he took her hand. "Chris stopped in at some party about three weeks ago. Just for a drink on his way home from the studio."

She stared at him blankly. *Chris hadn't said anything about stopping off at a party.* "This girl says he offered to drive her home, invited himself in for a drink, and raped her. She has witnesses that saw her leave the party with him."

"Mannie, you *know* Chris." Diane knew she was pleading, but she couldn't help it. "He's so polite. She probably asked for a lift, and he'd never turn her down. That doesn't mean he raped her, for God's sake."

"*We* know that. Chris's psychiatrist knows that. But if the story hits the papers, we can't guarantee anyone else will believe it. And it'll ruin his career. It'll be rotten for the whole industry. That's why we have to stop it right now. *Before* the charges are officially brought up."

"How?" She looked from Mannie to Zelda. "You mean, pay her off?"

Mannie took a long sip of water, paused, wiped his lips with his napkin. "The lawyers say no. She could turn around and use that, too. That little bitch has to be shown she can't pull this off. The fastest, best way to do that is for you to go to her lawyer. I've got his name."

Diane looked confused. "What am I supposed to say to her lawyer? Am I supposed to tell him my husband is a homosexual?"

"You tell that bastard that Chris could not have raped his client because he's impotent." Mannie saw the look on her face. "I'm afraid it's the only way. Damn it, tell this lawyer that Chris couldn't have raped that little bitch because he can't get it up. Tell him you'll go into court and testify to that."

"Mannie, will you go with me?"

"No, I'm sorry. I can't. But one of the lawyers will go with you. He'll meet us here in an hour. He's already set up the appointment."

"How's Chris? Is he holding up okay?"

"He's in shock. But if you handle this right he'll be off the hook." And the studio would be off the hook, too. Diane knew, of course, that Mannie wasn't rushing into action just to save Chris's neck. Big money was at stake. Big studio money. Mannie knew what he was doing.

Several minutes later the lawyer, Cameron Aldrich, arrived and settled down over a cup of coffee. Charming, sophisticated, descendent of a top Cali-

216

fornia family, and a product of Harvard Law School, he had the credentials Chris needed.

"I'm fairly certain we can make this girl and her lawyer back down," Aldrich said. "But you must go in there on the offensive rather than the defensive. You must appear outraged, ready to sue for libel. The key is your attitude."

"I'll do whatever you say." She wished she could share his confidence.

On the way to the lawyers' Aldrich gave Diane the details of her role. As he spoke, she sensed his curiosity about why Diane Dickenson, the richest girl in America, had married a Hollywood actor. She tried to concentrate on what she was to do within the next half hour. The police might be searching for Chris right this minute. Once word reached the press about the charges, Chris would be in headlines across the country. And she would be there with him.

From the lushly furnished reception room it seemed that the supposed rape victim had chosen her firm well. But it quickly became clear that her particular attorney was one of the newest to join the firm. His office was small and far down the hall.

"Please sit down." Bright-eyed and obsequious, he was thrilled to have the famous Diane Dickenson Ames in his office.

"I don't believe we'll be here very long," she said briskly.

For a few minutes she listened while the two lawyers discussed the case. Then she intervened.

"I'm sorry to interrupt you two, but we're wasting our time on this. You see, there's no possible way that Chris could have raped that girl." She paused,

217

enjoying their expectant looks. "He's impotent."
The room was completely silent. "He can't consummate a sexual relationship. I'm willing to testify to that effect. His psychiatrist will, too. Obviously Chris and I are both upset about this problem. And neither of us is thrilled about airing the intimate details of our marriage to the world. But if your client persists in upsetting him further with this absurd charge, then we'll have no recourse except to sue for libel."

After a long moment, the opposition's attorney cleared his throat and spoke. "Well, I think Mr. Aldrich and I should discuss this at greater length."

Diane smiled sweetly.

"Why don't you? But first, call the police and withdraw that charge. Immediately."

Her eyes dared him to refuse.

Chapter Twelve

"I think, Diane," Cameron Aldrich said as they left the office, "that you would have made a marvelous actress."

"Mr. Aldrich, Chris isn't guilty," she bristled. She was still trembling. "I didn't say anything that wasn't true."

"Of course not. But it could have been an ugly case that would have wrecked Chris's career if you hadn't handled it just right." He hesitated. "I hope everything works out for you and Chris."

Within three hours Chris arrived at the house. Though she was—as always—moved by how contrite he was, she couldn't help wonder why he hadn't mentioned stopping off at that party. He'd told her everything else.

In late August she and Chris left for Acapulco for a four-day vacation. They were to spend the time in seclusion aboard a yacht owned by one of Mannie's many friends. Diane hoped that here they might be able to rekindle their romance. Chris had been in therapy eight months. Maybe now that the insane rape charge was dropped, and they were away from Hollywood, he would want to come to her bed.

The yacht—at dock in Acapulco Bay—was served by a crew of twenty-six. It was 242 feet long, furnished below-deck in the delicate Louis XVI decor. There was a swimming pool and a game room, as well as an elegant lounge, dining room, and six guest cabins.

The weather was superb, the sky a brilliant blue by day, filled with stars at night. Chris was attentive, but she sensed a restlessness in him. Every night she lay awake, waiting for him to come to her cabin. Every morning she woke up alone.

A month later Diane decided to have a gallery showing of her paintings. Excited, she talked to Zelda Coleman. She had worked hard these past months. Her teacher had been encouraging. She didn't care much for most of her work, but there were a few paintings with which she was pleased, and she needed outside approval. She thought of what Laura had said: *"I have to know I've accomplished something on my own in this world."*

Though Zelda always insisted she was just a homebody, caring only for her family and house, she occasionally surprised Diane with her humor and acuity, and she had an eclectic—and wealthy— collection of friends.

"René LeClerque has a marvelous eye," she said. "He has one of the best galleries on the West Coast. Talk to him, Diane. He'll tell you if you're ready to show."

Reluctantly, Diane agreed.

A week later she sat in René LeClerque's private studio above the gallery, a half-dozen of her best paintings placed around the room. René—small, slight, bearded, sharp-eyed—walked from one painting to another, studying each, his expression unreadable. Diane fidgeted nervously. Zelda had said he would be honest with her.

He sighed slightly and turned to her.

"You have a fine feel for color," he said gently. "An eye for line. You are a talented amateur, my dear. But don't show. Paint for your own pleasure."

"You mean I'll never be more than a dilettante," Diane said, pale with disappointment.

"Enjoy your talent," he coaxed. "It's a gift, too." But his eyes were sympathetic. He knew the blow he had just delivered.

"Thank you, Mr. LeClerque. I'm grateful for your advice."

Back at home, she phoned Deirdre. Maybe she could persuade Deirdre to fly out for a couple of weeks. Deirdre had been commuting between Southampton and Manhattan all summer, enjoying showing off her new look at posh Southampton parties, but still convinced that every man who made a play for her was after her money.

"Deirdre, I'm going a little stir-crazy. Why don't you come out for a couple of weeks?"

"I can't right now. So what's with Chris?"

"He's still seeing the shrink three times a week. Nothing's happened so far for us, but he's optimistic."

221

"Why don't you come to Bermuda with me and Lenny, then? We're leaving tomorrow morning. I was going to call you anyway. Come on, we'll have a ball."

Diane hesitated. "No, I don't think so. I wouldn't want to leave Chris. Thanks anyway. I think he needs me here."

"Di, Chris is always at the studio. You could probably get a room right in our hotel. You need to have some fun . . ."

"Deirdre, where did Lenny get the money for this trip?"

"I told you, I was supposed to go with my cousin, who's still in the hospital with appendicitis. Since the trip was already paid for, I figured he might as well take my cousin's place."

"Oh, Deirdre, you know what I think about that—"

Diane had long since made her suspicions about Lenny known.

"But darling, he can do it a dozen times a night," Deirdre said with a melodramatic sigh. "He's a national treasure."

"Well, have fun, but be careful." She laughed. "And for God's sake, don't spend every minute in the hotel room!"

As she hung up, she worried again about what would happen when Lenny realized that Deirdre was really the Deirdre Swift whose grandfather had founded Swift Coal Mines.

Deirdre picked up Lenny at his furnished studio

222

and drove them to Idlewild for their morning flight. They'd leave the Thunderbird at the airport lot for the week. She felt nervous when she saw Lenny reading a copy of the *New York Times* . . . recently her name had been showing up a lot in the gossip columns, and she's always counted on Lenny's assertion that he read only the sports page.

"Hey, you're sure we don't need passports?" he asked for the fourth time.

"Yes, my darling, I'm positive. It's just routine identification. All you need is your birth certificate." Lenny thought this was the first time she had been to Bermuda. He didn't know about all those other times—in high season—when she had gone down there with her mother. The current governess and she in one suite, mother in another, always on different floors.

"I've never been out of the country before," Lenny said. "It's a funny feeling."

"I'm getting a funny feeling," Deirdre whispered.

"I'll take care of it when we're in the hotel," he grinned, a hand fondling her knee.

At the small Bermuda airport they went through customs in minutes and got a cab to take them to the parish of Hamilton. Lenny was uncharacteristically self-conscious, but Deirdre knew it wouldn't last long. They registered at the hotel as Mr. and Mrs. Leonard Jackson, Deirdre teasing Lenny that he didn't have to marry her now that they were registered at the hotel as man and wife. But secretly she wondered . . . *would* she marry him if he asked her?

Once they were in their rooms, he began to relax.

"It was damn nice of your cousin to come down with appendicitis," he said, lying back on the huge four-poster bed. "Nice you got a rich cousin."

He stood up and walked to the french doors opening onto their terrace, which overlooked the dazzling blue sea.

"Christ, I can get a sensational tan just lying on my butt out here!" he said. "Let's get into less clothes and soak up sun until dinner."

"Glad you came?" Deirdre asked while they got undressed.

"Hey, baby, you're something." With a satisfied glance at their reflections in the mirror—his body sleek and muscular, hers model-slim except for the bosom—he pulled her to him.

His mouth came down hard on hers, his tongue pushed past her teeth. For a moment, he pulled away. "Hey, you want it?"

"You know I do."

"Show me."

"Lenny, let's not play games."

"Games, huh?" He grinned. "Don't worry, baby, I won't lose it. I'm not one of those fifty-year-old characters who get it up once a month. How bad do you want it?"

"Bad," she whispered. She knew what he was leading up to.

"Then come and get it." He threw himself on his back across the bed, his eyes moving over each inch of her.

Moistening her lips, she drew herself up onto the bed. He took her face in his hands. "Show me how much you love me, baby. Then we'll do it the way

224

you like."

On their first night, Deirdre and Lenny had dinner sent up to their room. They dined on the terrace. For tonight, Deirdre forgot her diet and ate every bite of the mushrooms stuffed with crabmeat, broiled swordfish, and raspberry soufflé. Afterwards they returned to the room, wheeled the cart into the hall, and went to bed.

The next morning Deirdre pulled on shorts and a blouse, threw a pair of shorts at Lenny, and ordered breakfast sent up to their room. She felt radiant after their night of lovemaking.

They ate eggs florentine on the terrace. The brilliant blue of the sea blended spectacularly with the inlets.

"Shall we rent a pair of those silly mopeds and ride around town till we're hungry for lunch, Len?"

"I want to stretch out on this thing and burn to a crisp."

"Not all over, please." She giggled. "Neither one of us would be happy." She saw Lenny's eyes focus on a patch of grass below. Two bikini-clad girls who occupied the room below theirs had walked to the edge of their terrace to inspect the sea. "You can look, but don't touch," she said playfully, rubbing her foot against his leg.

"Who needs to touch?" He smiled lazily. "I've got you right here."

Even when she was fat, Lenny liked her. Not even knowing about the money. *Maybe she could get him to marry her.* She had until they headed back for New

York. In New York she might lose her nerve.

"Lenny, would you mind if I went into town to shop? My cousin told me that you can buy perfume and cashmere sweaters and all kinds of things much cheaper here. Liquor, too."

"Okay, babe—if you bring me back a bottle of gin. Think you can manage that?"

"Sure. If you promise not to get smashed. What good will you be to me if you're smashed?"

She changed into white linen slacks and a tailored black silk blouse, draped the matching jacket over one arm, and posed for his approval before leaving. She knew she looked great. Of course, he would die if he knew what she'd spent on this outfit, but it was worth every cent. Since her weight loss, she found that she couldn't stop looking in the mirror.

"Sure you don't mind?" she said. "I won't be gone more than a couple of hours."

"Stay as long as you feel like it." He stretched. "I'm out here to soak up sun. When I get back to town, I want everybody to know where I've been."

"I'll put the sign on the doorknob for the maid to come in and do the room. You'll be out on the terrace—she won't disturb you."

"Sure thing."

Deirdre was halfway into town in a taxi when she realized she had left her travelers cheques in the room, in her valise. She told the driver to take her back to the hotel and wait for her. She wondered what it would be like after she and Lenny were married. Then she'd tell him about her money. He wouldn't have to work anymore. They'd travel, make love in every country in the world. They'd have a ball.

She hurried inside while the taxi waited. She lifted her hand to ring their bell, then reached for her key instead. If Lenny was out on the terrace, he probably wouldn't hear her anyway.

She walked into the room. The bed was still unmade. She looked out on the terrace. He wasn't out there. Where had he gone? He said he wasn't going to budge. She looked out over the railing.

Where *was* he?

She leaned over a little further. There, on the terrace below, was Lenny, stretched out on a chaise. Perched next to him was a dark-haired girl in a bikini. His hand was on one breast while she rubbed suntan lotion on his chest.

Her face burning, eyes filled with tears, she turned away. How dare he? It didn't seem possible . . .

She went back inside the room and began to pack. What was the matter with her? Why couldn't she hold onto a man?

She threw her clothes into the two valises, hoping to be out of the hotel before Lenny returned to the room. She'd paid for the accommodations in advance. She left his return ticket on a dresser. Let *him* figure out what happened.

She hoped he burned his goddamn prick to cinders.

After the interview with René LeClerque, Diane never again set foot in the studio. She joined a health club; she took classes in landscape gardening; she went to services with Zelda on Friday nights at the Beverly Hills temple. Always, it was Diane who drove them.

"Everybody has a little *shtick*," Zelda said one afternoon. "Maybe it's my Lower East Side childhood—when I was a little girl on Jefferson Street, limousines always meant a funeral. Away from the temple I can forget. Whenever we drive up to the temple in the limo, I feel like crying."

One Friday evening, late in October, Diane slid behind the wheel of the Dual-Ghia and headed for the Coleman house. The Ghia had been in the shop for repairs for the past three days, and this morning the limousine had developed a carburetor problem. Chris refused to take the Chevy because Diane would then be grounded. He'd called the studio and arranged for a chauffeur to pick him up to take him to the studio this morning, to the psychiatrist when shooting was done for the day, and then to bring him home. He approved of her Friday evening routine with his producer's wife.

Waiting for a red light to change, she thought about how glad she was that Deirdre had broken up with Lenny. Deirdre'd even given up her apartment so that Lenny couldn't track her down. But Diane was concerned that Deirdre was overeating again. When Deirdre came out to the coast next month, she'd try to persuade her to join the health club, maybe get her to a doctor who'd put her on a sensible diet—not those pills.

At the Coleman house Diane found Zelda fighting with her housekeeper about going out for the evening.

"You talk to her," the housekeeper urged Diane.

"She's got such bad laryngitis she sounds like Andy Devine. She shouldn't go out into the night air. She ought to be in bed."

"So I'll go with Diane to temple. I'll be inside," Zelda said, her voice scratchy, her face flushed.

Diane was concerned. "Zelda, you look as though you might be running a fever." The housekeeper nodded vigorously. "Mrs. Rogers, make sure she goes to bed. And if you're not better by morning, talk to the doctor." At last, Zelda capitulated.

"I'll bring you a cup of tea and honey," the housekeeper said, pushing her up the stairs.

"I'll call the studio and see if Chris is through for the day," Diane said. Maybe she would drive him to his shrink's office.

She phoned the studio. Work was finished for the day. Chris had left. So he must be on his way to the psychiatrist's office. She'd leave word at the office for him to dismiss the studio chauffeur when he arrived. She'd wait downstairs in the car for him. She'd read the new *Town & Country* while she waited.

She found Dr. Everett's office number in the telephone book and dialed. Maybe Chris would like to go out for dinner tonight—somewhere quiet, far removed from the movie world.

"Dr. Everett's office," an ebullient feminine voice announced.

"This is Diane Ames," Diane identified herself. "Chris Ames's wife. May I please leave a message for Chris? I think he's due there shortly."

"He has no appointment, Mrs. Ames," the girl said politely. "He hasn't been a patient for about three months."

"I'm sorry," Diane stammered. Her heart pounding. "I'd forgotten."

She slammed down the phone and hurried out of the house. *Chris had been lying to her for three months. He'd walked out on the therapy.* He'd pretended to have pleaded with Dr. Everett to let him take time off from his therapy for the Acapulco trip. He had already left Dr. Everett.

She got into the car and headed home. What chance was there for Chris and her if he was lying to her? They'd have this out tonight. No more playing games. As soon as she was home, they'd talk.

She turned into the driveway. A studio limousine stood in front of the entrance. She could tell it was a studio car by the Menlow Films insignia on one door. Chris had probably invited the chauffeur in for coffee. He prided himself on being very democratic with workers at the studio.

As soon as the chauffeur left, she and Chris would talk. They would be alone in the house. At this hour the servants were either off on their own or in their cottage. If he felt that Dr. Everett wasn't helping him, why hadn't he come out and said so? Why hadn't he talked to her about finding another psychiatrist?

The door was unlocked. Diane walked inside. She glanced into the living room. Chris and the chauffeur weren't in there. They were out in the kitchen having coffee or a beer. All right. She'd go upstairs and wait until the chauffeur left.

Her mind in turmoil, she walked up the stairs. She would stay cool. She would listen to what Chris had to say. But unless he could make her understand why he left Dr. Everett—why he had lied to her—their marriage was over.

She paused at the entrance to her room. Rock 'n' roll blared from the record player in Chris's room. He had a habit of forgetting to turn it off when he went downstairs. She loathed rock 'n' roll.

Diane walked to the half-opened door to Chris's room and shoved it open. Then she froze. Naked, Chris lay on top of another naked man. Diane saw a chauffeur's uniform lying on the floor beside the king-sized bed.

For a moment she closed her eyes, trying to block out the image of the two of them locked in passion. She opened them. They were still there.

"Why did you lie to me?" The words tore out of her throat. "Why did you pretend we could have a marriage? Why did you beg me to come back to you?"

For an instant the two on the bed didn't move. Then Chris stood up.

"Diane, what the hell are you doing here? You're supposed to be out with Zelda!"

"I live here! How dare you bring him into my house?"

"I know it's your house. You never let me forget your fucking money!"

"Chris, why? Why?" What had happened to them?

"You drove me to men!" he spat. "You're as cold as an Arctic Circle iceberg. My super-rich beautiful bride. An iceberg."

"It wasn't like that! You've played games with me

from the beginning. We never had a chance—"

She turned and ran from the room. She wouldn't even bother to pack. Tonight she would stay at the Beverly Hilton. She could shop for what she needed in their boutique. Tomorrow she'd fly back to New York. Mr. Lewisohn would handle the divorce.

Chapter Thirteen

A dense fog hung over Manhattan. Usually Laura loved the view from her forty-second-floor cubicle, but today everything looked bleak. While she pretended to be reading over her stenographic notes, she listened to the voices coming from the office of Joe Freedlich, vice-president in charge of New York activities. Instinct told her that what was happening inside could have a powerful influence on her own life—if she played her cards right.

She had been an employee of Menlow Films for twenty-one months. She had moved up from receptionist to stenographer—once she'd raced through a speed-writing course, and then to secretary to Bill Garrison, the story editor. But she knew that in the railroad-car-long office of the chief of the New York division of the company, abrasive Joe Freedlich was in the process of firing his executive secretary. She had been with him for three years, considered a long run in Freedlich's office.

She couldn't make out the words of the exchange

inside, but the mood was clearly hostile. Washroom gossip reported that the secretary had been trying for a transfer to the West Coast office via a cousin who knew Mannie Coleman himself, and Freedlich had found out. He was outraged that his executive secretary had gone over his head—behind his back.

"You're fired!" Those words rang out. When Freedlich was upset, the whole staff suffered. "I won't have my employees going behind my back! Go take whatever belongs to you and get the hell out of here. Accounting will mail your check."

Laura winced at the sound of a door slammed shut. Seconds later, there was another slam. It sounded like Freedlich's secretary had left his office and closeted herself in her own for a brief cry of outrage before packing up her belongings. The entire office was unnaturally still. Not a typewriter was in operation.

The "girls" in the office were always griping about how Freedlich had never replaced his executive secretary from within the ranks. Some of them had been with Menlow Films for close to twenty years, though most were there for short runs. Joe Freedlich thought anybody who worked for a film company ought to be honored to be involved. He doled out raises as though they were personal gifts.

Laura's mind raced. Several weeks ago Freedlich had charged out of his office, hovered in her doorway, and yelled for her to come take dictation. He had dictated half a dozen letters to her. She had brought him error-free letters, grammar corrected; but he had signed without even looking at them and ordered her to leave the carbons for his secretary.

She wanted to be Joe Freedlich's executive secretary. She wanted it more than she'd ever wanted anything in her life. She could learn more from him than from fifty courses on filmmaking.

If she walked in there to talk to him about it, he might fire her on the spot for trying to move up without discussing it first with her boss. On the other hand, she knew that he hated Bill Garrison; the story editor was addicted to three-hour lunches, had no real feeling for what made a commercial movie script, and had been hired only because he was related to somebody high up in the West Coast office. Freedlich didn't dare fire him, but could appropriate his secretary. If he felt so inclined.

She decided that if she got fired, she'd look for another job in the field. She had experience now. She had taken those two courses on filmmaking at the New School. She read all the trade papers that came into the office. She'd learned to talk picture business as though she knew a lot more than she did. *You had to take chances to get ahead.*

With a swift glance in her mirror—she knew she was not a candidate for Joe Freedlich's casting couch because it was well known that he avoided women taller than himself—Laura stood up and walked toward his office.

Five feet two and weighing in at 160 pounds, Joe Freedlich simply glared as Laura told him that she wanted to fill the current secretarial vacancy.

"You talk to Garrison about this?"

"No. There seemed no point in disturbing Mr. Garrison if you turned me down." She caught the glint of vindictive satisfaction that crossed his face at the thought of stealing Garrison's secretary. "I'll stay on, of course, if you don't take me on. The country's still coming out of a recession. It's not the time to go job-hunting." Ira, who was forever talking politics, had taught her that much. If not for him she probably wouldn't know who was president. "I like working for Menlow Films," she continued. Freedlich seemed to expect a further pitch. "I like the picture business." True. She had become fascinated by the many sides of picture-making.

The phone rang. Freedlich cursed and waved a hand.

"Answer it. Get rid of whoever it is."

Laura picked up the phone.

"Mr. Freedlich's office." Freedlich leaned over the deep drawer of his desk and pulled out a bottle of Canadian Club. "Mr. Freedlich is not in his office at the moment. May I ask who's calling, please? Yes, thank you. I'll tell him—Oh," she feigned surprise. "Mr. Freedlich just walked into the office. Will you hold, please?" She covered the phone. "It's Mr. Coleman from Los Angeles."

Relieved that she had not brushed off Mannie Coleman—to Freedlich, Coleman was "the chief"— he snatched the receiver from her.

"Mannie, how are you?" When his eyes shot to his watch, Laura knew he was wondering what was important enough for Mannie Coleman to call at seven A.M. California time.

While they talked, Laura hurried from the office and down the hall to the lounge, where a carafe of hot water sat for coffee.

She made a quick cup of instant coffee, remembering that Freedlich took his black, without sugar. She returned to the office, knocked lightly, and walked inside. She knew Freedlich was still on the phone.

"We haven't seen anything in the New York columns yet," he was saying, clearly agitated. He reached eagerly for the cup of coffee. Laura headed for the door. Freedlich's voice trailed after her. "Maybe it's just a spat. Maybe she didn't walk out on him. Chris Ames is the hottest young lover on the screen. Do you think she found out—"

Even before Joe Freedlich told her to come back into his office, Laura knew she'd gotten the job. It was like Ira always said: moving up in the world depended upon being in the right place at the right time.

Changing from business suit and high heels into wool slacks, sweater, and loafers, Laura thought about what she had overheard. Diane had walked out on Chris. Ira had predicted it would happen. But Diane's marrying Chris had gotten *her* a job at Menlow Films.

She debated about leaving a light on in the kitchen. She hated coming home to a dark apartment. But instinct told her to stay over at Ira's place tonight, his last night in New York. It had jarred her when she realized he was serious about going to London to live for a year.

She'd thought when she planned on coming to New York that her life in the city would be one big party. She was young, attractive, and sexy—but the only men she met were unemployed would-be actors from the Off-Broadway scene, sweet but ineligible gays, or over-forty lechers who rushed for their commuter trains at the end of the business day unless they had a rendezvous scheduled at a sleazy Manhattan hotel. She could sleep around all she wanted with married men looking for action, but that just wasn't on her dance card.

Where were the good-looking, on-the-way-to-the-top young guys? How did girls in the city—girls like herself—meet the right kind of men? There were two she had met at classes at the New School, but both had been on the prowl for wives—the kind of wives who would be happy living in suburbia, taking care of the house and raising kids. She knew she'd die if she had to settle for that. She wasn't the only one—more and more girls today were deferring marriage in favor of glamorous and challenging jobs.

She had the job. Now she was looking for a jazzy social life. She didn't want to get married for a long time—not unless some gorgeous young millionaire chased after her, and that wasn't likely. It was girls like Diane Dickenson who met gorgeous young millionaires.

Ira was fun, but sometimes he got so damn intense. She'd been bored to death when he took her up to Columbia last spring to hear Allen Ginsberg read his poetry. She couldn't get excited about Jack Kerouac and the Beat generation—her favorite reading was *Vogue*, Sheilah Graham, and Cholly Knickerbocker.

Leaving the darkened apartment behind her, Laura headed down the stairs. She was going to miss Ira. If it weren't for him, she'd have practically no social life. She lived on the fringe of two worlds—Off-Broadway theater and films—and she wasn't actually a part of either.

She loved being here in the East Village, escaping at night from the skyscraper-lined canyons of mid-Manhattan to avenues and streets where a building over four floors high was a rarity. She liked its youthful feeling of optimism and excitement, walking down Second Avenue and recognizing actors as they emerged from rehearsal studios at Central Plaza or from a meal at Ratner's or Rappaport's—once, Ira told her, hangouts of the Yiddish theater stars in the days when Jacob Adler, Boris Thomashevsky, and Bertha Kalish were the idols of the Yiddish Rialto.

She loved working for Menlow Films despite the irascible moods of Joe Freedlich, because she knew that here she had one foot up the ladder. But while she was proud of her professional life, she found her social life frustrating. The fellows she met through Ira and here in the neighborhood—at the supermarket or having coffee at Mama's or in the laundromat—were all wrapped up in their precious careers. No man at the office was worth a second glance.

The "girls" at the office were anywhere from fifteen to forty years older than she. After work they hurried to their lives in Queens or Brooklyn. Several of them met one Saturday night a month to go out for a Chinese dinner and to a movie. She was never asked to join them. Occasionally she found herself wishing Cindy had not gone running back home.

Arriving at Ira's door, she sniffed the savory aromas that filtered into the hall. He'd told her his mother had enlarged his culinary repertoire with a new recipe. She lifted a hand to knock. Their private little signal: one long, two shorts, and another long knock. She wished Ira hadn't got that bug up his ass about traipsing off to live in London for a year with his old buddy from Columbia—a black guy, she remembered, who had been what Ira called the token black in their dormitory. Ira was involved in civil rights and the whole liberal scene. His big heroes were Martin Luther King, Jr. and Adlai Stevenson.

The door swung open. In his maroon silk robe and black leather scuffs, he looked like an actor in a movie seduction scene. She was always startled by how tall he seemed when she was out of her high heels. The maroon silk robe, a birthday present from his sister Kathy, told her he was in the mood for making love. Why not?

"Smell my magnificent roast?" He grinned. "I expected to have all the women in the house breaking down the door."

"Enjoy." Laura walked inside the kitchen and toward the oven. "From what I hear of English food, this might be your last decent dinner for a year."

"That's an eye round," Ira said while Laura viewed the long narrow roast with interest. Her budget did not include gourmet meals. Laura stayed in her tenement flat with its low rent and skimped on food to be able to take classes and buy more clothes than she could otherwise afford. She'd learned the art of eating cheap as a child. "Mom bought the roast as a going-away gift. I think she figured I'd have about a dozen people over tonight."

"I'll eat on it for the next two weeks," Laura guessed.

Over the delectably seasoned split-pea soup that Ira had brought from home in a jar, she told him about her promotion.

"It's not just the raise that makes me happy, Ira. As Freedlich's private secretary I'll learn a hell of a lot. It'll be rough for a while—I mean, every girl at Menlow Films will hate my guts for landing the job. But it's mine. I went after it, and I got it."

"We ought to have champagne to celebrate," he said. "But we'll have to make do with Chablis."

"Well, I have some news . . . it's supposed to be top secret . . . until Candace Collins or Winchell or Hedda Hopper breaks the news, but I don't see any harm in telling you: Diane Dickenson has left Chris Ames."

Ira's smile was compassionate.

"I'm not surprised. All that money and she *still* picked the wrong husband."

Laura tried to define the odd glint she always noticed in Ira's eyes when they talked about Diane. Sometimes she suspected he had a thing for Diane—but he had only met her that once. No, it must be the curiosity everybody had about somebody so rich.

"What do you hear from the new bride?" Ira's sister Kathy had recently married Craig Rosenthal, fresh out of Columbia Law and now employed by a prestigious firm. She had been surprised when Ira asked her to the fancy wedding at the Hampshire House. Kathy and Craig had wanted a small family wedding. Craig's parents had insisted on the Hampshire House and three hundred guests. Craig was their only child and they were determined to have an expensive wedding, even though they would shoulder most of the costs. Ira said he couldn't survive it without a kindred spirit at his side. Despite his parents' pride in their assimilation, she suspected they were uneasy about his bringing a *shiksa* to his sister's wedding. "Are they settled in at their house?"

"Trying to fit into life in Ardsley," he said. Craig's father had made the down payment on a four-bedroom split-level, but the newlyweds had to cope with high mortgage payments and upkeep. "It may be a half-hour from Manhattan by car, but Kathy says it's like living in exile—so far. She's sure that she and Craig will adapt."

"I bet Diane will come back to New York," Laura said. "After she's Renovated or whatever. God, she's just my age, and already she's been married and on the way to a divorce."

"You're obsessed with Diane Dickenson. She's just another girl. Just a girl, like you."

"In a way Diane and I are a lot alike." Laura collected the two soup plates and took them to the sink while Ira began to slice the roast. She pulled the pair of Idaho potatoes from the oven with tongs. "We both grew up kind of cut off from other kids. I never had the money to go with the other girls to the movies on Saturdays. Our big splurge was twenty cents a month for *Modern Screen*. I never invited anybody to my house to play or for a sleepover. The other girls made nasty cracks behind my back about our house. Only Diane accepted the laundry hanging in all of the four little rooms without thinking there was something weird about me."

"She wasn't looking at your house," Ira said gently. "She was looking for a friend."

"I was her first best friend, and she was mine. It only lasted for one summer, but I think it helped me get through the next lousy years. Of course, I was hurt as hell when she didn't write or anything. Not until we met again did I know what happened that summer." She'd told Ira about the rape attempt.

"Try my roast," he ordered, bringing the platter to the table. "My mother said nobody could go wrong with this." He eyed the succulent pink slabs of beef with pride.

"Umm, great."

But her mind was still on Diane. "I hope Diane isn't hurt by this divorce. I remember when she told me—back in Newport—how she wasn't allowed to go to school. She was tutored. She was lonely and a little bit lost, and I understood exactly how she felt. She had too much money. I didn't have enough. We were both unhappy—but she was unhappy in clothes from Bergdorf's and Saks and in a mansion on Fifth Avenue. I was unhappy in hand-me-downs from my mother's customers, living in a rundown cottage on the wrong side of town."

"Too few in this country will admit how many people don't have enough money to live like human beings. They ignore the hunger and lack of decent places to live and proper medical care." This was one of Ira's favorite tirades. "They don't want to know."

"Ira, get down from your soapbox," Laura said. "I want to enjoy this roast." She didn't know anything about civil rights, except what he was forever throwing at her. As for being poor, she knew plenty about that. "There's no Depression now—why can't people go out and work?" *She* did.

243

"Laura, you brag about having been so poor you ate rice or pasta for dinner every night in the week. There are people here in these great United States who don't have even that. How far do you think a welfare check goes these days?"

"I don't know—I've never been on welfare. Mom was too proud."

"Don't be so self-righteous," he chided. "A lot of people can't cope. Are we supposed to sit back and let them die? Eisenhower has blocked almost every welfare program the Democrats have tried to push through Congress. All he gives a shit about is balancing the budget."

"So you're running away to London to put all that out of sight." Laura loved teasing him.

"I need a year away from home to sort out things in my head," he said slowly. "I need it badly. And everything seemed to come together to make it possible. Those soft-core porn books I've been doing for the past few months—I know they're garbage, but where else can I make seven hundred dollars for two weeks' work? I couldn't do them on a regular basis," he grinned. "Not without throwing up all over my typewriter. But the six that I did gave me a bankroll. Then Russ wrote me about this sensational apartment he's rented for peanuts. I can live in London for a year on what I've saved up."

"It'll be a terrific experience to live in London for a year." It probably meant nothing to Diane, who had traveled all over Europe by the time she was twelve, but to them it was *the* great experience.

"Maybe I'm trying to emulate Fitzgerald and Hemingway and Wolfe," he mused. "Maybe I think a writer *has* to run away from home for a while."

"I'm just curious—why *did* Russ go to London? You told me he got a master's in journalism. Is he writing on a newspaper there?"

"He's doing research at the British Museum for a biography he plans to write, kind of his last fling before he comes home and goes down south to work in the civil rights movement. That's why he went after the master's in journalism. He figured he could be useful as a reporter."

"I'm surprised you're not down there," Laura jibed. "You, who wrote two plays of 'social significance,'" she quoted him, "and are plotting another."

"But who's producing them?" he challenged. "Broadway is a rat race. On Off-Broadway everybody's doing revivals. Ibsen, Chekhov, Shaw. Why not Ira Ross? I'm twenty-four years old. Is there a law that says I have to be fifty to crack New York theater?" He reached for another thick slab of roast. "In London I'll spend a year on nothing but writing my play. With luck I'll come home with something I can get on the boards. At least on Off-Broadway."

"I'll miss you," Laura said. It hadn't occurred to her that she would.

"I tell you what—any time you feel like coming over, Russ and I can put you up," he said. "But you're not going to leave Menlow Films. Not until you're New York story editor and angling for something bigger."

"You are so right," she laughed. Ira had taught her about recognizing priorities. Career came first, even before great sex.

"Let's get some music," he said with a look in his eyes that she recognized. "Something sweet and hot."

"Good thought," she said. Already she was imagining herself in bed with Ira.

He went into the tiny living room and put on a recording of a Cole Porter medley, then returned to the kitchen. When they finished the roast, he reached the freezer for the perennial half-gallon of coffee ice cream, into which they had made a substantial dent the last time she came down for dinner.

When they had eaten and washed and dried the dishes, Ira dropped an arm about her waist.

"Let's make love," he said. "After all, tomorrow night I'll be on a plane bound for London. You have to send me off right."

"Okay, set the alarm for seven. I'm not one of the idle rich like you. I have to go to work in the morning." *As Joe Freedlich's secretary.*

Lying awake beside Ira while he slept, Laura tried to imagine her life without him. She knew a lot of people casually. But Ira was the only person she felt close to. From the beginning they had made it clear to each other that marriage was not for now—it was something for the distant future. They both had far to go, and the determination and ambition to get there. But sometimes—like tonight—she wondered what it would be like to be married to Ira, *what it would be like not to be alone.*

Chapter Fourteen

Birch logs cracked in the grate of the marble-faced fireplace in Claudia's small but elegant sitting room. Diane sat in a smoky blue velvet wing chair, her shoeless stockinged feet tucked beneath her, while her aunt closed the door behind the maid, who carried out their dinner trays. At last they would have some privacy.

She knew her aunt suspected that something calamitous had brought her back to New York without some word before her arrival. Despite Claudia's efforts to appear delighted with her niece's unexpected appearance in New York, Diane saw the concern in her eyes as she returned to sit across from her.

"I've left Chris," Diane said. She couldn't believe it even as she heard herself saying the words. "I'm divorcing him."

"You've thought this out carefully?" Claudia asked.

"I've tried everything." She paused, trying to

figure out a way to make the truth more acceptable to her aunt. There was no way. "Chris was unfaithful to me. With men."

Her aunt gasped.

"You'll call Mr. Lewisohn in the morning," she said quietly, the faint pink of her cheeks betraying her shock. "He'll know how to handle this."

A few days later they went to see Mr. Lewisohn about the divorce. Diane was grateful that her aunt hadn't made any I-told-you-so remarks and was relieved that Miss Jeanne had retired and returned to Paris to live on her comfortable pension. Both Louella Parsons and Hedda Hopper had reported that Diane was in New York to visit with her reclusive aunt. Apparently the studio hoped to keep her break-up with Chris a secret until the voting for the Academy Awards was completed early next year.

Mr. Lewisohn listened with obvious sympathy while Diane haltingly explained her grounds for divorce.

"He can hardly contest," Mr. Lewisohn said gently. "I'd say a Reno divorce is your best choice. I'll clear the situation with Mr. Ames and his attorney." The studio's attorney, Diane surmised. "I'll make all the arrangements for an attorney to represent you in Reno."

"When should I leave?" Diane asked. Deirdre was due back from a Mediterranean cruise in two weeks. She'd ask Deirdre to go with her.

"Not for a while." Mr. Lewisohn squinted in thought. "I wouldn't want you to go to Reno before late March. The weather can drop down into the high teens out there in December and January. Even

February can be bitterly cold."

"Mr. Lewisohn, New York gets that cold then." She wanted to put Reno behind her. Most of his clients, she realized, were apt to be in warmer climates when winter descended on New York.

"Some time in March," he pinpointed. "It'll take until then to get all the paperwork set up. The attorney out there can arrange for proper accommodations. I'm sure he'll be able to find a suitable house for the six weeks you must be in residence."

"I'll go with you," Claudia said. "So you won't be alone."

Diane looked at them, startled. The prospect of six weeks in a strange city, alone with her aunt, was depressing.

"You have all your committees, Aunt Claudia. It wouldn't be fair to take you away. Deirdre will go with me. Please—I'll be fine."

Claudia seemed ambivalent, torn between relief and responsibility.

"If you're sure—" Claudia capitulated.

"I am."

"Now, regarding the marital settlement. I'm sure Mr. Ames will not expect a share of your estate under the circumstances." Mr. Lewisohn was faintly acerbic.

"No, he won't." *You never let me forget your fucking money!* She hadn't been like that. Had she? "But I want the California house to go to Chris in the divorce settlement," Diane told him. Her eyes avoided his. She knew she had unnerved both her attorney and her aunt.

"Diane," Mr. Lewisohn said, "may I remind you

that you have a sizable investment in the California house?"

She spoke quietly.

"I never want to set foot in that house again."

"Wouldn't it be wiser to donate it to charity?" Claudia said.

"Let Chris have the house." He could live with the memory of the few lovely days and nights they had shared. She couldn't. "His consolation prize." She managed a wry smile and saw the concern in her aunt's eyes. Aunt Claudia was worried that she was still in love with Chris. She was in love—but with a Chris who existed only rarely.

Two weeks later Diane sat with Deirdre over lunch in the roughly plastered, wainscotted main dining room at "21." Here they could dine in privacy. She would never get used to the stares of those who suddenly recognized her as Diane Dickenson. Stares that could be furtive or blatant, admiring or hostile.

Deirdre—again roly-poly and addicted to caftan-like dresses—listened wide-eyed and solemn as Diane brought her up to date.

"I told Aunt Claudia you'd go with me to Reno," Diane wound up breathlessly. "All right?"

"Sure I'll go with you." But there were tears in Deirdre's eyes. "I could kill that bastard Chris."

"It's not like that, Deirdre. When Chris married me he thought it would work. He hoped it would. At first I was angry. I'm not anymore—just hurt—*terribly* hurt that my dream has fizzled away into such ugliness."

"So," Deirdre smiled gamely. "When do we leave? That Mediterranean cruise was a dog. There was nobody aboard under sixty-five. Only the crew and me. And the crew was too busy keeping the passengers happy to have any strength left for extracurricular activities."

"It looks like you ate well," Diane said. "You need about a month at Maine Chance."

Deirdre shrugged. "So I'm fat. Maybe I'll look up Lenny again."

"Deirdre!"

"Why not? I told you. He can do it a dozen times a night. I haven't done it since I walked out on him in Bermuda late last September."

"That's not the sole purpose for living, Dee."

"All I know is that the happy times I've had in my life have been when I was flat on my back with Lenny," Deirdre said. "And don't tell me about all the times we thought we were having such a ball watching Tyrone Power or Rock Hudson from a seat in the Capitol or the Paramount. I'm talking about now. Grown-up stuff." She sighed. "I guess I won't be looking for him. If I was skinny again, I might. Clay says I'm crazy to mess with somebody like Lenny."

"Who's Clay?" Diane asked, alert to a newcomer in Deirdre's life. "You never mentioned him before."

"Clay Brentwood," Deirdre said. "You remember him. He took you to Mary Lou Caldwell's tea dance the fall we came out."

"I don't remember," Diane admitted. "I was so scared in those days about saying or doing the wrong thing. Every fellow I went out with until I flew with you to see Chris was faceless. I was play-acting the debutante."

"Clay and I do things together. I mean, casual things like going to the theater or some dinner or ball. I'm his escape from his mother. She can't wait to get him married off."

"You like him?"

"He's fun." Deirdre seemed uncomfortable. "But not somebody to marry. Though he is rich enough, so I know he's not after my money." She paused. "He's gay. I'm sorry—I was trying to avoid saying that."

"Why not?" Diane forced a smile. "You like him as a friend."

"The three of us could do things together if it wouldn't bother you," Deirdre pursued. "He'll take us places where we can't go without an escort, and it'll be fun." She grinned. "Not fun and games."

"What have you got planned for Christmas and New Year's?" Diane said.

"Mother rented a house down in Palm Beach. My grandmother's on a round-the-world cruise, so I guess it's Palm Beach for me. Want to come down there, too?"

Diane nodded.

"I promised Aunt Claudia I'd go down with her for the holidays. She's putting her house on the market. She's not happy away from the church and her committees."

Aunt Claudia clung to her church for survival. Why couldn't *she* do the same thing with the synagogue? Occasionally Diane wondered if her aunt had totally blocked out the fact that Palm Beach society was anti-Semitic.

They lingered over walnut soufflés and espresso

before leaving, pausing for a breath of crisp air outside the unpretentious brownstone—distinguished only by its New Orleans grillwork—while they waited for Diane's limousine to pull up at the curb.

"That's Diane Dickenson!" a feminine teenage voice squealed. Diane froze.

"Yeah!" another said excitedly. "I read in Earl Wilson's column that she was in town!"

"Can we have your autograph, Diane?" A book was thrust beneath her nose.

In a moment she was surrounded by half a dozen teenagers with autograph books. She tried to smile as she signed each book.

"The car's here," Deirdre said, tugging at her arm.

She was trembling when she was inside the car. They wanted her autograph because she was married to Chris Ames. Once the divorce was through, this craziness would be over.

"My God," Deirdre giggled, "it wasn't enough you were practically Debutante of the Year—you had to marry a movie star."

A few days later Clay Brentwood escorted Deirdre and Diane to a charity ball. Diane liked him on sight but couldn't remember dating him two years ago. At twenty-five Clay was slight, not quite six feet, pleasant-looking. His sandy hair was usually rumpled and longer than approved of by his son-smothering social-leader mother, widowed when Clay was seven. His blue eyes hinted at a keen mind, though he kept up the facade of mindless playboy.

He had a B.A. from Harvard, dabbled in painting, and had appeared for one season with a summer stock company. He refused to join his mother's brother—his Uncle Edward—in the investment banking firm founded by his great-grandfather. His father had been a blueblood whose empire was destroyed in the Wall Street crash. Crass rumors claimed his wife had driven him to suicide by her demands that he be a success in the financial world.

Bored after the first hour, the three of them fled from the charity ball to the Russian Tea Room, where they settled themselves at a secluded table to devour blini and sour cream. Diane was aware of a comforting sense of kinship between them. They were all super-rich, lonely, and insecure. Clay obviously took it for granted that Deirdre had confided in her about his homosexuality. He seemed relaxed.

With disarming candor they discussed their families—though Diane, as always, refrained from revealing her Jewishness. Though she used Aunt Claudia as an excuse, the truth was she herself wasn't ready to deal with it.

"My family missed the *Mayflower*, but they were on the next ship. Even without the DAR picture, though, they would have made it into the *Social Register*. With all that money, how could they fail to?" As for Clay, it was clear that he had only contempt for the *Social Register*.

"Will you be down in Palm Beach for Christmas?" Deirdre asked.

"That's the ritual," Clay sighed. "Mother opens up the house three days before Christmas. She stays

254

there until March, when she goes to the Homestead at Hot Springs for three weeks." Diane flinched. The Homestead at Hot Springs sounded too much like the Greenbrier and White Sulphur Springs. "Then she runs to Paris."

Deirdre looked disapproving.

"You won't stay in Palm Beach till March?"

"God, no." He shuddered. "How much can I take of Worth Avenue and society widows?" Palm Beach society was ruled by what Cleveland Amory called "an autocratic widow matriarchy." "I'll come back to New York a few days after I've recovered from New Year's Eve."

Diane was glad when it was time to go to Palm Beach. There she, Deirdre, and Clay were inseparable. But she was hounded by gossip columnists there, too, so she was relieved when it was time to return to New York. Clay's mother—oblivious to his homosexuality—made it pretty clear that she was hoping for a Dickenson-Brentwood alliance, which made Diane's "vacation" even more stressful.

Back in New York, Diane vowed to live in near-seclusion until it was time to leave for Reno. As it was, her every move was reported by Cholly Knicker-bocker or Sheilah Graham or Dorothy Kilgallen. In Hollywood Chris had finally admitted to a trial separation, though, he announced, "I love Diane and hope we can work things out."

Chris knew she would not be going to Reno until late March. He was hoping to keep the divorce under wraps until after the Academy Award votes were in. Mannie must be making life miserable for him, Diane thought; but even she knew that *any* Academy acknowledgment—a nomination—would make the new picture a box-office smash.

Deirdre was jubilant with the approach of her twenty-first birthday—in a weak moment her father had decided that at twenty-one she *could* handle all the income from her estate. Immediately she began inspecting posh apartments along Park Avenue—to buy, not to rent. She turned in the Thunderbird for a Dual-Ghia—though first she asked Diane if she would be upset at the sight of a car like the one Chris drove. On a whim, she bought a dozen silk nightgowns at Saks for $250 each.

A week before Diane was scheduled to leave for Reno, Sheilah Graham broke the news that Diane Dickenson had rented the palatial estate of an Arab prince in Reno. Mr. Lewisohn was upset. He insisted on maintaining round-the-clock security guards at the rented house, "to guarantee that no pranksters annoy you." The phones rang constantly. The servants were instructed to tell callers that "Mrs. Ames is out of the city."

On a damp gray morning in late March, Diane and Deirdre were driven to Newark to board a chartered flight to Reno. Diane's Reno attorney was to meet them at the private airport and escort them to the rented house.

Diane hoped that her stay in the divorce capital of the world would be uneventful. Reno was a small city—there would be no reporters at the airport, the way there had been when Chris and she returned to Los Angeles International from New York. The lawyer would meet them and drive them to the house. There would be no problem.

The plane landed. Diane emerged with Deirdre. A slender, graying man, elegantly tailored and barbered, came forward to meet them.

"I'm Leland Matthews, your attorney. I hope your trip was pleasant." Diane smiled in relief. Thank God, no reporters. Apparently the chartered flight had thrown the press off.

Mr. Matthews handed Diane and Deirdre into a shiny new Cadillac Coupe de Ville, arranged for their luggage to be carried to a waiting station wagon, and joined them in the rear seat of the car. He explained that the house he had rented in Diane's name was the *pied-à-terre* of an Arab prince who liked to spend occasional weekends in Reno because of the casinos. Here, security for the prince was less complicated than in Las Vegas.

"Mr. Lewisohn was especially pleased with the security system installed at the house at the time the prince made the purchase," he said. "And I've arranged for security guards to be on duty around the clock while you're in Reno. They'll be very unobtrusive—you'll hardly know they're about the property."

"Thank you," Diane said. Why was Mr. Lewisohn so concerned? Even Aunt Claudia had insisted—up until Diane's debut—that Philippe be armed when he drove her anywhere. *All because of a kidnapping when she was four?* It seemed ridiculous.

The house, on the outskirts of Reno, was a modern nine-bedroom masterpiece with an outdoor and indoor pool, an exercise room with steambath and sauna, and a tennis court. A domestic staff was kept in year-round residence, to be on duty whenever the prince chose to arrive. A gray Rolls-Royce was at their disposal. The exquisitely landscaped estate was surrounded by a high fence that would provide complete privacy.

Mr. Matthews explained that her appearance in court would be brief and uneventful. Meanwhile, he said, she must take some time to enjoy the sights.

"Drive over to Virginia City to visit the Comstock Lode, Mrs. Ames. It's only twenty-three miles from here. And Lake Tahoe, beautiful this time of year, is less than an hour by car. And there's still skiing if you're so inclined."

The large domestic staff was brought in for brief introductions, then returned to their duties about the house. Mr. Matthews gave them an elaborately detailed report on the city and offered his services as escort, though Diane had made it clear that she and Deirdre would not be likely to visit the clubs or casinos. Then Mr. Matthews left. Diane and Deirdre settled themselves in the ballroom-sized living room, its walls hung with Renoirs, Monets, Seurats, Cezannes, until the two maids who were unpacking for them returned to the lower floor. Then they went up to the ornate master bedroom suite, across the hall from Deirdre's suite.

"I wonder what this prince looks like," Deirdre mused while she sprawled across the king-sized bed, draped in a cream-colored satin bedspread with the royal emblem embroidered in gold and silver thread. "I'll bet Arabs are passionate."

"I'm afraid we're not likely to meet him." Diane laughed. She gazed out the window at the elaborate gardens below. Los Angeles—and Chris—was per-

258

haps an hour from Reno by air. She had thought that once she left Chris and was scheduled to divorce him she would put him forever out of her mind. Obviously, that wasn't possible. These six weeks in Reno would seem endless.

For the first four days Diane and Deirdre stayed around the house, swimming in the indoor pool, chatting in the sauna, and playing tennis. Diane had all the New York and Los Angeles newspapers delivered to the house, and together they read all the gossip columns. Diane knew this was masochistic, but she couldn't help herself. Rumor had it that Chris was likely to get an Academy Award nomination for best actor, but he was far from a shoo-in to win. Diane wondered why she couldn't put Chris out of her mind—and continued to look for news about her soon-to-be ex-husband. Every night they watched television, with Deirdre complaining about Nevada's poor reception.

"I never should have started up with Lenny," Deirdre said, diving into the fourth box of Lindt chocolates they'd consumed since their arrival, "and you never should have married Chris. We were so dumb, Diane. We fell for the first guys who we figured weren't after our money." She paused. "Though I *did* kind of figure the Thunderbird was my biggest attraction with Lenny. He loved to drive that car." She giggled. "Can you imagine if he found out I have a Dual-Ghia."

"It wasn't all bad with Chris," Diane said. "There were times when he made me feel so loved. I'd never felt like that in my whole life."

Deirdre looked horrified.

"For God's sake, Di! Don't tell me you're sorry about the divorce."

Diane shook her head.

"I know it's the right thing. But for a little while, after he begged me to come back and he promised to go into therapy, I guess I hoped we could make it work." Deirdre was the only person in the world she could talk this way to. Her mother had suggested therapy, but Diane knew that all she needed was a friend to listen to her. "Right now I'm hurt and angry, but I can't hate Chris. He's a special person, Dee. I'm not saying that to make myself feel better about marrying him—well, maybe partly that. But most of the time he's a fine, compassionate human being." Sometimes she even wondered if maybe he was right—maybe she *had* failed him.

"I know," Deirdre said drily. "Everybody in Hollywood loves Chris Ames. But Chris Ames doesn't know for sure who *he* can love."

Diane smiled.

"That's Chris's demon. I suspect a lot of women will try to convince him to go the 'normal' way, whatever that means anymore. But maybe that's the wrong way for him. Who are we to say?" At least Clay was honest. He didn't go around advertising that he was gay, but he didn't run after girls, either.

"God, I wish that crazy Lenny was here right now," Deirdre said. "I'd forget about the way he chases everything in skirts and hop right into the sack with him. I might even stop making a pig of myself." She picked up the box of chocolates and threw it across the room. "Di, what's the matter with us? Why is everything so rotten?"

"We've got to stop being sorry for ourselves, that's the first thing. Look at us! By the rest of the world's standards, we have everything going for us. Let's pick ourselves up and enjoy it! And you—stop trying to be the fattest post-debutante in New York! No more chocolates, no more desserts, and let's start exercising. We could go horseback riding! We'll ride for an hour every morning. Dee, it'll be fun; you'll slim down, and I could use some firming up." It would be a goal, something to keep them from obsessing about the past. "We'll use that exercise room every day. Come on, Dee, what do you say? Let's *accomplish* something in Reno." But even as she spoke them, she knew her words sounded hollow. *What would they accomplish?*

On their first morning on the horse trails, Diane knew this had been a mistake. For her, horse trails were haunted by memories of the early days with Chris.

"Di, I don't think we should ride anymore," Deirdre said on the way back to the house in the gray Rolls.

When they walked into the ornate marble-floored foyer, they were greeted by the housekeeper.

"There was a long distance call for you, Mrs. Ames," she reported. "A Mr. Brentwood. He asked that you please call him in New York."

For Diane, hearing Clay's voice over the phone was a comforting reassurance that her life had not gone entirely berserk. He had a disarming way of lifting her spirits, of making her laugh.

"I'm flying out there," he said exuberantly. "I'll arrive late tomorrow afternoon, your time."

"When?" Diane was surprised by how much she wanted him there. "We'll pick you up. You'll stay with us."

"I'm afraid that wouldn't be smart," he said. "You're out there for a divorce. The reporters would have a field day." There was never a hint in the society columns about his homosexuality. "I have reservations at the Riverside Hotel. I'll buzz you the minute I'm settled in."

Shortly past seven the following morning Clay called from his suite at the Riverside.

"I have a table reserved in the Theater Restaurant for eight-thirty. Meet me there. Afterwards we'll try our luck at the casinos, then go on to the Skyroom at the Mapes for the midnight show. How much have you dropped at the tables so far?" There was an edge to his voice, a forced quality to his gaiety, that told Diane he must have come to Reno after another savage battle with his mother, probably about money. While he would one day inherit the Brentwood fortune, rumored to be worth over a hundred million, he had to go to his mother for every cent; she controlled the income from the capital. She paid his bills—with loud lamentations and absurd predictions of future poverty.

Diane laughed.

"I have a confession to make: we haven't been away from the house. We've just been sitting around moping."

"For the next week that's not allowed. The Theater Restaurant at the Riverside, eight-thirty sharp."

Dressing for dinner, Diane chose a pink-and-gray satin evening dress with a strapless bodice and a black-velvet-accented waist. Clay had a good eye for fashion and was sure to recognize it as a Hardy Amies. She knew it would please him.

Gazing at her reflection in the mirrored dressing room, she fought down panic at the prospect of walking into the Theater Restaurant at the posh Riverside Hotel . . . as those eyes focused on her.

Then she had an idea: *the blonde wig.* That was it! She would wear her old wig and harlequin glasses.

"Oh my God, I don't believe it!" Deirdre burst out laughing when Diane appeared in the doorway. "Not even Clay would recognize you in that get-up."

For the first time since they arrived in Reno, Diane summoned the security guard who was to serve as their chauffeur. Feeling happy and adventurous for the first time in months, they clambered into the gray Rolls. Why shouldn't Deirdre and she go out with Clay, Diane asked herself defensively. This couldn't jeopardize her divorce. Not with Deirdre along.

As promised, Clay was waiting for them at a choice table in the Theater Restaurant.

Dinner was a gourmet feast. The players could have been on Broadway. From there Clay led them to the glittering casino, where twenty-one, roulette, and dice were the favorites. Diane had no gambling instinct, but she was happy to watch Deirdre, who enjoyed a bit of casual gambling.

It was after Clay took a chair at the roulette table that Diane became nervous, because he began to lose heavily.

She gave Deirdre a significant look.

"Clay, you promised to take us to the midnight show at the Mapes, remember?"

"Yeah, Clay," Deirdre pushed him away from the roulette table. He had already lost twelve thousand dollars. "It's late."

Reluctantly Clay gave up his seat at the roulette table. He smiled as he positioned himself between Diane and Deirdre.

"Mama dear will be pissed off when I phone and tell her she has to throw more money into my checking account. It was rotten of the old man to let her control everything until she dies. She'll probably hang on 'til she's a hundred and four."

"She hasn't gotten over your being barred from Monte Carlo," Deirdre laughed and Diane lifted an eyebrow. She hadn't heard about that.

"I stripped in a casino," Clay said casually. "They took me out behind a pair of screens." He sighed. "I don't remember a thing about it, but I got a report on every lurid detail. Now all of Monte Carlo knows about the birthmark on my rear."

Before Clay left them for the evening, he promised to come to the house for breakfast and take them on a sightseeing tour.

At noon the next day Clay arrived for breakfast. Two hours later the three of them settled into the Rolls for the short trip into town.

"There are two great things about Reno," he said. "No big-city traffic, and you can walk anywhere you like. I think we should leave the Rolls at the Mapes

Hotel. Too many people know it. In Reno we can be just three tourists without name tags." Diane smiled at him, appreciating his thinking of her.

The security guard tried to stop them from proceeding on foot from the plush Mapes Hotel, but Diane insisted. While they walked across the bridge over the Truckee River, which ran right through the center of town, she was aware that the guard was following them, albeit at a discrete distance. On orders from Leland Matthews, she surmised.

The atmosphere in town was casual, unhurried, and distinctly western. Here, Diane remembered Leland Matthews saying, the Old West still survived: there was legal gambling, twenty-four-hour-a-day saloon life, and everyone dressed in western clothes. When locals went horseback riding, they rode in western saddles.

The party of three strolled past the modern post office and the State Building, walked behind that to the library and a small park.

"That's the Washoe County Courthouse over there," Clay said. "Where you'll go for your divorce hearing, Di." He grinned. "A bellhop gave me a guided tour earlier this morning. He seemed especially anxious for me to know that there are lots more marriages in Reno than divorces."

Diane tried unsuccessfully to ignore the parade of dewy-eyed young brides emerging from the courthouse, orchid corsages on their shoulders and grooms with white carnations on their lapels. They all looked so happy.

"All you have to do to get married in Reno is to go into the courthouse there, get a license, then go upstairs to the judge and plunk down the ten bucks for him to marry you. Anybody interested?" He turned from Diane to Deirdre.

Diane's brief happiness disappeared. In a little over five weeks she had to go into that courthouse and apply for her divorce. She knew what Chris was—why did she feel this awful sense of loss at divorcing him? Her eyes blurred as she watched a young couple, the bride clinging to her groom's arm, emerge from the courthouse and pause, as though to etch the day forever in their memory.

Diane tried to match Deirdre and Clay's high spirits as they visited Harrah's, with its slogan "Your Reno Host"; and the Golden Nugget—with the greatest collection of gold nuggets in the world.

Exhausted by nightfall, Diane and Deirdre went home to nap briefly and dress before meeting Clay again for steaks at the Christmas Tree, where, Clay told them, they would meet the owner's friendly lion cub and an enormous St. Bernard named Clancy.

Diane and Deirdre were sorry to see Clay leave Reno after his week's stay—unless they chose Leland Matthews as their escort, that meant the end of their nightlife.

After Clay's departure the days dragged. To pass the time Diane and Deirdre went into town to gamble or shop, Diane always in her disguise.

They followed Leland Matthew's advice and visited Lake Tahoe, a lovely blue-green lake rimmed by lush pines of the High Sierra. A week later they drove to Virginia City. The television set sat silent the night of the Academy Awards ceremonies. Afterwards Diane let Deirdre listen to the radio report the winners. Chris had been nominated; he had not won. But the nomination would be a terrific boost for his career.

At last Diane's day in court arrived. At ten-thirty A.M.—nervous and cold, despite the warmth of the morning—she, Deirdre, and Leland Matthews drove to the side entrance of the Washoe District County Courthouse. She was startled by the hordes of people milling before the entrance—among them photographers and reporters.

"It's going to be all right," Matthews said. "We did our best to keep it quiet, but I guess word leaked out."

"Why do they care?" Diane said. Would they ever leave her alone? "What's so important about my divorcing Chris?"

She allowed herself to be handed out of the Rolls, Deirdre and Matthews on either side of her. The security guard walked a few paces ahead. At that same moment half a dozen deputies emerged from the side entrance to flank the small party.

"There she is!" a woman shrieked. "Diane Dickenson!"

Diane let herself be guided past the crowd toward the rear of the building. At one point she stumbled and would have fallen down the stairs had Mr. Matthews not steadied her. In the corridor leading to the courtroom, more reporters waited. Flashbulbs erupted with machine-gun precision as she was escorted to the courtroom.

Once the Dickenson party was inside the courtroom, the door was locked. Diane silently thanked

Mr. Matthews for arranging a closed hearing. Only the necessary courtroom personnel was present. Chris was represented by his attorney. The legality of her residence in Reno was established. The judge questioned her briefly. Fifteen minutes after walking into the courtroom, Diane was granted her divorce.

"Baby, you're free!" Deirdre threw her arms around her. "Welcome back, Diane Dickenson!"

Chapter Fifteen

Laura stood beside Joe Freedlich's desk, waiting for her call to be put through to Mannie Coleman's office. She was proud of the way she had learned to handle herself in these first few weeks of her job as Freedlich's secretary. While Freedlich never bothered to offer praise, she knew he was satisfied with her services.

"Yes?" Marge Mendelsohn was on the line, crisp and slightly impatient at the interruption from the New York office.

"Good morning, Marge," Laura said. "This is Laura Devlin at Menlow New York. Mr. Freedlich would like to talk to Mr. Coleman about the distribution figures. Is he free?"

"Good morning, Laura. Sure. Put him on."

With Freedlich on the line, Laura left his office to return to her own. She heard raised voices in the office of her former boss, then saw a young woman—the first reader—storm out in tears.

"I'm getting out of this nuthouse! Garrison is out

of his mind!"

For a moment Laura debated . . . should she get involved? Then, slowly, she walked into Bill Garrison's office. While Garrison had been irritated by her move up, they maintained a guarded but friendly relationship.

"Problems, Mr. Garrison?"

"We've got more temperament in this goddamn office than Coleman has to put up with on the studio sets! You know what pissed off that twit English major from Vassar? I asked her to take home the bound galleys of a novel and read 'em and bring in a report tomorrow. But she couldn't do that," he drawled sarcastically. "Miss First Reader is going to see *The Miracle Worker* with Anne Bancroft."

"I'll read them for you," Laura said casually. He stared as though seeing her for the first time. "It'll save me a trip to the library. I have nothing at home to read. I go through four or five books a week. It'll be kind of fun to read a book before it's been published."

"What kind of report will *you* bring in?"

"I'm the typical moviegoer. I loved *Some Like It Hot* and *Room at the Top*." Both were box-office smashes. "I'll write up a report from my viewpoint. I took two courses in English Lit. at NYU last year. We had to do reports on contemporary fiction."

His phone rang, a jarring intrusion. His secretary was on her coffee break. Scowling, he picked up the receiver.

"Hold on a moment." He covered the phone and reached for a manila envelope at one corner of his desk. "If you want to spend your time reading galleys, fine. Tell Maureen to give you a couple of old

270

reports so you'll see how to do it."

"Sure thing." She smiled, took the envelope, and sailed back to her own office.

Bill Garrison wasn't worried about her wanting the first reader's job, she realized. He knew she earned more where she was. But he had no suspicion that she was aiming for *his* job. It might take her two or three years, but she was young enough. She had plenty of time.

As usual, she had lunch at her desk, taking time to dip into the galleys. As she read she doubted that the West Coast office would be interested in it, but Ira had taught her not to make judgments too quickly.

The remainder of the day raced by. Laura enjoyed the office's pressured atmosphere. She made a point of staying until Joe Freedlich had charged through the door for Grand Central and the commuter train for Westport.

By the time she arrived at the subway station, the rush-hour crowds had thinned out and she got a seat for the brief ride to Astor Place. On the street, she picked up copies of the *Journal-American* and the *New York Post* at a newsstand on Second Avenue. Every night with her after-dinner coffee she read Dorothy Kilgallen, Cholly Knickerbocker, Leonard Lyons, and Earl Wilson.

Occasionally she glanced at the political news, a result of Ira's influence. The newspapers projected Vice-President Nixon and John Kennedy—the rich senator from Massachusetts—to be the major-party candidates. Ira wrote that he hoped Adlai Stevenson would run again. He was against Kennedy because, he said, as congressman and senator from Massachusetts, Kennedy had done nothing to stop Joe McCarthy. Ira said people had heard Joseph Kennedy make anti-Semitic remarks, and that John Kennedy was strongly influenced by his father. She supposed she ought to be interested in politics. But right now she was more concerned about her personal campaign at Menlow Films.

The May evening was deliciously warm, with no hint of the sultry heat that would soon envelope the city. She enjoyed the walk home, felt comfortable in the East Village, with its lineup of Off-Broadway playhouses and eclectic array of restaurants and candy stores. She had never felt comfortable in Newport. There she had always been an outsider. Here, with other ambitious young people, she felt at home.

She walked into her bleak East Fifth Street tenement, her mailbox key in hand. Since Ira had left, she had received only a postcard and three hastily scrawled letters. Though she didn't miss him during the hectic hours of the office day, at night and on weekends she found that he crept into her thoughts more than she cared to admit.

She unlocked her mailbox. Mostly bills, as usual. Sometimes she felt like a nonperson, receiving so much impersonal mail. There were catalogues from the New School for Social Research, the business school where she had taken her course in speedwriting, mail marked "Occupant, Apartment 14." Cindy rarely wrote anymore—she was all involved with her social life, dying to get married and out of the family household, where she fought constantly with her mother. Why did they fight anyway? Laura wondered. They both wanted the same thing for Cindy: marriage to a doctor or lawyer—a "professional man."

But tonight there was an airmail envelope in the mailbox, and Laura glowed when she read the return address in the upper corner. Ira. Reading a letter from Ira was like talking to him. Almost.

As she locked her mailbox and opened the front door, she remembered that she was going to an Off-Broadway opening tomorrow night with a friend of Ira's. Everybody she saw socially she had met through Ira. She knew that some actors thought that dating her might lead to a screen test. Their obsession with "contacts" bothered her. Was that why she had turned down Peter Grayson's invitation to bed last week?

Why *had* she turned him down? She was beginning to feel like a virgin again. Was it Ira? Climbing the dark, uneven stairs to her apartment, she wondered about this. Truth was, she couldn't afford to be serious about Ira. She couldn't afford to be serious about *any* man—unless he was instrumental in helping her up the ladder at Menlow Films. But in three weeks she would be twenty-one. She was a woman. She needed a man in her life. At least occasionally.

She shifted the manila envelope containing the bound galleys under one arm and unlocked the door. Flipping on the overhead light, she realized again how she hated this fleabag of an apartment. Where else could she live for forty-two dollars a month?

She wriggled out of her coat and ripped open the airmail envelope, reading as she dropped into a chair. Ira was still intrigued with London. The young British, Ira had written in his first letter, were hostile toward their class structure. London was teeming with the talented who were fighting their way out of the East End slums and the depressed provinces.

Right now London is the most swinging city in the world. At least, for our generation. They've stopped railing against the Establishment to be themselves. You'd love the boutiques opening up on Carnaby Street—and the clothes! People our age are beginning to move into the entertainment field and fashion and photography. They can work there even if they left school at fifteen—that's allowed here—and don't speak with an Oxford accent. I've seen some terrific new plays by nobody I've ever heard of, and there are some new musical groups showing up in London that will give the Beach Boys and Chubby Checkers a run for their money if they ever decide to cross the Atlantic. And some are making sensational films.

Ira would always be interested in the artistic end of the entertainment business, Laura thought. That's where they differed; she was fascinated by what would make a box-office smash, bring people into the movie houses. With Ira, everything had to say something special. It wasn't enough to entertain. She went on reading.

After all these months I'm still sightseeing.

History comes to life here. I stood on the spot
where Anne Boleyn had her head chopped off,
and then I climbed the Bloody Tower. Wow!
But there's history in the making, too. Each year
since 1958 London has seen the Aldermaston
March for nuclear disarmament. This year
100,000—including me—marched.

She finished reading the letter, put it aside to
reread later, and went into the bedroom to change
from her office suit and blouse into slacks and T-
shirt. When she returned to the kitchen, she put the
remains of last night's tuna noodle casserole in the
oven.

While she waited for the casserole to heat up, she
reached for the *Journal-American*. Diane's name
leapt at her from Cholly Knickerbocker's column.
She had been seen at El Morocco, Quo Vadis, and the
Stork Club with Clay Brentwood. Apparently they
had become an "item" since Diane's return from
Reno.

The thought of Diane's jumping into another
marriage disturbed her, even though she knew that
Clay Brentwood was rich and considered one of the
country's most eligible young bachelors. It must
have been an awful shock for Diane to find out about
Chris's homosexuality, but it didn't seem right to
run into another man's arms just weeks after her
divorce. Anyway, with all that money, she didn't
have to marry rich.

But Diane Dickenson didn't think like Laura
Devlin, did she? How *did* a girl with seventy million
dollars think? What did she do every day? She

couldn't just sit around counting her money. After a while it had to be pretty boring—looking for more things to buy, more places to visit, more parties to attend. Laura tossed the paper on the floor. Maybe all those people who made up the jet set kept running because they were afraid to stop.

The phone was ringing. Slowly Diane woke up. Her eyes closed, she fumbled around her night table for the phone.

"Hello—"

"Di, the apartment's all mine!" It was Deirdre. "The lawyers just called to tell me."

"How are you so wide awake at this hour of the morning?" She squinted at the French ormolu clock setting on the fireplace mantle. It wasn't morning at all—it was five minutes past noon.

"How could I sleep when I knew the lawyers were closing on the apartment? *My own pad.* Of course daddy's furious that I'm buying it, and more furious that I won't hire this chi-chi decorator who just redid *his* apartment. She's about thirty and gorgeous. I'm sure he's sleeping with her."

Diane pulled herself up and leaned against the headboard.

"Who *are* you hiring, then?"

"I'm going to do it myself. With you, of course, to help me. If you tell me not to buy something, then I won't. You've got sensational taste. Didn't you do your house out in California yourself?"

"But Dee, we're leaving for Southampton in a week—" Still, the prospect of decorating Deirdre's eleven-room apartment on Park Avenue *was* intriguing.

"Oh, you'll get bored out there," Deirdre said confidently. "You always do. So we'll come in a couple of times a week to choose things for the apartment. Don't worry—it's not like Barbara Hutton's twenty-six room duplex, but it'll do. We'll have a housewarming in October," she decided. "After everybody comes back from their summer spots."

"How about asking Clay to help?" Diane said. "Remember how well he redid his Uncle Edward's whole apartment after the decorator finished? It's beautiful."

"I'll be over in forty minutes. Stay close to me, Di— I have an awful urge to go look up Lenny."

"Dee, stop it. You don't need him." Diane said vigorously. "When we get out to Southampton, we're going to walk miles on the beach every day. You're going on a strict diet. No cheating."

"You know what? I don't even care if I get skinny again or not. I'm just so damned bored. Maybe in August we can run over to St. Tropez. Clay was there last summer. He said it was great."

"Maybe. Early in August, though. My mother won't be there then. She's spending August on somebody's yacht, touring the Greek Isles. For July she rented a villa on the Mediterranean. She asked if I'd like to fly over for a few days, knowing, of course, I'd never say yes. According to the gossip columnists, Olivia's latest lover is the same age as Chris."

"Di, get out of bed and get dressed," Deirdre said. "Clay will pick us up at your house at one o'clock. We're having lunch at the Colony with his mother."

277

"Deirdre, no." She couldn't bear an afternoon of Mrs. Brentwood's clumsy matchmaking efforts. Not today. Diane smiled. Would Mrs. Brentwood of the DAR be so eager if she knew Diane Dickenson was really Diane Seligman?

"We have to, Di. For Clay. Wear something that'll make every woman at the Colony hate you. That sexy Galanos. It makes you look so sophisticated and aloof."

Diane laughed.

"All right, you win. But you owe me one, Dee."

As she dressed, she decided to call Laura that night and ask her out to lunch later in the week. God, it was such a long time since they'd had lunch together. They ought to see more of each other, she thought guiltily. Laura had been a friend when she needed one. Desperately. It was funny, really—though they saw each other so seldom, she had the feeling that Laura would always be a part of her life.

At Sardi's, Diane listened intently as Laura told her about her small success at Menlow Films.

"I think it's marvelous that you're doing so well," she said. And she meant it. But she was just a little envious, too; she had nothing so absorbing in her own life. Chris had filled that void in her life—all too briefly.

"Did you ever pursue those painting classes?" Laura asked, obviously pleased by Diane's approval.

"I went to classes. I worked like mad. And then I found out I have just a little talent. Enough to make me want to paint. Not enough to be a professional. I think that's worse than none at all." She forced a laugh, but the old pain of disappointment came through. "Once when Chris was tired and upset about how the shooting was going on a film, he said, 'Poor little rich girl, making like Picasso.'" Funny, she thought she'd forgotten that.

"Everybody says things they don't mean when they're upset," Laura said. "But I wouldn't be too happy hearing that." She hesitated. "I'm sorry it didn't work out with Chris and you."

"I guess everybody at Menlow Films knows why." Her eyes searched Laura's.

Laura looked embarrassed. "Yes."

"Then why didn't somebody tell me?" The words burst out. "Why didn't *you* tell me?"

"Diane, you were married already by the time we met again. I wasn't working for Menlow yet. But Ira knew about Chris. The Off-Broadway director they'd both worked with told him."

"Looks like it's the old story: everybody knew except the bride," Diane said. Of course, in Hollywood there was a pact to keep anything considered scandalous under wraps for the sake of the whole industry. "What's with your friend Ira?" It was funny the way he stayed in her mind, though they had met just that once. She'd liked the way he was low-keyed and natural when everybody else was high-pitched and phony.

"Ira's living in London. He's been there since last November. He's writing a play. He expects to be there for a year."

"Well, I hope it's a big hit." But Diane felt defensive. Here was Ira, probably very talented, but with no money. She had more money than she could ever use, and no real talent. She'd give up all the money, she thought recklessly, for talent. It didn't have to be painting. It could be anything that would make her feel worthwhile as a human being.

"Ira keeps telling me to come over and visit," Laura said. "But right now I'm not going further from the job than Fire Island for a weekend."

"I think it's great that you're so involved with your job."

Most of the girls who had graduated with her from Miss Framingham's and had not gone on to college kept busy with charity balls and luncheons. Though she avoided all that, at least she donated money, she recalled conscientiously. Mr. Lewisohn took care of that. It wasn't as though she were shunning her obligations; money was what they needed. What did *she* need?

"What a beautiful dress that woman is wearing!" Laura gazed, fascinated, at a new arrival. "Wait a minute, who is she? She looks familiar—"

"That's Candace Collins," Diane told her, tensing because she knew Candace would table-hop over to them. Right now she was surveying the room.

Candace spied Diane. With a scintillating smile she was striding toward them.

"Diane, how lovely you look!"

"Thank you, Candace." Diane managed a smile, hating the hypocrisy, knowing it was necessary.

"I was sorry that you and Chris broke up." Her smile was sympathetic, her eyes triumphant.

"Chris is married to his career." They both knew the truth. "I couldn't bear the Hollywood life."

"Any truth to the stories about Clay Brentwood and you?" she asked archly. "Are you going to take him out of circulation?"

"Clay and I are just close friends. We share a lot of interests. In fact, we may open up an interior decorating shop together." *Why had she said that?* Tomorrow morning she'd be reading about it in Candace's column. Poor little rich girl, making like a business girl. Clay wouldn't mind—he'd just laugh.

The waiter arrived and Candace moved on to another table. Diane felt depressed. She was glad she and Deirdre were leaving for Southampton next week. Walking along the beach at sunrise, she would make herself forget Chris. The beach was her therapy.

Knowing about Chris's indiscretions should have been enough to wash him out of her mind. It wasn't. Still, with each passing week she thought about him less. Maybe soon she wouldn't think about him at all.

Chapter Sixteen

Deirdre phoned in the afternoon to say that she had to have dinner with her father and his "decorator whore."

"He says *I* have to explain why I won't hire her to decorate the apartment." Deirdre sighed. "So you and Clay go on without me. Oh—ask him about where we should stay at St. Tropez. We have to make reservations right now, or we'll be sleeping on the street."

Diane didn't know quite what to do. If any of the columnists saw Clay and her alone tonight—without the perennial presence of Deirdre—they'd be sure they were romantically involved. Clay had once joked that they should get married to protect themselves from everybody else. Now she understood he'd meant to protect himself from his homosexuality and her from the pursuit of fortune-hunters.

She took special care dressing, knowing that Clay enjoyed seeing her beautifully turned out. She chose a short evening dress of sky blue chiffon, cut high at the neck and low at the back, its low-waisted bodice easing into a pleated skirt.

Clay picked her up promptly at seven o'clock and took her to the Café Pierre for dinner, knowing that both of them enjoyed dancing to the music provided by Stanley Worth and his quartet. Afterwards they went to the Blue Angel and saw a young comic—one of Clay's favorites.

When Diane told him about the trip to St. Tropez he told her that it was already too late to get reservations.

"But it's all right," he said. "I know a villa you can rent for the whole month. Mother was going there— she's been going to the Riviera for the month of August for years and decided on St. Tropez this summer—but when she found that St. Tropez was getting a reputation as the playground of the young, she decided to look for a house at Antibes. Can you imagine Mother rubbing shoulders with Brigitte Bardot and Françoise Sagan?"

"She hasn't sublet the St. Tropez house?" Diane asked. A house of their own would be marvelous.

"Not yet. I'll tell her you'll take it." He winked. "I may even make her cut the price for you. Maybe I'll fly up for a few days after the Tangier houseparty. I may need a place to flake out and recuperate after that. I can't tell you who's coming, but it'll be *très* elegant."

So the arrangements were made for Diane and Deirdre to rent the fully staffed villa overlooking the shimmering blue water of the harbor. It would be an interesting change from Southampton, Diane decided, though the beach house was beautiful in June, especially with the azaleas in glorious bloom. She loved the privacy afforded by the fourteen-foot-tall privet hedges. But all was not perfect: she'd planned on playing tennis three or four times a week at the beach club—before she remembered that the club was decidedly hostile to Jews.

Aunt Claudia kept up the family membership at the Beach Club because it had been a tradition in the Carstairs family but Diane never felt entirely comfortable there since she'd learned about the club's anti-Semitic policy. Aunt Claudia lived in her own little world, even at Southampton. She wasn't involved in the endless round of parties. She didn't spend her days worrying about what to serve with the caviar, what to wear to the Rockefellers' dinner party, what she should do to improve her tan.

Clay talked about St. Tropez day after day—while they raced around New York searching for just the right wallpaper, draperies, furniture for Deirdre's new apartment or lounged on the deck of his mother's Southampton house and discussed what was to be chosen next. She was enjoying decorating the apartment, especially since Deirdre had exempted herself from the decision-making process.

At intervals Diane was caught up in the drama of the presidential campaign, though neither Clay nor Deirdre displayed any interest in what was happening. This would be the first election in which she could vote. Zelda Coleman had convinced her that Adlai Stevenson was the man to vote for, and during the Democratic convention she could not be pried from the TV set. She was desolate when he lost to

John Kennedy.

On August first—after a three-day stopover at Claridge's in London so that they could shop at Hardy Amies's boutique on Savile Row for fall clothes—Diane and Deirdre moved into the rented villa, high on a hill with a magnificent view of the harbor. Deirdre was thrilled to discover that there was an Alfa Romeo at their disposal, but she dismissed the offer of a chauffeur to drive them around St. Tropez.

"We're too young for that," she told Diane high-spiritedly. *"I'll* drive us." In Dior caftans and bare feet.

To their delight Clay arrived unannounced on their third day in the villa. He had taken a detour on his way to Tangier.

"I knew you two would hole up here like a pair of nuns," he chided. "St. Tropez is for living."

"You wouldn't think so," Diane laughed, "from all those bodies lying on the beach.

"We'll have cocktails at the Café Sonequier," Clay said. "And work our way up to dinner at Les Mouscardins. We'll cha-cha in the *caves*. I hope you've learned to cha-cha."

"You'll teach us," Deirdre said. "Right now."

In casual attire that would have been frowned upon in the best New York bars and restaurants—but in St. Tropez rope sandals, striped fisherman's shirts, and slacks were practically the uniform—the three set out for the evening's festivities. The artist in Diane felt an urge to paint the splendor of the harbor, the quays, the line-up of pretty Mediterranean houses that faced the water.

The faces at the Café Sonequier—which looked out upon the harbor—were mostly very young. The voices were multilingual, though French was predominant. Here and there Diane spied a familiar face. What a tight, circumscribed world we live in, she thought. But it wasn't the real world. Laura Devlin lived in the real world. Money protected Deirdre and Clay and herself from that world. And then a horrible thought occurred to her: *she was living her mother's life.*

They exchanged casual greetings with several people they knew from New York. Clay talked briefly about his houseparty in Tangier, then pushed Diane and Deirdre out of the café and on to their next destination. He seemed to be having a marvelous time, but Diane noticed that before leaving he gulped down a pill with a glass of water.

Every table at Les Mouscardins was occupied. The atmosphere was elegant, salonlike, though people were dressed casually. Diane had changed into a simple linen dress with her Harry Winston pearls. Deirdre was dressed in her usual colorful Dior caftan. Diane sensed her anxiety as she gazed at the sleek, tanned young bodies of the girls.

From the restaurant they moved on to one of the popular *caves*—dark, stone-walled basements that had been turned into small cabarets with tiny tables and chairs. Stereo music shrieked from every side as couples danced on the minute area provided for this activity. Clay danced first with Deirdre, then with Diane. Diane looked around the room; all the young people here in St. Tropez were those important in theater and films and fashion. *They were doing things.*

"Let's move on to the Tropicana," Clay said. "We've been here long enough."

They roamed from one *cave* to another until Diane decided it was time to call it a night. On the way back to the villa, they stopped at the crest of the hill to admire the harbor, aglitter with the lights of private yachts.

"I heard that Prince Amid What's-his-name—from that tiny little Arab country near Iraq—came in today on his yacht." He stared down at the night-dark bay. "Wonder which it is."

"Isn't that the prince whose house we stayed at in Reno?" Deirdre turned to Diane. "Let him know you're here. Maybe he'll invite us to a party on his yacht."

"I hear he's so-o handsome," Clay said. "He runs with an Italian opera star."

"Not anymore," Deirdre said. "He dropped her for some French sexpot who's supposed to be hotter than Brigitte Bardot." Deirdre was addicted to the scandal sheets. "He looks like a movie star himself."

"So what about it, ladies?" Clay said. "Send one of the servants to the yacht with an invitation to come up for cocktails."

Diane looked horrified.

"Clay, no."

"Oh come on, let's do it," Deirdre said. "I've never met an Arab prince. It might be fun."

"Dee, he's not going to show up in a turban and white robe," Diane said. "He's not this generation's Rudolph Valentino."

"Spoilsport."

Clay was sulking. "Deirdre and I would love to meet him."

"There's plenty to do in St. Tropez without chasing after Prince Amid," Diane said. "Tomorrow let's drive to Grimaud and visit the castle."

"God, that's so touristy."

He rolled his eyes.

Deirdre shrugged.

"Let's worry about it tomorrow. It might even rain."

At the villa, Clay, cold and uncommunicative, went to his room. The next morning, when Diane went downstairs for breakfast a little after eleven, he was already at the table.

"Have you looked outside?" he said, last night's mood apparently over. "We've got a day that's a painter's dream."

"How can you look so good after what you drank last night?" Clay loved being told how good he looked—already he worried incessantly about old age.

"If we can rouse Deirdre, we'll drive over to Grimaud," he said casually. "But we must be back by four so that you two can have time to dress for cocktails."

"Clay, nobody dresses for cocktails in St. Tropez."

"They do if a prince is coming to the house." He grinned. "I sent a note down to the yacht in your name first thing this morning. I saw Prince Amid walking around the deck. He'll be here at five."

"How did you know it was Prince Amid?" Diane asked.

"Binoculars, my sweet. We've all seen his photograph often enough to recognize him. Hmm." He sighed. "Such a gorgeous chunk of man, even if he wasn't an Arab prince."

"Clay, you shouldn't have done that," Diane said. But she should have expected it after last night. Sometimes Clay was like an overindulged little boy. "Now tell me exactly what you wrote and what he said."

Diane wore the white silk top and matching white silk pants cropped just above the ankles that she had bought at Magnin's for cocktails. The simple cut flattered her lean, narrow figure, and brought out her delicate tan, her dark hair. Sapphire earrings highlighted the blue of her eyes.

"Didn't I read somewhere that Amid is one of the richest princes in the world?" Deirdre asked. "As well as being one of the best-looking. And I heard he speaks six languages, incuding English."

"A title doesn't mean anything," Diane said. Her mother had been married to a prince and a marquis. "Nobody gets excited about them anymore."

"They do when the title belongs to a reigning family. Like Prince Rainier and Aly Khan and Prince Amid." Deirdre looked away dreamily. "And Amid is only thirty-two."

Diane and Deirdre lounged on chaises on the side terrace. Eager for the arrival of Prince Amid, Clay sat at the concert piano in the music room and played—surprisingly well—a medley of Cole Porter tunes. Diane wished he would play something else— Chris had adored Cole Porter.

Deirdre jumped up at the sound of approaching cars. Three in all—the front and rear cars were probably filled with security men. The prince would be riding in the Aston-Martin.

"Diane!" Clay's voice was rich with excitement. "He's here!"

They were a welcoming committee of three as the butler opened the door to admit Prince Amid. He was not tall, nor was he movie-star handsome, but he was a good-looking, well-built man. Diane immediately felt the power of his personal magnetism, his *joie de vivre*. There was a mercurial air about him, but his dark eyes hinted at a romantic soul. No wonder international beauties pursued him!

"We're so pleased that you could join us." Diane extended a hand. "I'm Diane Dickenson."

"How lovely that you have invited me into your house." He lifted her hand to his mouth.

She laughed a little uncomfortably.

"It seems only proper, considering that I lived in yours for six weeks."

She introduced Prince Amid to Deirdre and Clay, both of whom were clearly smitten by their guest. Diane noticed that four security men were moving around the gardens. A pair stood at the entrance to the house.

They settled themselves in the lushly modern living room. Amid was intent on charming Diane while diplomatically drawing the other two into the lively conversation. He startled Diane by announcing that he had met her mother on several occasions.

"At a ball in Monte Carlo, if I remember correctly.

291

At a houseparty in Deauville. And once in a casino at Cannes. I know that she is your mother," he confided, "because of the report the lawyer sent me when you leased my house in Reno." He chuckled. "Lawyers burden one with such unnecessary details. Did you enjoy the house?"

"It was beautiful." She smiled. "But my reason for my being there wasn't." Surely he knew why she had been in Reno.

"I like your American Southwest," he said while the butler served champagne and a maid circulated with a tray of hors d'oeuvres. "I especially like Phoenix. And above Phoenix is that magnificent Oak Creek Canyon—I believe the natives call it Red Rock country." Diane sensed he was ignoring the others—and she was rather enjoying the attention. "Someday perhaps I may be able to show it to you."

At a signal from Clay, who was playing host, the butler placed a bottle of chilled champagne in an ice bucket. A second maid arrived with a tray bearing a caviar pie along with bone-china plates and silverware.

Before Prince Amid left to join his mother for dinner, he invited the three of them for a day's cruise on his yacht two days hence.

"My mother is flying tomorrow to Biarritz. She came to St. Tropez only to visit with me for three days. She loves Biarritz. There she can spend the morning on the beach and then go to Bayonne in the mountains—only a few kilometers away—for lunch. And she adores Le Palais Hotel in Biarritz. My mother deplores the casualness of St. Tropez. She much prefers the traditions of an *époque de grande luxe.*"

"She sounds like my mother," Clay said. "My mother was horrified when she discovered what St. Tropez was like these days. She's spending the summer in a villa at Antibes."

When the prince had left with his entourage, the other three drove to Les Mouscardins for dinner. All through dinner Clay talked about Amid. He was fascinated by Amid's dark good looks, his charm.

"Di, he's mad about you. I could feel the electricity between the two of you."

"Maybe—" She paused. "Isn't he mad about some French sexpot who's supposed to be the next Brigitte Bardot?" Diane said. Nevertheless, his obvious interest in her had been flattering. "But it'll be fun to spend the day on his yacht." She would *not* think about the yacht at Acapulco, where she and Chris had slept in separate cabins.

She was glad now that Clay had invited Amid for cocktails. His enthusiasm for their new friend was contagious. They planned to sail from St. Tropez to the Hyres Islands and back.

Amid's chauffeured Aston-Martin picked them up at the house at eight-thirty the following morning.

From the moment he welcomed them aboard, he was the perfect host, though it was clear to all aboard that Diane was the focus of his attention. The knowledge saved her. Chris had placed doubts in her mind about her desirability. Even now, Chris's words woke her up in the middle of the night: *"You drove me to men. You're as cold as an Arctic Circle iceberg."*

Prince Amid didn't think she was cold. He could

have practically any woman in the world, and he seemed to want her.

At midnight, with Amid insisting on seeing her personally to the rented villa, they said goodnight in the white marble foyer. Clay and Deirdre had discreetly disappeared. Gently, almost tentatively, Amid took her in his arms and kissed her goodnight. It was a soft, passionate, loving kiss. Diane felt happier than she had in months.

The four of them became inseparable until the time came for Clay to fly to the houseparty in Tangier. When Diane danced with Amid on the miniscule dance floors of the *caves*, she could feel her heart pounding against his chest. Secure in Amid's embrace, she barely noticed the stares as they entered a restaurant or *cave*.

The day after Clay left for Tangier, Amid insisted on flying them to Paris in his twin-engined North American B-25. They would leave in the morning and stay at his Paris house.

Amid's "house" turned out to be a thirty-six-room mansion located just off the Place Vendôme, a quick sprint to the Ritz. Amid enjoyed holding court at George's Le Bar, located at the Rue Cambon entrance of the Ritz. Inside the Paris mansion, exquisite tapestries embellished with precious jewels—diamonds, emeralds, and rubies—hung from every wall. The floors were covered with priceless Aubusson rugs. Silk and velvet drapes hung from the tall windows.

Amid escorted Diane and Deirdre to their respective suites and told them to rest. In a few hours they would leave for cocktails at the Ritz, then dinner at

Maxim's. In the interim Amid had to confer with some of his father's emissaries.

Giggling Arab maids in native costume unpacked Diane's and Deirdre's bags. Clearly Amid entertained feminine guests often. Diane wondered why she and Deirdre had come to Paris—it wasn't like her to be so impetuous. But she'd stopped thinking rationally these last few days.

She lay back against the satin bedspread, trying to sift through her feelings. Amid had kissed her perhaps a dozen times, with a passion on the last three occasions that awoke long-dormant feelings in her. *Forget Chris,* she told herself. *You aren't frigid.*

"Diane?"

"I'm in the bedroom, Dee."

"I wasn't sure you were alone." She giggled coming in. "I thought maybe I was under temporary house arrest while Amid chased you around the bedroom." Her eyes were soft. "He wouldn't have to chase, Di, would he?"

"Dee, this is crazy—I don't even really know this guy!"

"Nonsense! Stop thinking and just enjoy yourself. After Chris you deserve some fun."

"Come sit down here." Diane patted the side of the bed. "I feel like something out of the *Arabian Nights.*"

A maid arrived with a tea tray.

"God, how many calories are in this?" Deirdre said, reaching for a pastry of chopped nuts, fruit, and honey. "If I keep this up I'll be out of caftans and into a tent."

"Do you suppose Amid would mind if we went to

the House of Dior to shop one afternoon?" Diane said. "Yves Saint Laurent showed his new collection last month. It's supposed to be wonderful—very avant-garde."

"My mother went into mourning when Dior died and Saint Laurent took over. She says he designs for pubescent girls. *You* can get away with his knee-high bubble skirts and waists dropped down to the hips."

Diane laughed.

"I bet my mother will wear them. She threw away her calendar years ago. She still thinks she's twenty-seven."

"Di, I don't think you're going to buy anything from Saint Laurent's new collection. You have to hang around for two or three weeks for fittings, unless you have your own mannequin there. And we *do* want to get back to St. Tropez, don't we?"

Soon word came from Amid to dress and be ready to leave the house within an hour. They were to meet him in the ground floor salon.

Excited by the prospect of seeing Paris—for both of them, the last time had been during their predebutante years—Diane and Deirdre changed quickly and were ready to go ten minutes early. The moment they arrived at the ground floor foyer, a door at the side opened and Amid emerged. Instantly Diane realized that this room was a tiny Moslem mosque. In that brief moment she could see the prayer niche and pulpit, and the fountain designed for ritual ablutions. She realized that she hadn't even thought about Amid's religion.

"We'll go to the Ritz for cocktails," he said taking her by the arm. "Then we go to Van Cleef and Arpels.

Of course they'll be closed, but they'll let us inside as a favor to me. I want to buy you something, Diane—whatever you want."

At the intimate little *boîte* hosted by George—apparently royalty and socialites alike brought him their Paris problems—they were greeted warmly and deferentially by George himself. Though most of Paris's well-to-do were away for the hot month of August, several notables were there who were delighted to exchange a few words with Amid and his party. Diane didn't like the way they looked at her—as if she were the latest of his acquisitions.

From the Ritz, they drove in Amid's chauffeured Mercedes limousine to Van Cleef and Arpels, also on the Place Vendôme, where they were admitted with gracious smiles while a pair of Amid's security guards—who always followed in a second car—positioned themselves in front of the store.

They were led to a private viewing room, where jewelry lay on velvet trays for their perusal. Suddenly Diane felt self-conscious at accepting an expensive gift from Amid. What exactly did he want from her? Nothing had happened between them, except for a few passionate kisses.

"Perhaps Mademoiselle would like to try this on?" the jeweler suggested, indicating a spectacular necklace of gold, pearl, and diamonds.

Diane hesitated.

"It is lovely." Immediately Amid lifted the necklace from the tray and fastened it about her neck.

"Di, it's gorgeous!" Deirdre said, relishing the whole scene.

"Perhaps Mademoiselle would wish also to try on

297

these?'' the jeweler said. Diane shook her head.

"No, thank you. This is exquisite.'' Her mother would consider it too sophisticated for anybody under thirty, but then, she and her mother didn't agree on much. And Aunt Claudia would be shocked that she was accepting so expensive a gift from a man—but to Amid a hundred-thousand-dollar necklace was a trinket.

To please Amid she agreed to wear the necklace; against her simple black dress, it looked stunning. On their way out, Amid picked up a gold *minaudiere* for Deirdre. Diane couldn't help smiling as Deirdre, who could easily have bought herself a dozen, practically fell to her knees thanking him.

Dinner at Maxim's, in the art nouveau dining room filled with stained glass, Belle Epoque murals, wood panels, polished brass, and ornate mirrors, was delicious, and Deirdre was thrilled that they were sitting in the Royal Box. Afterwards, Amid escorted Diane and Deirdre to the black Lucite splendor of New Jimmy's.

"We must see this girl, Régine, do *le twist,*'' he said with anticipation as they were being seated. "Everybody says she's marvelous.''

"I read in somebody's column that the duke of Windsor says that doing the twist is good for the duchess's arthritis,'' Deirdre said. "It probably helps keep her thin,'' she giggled. "Wasn't it the duchess who said no woman can be too rich or too thin?''

When they returned to the prince's mansion,

Deirdre discreetly went to her own suite. Amid stayed behind.

"Tomorrow we'll drive to my mother's small villa near Lery," he said, after they had kissed. "This Paris heat is too much for more than a day or two. I could never forgive myself for exposing you to such discomfort."

"I remember Lery when I was a little girl," Diane said. "I went with my mother for lunch at a country restaurant with stained-glass windows."

"That's Beau Séjour. We'll lunch there, *mon amie.*"

That night, Diane lay awake for hours. What was happening to her? Amid's pursuit of her was confusing—and yet, after Chris, it was nice to be wanted. She wondered why Amid hadn't tried to make love to her. Maybe he was—no, that was ridiculous. She was getting paranoid.

The following morning they left Paris for the villa near Lery. Amid made it clear that his mother would not be there. During the ride, he sat so close to her in the Mercedes that she felt herself growing warm with excitement. She was *not frigid. Definitely not.*

Once she and Deirdre were settled in their rooms at the villa, furnished in his mother's favorite Louis XV and surrounded by acres of formal gardens, Amid took them out to lunch at Beau Séjour.

The French countryside was beautiful, fragrant with the scent of summer flowers. Amid's eagerness to please her made her feel cherished. Safe.

"We'll have a small dinner party at home tonight," he told them. "The three of us and Pierre Lemercier."

He smiled at Deirdre. "Pierre's a racing-car driver. He'll probably drive at Le Mans next season."

Deirdre brightened. A racing-car driver would be high on her list of exciting men.

At Amid's urging they retired to their suites at the villa for late-afternoon naps while he made plans for tonight. As soon as she heard Amid drive away in his mother's black Citroën, Deirdre joined Diane in her room.

"Di, he's going to make his play tonight, I can tell." She sat down at the foot of Diane's bed. "That's why he invited the racing car driver over tonight. To keep *me* amused. So he can have you all to himself." She looked at Diane. "You aren't going to turn him down, are you? Not after that gorgeous necklace!"

"Dee," Diane said crossly, "the necklace has nothing to do with it." But she was scared. Did she want to sleep with Amid?

Amid had had an affair with a French movie star, with several jet-set beauties, with an Italian opera star—but instinct told her that this was different. He'd said casually on the drive out here that his mother and father were impatient for a grandchild. An heir to the throne. She hadn't told Deirdre, but she suspected that he planned to ask her to marry him.

Shortly past nine, when Pierre Lemercier had arrived and been welcomed with Dom Perignon, the two couples sat down to dinner in the baroque dining salon. Diane was pleased to see that Deirdre enjoyed the attentions of the young racing-car driver, whom Amid had obviously known for several years. As anticipated, dinner was a culinary masterpiece, accompanied by a parade of the finest French wines.

Diane was relieved that little was demanded of her beyond appearing attentive to Amid's flow of amusing anecdotes. Tonight his magnetism was electric, his frequent amorous glances exhilarating. After dinner Pierre took Deirdre out into the garden. Diane suspected this had been prearranged between the two men.

"I have something special to show you," he murmured, reaching for her hand. "I'm sure you'll enjoy them."

"Them?" Diane lifted an eyebrow in curiosity. "Amid, what are you talking about?"

He smiled mysteriously.

"You'll see."

His arm around her waist, Amid led her upstairs and down the long wide hall to the west wing of the villa, to his private apartment. His sitting room, three walls adorned with Göbelin tapestries, was huge and lushly appointed. Hand-painted lamps cast a muted light. A champagne bucket packed with ice and yet another bottle of Dom Perignon sat on a table decorated with gold inlay in a tortoise-shell background. At one side of the room a small petit-point sofa faced a sweep of burgundy velvet drapes.

"Sit here, Diane." He pointed to the sofa and walked over to pull the drapes wide.

Sheer curtains masked a pair of french doors and Diane could now see that they led to a wide terrace, lighted against the night.

Amid sat beside her.

"They can't see us. The curtains are specially treated." He leaned forward to tap lightly on a door.

Instantly there was a crash of cymbals. The sound of sensuous music. A tall golden-skinned, small-breasted girl clad only in a jeweled G-string and gold bracelets leapt into view. She moved with sinuous, seductive grace as three males wearing what appeared to be gold brocade fig leaves encircled her. They were four magnificent bodies gyrating in unison, three men in pursuit of one woman.

Amid left Diane's side to return with two glasses of champagne. Diane sipped self-consciously while she watched the entertainment. It was puritanical to be disturbed by their almost nonexistent costumes. In moments she was mesmerized by the erotic dancing, the passionate music. The girl enticing the three men, proud of their pursuit. Diane was conscious of Amid's arm about her waist, his lips touching hers. She felt his heated breath as his lips brushed the side of her throat and the hand about her waist moved to her breast.

All at once the lighting on the terrace became subdued. The girl reached her arms above her head in an air of glorious surrender. Her eyes half-closed, her mouth parted, she allowed herself to be pulled into the arms of one of the male dancers, and they moved as one—breasts, hips, thighs touching—while the other two hovered in an aura of frustrated passion.

With a sharp outcry the two men reached to denude the other two. Diane's eyes widened in shock, even while Amid's mouth trailed from her throat to the valley between her breasts. The girl was impaled between the two men. The three of them moving as one. Passion etched on their faces and in their thrusting bodies. The third male dancer encircled them in frenzy and then climbed the ivy-covered trellis directly behind them.

"Diane, let me help you out of your dress," Amid whispered. "I can't bear not to see you."

In a champagne haze Diane allowed him to draw her to her feet. Amid pulled the zipper down the back of her white chiffon dinner dress and coaxed it from her shoulders while her eyes clung to the heated tableau on the terrace. The dancer on the trellis leaned forward in heat to take the girl's face between his hands and draw it to him. The music accentuated his passionate outcry as her mouth engulfed him.

Ignoring the dancers now, Amid lifted Diane in his arms and carried her into the bedroom and to the ivory canopied bed. While the music and dancing continued unheeded on the terrace, Amid made love to her.

With Diane in his arms, Amid talked about the future.

"We'll be married in October at the palace. There'll be a week-long celebration in my country— they've waited long for me to choose a wife."

"Amid, this—this is too fast." She had suspected he would ask her to marry him, but she wasn't ready. "We've known each other little more than a week."

He sighed.

"All right," he said indulgently. "We'll wait a month if you insist. Then I will ask you again, and we will make a formal announcement. You must

303

become a Moslem, you know, for us to marry."

"Give me a month to think about it."

"Yes, my love." He pulled her closer. "We'll have a wonderful life—we'll spend most of our time in Paris, London, and Lausanne. Of course my mother will be upset that you've been divorced, but my father will approve. He has waited a long time for a grandson."

"Amid, this is too much, I'm not ready to say yes."

"Then we'll wait, my darling. But I am a very determined man." He smiled. "And I always get what I want."

"I should go back to my room—" All the servants made her uncomfortable.

"Of course." He kissed her gently "The servants are not to know that we have made love before you have become my princess."

Diane did not return to her own suite. Instead she knocked tentatively on the door of Deirdre's rooms, worried that she might be intruding, yet eager to tell Deirdre about Amid's proposal.

"Entrez," Deirdre called out blithely.

Diane opened the door and hurried into the sitting room. Deirdre sprawled on the sofa in what she called her "Theda Bara" black negligée.

"You look ecstatic," Deirdre said. "Let me guess—Amid made love to you and it was great."

Diane laughed.

"Is it that obvious? Well, it was heavenly. And he asked me to marry him."

"Di!" Deirdre leapt to her feet. "Oh, my God, you'll be a princess. Like Princess Grace. I can't believe it. If it was anybody but you I'd be dying of

304

envy." She threw her arms around her.

"Hold on there—I didn't say yes, Dee. I need a little time. He said he'd give me a month. What about you and Pierre?"

Deirdre shrugged.

"He makes love like he's driving a racing car. He left me at the starting gate. Lenny's lots better." She hesitated. "And you know, somewhere between the time he arrived and the time he left, he acquired a Piaget watch—a present from Amid. I think it was in lieu of payment." Briefly she looked hurt. "When we get back to the States, Di, let's make reservations for Maine Chance. I'm tired of looking like a blimp."

"Dee, forget about it. You'll never see that creep again. Anyway, it's not as if you were in love with him."

"You're right." Deirdre grinned. "So tell me about *your* night. Everything."

Diane reported all but the most intimate details, knowing Deirdre would be enthralled with her story of the evening's professional entertainment. Deirdre plied her with questions. She was already envisioning the palace wedding, the international-name-studded wedding reception that would bring heads of state from around the world.

"Dee, do I have to tell you again? I haven't said yes yet."

"You will," Deirdre said confidently. "Prince Amid and Princess Diane. I can't believe it!"

"I've got to get some sleep." Diane rose to her feet. She heard a car driving up, heading for the garage. Probably one of the servants returning from a late rendezvous. "I'm not used to all that champagne."

Back in her own suite, Diane thought she would fall asleep the instant her head touched the pillow, but she couldn't stop thinking. Finally, at two A.M. she got up and looked for something to read.

On a small table in her sitting room, she discovered the current editions of *Vogue, Paris Match,* the *Daily Express,* and the *London Times.* She flipped through *Vogue* and *Paris Match,* and took the *Daily Express* back to her bedroom. When she saw the gossip item about Amid and herself in the London newspaper, she tossed it aside.

Restless, she stood at a pair of french windows that led to a miniscule terrace and gazed out into the star-splashed night. Impulsively she thrust open one door to admit the cool country air, and flinched. The air was fragrant with the scent of roses. Roses always reminded her of the time she lay in her rose-scented hospital room, trying to accept the fact that the baby she had carried a few hours ago had been scraped away.

Amid meant for them to have a baby as soon as possible. To make his parents—and their country-men—happy. *Amid wanted children.* That meant a great deal to her. More than he could know.

Maybe she shouldn't make him wait a month. Now. Go to his apartment and tell him now. *"Yes, Amid, I'll marry you."* She reached for the white satin robe that lay across the foot of her bed and darted from her room and out into the darkened hall. Amid had told her he seldom fell asleep before dawn.

She paused breathlessly before Amid's door. She should have taken a moment to put on lipstick, at least. Never mind the lipstick. Churning with the excitement of her decision, she knocked twice. The sound was startlingly loud in the 2 A.M. silence.

"*Entrez,*" Amid called out. His voice seemed to come from a distance.

Diane opened the door and hurried into the sitting room. Her face luminous, lovely in anticipation of Amid's pleasure. And then her eyes followed the parade of clothes that made a path to the bedroom. Women's clothes.

"René, what has taken you so long? I asked simply for a late supper," Amid scolded, and stopped dead at the entrance to the bedroom.

"Deirdre and I wish to drive to Paris immediately." Diane was imperious in her hurt. "Please order a chauffeur to bring a car to the front of the house within twenty minutes."

She swerved away and headed out into the hall. But not before she saw the curious face of Amid's Italian diva peering over his shoulder. So much for Diane Dickenson becoming Princess Diane.

Back in Paris, Diane and Deirdre were able to acquire the Ritz's choice second-floor suite with a terrace overlooking the Place Vendôme. For a few hours Diane worried about the proximity of the Ritz to Amid's Paris house. But she knew he wasn't likely to return to Paris. She hoped.

As soon as they were settled in their suite she arranged to have the Van Cleef and Arpels necklace delivered to Amid's Paris house. Sooner or later he'd realize it had been returned. They would stay in Paris only a few days—just long enough to spend some time in the fabulous shops on the Rue du Faubourg St. Honoré.

Once, she tried to contact Miss Jeanne, but like many other Parisians she was off in the country. On their third and final afternoon in Paris Diane bought an exquisite Limoges vase and had it sent to her Grandmother Seligman at the Goldman Nursing Home. She needed to feel connected to that part of her past, especially now, since she'd come so close to becoming a Moslem and giving up her Jewish roots.

The fact that she had almost taken yet another step away from the heritage her family sought to deny terrified her. She wanted to go home.

Chapter Seventeen

Ira locked his SCM portable and put it next to his luggage. He would be leaving for home in less than twenty-four hours. He couldn't wait to be back in New York, sitting in the family apartment on West End Avenue. He checked his watch. Six-thirty. Time to meet Russ for dinner, their last dinner in London. It didn't seem possible.

As he locked the door to the flat, he thought about what lay ahead for each of them. Russ was traveling down to Atlanta to become involved in the civil rights movement. *He* was going back to New York to do battle with the theater. The discrepancy bothered him. Why did he always have the guilty feeling that he ought to be doing something more useful with his life?

At least he'd been keeping up with the news back home.

Last February, a student in Greensboro, North Carolina, fought to integrate the lunch counter at an F. W. Woolworth store. Two weeks later sit-ins had taken place in fifteen cities in the South. By late March, students at Yale, Harvard, Boston, MIT, and Brandeis were simultaneously picketing twelve Woolworth stores in Greater Boston. By summer there were sit-ins across the country . . . read-ins at libraries, sleep-ins in segregated motels, and wade-ins at segregated beaches. It was clear that many whites in America were incensed about segregation.

But Ira had been particularly affected by the troubles at Berkeley. Busloads of students from the University of California had stormed City Hall in San Francisco to protest what had appeared to be another outbreak of McCarthyism. The House Committee on Un-American Activities, checking into communism in California, had subpoenaed a bunch of school teachers and a student suspected of leftist activity. Violence had broken out when the students were denied entrance to the crowded hearing room and tried to make their way inside; the police had resorted to water hoses and billy clubs.

Ira had spent almost a year writing *We Hold These Truths* and he was proud of it. But often he asked himself if he ought to take his place in the picket lines. Russ kept telling him he'd never get such a controversial play produced.

He stepped out onto the street and headed left, toward the Russell Hotel Restaurant.

When he arrived, Russ was already sitting at a table, reading.

"Do you realize this may be the last meal we'll ever have in a London restaurant?" he said as Ira sat across from him. "Unless we come back sometime in the distant future."

"You know, I hate to admit it, but I'm ready to go home. I miss American hamburgers, tall glasses of orange juice, bagels, Ratner's onion rolls. I miss my family." He had expected his parents to come over for two weeks during the summer, but with Kathy pregnant they were reluctant to leave New York. "I'm glad Nixon lost, but I feel bad that Stevenson got pushed out by John Kennedy. I wish to hell I'd been there when Eleanor Roosevelt made her pitch for him at the convention. That's one great lady."

Russ shrugged.

"At least we've heard most of the Nixon-Kennedy debates, too." Neither of them was keen on Kennedy, and they actively distrusted Nixon. "Yeah, it was nice of the BBC to carry debates between American candidates," Ira said. "Smart, too." Starting last month, late on Saturday nights, interested British citizens had a chance to hear Nixon and Kennedy. Not that many were interested.

The waitress took their orders—two steak-and-kidney pies, two drafts.

"You know what pisses me off about Kennedy?" Ira said. "The way that whole super-rich clan ran roughshod over Stevenson. The way they played John Kennedy's Pulitzer Prize to the hilt. I'd take any odds the book was ghostwritten." But this was the era of the super-rich politician. In New York the new governor was Nelson Rockefeller, who drove around Albany in a Chrysler with a custom-built Ghia body.

"What the hell." Russ raised his glass. "Here's to London. And going home."

*   *   *

Weighed down with luggage, Ira staggered out of the elevator and walked to the door of his parents' apartment. The smell of a stew cooking filled the carpeted hallway. A commentator was spouting the evening news. Ira smiled. Dad was addicted to the newscasts. Tonight his parents had wanted to pick him up at the airport, but he'd asked them not to. He wanted—needed—to make the trip into Manhattan alone.

He put down his two valises and rang the doorbell, surprised to see the bright new *mezuzah* fastened to the door frame. That must have been Kathy's doing. From her letters he gathered that suburbia was sending her back to her Jewishness. Apparently she and her husband Craig were even looking for a Westchester temple to join. You could be thoroughly Jewish in New York City without religious affiliation, she'd pointed out; but living outside of the city was—for a Jew—like living in exile.

He heard a jumble of excited voices inside. The door was thrown open.

"Ira!" Mom—small, slender, warm—threw her arms around him. "Oh, darling, it's good to see you!"

Then he was surrounded by his father and sister while Craig, his brother-in-law, managed a brotherly handshake. In America—except for over-fifty Jews, Italians and Frenchmen—males avoided the exchange of kisses that was accepted in Europe. He himself had never felt abashed at kissing his father.

His mother and father peppered him with questions. In one of the bedrooms the baby was crying.

"Hey, what about my niece?" Ira demanded.

"Don't I get to see her?" It was hard to accept the fact that Kathy was a wife and mother. *His little sister.* He felt a twinge of envy. She'd always been the child who gave their parents what they wanted most—now she'd given them a grandchild. She had a safe niche in teaching. She'd be back working for the board of education and building up that pension as soon as she had her family set and the kids in school. She had married a fine Jewish boy. What had *he* done for them? Despite their overall support, he sensed their concern for him, and he knew they wouldn't understand the substance and message of his play.

As they sat down in the living room, Ira realized how much he had missed his family in London. In New York, even when he didn't see them for weeks at a time, he knew he could always pick up the phone and call them. Given his financial situation, calling from London had not been an option. His parents had called him twice, on his birthday and on their wedding anniversary. Although they had been disappointed, they accepted his decision to live abroad. But they would never really understand why he refused to be a teacher or accountant or lawyer, why in fact he shied away from any kind of civil service job. Any desk job. They were the Depression generation—to them, security was everything.

As he held his four-month-old niece, he realized it would be at least ten years before he'd be in a position to marry—and then it would probably be to a divorcée or a widow with a couple of kids.

"Janis looks like mom and you," Kathy said. Everybody had always said he was the image of mom, and Kathy the image of dad.

Janis began to cry.

"Am I holding her right?" Ira said. He'd never held a baby before.

"She's hungry," Kathy said, reaching for the squirming infant. "I'll take her into the bedroom and nurse her."

"After she's fed she'll go to sleep," his mother said. "Then we can sit down to dinner. That okay with everyone?"

"Your room's all ready for you, Ira," his father said. "I guess you'll be staying here?"

"Yeah, for a few days." He tried to sound casual. "Then the sublet moves out of my place downtown and I move in." Whenever he was with his parents he felt guilty that he wasn't fulfilling their expectations. He knew that they'd been disappointed when, after Columbia—which had cost them a great deal more than City College would have—he had emerged without a profession, at least in the traditional sense. But the years at Columbia had been valuable. There he had come to grips with what he expected from life. Would his parents ever understand that he needed more than security and a guaranteed pension after thirty years?

"What are you going to do now that you're back?" his father asked. He saw his mother shake her head at his father in stealthy reproach.

"Back to the old grind on Off-Broadway, I guess. I've finished a play." He waited for a reaction; there was none.

"Have you given any thought to going back to school?" his mother asked. "Like a degree in journalism at Columbia? *That's* writing. You could

314

live at home. We'd help with tuition."

"Mom, I'm twenty-five years old." His father nodded grimly. "If I went back to school, I'd manage it on my own. I'll stick it out with theater. I'm not interested in journalism."

"You weren't even home to vote," his father said. "I'll bet you forgot about getting an absentee ballot."

"I didn't forget, dad. I wasn't happy about it, but I voted for Kennedy." His family had been devoted to Adlai Stevenson since 1952.

Dinner was fun, this time his father urging him to eat. In earlier years Ira and Kathy had been mortal enemies, but now he felt a brother-sister closeness between them. He had never had a chance to come to know Craig, but mom said he was a fine husband and father.

Earlier than he expected, Kathy and Craig began to gather together the paraphernalia that was part of traveling with a baby.

"May I remind you all that tomorrow's a work day?" Kathy said as she packed up Janis's diapers. "Craig has to be up at six-thirty. I know it's supposed to be only thirty minutes to Manhattan from Ardsley, but that's to the city line—and that's when there's no tie-up on the highway in the morning."

"Which never happens," Craig said drily.

"Wouldn't you rather live in New York?" Ira asked.

"With kids it's better in the suburbs," Kathy said. "Decent schools, a place for them to play." But she didn't look quite convinced.

"We raised two kids in Manhattan," her father said grumpily. "We moved in from Brooklyn when you were seven and Ira was four. You didn't turn out so bad."

"Joe, they like it in Ardsley," Ira's mother scolded. "Not everybody has to live in Manhattan."

When Kathy and Craig and the baby had left, Ira called Charlie Winston to remind him that he was reclaiming the apartment in three days. Charlie was trying to raise money for an Off-Broadway production. For almost an hour they talked about the theater scene. Then he called Laura. She wasn't home. He'd try her later.

"Ira, come have some cake and coffee before we go to bed," his mother called from the kitchen.

It was good to be home, Ira thought, while he listened to his parents fill him in on the lives of uncles and aunts, cousins and friends. And then the old guilt came back. He was twenty-five years old, and in his parents' eyes he was nowhere. Why did they make him feel that he had to have a steady job, a wife, and family? When he'd told mom he was bringing a girl to Kathy's wedding, she'd been so hopeful—until he told her Laura's last name was Devlin. He'd comforted her with his assurance that Laura was "just a show-biz friend."

When they finished with their coffee and cake, he left the kitchen and phoned Laura again. He'd had pleasant sexual encounters with London girls—he admired their candor and independence—but the relationship with Laura, while not involving ties, had a continuity that he found comfortable.

He knew he'd missed her when he heard her cheerful hello.

"Guess who's back in town, babe?"

316

She sounded excited. "Ira? Are you downstairs?"

"No, I'm at my parents' apartment. The big family reunion scene. I'll be here until Charlie moves out day after tomorrow. I called you earlier. Where were you?"

"I went to the theater with Diane Dickenson. We saw *A Taste of Honey*. It made me think of you in London. I can't believe you're really back!"

"Well, I am. Make dinner for me tomorrow night?"

"Sure. I'll be home from the office by six-thirty or seven. Help me find a sensational vehicle for a movie, and I'll have that story editor's job in six weeks."

"My play?" He knew the answer.

"A movie on integration?" she clucked. "Box-office poison."

Philippe dropped Diane at the Fifth Avenue mansion and drove the car to the garage. Diane climbed the stairs to her rooms; she never used the tiny elevator that had been installed years ago for her grandmother. The lights were out in her aunt's rooms—she had to be asleep, for which Diane was grateful. She wasn't in the mood for a bedtime chat.

Tonight her mind was on Clay. Lately she'd been worried about him. He was drinking too much and popping pills—phenobarbital, Nembutal, Seconal, and God only knew what else. He said he couldn't sleep without them, but she was terrified that he would mix alcohol and drugs. Just two nights ago she had dragged him away from that bar in the Village and dropped him off at his house—with a stern lecture about the pills and drinking.

Diane was looking forward to seeing Deirdre, who would be returning in three days after a month at Maine Chance and a brief visit with a cousin in Scotsdale. She said she had dropped twenty-six pounds and meant to take off another ten. Of course she couldn't wait to go shopping for a complete new wardrobe.

Diane decided that if Deirdre wasn't too tired from her flight, they'd go see *The Wall*, the Millard Lampell play from John Hersey's novel, that night. She had ordered tickets with the thought of taking Aunt Claudia, belatedly realizing her aunt would not want to see a Broadway play about the terrible experience of the Jews in the Warsaw Ghetto. Clay refused to go to anything except musicals. They had already seen *Irma La Douce* and *Bye Bye Birdie* twice.

In her private sitting room Diane discovered a memo from Mrs. Byrnes, the housekeeper, instructing her to call her mother in Monte Carlo "no matter what time." Aware of her mother's flair for melodrama, she sat down by the telephone and dialed. Did her mother really want to hear from her at this hour? It was about five o'clock in the morning in Monte Carlo.

Her mother's voice came over the wire high-pitched and tense. "Hello?"

"Hello? Mother? It's Diane—"

"Darling, you must fly immediately to Paris. I'll be leaving in four hours. Charles died quite suddenly. The funeral is scheduled for day after tomorrow. Let me know what flight—"

"I'm afraid I won't be there, mother." All at once she was trembling, a terrified little girl again.

"You have to be there! How would it look? He's your stepfather. People will expect you to be at his funeral."

"I'm sorry. I can't. I won't pretend to mourn for him. How could I, *after what he did to me?*"

"He was drunk," Livvy said. "Nothing actually happened."

"I spent three years in therapy because of what happened. He should have been thrown in jail."

"You mean you're going to let me go through the trauma of that funeral alone?" Livvy demanded.

"I will not be at the funeral." Why couldn't she ever talk to her mother without becoming furious? She doubted her mother was going to be alone in Paris. What about that twenty-seven-year-old polo player her name was being constantly linked with these days? He'd be tucked away in her hotel suite, no doubt. He was probably with her in Monte Carlo this minute.

"All you ever care about is yourself!" her mother screeched. "You're cold and unfeeling—no wonder you couldn't hold Chris Ames!"

"Goodnight, mother." Quietly she hung up.

She sat still for several minutes. Was her mother right? Had her marriage failed because she didn't know how to hold Chris? But the whole world, it seemed—except for her—had known about Chris's problem. *How could she have held him?*

As always, after an encounter with her mother she was upset. She knew she would have difficulty falling asleep. She could hear Clay saying, "Darling, a tiny little pill and you'll have hours of gorgeous sleep." His mother always had a drink before bedtime for her insomnia. Diane had a drink whenever she fought with Clay and whenever she felt she had been slighted by friends or tradespeople.

She would get into bed and read, Diane decided. No pills. No drink. With a stubborn but futile effort to push her mother's accusation out of her mind, she prepared for the night, settled herself in bed against a mound of pillows and started reading *To Kill A Mockingbird*, the new bestseller by Harper Lee that Deirdre had passed on to her. Thank God for the escape she found in books.

It was close to dawn before she started to doze. Tomorrow, she promised herself, she would have Philippe drive her up to the Goldman Nursing Home in Westchester. She needed to sit for a while beside the bed of her Grandmother Seligman.

If Chris had not been so afraid of Mannie Coleman and had let her have the baby, she wouldn't feel so alone. If they'd had the baby, he might have been able to become again the Chris Ames she had met in White Sulphur Springs.

The morning was gray and raw, the trees winter-gaunt and desolate except for a patch here and there of brace evergreens that defied the weather. Diane dozed all the way to the Goldman Nursing Home.

If Philippe ever wondered about her covert visits here, he never said so. She left the limousine and hurried up the path and to the entrance. She doubted that her grandmother remembered her from visit to visit, but each time she was greeted with a shy smile and talk about "my boy David." The roses delivered each week were always beside her bed, the diamond-encrusted Jewish star on a gold chain always hanging around her grandmother's neck.

She crossed the lobby and walked to the reception desk. At the nursing home no one knew that Mrs. Seligman's occasional visitor was Diane Dickenson. She always identified herself as Diane Seligman.

"I'd like to see Mrs. Seligman," Diane said to the woman at the desk. "I'm a member of the family."

The woman looked upset.

"So *you're* the one who sends the roses. We told the florist not to deliver them anymore—"

"She's been moved?"

"You—you must have been out of touch with the family—"

"I've been touring in Europe for several weeks. I just returned late last night." Her heart was pounding.

"I'm very sorry, Miss Seligman. Mrs. Seligman died three weeks ago. The family should have contacted you."

"Thank you." Diane was pale, her voice barely audible. "I didn't know."

"She died holding a red rose in her hand," the woman said. "She just closed her eyes and went to sleep."

"Thank you." Without another word, Diane turned and walked swiftly to the door and out the building.

Snow was falling in huge flakes as Philippe drove back to the highway. Diane sat with hands clasped together, fighting tears. She felt an ineffable sense of loss.

On a Friday afternoon in mid-December Diane

was at Idlewild to meet Deirdre's flight. Deirdre came through the gate in a designer suit she had picked up in the Maine Chance boutique and which, she declared, was the only thing she owned that fit her now.

"Di, I will *never* allow myself to be fat again," she promised while they paused in the baggage area. "I can't wait to see Lenny's face when I walk into that new place he's working."

"Dee, you're starting up again with Lenny?" Diane was surprised—Deirdre hadn't mentioned his name in months.

"Maybe," she hedged, her eyes avoiding Diane's. "We'll talk about it later."

Back at Deirdre's apartment, in the sitting room, they had tea and watercress sandwiches.

"How's Clay?" Deirdre asked.

"I'm worried about him." Diane sipped her tea. "He's drinking too much, and popping pills."

"This is close to the time of year when his mother heads for Palm Beach. He'll be better when she's gone."

"What about Lenny and you?" Diane said. "I thought you said after Bermuda that you'd never see him again."

"So he cheats." Deirdre shrugged. "At least in bed with him, I feel like a woman."

"He's not the only man alive, you know," Diane said impatiently. "You'll find somebody else. You're not tubby little Deirdre anymore. Look in the mirror. You're very pretty."

"In a colorless kind of way." Though Deirdre was ecstatic at being slim, she had no confidence in her appearance. "Anyhow, what's the difference? Every man we meet looks at us and sees all that loot. Lenny liked me without knowing who I was."

"But not enough to be faithful," Diane shot back.

"When you fell in love with Chris, you were happy because he didn't know you were Diane Dickenson. You knew he was in love with *you*, not the money." She paused. "So it was a mistake, but you both thought he was in love with you. I could marry Lenny knowing he wasn't after my money."

"Dee, you can do better than that arrogant sodajerk!"

"The characters we meet . . . Either they have enough money so they don't do anything except party or they play at being stockbrokers or raising thoroughbreds or dealing in real estate. They bore the shit out of me." She tilted her head to one side and inspected Diane. "What about you? Isn't there anybody that turns you on?"

"No," Diane said. Too quickly, because she saw a knowing glint in Deirdre's eyes. "Anyhow, after Chris and Amid I'd be scared to marry again." She didn't want to be like her mother—or Deirdre's. Chasing from one man to another.

"Aha!" Deirdre looked triumphant. "There *is* a guy!"

"It's just a funny thought that pops into my head every now and then." It was absurd to be interested in somebody she'd seen for about two hours at a party. "I met this friend of Laura Devlin's." Deirdre knew about Laura and Newport. "At the party after the premiere of *Rendezvous with Life*. You were down in Palm Beach. He was the only person there who seemed real. He didn't talk much, but I liked what he said. I felt comfortable with him. If I hadn't been so in love with Chris, and if I hadn't thought he was Laura's boyfriend, maybe I would have been interested."

"Is he Laura's?"

"Laura says they're just friends. She says she's too career-conscious to get serious about any man."

"Why don't you throw a little party and ask Laura to bring him?"

"Maybe. But he's been in London for about a year. I think he's still there— Anyhow, I don't want to get involved with anybody. At least, not for a long time."

"Why don't you ask Laura when he's coming back? He won't stay in London forever."

"I don't even want to think about Ira. And if you're smart, you'll forget all about that crazy Lenny."

Deirdre smiled.

"I must confess, I did call him from Scottsdale. He's living in the same place. I'm seeing him tomorrow night. And don't tell me not to see him. I haven't been laid in so long I've forgotten how—and don't tell me about the racing-car driver. Di, Lenny can do it a dozen times a night."

"Dee, why don't we fly down to the Bahamas for a week?" Diane said, desperate to remove Deirdre from Lenny's turf. "I'm sick of the cold weather."

"Nice try, baby, but not now." Deirdre shook her head. "Tonight I'm yours, but tomorrow I'm making up for lost time with Lenny."

Chapter Eighteen

Laura was always the first to arrive at the office. But this morning Joe Freedlich was there ahead of her. He was hunched over the telephone, his bushy eyebrows almost meeting in a frown while he nodded in the familiarly impatient manner that told her he was upset by what he was hearing. It was six A.M. on the Coast. This had to be something serious—probably a carryover from last night.

"All right, we'll be ready for them, Mannie. We got nothing to hide from a team of accountants. But I wish we'd had some warning that you were selling the studio. What does an oil company know about making pictures?" He sighed. "I know, it's a big conglomerate with lots of interests. But I tell you, Mannie, it won't be easy to do business with them. They'll have a finger in everything."

Laura went off to make a cup of coffee for Freedlich. When she came back, he was still on the phone and gulping down a tranquilizer, without water. He reached eagerly for the coffee.

"All right, Mannie," Freedlich said, more conciliatory now. "I'll call a board of directors meeting in New York and go over the budget for the line-up of new pictures. But who's this guy Kramer who's to sit on the board now? What has he done besides sell oil or breakfast cereal?"

Laura started to leave for her office, but Freedlich gestured for her to refill his coffee cup.

She went back to the lounge and brought Freedlich his coffee. He was just putting down the receiver as she stepped into the office.

"We've been sold out," he said through clenched teeth. "To Clayton Enterprises. That fucking bastard managed the whole deal under wraps. But it won't be what Mannie expects. They can fire him any time they want. So he made himself a terrific bundle—he'll die if he can't run the studio the way he wants."

"When shall I schedule the board of directors meeting?" Laura asked.

"Tomorrow at two. Don't make any plans—we may be here half the night. If it goes past six, call the Stage Deli and order food. At ten o'clock a team of accountants is coming in to go over our books. At eleven o'clock some guy named Bernie Kramer is coming to talk about 'the future of Menlow Films.' Kramer's the new member of the board. He'll commute between here and California. He reports to the chairman of the board of Clayton Enterprises. What I want to know is, who the hell is Bernie Kramer?"

"He's an independent producer," Laura said. "He did that quickie about a cotton-mill strike—remember? It made a fortune at the box office."

Now Freedlich looked nervous. "He does offbeat films on low, low budgets. Now and then one makes it big." She'd read about him in *Variety* and *Billboard*. Freedlich read all the trade papers, but he usually ignored the small items about supposedly unimportant films.

"So Mr. Kramer is coming in to tell Menlow how to turn out a box-office smash for under a million. How'd that son of a bitch push his way into Clayton Enterprises?"

"Maybe family connections," Laura said.

"Find out everything you can about Kramer before he comes in at eleven and let me have it," Freedlich ordered. "We can't afford to screw up with this guy."

As always, Freedlich's panic was contagious. Promptly at ten the team of three accountants arrived, throwing the entire accounting department into a frenzy. While the accountants were making their check of the books, Bernie Kramer arrived. He wasn't quite what Laura had expected. Somewhere in his late thirties, he was dynamic, good-looking, and, she suspected, ambitious as hell.

At a quarter of twelve Freedlich called Laura to reserve a table for Kramer and himself at Sardi's for twelve-thirty. It was clear that Kramer would be at Menlow Films for the rest of the day. Laura was aware of several covert glances from Bernie Kramer in the course of the next few hours. She guessed that he might be interested in Joe Freedlich's secretary for whatever information he could pump out of her.

For the rest of the day, tension at Menlow Films was thicker than a London fog. Everybody knew one thing: the takeover by Clayton Enterprises meant nobody's job was safe. At two P.M. sharp the board of directors meeting began. As always, Laura sat on one side of Joe Freedlich, her shorthand notebook in hand. Bernie Kramer sat on the other. Silverstein, the attorney, sat at the opposite end.

This was not an ordinary board meeting. Bernie Kramer made no pretense about his taking over, though officially Freedlich was in charge. He was Clayton Enterprises's boy, and no one was allowed to overlook this for a moment.

"The budget for the new Chris Ames film is way out of line," Bernie said briskly. "Slash it."

"Mannie Coleman will be upset," Freedlich said in a rare effort at diplomacy. "Chris Ames is his biggest star now. He shoots the works for Chris."

"He'll have to shoot lower." Bernie was scribbling notes. "And reschedule the film. I've been talking to Twentieth-Century about a loan-out. They'll pay us half a million for Chris for one picture. They've got a script that fits him like a glove."

"Chris will hate working on a loan-out," Freedlich said. "He's terribly insecure in unfamiliar situations. And Mannie won't be happy."

"They'll survive," Bernie said, looking around the table. He knew he was in control.

"There's a legal problem," the attorney said slowly. "Chris Ames's agent worked out a contract that says Chris can't be loaned out without his consent."

"Fuck the contract," Bernie snapped. "Actors are shmucks. He won't remember the clause. And his agent is Buck Reilly. Buck won't give us any trouble. He wants to do business with us."

For the remainder of the meeting—which ran past nine o'clock, over the Stage Delicatessan's choice pastrami and corned beef—Laura debated about how to handle the information she'd acquired about Chris's contract and the studio's plan to bypass it. Chris had gotten her the job here—she owed him something. Also, instinct told her that it would be to her advantage in the future to make Chris grateful to her. Somewhere along the line she might find that damned useful. This could be one of those crucial decisions in building a career.

"That's a wrap," Bernie decided finally. "Joe, I know you'll do a great job on cutting back on the budgets. Get rid of the fat, and we'll come in with some healthy figures."

Freedlich returned to his office. Laura guessed he'd pull out the Canadian Club for a bracer before he went home. He wasn't a lush; this *had* been a bitch of a day. Laura pulled on the Bergdorf's coat that had cost her two week's salary and headed for the elevator.

The heat had been turned down in the buidling for the night. Most of the offices in the building were closed. A damp chill filled the halls. When she got home, Laura decided, she'd call Diane and talk to her about Chris. It was up to Diane to pass along the information. Knowing Diane, Laura suspected she might be uncomfortable, but she'd do it.

In the downstairs lobby she spied Bernie Kramer in conversation with the night watchman. He looked up as she walked toward the doors.

"I'll drive you home," he said casually. "I'm parked right outside. It's gotten damn cold in the last hour."

"Thanks." She smiled warily. Was he about to make a pass, or was he after information?

He reached to open the door for her and pointed to a black Mercedes at the curb.

"You're taking a chance," she said, laughing. "I might live at the ends of Brooklyn or the Bronx."

He grinned.

"You live on East Fifth Street, you're twenty-one, and you come from Newport, Rhode Island."

"You've been studying the personnel files." She inspected him with fresh curiosity. She knew he was married; she had immediately spotted the heavy gold wedding band. Exactly what could Bernie Kramer do for her?

"Part of my job to know personnel." He opened the door and helped her inside.

But as she thought about it, she decided that Bernie Kramer *could* be useful. He reported to the chairman of the board of Clayton Enterprises. That meant he'd be making major decisions for Menlow Films. He could edge her into Garrison's job as story editor—not right away, but in time. All she had to do was make herself useful to him. And this had nothing to do with the two of them crawling into bed together. This was going to be a professional relationship.

On the drive across town and down Second Avenue, Kramer questioned her about her daily routine at the office. They understood each other; this was a special assignment that would have a later payoff. When Bernie pulled up in front of the rundown tenement, he reached for her hand and squeezed it.

"You're not just sexy, Laura—you're bright. I like

that in a girl. We can help each other."

"Thanks for the ride." Her smile sealed the association. Nobody at Menlow Films knew more about what happened there than she did. Bernie was sharp to have recognized that so quickly.

"I'm flying back to California for the holidays," he said. "Let's have dinner one night when I return to the city."

When her private phone rang, Diane thought it was Clay. He was supposed to have picked her up forty minutes ago. He was taking her to the Blue Angel tonight. He had promised he would not have more than one drink but she worried that he might anyway; he was uptight about spending the holidays with his mother in Palm Beach.

"Clay," she said without thinking.

"Hi, Diane. It's Laura."

"Laura, how nice to hear from you. Clay Brentwood was supposed to pick me up almost an hour ago. I thought he was calling to say he was on the way. How are you?"

"Fine. Look, Diane, something crazy has come up. It's about Chris—"

"I don't see Chris ever," Diane said quickly. But of course with the approach of Christmas she couldn't help thinking of him.

"We just found out today that Mannie Coleman has sold Menlow to a conglomerate," Laura said. "I think they're trying to pull a fast one on Chris. I thought he ought to be warned, but I felt kind of strange about calling him directly. I probably couldn't even get through," she laughed.

"If it's important, I'll get word to Chris." She hesitated. "I'll talk to his agent."

"No," Laura said. "Buck Reilly is in on it. This has to go straight to Chris."

"If it's all that important, I'll call him." How long would it take to wash Chris out of her mind? "Tell me what he has to know."

Briefly Laura described the situation to her. Diane had learned enough about the picture business to understand that Buck Reilly might fight for great terms and money for a client, but he wouldn't cut his throat for the client when a major studio was involved. He had to do business with the studio for other clients.

"You're a real friend, Laura," Diane said softly. "I'm sure Chris would never think of checking out his contract. He'd fall right into the trap. I'll call him right away." It was just an act of friendship, she soothed herself. She could bring herself to talk with Chris for the few minutes required.

"I suppose it looks like I'm being disloyal to Menlow," Laura admitted. "But Chris got me the job there."

"I'm sure he'll be very grateful." What had possessed Mannie to allow himself to sell the studio? His whole life—and Zelda's—revolved around it. He might still be the chief, but Clayton Enterprises controlled all the strings. "I'm flying down to Palm Beach with my aunt for the holidays, but when I come back, Laura, let's get together. Why don't I have a small dinner party? At one of those little restaurants in the Village that Clay's always discover-

332

ing. There'd be six of us; Clay and me, Deirdre and her friend—" Maybe if Deirdre saw that crazy Lenny in different surroundings, she would see him for what he really was. "And maybe you'd like to bring your friend Ira or someone," she wound up, faintly breathless.

"That sounds great." Laura's voice was electric. "Ira just got back from London. I'm sure he'd love to come."

"Great. How about the second Friday in January?"

"Fine," Laura said. "I'll tell Ira."

"I'll call you with the time and place a few days before," Diane promised. "Clay has a real talent for finding fun restaurants."

She was going to spend a whole evening in Ira Ross's company. She knew it was ridiculous, but she had the feeling her whole life was about to change.

Her heart pounding each time she dialed, Diane tried to reach Chris four times that night—twice at home, before Clay arrived to take her off to the Blue Angel, once from a public telephone in the ladies lounge, and again back home. She knew he was still living in the house he had acquired in the divorce settlement. Candace Collins had run an item about a surprise birthday party he had given for Mannie there last month.

At close to three A.M., still too tense to sleep, she picked up the phone and dialed again. The phone rang half a dozen times. She was about to put down the receiver when he answered.

"Hello?"

"Chris, it's Diane." There was a long pause. "Laura Devlin asked me to call you about something she thought you ought to know," she stammered. "She's still working for Menlow—"

"What is it, Di?" Now he sounded more alert.

As succinctly as possible, she repeated what Laura had told her.

"The rotten bastards," he swore softly. "I'll get rid of Buck as soon as I can. And nobody's loaning me out. Mannie knows I can't handle that."

"They can't, Chris—not under the terms of your contract." It felt so strange to be talking to each other this way! But she felt oddly peaceful. She'd had to talk to Chris again to make the divorce seem real.

"Tell Laura I'll never forget what she's done for me. Anytime she needs a favor, I'll be there."

"I know you will, Chris." This was the sweet, compassionate Chris she had known in their earlier days. The Chris everybody in Hollywood liked. "I hope everything goes well for you."

"And for you too, Diane," Chris said softly. "You deserve the best."

She would be able to face this Christmas in better spirits. Except for that first Christmas with Chris, she had always dreaded the holiday season. At Christmas everybody seemed caught up in family and she felt left out.

She had persuaded Aunt Claudia to fly to Palm Beach for Christmas and New Year's. Always up to date about goings-on in their social circle, Clay had found an available beach house with plenty of privacy.

Now Diane regretted her impulsive plans for the

dinner party early in January. At the moment it had seemed a good way to meet Lenny, especially since Deirdre kept pushing the idea of a foursome—including Clay—on her, but that was a little too intimate to suit her.

With another couple present, she wouldn't feel so trapped. But she was dying to meet Lenny—apparently Deirdre had lied to him about how they'd met . . . something about them going to school together because her rich aunt had paid her tuition. The mother of the cousin who had pulled out of the Bermuda trip. As far as Lenny knew, Deirdre was a poor relation. Of course he knew about Diane Dickenson, especially since after her much-publicized debut and marriage to Chris she had been mentioned frequently in the scandal sheets.

She realized now that the real reason for the dinner party was to see Ira again. But that was ridiculous—there she was, romanticizing again! When would she grow up and stop looking for a knight on a white charger? She shivered, remembering how close she had come to marrying Amid.

If Ira even remembered her, it was only because she had been married to Chris. And if he did come to the party with Laura, it would probably be out of curiosity. *He might not even come.* Laura said he was working as stage manager for some Off-Broadway play that was about to go into production. Maybe he would be too busy; maybe Laura would bring somebody else.

When she told Deirdre about their dinner party, she was delighted. For a long time she'd been convinced that once Diane met Lenny, she'd be more supportive of their relationship.

At Deirdre's prodding, Clay had gone into the luncheonette where Lenny worked for a covert inspection. His appraisal afterwards had been blunt.

"He thinks he's a hotshot stud. He thinks he's doing a favor to any girl he sleeps with."

Deirdre had been furious.

Though Clay hated spending the holidays with his mother in Palm Beach—an annual ritual—he seemed less bitter about this year because it was expected that the newly elected President Kennedy, his fashion-plate wife Jackie, and their two children—including the newborn John, Jr.—would be at the Palm Beach house of the elder Kennedys for Christmas.

Diane found life very easy in Palm Beach. Most days she and Deirdre shopped almost every day on chic Worth Avenue. Diane made a point of having dinner every night with Aunt Claudia, but there was plenty of time left over to have fun with Deirdre and Clay. The trio took in some of the holiday parties, where all the talk was of Jack and Jackie. It was all wonderful fun, but Diane couldn't escape the feeling that each of them was running away from something.

On several occasions, caught up in the splendor of the Palm Beach scenery, Diane found herself tempted to paint again. But the temptations were short-lived. She couldn't accept being a dilettante artist. But she did consider signing up for some courses in interior decorating in the fall. "Just for fun," she told Clay and Deirdre. She and Clay had redone Deirdre's apartment. When they returned to New York, they would redo her own suite at the Fifth Avenue house. They both knew Aunt Claudia would be furious with any other changes in the house.

She had been relieved to leave New York behind; now she was glad to be coming back. But she began to notice a monotonous rhythm to her life. She was irritated, too, that Clay kept changing his mind about where she should take her guests for what he called her "pot-luck dinner party." A week before the party, Diane finally pinned Clay down, over lunch in the charming, dark-green-walled back room of the Russian Tea Room.

"God, Diane, you're making more fuss about this creepy little dinner than if you were planning a dinner for a hundred at the Pierre."

"Come on, Clay, I'd hate a dinner for a hundred. You know that. I think this will be fun. And I'm hoping Deirdre will get a clearer view of Lenny when she sees him with *real* people."

"God, let's hope. Okay, we'll have dinner at this place on Perry Street, La Petite Maison." He reached into a jacket pocket for a pen and scribbled down the address for her on a scrap of paper ripped from a bill. "*Très* unfancy, full of locals. The food is good." He gave her a sly look. "Your friends will be comfortable."

"Now Clay, I want you to behave yourself."

"I'll be good," he promised.

Two days later she and Deirdre went to lunch at La Petite Maison.

"It's not that I don't trust Clay, Dee," Diane said. "I know he's a birddog about finding offbeat restaurants, but I'd feel better if you and I dropped in there first." She knew it was ridiculous to be so uptight because she was going to see Ira Ross, but she couldn't help it.

They took a taxi to the restaurant. Eager to fit in with the rest of the clientele, they wore skirts and sweaters, simple tailored coats and boots—what Deirdre called their "schoolgirl look." Diane had phoned for reservations as Diane Davis, though given the indifference of the woman on the phone it seemed unnecessary.

They were greeted by a tanned young man who escorted them to one of the dozen or so tables in the room. The walls were white and rough-plastered and hung with ears of maize and garlic chains. The tablecloths and napkins were a ruby red. A warm French bread and a tiny pot of butter was brought to them before they ordered from the large, handwritten menu.

"Dee, what do you think?" Diane leaned forward. Deirdre looked around.

"I think Lenny will like it." But Diane could tell that she too was pleased. "You should see the joints where he takes me to eat." Where Deirdre invariably picks up the check, I bet, Diane thought. "And he's *so* impressed that I know Diane Dickenson."

"You're sure he doesn't know Deirdre Swift?"

"I told you. He never reads anything except the sports pages on the *News* and *Mirror* plus *Confidential*. And *you* make *Confidential*. I don't."

Diane changed her outfit four times before she was satisfied. With her deceptively simple black crepe dress she wore pearl earrings and a single strand of Harry Winston pearls.

Clay picked her up in his Corvette. He was in high spirits after finding a small apartment for himself. "In Greenwich Village," he emphasized with a flicker of amusement. "I'm not ready yet for a tenement flat in the East Village. I just want a place I can escape to when the pressure at home gets too heavy." He remained in the family mansion because his mother insisted that she was terrified of living alone with the servants.

"'Suppose I'm sick in the middle of the night,'" he mimicked his mother. "'The servants won't even wake up if I call.' We're separated anyway by thousands of miles half the year—thank God!" He gazed upward for an instant. "But she just can't bear the thought of my having an apartment of my own." His voice hardened. "Unless a wife goes with it."

"Clay, why don't you rent an inexpensive little place that you can handle on your own and just don't tell her?" Diane understood how Clay felt. There were times when she couldn't wait to leave the Fifth Avenue house, but she knew that her aunt wouldn't stay there unless she remained. She couldn't envision Aunt Claudia living anywhere else. Somehow the divorce had brought the two of them closer—the one good thing that had come out of her marriage.

As they walked toward the table they saw that Deirdre and Lenny had already arrived. They were arguing good-humoredly about the rising popularity of Neil Sedaka and Ricky Nelson. While Deirdre made ebullient introductions, Clay sat next to her, pulling Diane down beside him. Diane was glad that Ira would be next to her, and Laura between Ira and Lenny.

From the moment she met Lenny, Diane realized that she had to be polite but withdrawn—the slightest show of friendliness and Lenny would be in hot pursuit of her. Actually, she thought, not of her, but of the Carstairs fortune. He was uncomfortable around her, but greed practically oozed from his pores. He did have a certain raw sexuality that could probably make him a fortune with lonely ladies "of a certain age"—if he were sharp enough to know how to approach them. But she wasn't sure he was clever enough for that. He was exactly as Clay had described him.

Deirdre was uncommonly subdued; her smile was strained. Deirdre was scared that Lenny would drop her to chase her best friend. But Diane had made it clear that she considered Lenny a creep. Meeting him hadn't changed that. Poor sweet Deirdre, she thought tenderly. She had so much to offer and so little respect for her own worth.

Moments later, Laura and Ira appeared. Diane was warmed by the glow in Ira's eyes when they met hers. She was aware of an exciting, unspoken communication between them. The last time they met she was married to Chris. Now she was unattached. Available.

She was unnerved by Clay's faint air of superiority when she introduced him to Laura and Ira—not toward Laura, but Ira. *Why?*

A waitress came over to the table and took their orders. Clay's arrogant attitude, his disconcerting possessiveness of her, was spoiling her evening. Why was he acting this way?

Ira brushed off Clay's condescending questions about his year in London.

"No, I never had Sunday lunch at the Causerie in Claridge's. Nor dinner in the Connaught dining room, nor after-theater supper at the Savoy Grill. I lived in London on a pretty strict budget. *Europe on $5 a Day* was my bible."

"How quaint," Clay sniffed. Diane kicked him under the table. "How creative."

"No," Ira said calmly, refusing to be ruffled. "I'd call it practical."

"I'll bet you were fascinated by the manuscript room at the British Musuem," Diane said. "I mean, your being a writer—"

Ira smiled.

"They called it the Manuscript Saloon."

"Even to a near-illiterate like me it was exciting," Diane said. "I remember standing there gaping at the deed to Shakespeare's house." It seemed like a thousand years ago.

"I must admit, I went out of my mind there," Ira said. "There, and in the Poets' Corner at Westminster Abbey. I didn't come down to earth for weeks."

"But you did find time to write a play," Laura said.

"Yes. Which, by the way, is now making the rounds of producers' offices." Ira looked grim. "But with the way the costs of putting together a production are skyrocketing, it's almost impossible for a new playwright to make it to the boards. Still, I'm glad I took the year off to do it."

Diane felt Laura's eyes resting on her and suddenly she understood. Laura and Ira were hoping she would put up the money to produce his play. *That* was why Ira had accepted the invitation to dinner.

Lenny turned to Laura.

"Deirdre says you work for a movie company. You ever get a chance to see the movie stars?"

Laura looked disappointed at the turn the conversation had taken.

"Now and then somebody shows up at the New York offices. But most of the action is on the Coast."

Diane had stopped listening as she tried to understand the situation. Ira was like all the others. He wasn't interested in her; he was interested in what her money could do for him.

"Clay was in summer stock one season," Deirdre said. "He was good, too."

"I was fair." Clay frowned. "If I can't be great, I don't want to be involved." He'd only been in the play to annoy his mother, or so he said; apparently Mrs. Brentwood considered all theater people immoral. "Diane should be an actress, don't you think?" He dropped an arm around her. She flinched. *Why was Clay behaving this way?* "She's got that movie-star look."

"Clay, don't be ridiculous."

"She's lovely," Ira agreed, his eyes resting admiringly on her, "but not everybody wants to be an actress or a movie star."

"What about you?" Lenny asked Laura. "You're right there, on the inside track. You've got a shot at it. Wouldn't you want to be a movie star?"

"No." Laura smiled. "Eventually I want to move into production." Diane sensed that though Laura was being polite to Lenny, she clearly had sized him up and found him wanting. "I like seeing all the pieces come together and then—zingo—you have a film."

At the table to their right a party of four were arguing about the recent presidential election.

"Come on," one said, "Kennedy won with a margin of one-tenth of one percent of the popular vote. If they hadn't spent all that money, he'd never have made it. Flying around from city to city during the campaign in that Convair owned by his family—so it didn't even count as a political contribution."

"I like Jack Kennedy," Clay said. "He's got such dash."

"I can't forgive the ruthless way the whole Kennedy clan pushed around Adlai Stevenson at the Democratic convention," Ira said. "And I can't forgive Jack Kennedy for not appointing Stevenson secretary of state." Obviously, Diane thought, Ira really cares about the way this country is run. She admired that.

"My mother's furious because I voted for him," Clay went on. "She says he may have bushels of money, but he's still shanty-Irish."

"So am I," Laura laughed. Diane winced. Clay knew that Laura was Irish. With a name like Devlin, what else could she be? "Of course," Laura said wryly, "I don't have the Kennedy money."

"Now that we have a Catholic president, some people are scared to death we'll have a kosher White House next," Clay said. Diane stared at him. He seemed determined to offend everyone tonight.

"What would be wrong with that?" she said. "New York had a Jewish governor for three terms.

Everybody remembers Governor Lehman with great respect." Clay was acting like a spoiled little boy, determined to make himself disliked.

"You don't remember him," Clay challenged. "You were a baby."

"The history books remember," Ira said quietly. "Lehman was governor from 1933 to 1942, and my parents tell me how every Jew in America— including themselves—went to sleep a little happier every night, knowing that Lehman was in the governor's mansion in New York. In Germany, Hitler vowed to eliminate Jews from the face of the earth."

Clay looked like a little boy who had been slapped. He wasn't the nasty, narrow-minded bigot that he appeared. He looked around the table for an ally. Diane was relieved when their waitress appeared with their drinks.

"I've been hearing fascinating stories about the new East Village." Clay tried to play the convivial host. "All those coffeehouses where bearded poets get up and read their latest work, and new comics and actors and dancers do their bits."

"The East Village is great," Laura said. "In addition to the playhouses and the coffeehouses, it has the best bagels, the best lox, and the greatest gefilte fish in the country—things I never knew when I was growing up in Rhode Island."

Ira chuckled.

"Zabar's up in on the West Side does pretty well with those, too. But you can't beat the East Village for low rents. My parents were shocked when I slaved

to unearth an apartment down here. Their immi-
grant parents had slaved just as hard to get out of the
Lower East Side, and here was their son, reared
gently on West End Avenue, fighting to get back.''

Diane was surprised that Ira referred to his Jewish
parents. She had never thought about his ethnic
background. Now they shared another bond. But
then she remembered what had brought him to this
dinner party.

"It must be a whole lot different living over in the
East Village than in London,'' Clay said, trying to be
more pleasant. "Are you having a hard time
adjusting?''

"It's not actually *that* different,'' Ira said. "In
spirit, anyway. In London the young people are
fighting for something new in the arts, and the same
thing is happening in the East Village. The English
are ahead of us, but the spirit is similar.''

"What do you do when you're not looking for
somebody to produce your play?'' Now it was
Lenny's turn to be snide.

"I'm working with an Off-Broadway company in
the East Village,'' Ira said. "I started off as stage
manager and assistant director, but this morning the
director walked out and I'm picking up the pieces.
It's an Equity company, so we'll be reviewed.''

"Another revival.'' Laura looked bored. "Off-
Broadway should be doing lots of originals. Movie
companies like Menlow are dying for fresh material.
Off-Broadway makes a great showcase for play-
wrights as well as actors.'' She paused and turned to
Ira. "I know you're dying for a shot at Broadway, but

wouldn't you settle for an Off-Broadway production?"

"I think any playwright would grab at it," Ira said.

"Would it take a lot of money to produce an Off-Broadway play?" Clay asked with a flicker of interest. Diane frowned. Why was Clay trying to make Ira believe he was a potential investor? His mother had complete control of his money.

"It isn't what it was like five years ago." Ira looked interested, but Diane suspected that he knew Clay was playing games with him. "The big problem five years ago was renting a place that could be used as a playhouse. Now it's much more respectable and much more expensive, though nothing like uptown. Equity makes a lot of concessions."

Diane kept her eyes focused on her glass of white wine while the others talked about the Off-Broadway scene. She suspected that the attractive young waitresses were out-of-work actresses; she saw the flicker of interest on the face of the waitress serving them.

Ira spoke at length about Off-Broadway's role in New York theater, its tremendous potential. He was clearly knowledgeable about all phases of theater, but Diane sensed that he was not entirely happy as a director.

"I love having all the playhouses in the East Village," Laura said enthusiastically. "It makes it a fun place to be."

Diane kept silent. Did Laura think she might put money into an Off-Broadway play just because the East Village was "a fun place to be"? Mr. Lewisohn was super-conservative with her investments; she was sure he would reject her putting money into a play. Why was Laura pushing this way?

She toyed with her salad, her appetite gone. She had thought Ira Ross might just be interested in *her*. Again she was wrong.

Chapter Nineteen

After dinner, when Deirdre and Lenny asked Laura and Ira to take them on a tour of East Village coffeehouses, Clay quickly invented an obligation that required his presence—and Diane's—uptown. Diane sat in silence beside Clay while he maneuvered the Corvette through the heavy Friday night traffic. Not until they were out of Greenwich Village and heading north on Sixth Avenue did Clay speak.

"You're angry, aren't you?"

"Clay, you promised to behave. Why were you so snide to Ira? And why did you act so possessive of me?"

Not that it mattered that Ira might think there was something between Clay and her—she'd probably never see him again. Except that she could tell by the way Ira had looked at her that he wanted to see her again. It seemed as though he just couldn't bring himself to ask.

Clay stopped for a red light, his hands gripping the wheel. He still hadn't answered her question.

"I'm sorry, Di—I guess I panicked. I was scared."

"Of what?"

"I saw how Ira looked at you when he sat down. Like he had died and gone to heaven. I had this vision of you flipping for him and forgetting you ever knew me. I don't want to lose you, Diane. Tonight I realized how damned important you are to me."

Diane put her arm around him.

"Clay, nobody can come between us—you're like my brother. Deirdre, you, and I. We'll always be a trio. This century's Three Musketeers."

"I don't know why I do the crazy things I do sometimes," he said, his voice hoarse. "Sometimes it's to bait my mother. Other times—I just don't know. Like what happened in Paris, after I left Tangier last August."

"What are you talking about?" Clay hadn't even mentioned being in Paris last summer.

"I showed up one night at the Crillon's grillroom in drag—when they were expecting the duke and duchess of Windsor at any minute. So I've been banned from there ever since."

"Clay, why? Were you—had you taken pills or something?" If anything, Clay was polite. It wasn't like him to make an ass of himself.

He shrugged.

"There was some hash and coke at the houseparty in Tangier. But I hadn't had any in Paris." He paused. "I don't think—"

"Clay," she spoke softly, "I think you ought to see a shrink. Soon."

"I tried that. Twice, in fact."

She squeezed his arm.

"Try it again. You owe it to yourself."

He took one hand off the wheel and reached for hers.

"Still mad at me?"

"No. But get yourself straightened out, Clay. You're very important to me."

"Let's drop in at the Latin Quarter, okay?" As quickly as it had descended, or so it seemed, his mood disappeared. "It's too early to go home on a Friday night."

"All right. But I expect you to set up an appointment with a shrink Monday morning. I mean it, Clay."

For a moment she remembered how Chris had lied to her about seeing Dr. Everett. She had blamed herself for not making sure that Chris kept his appointment—as though *that* might have saved their marriage. But Chris had been the romantic fantasy of a young girl. She was a woman now.

By the time everyone had agreed to call it a night, Ira had a splitting headache. The air in the coffeehouse on Bleecker Street had been thick with stale cigarette smoke. The singer was pretentious and untalented. The heat in the room was stifling. He longed for a brisk walk in the cold January air, but Deirdre was already leading them toward the garage, where her car was parked.

The sidewalks were crowded, even though it was one A.M. It seemed that the coffeehouses were filled with teenagers from Long Island and Westchester County. Tonight he missed London. At least there he had felt no pressures. It had been a year of living one day at a time, writing, talking, arguing with friends about the state of the world. No obligations. Now he was home. He had lots of decisions to make.

"Why don't we all go up to my pad for coffee?" Deirdre said, with a sly glance at Lenny.

"I think I'd better get home," Laura said. "I have to be in the office early tomorrow morning."

"We'll drop you off." Deirdre turned to Lenny. "You drive."

Ira had felt uncomfortable when Deirdre had insisted on picking up the checks at the three coffeehouses. Lenny, on the other hand, seemed to take it for granted.

He couldn't help noticing how Diane had clammed up the minute they started talking about his play. Hell, she thought he was after her to put up money for a production. He had never even considered that. Ever since he'd first met Diane, she'd been in his thoughts. Of course, she had done a lot of growing up since then. And she was probably sure that every guy who looked at her twice was after her money.

While Deirdre paid the check at the garage, Ira saw a minute exchange between Laura and Lenny. From her quick frown—though he couldn't hear the verbal exchange—he guessed that Laura was rejecting a pitch. He had known guys like Lenny on the Off-Broadway scene. They were usually shacked up with some girl while they made rounds, sure that they would make a quick hop from Off-Broadway to Hollywood.

Lenny drove too fast to East Fifth Street. The car

radio played too loudly. Deirdre flinched when he ran a red light, but she was too scared to say anything. Ira couldn't figure it out: Why would a good-looking and super-rich girl like Deirdre Swift put up with a jerk like Lenny?

Lenny brought the car to a screeching halt in front of their apartment house.

"It's been great fun," Laura said to Deirdre while Ira reached for the door handle. "Thanks for everything."

"Yes, let's do it again sometime," Deirdre said.

At last the two couples parted. The car sped away into the night. Laura and Ira walked up the stoop of the house and into the smelly, dimly lit corridor.

"My place for coffee?" Ira asked.

Laura hesitated.

"I'd better not. Joe's so uptight these days that he's been making some weird mistakes in his reports. I'll need a clear head in the morning. I messed up on the big try," she said as they approached Ira's landing. "I was hoping Diane might offer to put up money for an Off-Broadway production for you."

Ira stopped dead.

"Did you go to dinner with that in mind?"

"Come on, Ira, what would that money mean to Diane? Probably the price of one luxury jaunt to Europe." Laura sighed. "I don't think I handled it right."

"Diane got the message." Ira was terse. "In a split second her whole attitude changed."

"Ira, I'm sorry."

"Forget it." He reached for his key. "I'll probably never see her again."

"She'll call me." Laura was confident. "Maybe we don't see each other often, but I've got this crazy feeling that Diane will always be involved in my life." She giggled. "I don't expect to inherit her fortune or anything like that, but Diane is responsible for my being at Menlow Films. And if I ever need a favor from Chris, all I have to do is whistle. Chalk that up to Diane, too."

He reached for her.

"Sure you won't come in for coffee?"

She laughed.

"I don't dare. We'll be fooling around the rest of the night, and I'll be too sleepy to work in the morning."

"That jerk Lenny made a pitch," he said when he released her after a passionate goodnight kiss.

"He makes a pass at every girl. I told him to go peddle his papers somewhere else. What the hell does Deirdre see in him?"

"What she'll probably be seeing, from a horizontal view, within the next half hour," he grinned. "Aren't you a little bit jealous?"

"Business before pleasure," she murmured. "Goodnight, sweetie."

Deirdre sat silent in the overheated car while Lenny sped north on near-empty Third Avenue. He had been fascinated by Diane and Laura, she tortured herself. He had been ready to hop into bed with either of them. Even when she was skinny enough to be a fashion model—if she were six inches taller.

"Hey, babe, you meant it?" Lenny broke the

silence while he waited for a red light to change. He was aware of a police car directly behind them.

"Meant what?"

"About going up to your place tonight." Most of the time she reminded him that it wasn't really her apartment but her "cousin's," and she lived there because she was her cousin's "companion."

"Yeah." Her mind was charging ahead. *She knew how she could hold on to Lenny forever.* Why not, if he made her happy? "It's on Park in the Sixties."

"Your cousin won't be there?"

"No."

"Sensational." He took a hand from the wheel and caressed her thigh.

They pulled up to the entrance of the all-night garage.

"Good evening, Miss Swift," the attendant greeted her pleasantly. "Good evening, sir."

Looking self-conscious, Lenny handed over the keys and got out of the car. Hand-in-hand he and Deirdre walked to the posh Park Avenue building where she lived. They exchanged brief greetings with the doorman and headed across the rich wall-to-wall carpeting of the decorator-furnished lobby to the bank of elevators.

"Your cousin knows how to live," Lenny approved, impressed by the obvious affluence on every side. His eyes settled now on Deirdre. "Is she coming home tonight?"

"No," Deirdre said softly.

"So tonight we can make love on Park Avenue."

"Does that make it any different?"

"Honey, everything on Park Avenue is different."

In the elevator, where they were the sole occupants, Lenny pushed her up against the wall.

"Lenny, somebody might be getting on," she protested, but she was already excited.

The elevator stopped at their floor. Lenny was astonished that there were only two apartments on the floor. Deirdre got her key, found it, handed it to him. He unlocked the door and pushed it open. She flipped on the foyer wall switch and watched his eyes widen in approval while she took off her coat and dropped it on a chair.

"Man, this looks like somethin' out of a movie. How many rooms?"

"Eleven." She walked into the small sitting room off the foyer where the bar was located.

"For two chicks?" He lifted his eyebrows in amusement.

"Would you like a glass of champagne?" she asked, walking to the sleek ebony bar with its own refrigerator unit.

He grinned.

"Sure. Why not?"

While Lenny roamed around the room, Deirdre brought out a $150 bottle of Lafite-Rothschild because, after all, this was a special occasion. And daddy always said a special occasion demanded Lafite-Rothschild. She could still imagine him in one of his silk smoking jackets—adroitly designed to conceal his martini paunch—pouring Lafite-Rothschild for himself and his latest twenty-five-year-old conquest.

She lifted the mirror-lined top of the bar for the Baccarat champagne glasses.

"Lenny—" She extended the bottle of champagne, knowing he would appreciate the fact that it wasn't beer, but wouldn't understand that this was a king among champagnes.

"You won't get your head handed to you for opening this?" he asked while he manipulated the cork.

"No." She paused. Took a deep breath. "Lenny, this is my apartment. Everything in it is mine." She watched while his eyes widened in skepticism.

"You're putting me on," he said. "You mean, with your cousin away you do what you want." *That* he could understand.

"Lenny, I'm Deirdre *Swift*," she emphasized. "My great-grandfather was Josiah Swift, who owned the Swift Coal Mines. This is my apartment."

Slowly he put the bottle of champagne on top of the bar, his mind trying to cope with this new situation.

"No cousin?"

"No cousin." She managed a wisp of a smile.

"Then why have you been playing these crazy games?" Belligerence battled with pleasure.

"I wanted to know you liked me because I'm me. Not because I'm rich."

"Baby, being rich has never been a handicap."

"Pour me a drink, Lenny."

Lenny reached for the bottle and two glasses.

"Point me in the direction of the bedroom," he ordered.

In the blue bedroom high above winter-garbed Park Avenue, Lenny poured champagne into two glasses, handed one to Deirdre and now inspected the furnishings: turquoise velvet wall-to-wall carpeting beneath their feet and draperies of a matching turquoise at the windows; a queen-sized bed covered by a blue-dominated Spanish rug; a pair of gilded Persian chairs flanking a seventeenth-century Spanish painted cabinet. Between two windows stood a Louis XIII armchair and an inlaid Moorish table, above which hung a mirror with a matching frame.

"Drink up," he said while he slid his unoccupied hand inside the neckline of her dress. "Then let's try out the bed."

"I thought you'd never ask," she murmured. *Everything was going exactly as she'd planned.*

She would have liked some romantic undressing, but Lenny never bothered with that. She stripped to her skin, letting her clothes fall in a heap at her feet. She waited while he kicked his clothes into a corner and closed the drapes.

He moved closer.

"You're crazy, you know that?"

"Why?" Her voice deepened as he pressed against her.

"Thinking I'd run away because you're this little rich bitch."

His mouth came down hard on hers. Then he pulled away and lifted her up and carried her to the bed. His one gesture of romanticism, though she suspected that to Lenny this was just to show off his male strength.

"Got any music around here?" Lenny always liked music when they made love.

"There's a radio in the cabinet there." She pointed

across the room.

In a moment the room reverberated with the sounds of *The Four Seasons*. Lenny always played music too loud, but in this building they didn't have to worry about neighbors complaining. Before he joined her on the bed, Deirdre intercepted his pleased inspection of himself in the mirror that hung above the Moorish table.

"You're a hot little number," he said while he hovered over her, thrusting her thighs apart with one knee. "And I'm just the guy to keep that flame going."

"Lenny, shut up," she whispered and reached for him. "Shut up and show me."

Deirdre and Lenny lay beneath her turquoise silk sheets. He was on his back, snoring lightly. He'd wake in a minute. She'd see to that. They hadn't talked much, but Lenny said he'd call in sick around eight o'clock. He was due in this Saturday morning at nine.

She felt warm and relaxed and loved. She wanted to be with Lenny every minute of the night and day. And it would be that way because she could give Lenny everything he wanted in life. Tomorrow she'd buy him that beaver-lined raincoat he'd been talking about ever since he saw it on some movie-star stud.

She felt a fresh surge of passion as she imagined Lenny's delight when she bought him the coat. She tossed aside the turquoise sheet and placed a hand between his thighs. He wouldn't be asleep for long.

A smile touched her face, devoid of makeup from the shower they had shared between bouts of lovemaking, when she heard his light snore turn into a mumble.

"Baby, what are you doing to me?"

"Let's fuck."

His eyes were open now. Smug and secretive.

"I'll think about it," he drawled.

"Lenny!" But he was already getting excited.

"Make me hot, babe," he whispered, "you know how to do it."

"You *are* hot," she protested, but she knew what he wanted. She didn't really like doing it. He boasted about how some bartender told him the duchess of Windsor did it with some rich fag.

"Make me hotter," he ordered, drawing her face down. "Baby, in a few minutes we'll go right through the roof."

She obeyed while he murmured heated encouragement.

"Now!" he said hoarsely and reached to shift her above him. "Come on, baby, let's go!"

Her eyes closed, her hands on his chest while his own cupped her breasts, they moved together until he cried out in passion. Whatever Lenny wanted, Lenny would have.

Now Deirdre lay beside him, her head on his chest, her fingers trailing through the burnished hair on his chest.

"I wish you could move in here with me," she said, knowing this was what he wanted to hear.

"Why can't I?" It was obvious that the prospect was enticing.

"This is a co-op. The board of directors would throw me out." She paused. "Unless we got married."

She felt him tense.

"Okay," he said. "So let's get married."

There it was. She paused.

"Yes. We'll elope. Soon." Dad would have sixteen fits if she said she was marrying Lenny. Mother would have hysterics. But she was over twenty-one. She could marry anybody she liked.

"Right away!" Lenny pounced. "We'll drive down to that place in Maryland where you can get married the same day. We'll be married before lunchtime." He pulled himself into a sitting position. "We'll get dressed, go for the car, have breakfast somewhere on the highway. Baby, we'll have a ball." Like a general on a victorious field of battle, he swung himself off the bed and picked up his clothing.

Deirdre sat absolutely still, trying to imagine life as Lenny's wife. They'd get married in Maryland and go right off on a honeymoon. Maybe back to Bermuda. No, not Bermuda. Capri. The sun always shone in Capri in January. Lenny loved the sunshine.

"Lenny," she stopped him on the way to the shower, "do you have a passport?"

"No. Why?"

"We can't honeymoon in Capri unless we both have passports. I know—" She looked triumphant. "We won't need a passport in Nassau."

While Lenny showered, Deirdre pulled fresh clothes from drawers and hangers in her dressing room and headed for the guest bathroom across the hall, feeling vaguely guilty that she wasn't phoning Diane and Clay. She knew why she wasn't: Diane and Clay would try to stop her from marrying Lenny.

She'd telephone the house early, before Diane was awake, and leave word that they couldn't have lunch today or see Elaine May and Mike Nichols again tonight. Di would figure that Lenny'd had his day-off switched and was spending it with her. Which she was, she giggled in elation. After this they'd spend every minute together.

After she and Lenny were married, she would phone Diane and Clay from Maryland and tell them. Daddy was in Paris on business. Later she would tell him about Lenny and her. Where *was* mother? she wondered as she stepped into the stall shower. Mother was either at Maine Chance or at that place in Switzerland where they gave injections to rejuvenate aging tissue.

She turned the water on full and hot, relished the pounding against her shoulders. They wouldn't even bother taking more than a weekender, she plotted. They'd buy clothes in Nassau. She'd call the lawyers from Maryland and have the funds transferred to a bank down there.

Lenny was right. *They'd have a ball.*

Chapter Twenty

After her morning grapefruit and coffee Diane phoned Clay to tell him that Deirdre would not be joining them for the theater that night.

"She left a message early this morning, something about going off to spend the day with Lenny. I didn't like the sound of it."

"Why doesn't she take him up to Stowe to ski?" Clay said. From his sharp tone Diane guessed it was more than distaste for Lenny that disturbed Clay this morning. "The bastard might break his neck."

"Feel like lunch?" she asked.

"Sure." He grinned. "At Le Pavillon." Clay had a taste for gourmet food. Chris had considered a steak and french fries a choice meal. "I'll call and make reservations. And tonight after the theater we'll go to Le Club."

"Clay, you know I hate discotheques."

"It's Olivier Coquelin's private club," he said loftily, "for which I paid a fancy membership fee."

She sighed.

"All right. Lunch at Le Pavillon at one-thirty."
She knew that Clay always insisted on lunch at one-thirty or later, insisting that by then Henri Soulé would release the tables that had been permanently reserved through the years for such patrons as the duke and duchess of Windsor, the Cole Porters, and Mainbocher. For Clay half the pleasure of gourmet dining was in being seated at a choice table. "Provided you get a reservation."

"If you don't hear from me in ten minutes, we have a reservation. And after the theater we'll drop in at Le Club." He caught her look of reproach. "Not for long," he added quickly. "I'd just like to stop by to see if anybody exciting is around."

"How can you see?" Diane said. She loathed the dark shadows of the pseudo-hunting lodge, the deafening sound system.

"Wear something wonderful to lunch," Clay said. "I love the looks of envy a gorgeous woman gets when she walks into a restaurant."

At slightly past one-thirty, Diane was led to Clay's favorite luncheon table at Le Pavillon. To complement the cerise damask upholstery of the chairs and the matching roses about the room she wore a black crepe Jacques Fath and her pearls. If she'd been having lunch with Deirdre alone, she would have worn the new Mary Quant.

"You look depressed," she scolded. She was aware of curious eyes focused on their table, but it didn't bother her; people who knew Clay well realized that theirs was only a close friendship.

"It's mother. I had another battle with the old bat—" Clay sighed.

"I thought she was in Palm Beach—"

"She is. We fought over the telephone. For sixty-eight minutes." He grinned maliciously. "She hates running up large phone bills. There's no AT&T in our portfolio."

"Clay, why do you fight with her? Why don't you just listen to her?"

He looked appalled.

"Just listen? When she's screaming that if I don't get married and have children, who the hell's going to inherit our money? I said, 'Frankly, my dear, I don't give a damn.'"

"Clay—" she hesitated. "Have you done anything about seeing a shrink?"

"Di, what's the goddamn rush?" His face flushed.

"Clay, I mean it for your own good," she said quietly. "You've got to get off all those pills. And you've got to stop drinking."

"I've got an idea!" He brightened. "Let's sign up for some courses in interior decorating. I'm bored with everything else."

"Check around and see what's available," she said. "I'll go along with that." Chris had teased her out of opening a shop in Hollywood. Clay would join her in a partnership any time she made the suggestion. Could they make it successful?

"Oh, I forgot to tell you because I was so pissed off at the old lady this morning." Clay's mother had been thirty-eight when he was born; to him she was ancient now. "We're driving down to Washington for the Inaugural Ball. One of the five being held. We'll go to the one at the Mayflower Hotel. Mother managed to acquire a pair of tickets. They'll be delivered tomorrow."

Diane stared.

"But your mother's a Republican."

"The Auchincloss connection makes it respectable for us to go to a Democratic Inaugural Ball. In case you didn't know, the Auchinclosses fill two full pages in the New York *Social Register*. Besides, I think Jack Kennedy is sexy."

"I hate what the Kennedys did to Stevenson," she said, aware that she was parroting Ira Ross. It was ridiculous how often he invaded her thoughts.

"Stevenson is sexy, too," Clay said. "For an older man."

"Clay, you know we'll never find last-minute hotel accommodations in Washington."

"No problem," he said grandly. "My great-aunt Jessica has a house in Georgetown. We'll stay there. We'll drive down the night before and come back the day after. It ought to be exciting. It's a triumph for the younger generation. Did you know that except for Ulysses S. Grant, Jack Kennedy is the only president to be inaugurated while his parents are still alive? And he'll be the youngest president in the history of this country. Maybe that's what this country needs now."

"Since when have you become so concerned about politics?" Diane teased. But she too had been fascinated by what the new president labeled the New Frontier. Most people in Clay's and her world—except for the heads of big business corporations—seemed to watch politics from a distance. As though it were of little consequence to them who lived in the White House.

"It's something to think about," Clay shrugged, as though embarrassed at being caught in a serious pursuit.

"I'm afraid I can't dawdle too long today," Diane said, knowing Clay's fondness for three-hour lunches. "I've been asked to serve on a committee for the April in Paris Ball. I have my first meeting at three-thirty."

He smacked his hand to his forehead.

"Oh my, will *Maman*—yours *and* mine—be impressed! Every debutante in New York who hasn't been asked will be jealous."

Twilight settled around the city as Diane arrived at the house. She remembered that her aunt would not be home this evening. She could have dinner on a tray in her room; that would give her plenty of time to dress for the theater.

"Miss Diane, Miss Swift has called three times in the last hour," the new housekeeper reported. "She said she'd call again shortly."

"Thank you, Mrs. Avery." Diane smiled. "And would you please ask Molly to send a dinner tray up to me as soon as possible? Just a sandwich or something. I'm going to the theater tonight."

Birch logs, kindling, and rolls of paper had been laid in the grate of her fireplace. Diane lit a fire. The telephone rang in her bedroom. It had to be Deirdre. Maybe she would go with them to the theater tonight after all.

"Hello?" She sat on the edge of the bed.

"Di, I've been trying to get you for hours," Deirdre

scolded. "I have the wildest news. Now don't be angry—"

Alarm shot through her.

"Dee, what did you do?"

"I'm down in Elkton, Maryland," Deirdre said blithely. "I know I should have brought Clay and you down with me, but I was afraid you'd try to stop us. At two o'clock this afternoon Lenny and I got married."

"Oh, Dee. No."

"Come on, Diane. I know Lenny isn't your favorite person, but can't you at least wish me some happiness?"

"Of course I do," Diane said weakly. Lenny must have found out about the inheritance. "When are you coming home?"

"Darling, first the honeymoon," Deirdre exulted. "We're going to Nassau. I haven't reached my mother or father yet. I'll let the lawyer tell them and my grandmother. I had to call him anyway to transfer money to Nassau for us. I know it's high season, but I hope we can rent a cottage for a month. Di, I'm out of my mind, I'm so happy. It'll work out. You'll see."

They talked for several minutes before Diane heard Lenny's voice ordering Deirdre to get off the phone and back into the car.

"Sorry, Di, Lenny wants us to check into a motel and catch some sleep. We were up all night. I'll call you from Florida. We'll garage the car there and fly to Nassau."

"Tell Lenny to drive carefully." Clay had told her about his fast driving.

"Come on, stop worrying," Deirdre said. "We'll

be fine."

Diane put down the phone. She had to call Clay. Then the phone rang again.

"Hello?"

"Have you seen the late edition of the *New York Post?*" It was Clay, his voice grim.

"No. Why?"

"Let me read you the headline. 'Swift Heiress Marries Sodajerk. Dee Says, 'I'm Sublimely Happy.'"

"I just talked to her. Clay, there's nothing we can do. She's over twenty-one."

"I'd like to castrate the bastard. He'll be chasing after other girls the minute they get back to New York. Can't she see he's after her inheritance?"

"All she can touch until she's thirty is the income, Clay. That's something."

"He'll go through that fast enough. He'll push her to take out loans against the inheritance. He's a creep. How long can she stay with him?"

"She thinks she's in love, Clay. All we can do is stand by."

The morning of the presidential inauguration was cold and gray. Diane realized this the instant she woke up because no ribbon of sunlight peeked through her bedroom curtains this morning.

Hastily she reached to switch on the radio to catch the tail end of the nine o'clock news.

"—Blizzard heading into the Northeast from Virginia. It is predicted that eight to ten inches of snow will blanket the area from Washington, D.C., to Boston before the blizzard blows out to sea—"

Diane reached for the phone to call Clay. He usually slept till ten or eleven, but the weather warranted waking him, she comforted herself. It would be crazy for them to try to fight their way to Washington by car in the face of a blizzard. But Clay was awake; he had heard the weather report and was unruffled.

"We'll make it," he said blithely. "I have chains on the tires. But let's leave by ten instead of waiting until afternoon. I'll call my Aunt Jessica and say we'll be there ahead of schedule."

"Maybe we ought to fly down or take the train." She didn't share Clay's enthusiasm for battling a storm.

"Darling, there won't be a seat to be had today. Everything into Washington has been booked for months. We'll drive down. Come on, it'll be fun."

She knew Clay was determined to make this a festive occasion, to take both their minds off Deirdre's marriage.

Shortly before ten that morning, they were in Clay's car. By the time they were on the New Jersey turnpike snow had begun to hit the ground, but Clay refused to be disturbed about a possible blizzard. He talked about the new mood in the country with the New Frontier evoking commitments from the young and the not-so-young.

"I loved what Kennedy said about his New Frontier at the Democratic convention," Clay said. "'Not a thing of promises, it is a set of challenges. It sums up not what I intend to offer the American people, but what I intend to ask of them.' And he's bringing in some of the best brains in the country—and *young* advisers. The Sixties will be a decade that will take a real stand. You can feel it in the air."

Disturbed by this rarely seen side of Clay and feeling an inadequacy in herself, Diane reached to switch on the radio, fiddled with the dial until a Jerome Kern medley filled the cozy warmth of the car. Today she'd take a respite from reality. Why couldn't she just sit back and enjoy it? She was glad now that Clay insisted they drive down to Washington.

When they approached Philadelphia, Clay suggested they stop for lunch.

"Do you think we should?" Southbound traffic was heavy, and they were driving into hazardous weather. Already the roads were slippery in spots.

"I know this sensational place," he said. "It's off the highway at the next exit. We have time."

Clay always knew some gourmet restaurant, no matter where they were. It was one of his numerous small talents. They left the highway and sought out the restaurant, lightly populated today. They had a superb luncheon before a blazing fire while traffic trickled past. But when Clay ordered a second cup of coffee, she said, "Clay, we have to get back on the road. God knows what it'll be like in Washington."

He laughed.

"Darling, stop worrying. We'll make it through. Relax."

But Deirdre's elopement had stirred up so many memories for Diane, she couldn't relax. Barely three years ago she and Chris had eloped. It didn't seem just three years ago that Deirdre had flown with them to Vegas. It seemed another lifetime.

At regular intervals in the sluggish traffic, Diane anxiously inspected the ominous sky. As they moved south, they were encountering what showed every sign of becoming a full-scale blizzard. Soon visibility became poor. Winds increased.

"Maybe I ought to try to find a phone to call Aunt Jessica," Clay said. "I told her we'd be there no later than four o'clock."

"She'll understand," Diane said. "We'd better stay on the road."

Though she always told herself she hated driving in bad weather, she felt oddly exhilarated by this adventure with Clay. He was a superb driver, manipulating the car skillfully over the snow-packed roads made doubly hazardous by patches of ice beneath the white powder. Already snowplows and sanders were out on the highways unusually heavy with inauguration-bound travelers.

At intervals Diane switched the radio stations so they might hear bulletins about the road conditions into Washington. Workers in the city were being dismissed early because of the intensity of the blizzard. At places the roads into the city were impassable. Diane and Clay geared themselves for long waits in traffic.

Chapter Twenty-One

At last, almost eight hours after Diane and Clay left New York, they were inching their way along the road into Georgetown. The traffic was light now. There were abandoned cars on either side of them. The snow was a biting, blinding sheet of white.

"Just another block or two." Clay sighed in relief. "I told you we'd make it."

"If this keeps up, we may wish we hadn't," Diane laughed. But she loved seeing the elegantly restored houses of historic Georgetown.

"There it is." He pointed in satisfaction to a well-tended old-fashioned red-brick townhouse with a tiny plot of snow-covered earth before it and a low wrought-iron fence setting it off from the narrow sidewalk.

"What about the car?" Diane asked.

"Aunt Jessica will have someone take it to her garage. I doubt if we could dig it out tomorrow if we left it here."

Relieved that she had worn boots, Diane struggled

out of the car and onto the snow-blanketed sidewalk, while Clay emerged from the other side and trudged to the trunk to get their luggage.

"It looks so peaceful," Diane said. "Like an old-fashioned Christmas card."

"Aunt Jessica is the least old-fashioned octogenarian I've ever encountered," Clay chuckled. "The only living member of the family who's worth a damn."

A tall, white-haired, black houseman responded to their ring.

"Mist' Clay," he said, mingling respect with friendliness, and reminding Diane that she was in the South. "It's so good to see you again. Your aunt's been lookin' forward to your visit." He smiled respectfully at Diane. "And to meetin' your young lady. We was worryin' about you gettin' here all right."

"We did fine, Jefferson," Clay said with gentle affection. Diane had a vision of Clay coming to this house through the years, since he was a little boy. While he had never talked about his aunt in Washington, D.C., she guessed that she held a special place in his heart—maybe too special to talk about.

"If you give me your car keys, Mist' Clay, I'll have Daniel put it in the garage. You don't want it settin' out in that snow."

Clay handed over the keys.

"Thank you, Jefferson."

"Your aunt's waitin' for you in the family sittin' room," Jefferson said, and hurried off to send Daniel for the car.

For a few moments, when they walked into the

English Regency-style sitting room where the elderly Mrs. Parsons waited to receive them, Diane wondered uneasily if Clay's mother had given his aunt the wrong impression about her relationship to Clay. But in speaking with the small, spare, aristocratic Jessica Parsons, whose fading blue eyes still managed to convey shrewdness and a sense of humor, she knew this was someone to cherish.

"The city officials are insisting the inaugural parade will go on as scheduled," Jessica said. "Even if they have to push a bulldozer in front of the president. But there are plenty of skeptics. This is the worst inaugural weather since William Howard Taft took office in 1909. And I was there," she said with pride. "Right on the inaugural platform. I'll watch this one on television. I've been out for every other one since Teddy Roosevelt's. That's enough."

"Aunt Jessica, you're bragging again." But she ignored him.

"Pity we had to have a blizzard. The National Park Service has been out there spraying green on the grass at the Washington Monument to make it look like spring and spraying chemicals on the trees that line the parade route to make sure the starlings don't roost there. The snow took care of all that." She inspected Clay with a quizzical smile. "How's your mother?" Diane suspected little love was felt between Jessica Parsons and her niece by marriage.

"In her usual form when I talked to her on the phone a few days ago. According to her, Palm Beach is going to the dogs."

"Still trying to push you into investment banking with your Uncle Edward?" Without waiting for a reply—knowing the inevitable—she lifted a hand to signal the houseman who lingered at the door. "Let's have a glass of wine before you go upstairs to your rooms. The worst time in my life in Washington was during Prohibition." She turned to Diane. "What was being made in the cellars of Washington was ghastly, and I refused to risk my eyesight or my life on bootleg whiskey." She surveyed Diane in candid curiosity. "What do you do when you're not chasing around to inaugurations?"

"I'm in volunteer work in New York," Diane said, suddenly self-conscious about the emptiness of her life. She looked to Clay for support.

"Diane and I are starting classes in interior decoration in February," he said. "We just may go into business. Diane has a real flair for it. So have I."

"The trouble with people in this family," Jessica said to Diane, "is that not one of them has ever had any get-up-and-go. Except for my father, that is. Before him they had plenty of breeding and pride but no money. Frederick Brentwood shocked the hell out of his family by taking off for the California Gold Rush in 1849. Before he was twenty he was a millionaire. He built one of the greatest fortunes in this country, but my husband and brothers lost most of it in the stock-market crash. Good thing for you, Clay, that my nephew Roger married one of the rich Langfords."

"There's no Gold Rush to run after anymore," Clay reminded, "or I might just take a crack at it."

The houseman arrived with wine, and the conversation focused on the inauguration. Jessica embarked on a lively dissertation about American politics. Diane was impressed by how much she knew.

"Who'd you vote for?" Jessica turned to Clay. "That young man who steamrolled his way into the White House?"

Clay laughed.

"Aunt Jessica, that's privileged information."

Mrs. Parsons turned to Diane.

"I—I didn't vote," she stammered. "I guess it was pretty silly of me, but I figured what would my one vote mean?" Guiltily she realized this was the first time she was able to vote for a president. And she hadn't.

Jessica looked horrified.

"Young lady, do you know what women went through to get the vote?" Then she launched on a colorful reprise of the women's suffrage movement. Diane could envision her marching down Pennsylvania Avenue, chaining herself to the gates before the White House, lecturing atop soapboxes.

Finally Clay interrupted his aunt's diatribe to suggest that they shower before dinner.

"All right, you can go," Jessica rumbled good-naturedly. "If you feel up to facing the snow, I have tickets for you to attend the Inaugural Concert over at Constitution Hall. Provided, of course, that the musicians can make it into the city."

"Don't be silly! We'll stay home and talk to you," Clay said. "We can go to plenty of concerts in New York. How often do I see you?"

"That's your fault," Jessica said. "But while you're here, I mean for you to see what's important. I have a pair of seats for the swearing-in tomorrow morning. Your mother gave you tickets for the ball at the Mayflower. If you're in the mood—and they clear the snow off Pensylvania Avenue—then you can see as much of the parade as amuses you. And of course there are parties all over the place if you'd like to socialize."

"All we're interested in seeing are the swearing-in and the Inaugural Ball. We'd rather spend the rest of the time with you."

Jessica smiled.

"Fine. Shall we have our baths?"

A maid showed Diane to her room, drew a bath for her, and asked her which dress she should press for Diane to wear to dinner. The mood in the house—gracious, measured, elegant—seemed far removed from the excitement that must be enveloping most of the city on the threshold of a presidental inauguration.

Before going down to dinner Diane pushed aside the drapes at one tall, narrow window and looked out into the night. The snow was coming down in big flakes and was sticking.

She could tell by the sway of the trees that it was very windy, and she wondered briefly who would be able to attend the inaugural festivities if the weather continued like this.

Over dinner in the classically elegant dining room Jessica held court.

"It's the stupid way you're all raised, this obsession with making all women wives and mothers. Oh, I was brought up in the same way. My brothers were horrified when I became involved in the suffrage movement. It simply wasn't done in our circles. They upbraided my husband regularly for indulging me in what they considered my little eccentricities. But by God, I needed something more in my life than society balls and dinners and the opera season. The high point of my life was marching down Fifth Avenue beside Mrs. O. H. P. Belmont—she'd been Alva Vanderbilt—back in 1912. We might have been Old Society," she said with pride, "but we were also the New Women."

Diane recalled when Mr. Lewisohn had told her that August Belmont—who became Alva Vanderbilt's father-in-law—was Jewish. But like her grandparents, he had abandoned his faith to become an Episcopalian. She remembered Ira's pride in Governor Herbert Lehman. She smiled to herself. Aunt Jessica would not be shocked to learn that Diane Dickenson was really Diane Seligman.

"At least your Uncle Ernst—God rest his soul—didn't settle for an inane, useless life," Jessica said. "He served his country in Congress for thirty-two years—and I was part of that service, as Ernst was the first to admit. We were a team."

They were having coffee when they heard voices in the marble-floored foyer.

"It's all right, Jefferson." A man's voice. "Mrs. Parsons won't mind my interrupting."

A tall, lean man of about fifty, dressed in a tuxedo, charged into the room. He was an arresting-looking man, with salt-and-pepper hair and what Diane suspected was a perennial tan.

"Jessica, my wife didn't make it up from Atlanta for the Democratic fund-raising gala tonight, and I thought you might like to go with me. I've got a car

379

out there with four-wheel drive and a man at the wheel who can make his way through the worst blizzard God can create. Sinatra's going to be there and a flock of Hollywood stars—" He paused. "I'm sorry, I didn't realize you were entertaining guests—"

"Tom Mason—" Jessica waved a hand around the table. "This is Diane Dickenson and my nephew Clay."

She turned to Diane. "Tom lives next door—though actually he doesn't really stay there very often." Diane studied the newcomer. Wasn't he that cotton-mill magnate who was always fighting against attempts to unionize his mills? She thought she'd read about him in *Life* and the *New York Times*.

She thought she saw a glint of recognition in his eyes when they rested on her. Belatedly she wondered if Chris was among that "flock of Hollywood stars" appearing at the gala. It was being staged by Sinatra and his Rat Pack.

"Jessica, you've been a substantial contributor to the campaign fund. Surely you received tickets. Even if you didn't with this weather there'll be plenty of people who won't show." His eyes strayed to Diane. "We could all go." Diane was flattered by the interest she saw in his penetrating brown eyes.

"I have a pair of tickets, but we'll forego this one," Jessica said firmly. "With the way that snow's coming down, it'll probably be an hour or two late getting started—and they do go on forever."

"It will be a rough drive," Mason said. Diane sensed he wasn't the kind of man to be stopped by the

380

elements. Again his eyes rested on her for barely a moment. "There are stalled cars all along the road. Still, Washington has to keep the city open for the inauguration. They'll have to clear a road from Georgetown into the city so the president-elect can arrive to be sworn in. Crews are out plowing and salting the streets like mad."

"We'll watch whatever TV has to offer," Jessica said. "Nice thing about TV: we don't like it, we can turn it off. And we have color TV. It'll be like sitting right on the inaugural platform."

"Next inauguration, Jessica," he said, "we'll do this whole thing together."

"If I'm around, ask me," she said. "And I expect to be around for two or three more."

Quietly, Mason slipped out of the room.

Diane was astonished that Jessica Parsons had contributed to the Democratic campaign. It must have shown on her face.

"I contributed," she confirmed, "but not the way I'd like to have done. Obviously, the stock-market crash put a real crimp in our finances. I'm probably the only member of the family who's an avowed Democrat. I know," she nodded to Clay, "you voted for John Kennedy. But this was just your first Presidential election. I've been a Democrat since FDR. What did you think of Tom Mason?" Her gaze swept from Clay to Diane.

"A terrific friend or a dangerous enemy," Clay said.

"Right on the head." Jessica nodded in approval. "He contributed heavily to the Democratic campaign. He's from Georgia—that's Democratic country. He has cotton mills all over the state. But I know he gave just as much to the Republicans. Washington is a gossipy town."

"So he plays both sides and he's sure to come up a winner." Clay was amused. "Good business."

"Oh, Tom's made his own congressmen in the past ten years. He runs to Washington every time some bill that's important to his mills comes up. And that business about his wife not making it up for the inauguration—I don't think there's been any marriage between them for the past twenty years. She's devoted to their two daughters and gardening. In the seven years he's owned that house next door, she's never been up here. Not even when he needed her to be a hostess at political dinners. Usually he has some congressman's wife stand in for her."

Clay laughed.

"To their faces Nixon is probably 'Dick' and Kennedy is 'Jack,' and behind their backs they were 'those sons of bitches running for president.'"

Jessica suddenly looked serious.

"You've got to give Tom Mason credit. Here's a man who's pulled himself up from nothing. His parents and grandparents and all the others before them were sharecroppers. They might have lived in Georgia since before the Civil War, but Tom Mason's ancestors never made it into the 'best' homes—and that rankles. That's why he asked if I wanted to go with him to this affair. As a former member of the DAR and an old friend of Alice Roosevelt Longworth, I lend class to one of the shrewdest businessmen the South has ever spawned." Her eyes twinkled. "Tom doesn't know I withdrew from the DAR when

382

they prevented Marian Anderson from singing in Constitution Hall back in 1939. And do you know who's singing the national anthem at the start of the gala tonight? Marian Anderson. If it weren't for this damnable weather, I'd go and stay just long enough to hear her."

"I guess that's a sure sign that the New Frontier is moving ahead," Diane said. "I don't know too much about what's happening in the world." Her smile was rueful. "I read the front pages of the *New York Times* so I know what Governor Orval Faubus tried to do to those brave little kids in Little Rock. I know about Castro overthrowing Batista, and about the awful danger of nuclear tests, and how one plane today can carry more destruction than every plane in all the air forces of the world during World War II. I know about things, but it's always been as somebody sitting on the sidelines."

"And now you want to be part of the world." Jessica glowed. "That's the beginning, my dear. Do something with your life besides spinning in the social whirl. You too, Clay. You don't want to reach my age and ask yourself, where did it all go? I *know*," she said. "I was part of what was happening."

"Do you think this snow will let up in time for the inauguration tomorrow?"

"The sun will be out tomorrow," Jessica said. "Crews will work all night to cut paths through the snow. This city will never allow a blizzard to stop it from celebrating a presidential inauguration."

Laura typed the last line of the report to Mannie

Coleman and pulled it out of the typewriter. Now she noticed how quiet the offices of Menlow Films were. She glanced at her desk clock. It was almost seven P.M. Almost everyone had been sent home at four because of the weather conditions.

She collated the three copies of the report, threw one copy into her file basket, slid another into a manila envelope to go to California, and picked up the third to take in to Bernie. If Joe was irritated that Bernie was taking her away from him, he certainly didn't show it—probably because he was terrified that Bernie would complain about him to Clayton Enterprises' board of directors.

Bernie was in his office, his feet propped up on a pulled-out desk drawer, one of the inevitable cups of coffee at his elbow while he talked on the phone. He glanced up with a glint of approval when Laura came in.

"Look, I have to go in to a meeting. Enjoy the sunshine—we're freezing here in New York." He frowned in a show of strained patience. While he played on the side, he intended to keep his marriage intact. "Yeah, I'll call you in a couple of days. Tell the kids I'll be back there in another week or so." He put down the phone and allowed his eyes to travel their familiar route over Laura's slim, curvaceous figure. "Did I ever tell you that you're a sexy broad?"

She smiled.

"Just a few times."

"Listen, I called the Stage Deli and ordered food sent up. Even in this weather they'll get through for regulars like Menlow."

"Here's the report." She tossed it on his desk.

"Some storm."

Bernie shrugged.

"We should worry." His voice was nonchalant, but his eyes were disconcertingly probing. She hated not knowing what he was thinking. "It's warm inside. Dinner's coming up. If you want to watch the gala from Washington later, I have a TV here in the office." He also had a sofa that opened up into a queen-size bed in which he occasionally spent the night when he worked late.

"I couldn't care less about what's happening in Washington," she said. Except it did please her that a third-generation American whose great-grandfather had been a tenant farmer in Ireland had been elected president of the United States. But right now she was more concerned about Bernie. She wished he'd stop this sparring and say what was on his mind. But she knew she could only wait until he was in the mood to open up.

The night buzzer went off.

"That's our food." He swung his expensively trousered legs to the floor. "I'll get it."

Laura trailed him to the door and waited for him to return.

"God, I'm starving," he said with relish as he returned. "Thank God I can eat like a horse without putting on a pound." Laura knew he did a hundred push-ups every morning.

"Shall we dine at your place or mine?" she said.

"Here," he said. "Go put up some coffee. I'll set up the table."

By the time she returned with two mugs of coffee, Bernie had set up the Stage spread on the coffee table before the sofa that dominated one wall of his office. For a few minutes they were content to concentrate on the massive pastrami-on-rye sandwiches, crisp fries, and kosher-style pickles.

"We won't break the news for another week or two, Laura," Bernie punctured the companiable silence, "but Garrison's being sent out to the Coast. I can't fire him without creating a big stink, so I'm promoting him."

Laura sat motionless. Was Bernie bringing in somebody from the outside, or would she inherit Bill's spot? Bernie knew she was dying for that job. Moving up to story editor would take her out of the secretarial level. She'd be an *executive*. The money wasn't a hell of a lot more, but it was a tremendous step up the ladder career-wise. She would be in a decision-making position. At her age, that was sensational.

"Bill was hoping you'd ship Lowell to California and he would move up to executive story editor," Laura said, trying not to betray her excitement.

"No way." Bernie was firm. "I want somebody in that seat who's loyal to me. Bill's loyal to whomever will do him the most good." Laura was puzzled. What kind of loyalty did Bernie expect from the story editor? "I never know what goes on in Jim Lowell's head. I figure with you as story editor I'll be able to find out."

"Who knows this?" *It was happening. Just as she knew it would.*

"So far, just you and me. That's why it has to stay under wraps for the next week or two. I told you, baby. We can do business together." His eyes settled on her bosom as she leaned forward to help herself to a slice of apple strudel.

"Thanks, Bernie," she said softly.

"Don't you know a better way to say thank you than that?"

Their eyes met.

"I won't sleep with any man just to get ahead in the world." She knew this was the right approach.

"What about because you like the guy?"

She smiled. And moved closer.

"That's a different story."

After dinner Jessica and her two guests moved, with their coffee, into what she humorously called the music room.

"The music all comes from the radio or the television set. I haven't touched the piano in twenty years. Clay, see what you can get on the news."

Clay found a channel featuring local news. So far about sixty musicians of the hundred members of the National Symphony Orchestra had been able to reach Washington. The gala at the National Guard Armory had not yet started and was already an hour late with about two-thirds of the sell-out audience not showing. Highways were blocked. Cars were marooned in snowdrifts.

"Before the blizzard is over," the newscaster reported, "it's estimated that ten thousand cars will have stalled and been abandoned. Tonight one thousand people will sleep in Union Station. The Sheraton-Park Hotel is putting up fifteen hundred cots in ballrooms to serve the stranded—"

"What an introduction to the presidency for John Kennedy," Diane said softly. "Do you suppose it's nature's way of warning him about the four years ahead?"

Where would *she* be in four years? Like Jessica Parsons, she needed more in her life than society balls and dinners and the opera season. She thought about Tom Mason, who had pulled himself up from nothing to a position of power in the business world, a man who came to Washington to fight for the issues important to him—and who, she suspected, often won. She thought about Clay's great-grandfather, Frederick Brentwood, who ran off at seventeen to the Gold Rush in California.

God only knew what would happen to her.

Chapter Twenty-Two

Wearing a flannel bathrobe over his slacks and one of the Shetland sweaters he'd picked up in London, Ira ground coffee beans in a coffee mill—a welcome-home present from Laura—and transferred the results to a percolator. He swore as he spied a roach crawling behind the antique kitchen stove and reached for a sheaf of newspaper to kill it. He'd have to spray like hell tonight.

He'd thought he could come back to East Fifth Street and settle in comfortably. But the few days he'd stayed at the apartment with his family had highlighted his growing distaste for slum living. It astonished him that Laura stayed on upstairs. The way she was pushing ahead financially she could afford a studio in one of those new luxury buildings going up all over Manhattan. Where there would be plenty of heat and hot water and no roaches. But Laura invested every spare dollar in her wardrobe and courses on filmmaking.

He brought out eggs and butter from the yellowed

refrigerator, reached into the breadbox for a bagel. The TV in the tiny living room was blaring out news from Washington. All last night crews had worked to open up streets blocked by the snow, to remove cars abandoned in the drifts. And this morning sun smiled down upon the city.

According to the local early-morning news, ten inches of ice and snow had paralyzed the city. Most businesses and offices in New York were closed because of the weather. The city schools were closed for the inauguration. Railway and bus traffic was suspended. La Guardia Airport was closed down, and out of 1,600 flights originally scheduled to leave Idlewild and Newark, only a dozen were expected to be made.

As Ira dropped the eggs into the frying pan, his phone rang. God, he thought, don't let it be somebody else in the cast dropping out! He had sweated out two replacements so far, and they were opening in five days. He wasn't worried about losing the Equity actors—they were bound by contract. But the non-Equity actors could walk out on a moment's notice.

He turned the gas flame low and walked into the bedroom to pick up the phone. "Hello."

"Did I wake you?" It was his mother. She knew he he could sleep till ten and still be at rehearsal by eleven. It was only ten of nine now.

"No, mom. I've been up since eight."

"You're rehearsing even with the snow emergency?"

"I called everybody last night and told them to be there. I don't care if they have to come on skis.

Actually, though, everybody lives within twenty blocks, so it looks like they'll make it."

"Well, dad and I have been glued to the TV since seven o'clock. It's a shame you can't watch the inauguration. I thought it was lovely that Kennedy asked Robert Frost to read 'The Gift Outright' at the inauguration ceremonies, don't you? It shows a feeling for the arts."

"It'll be a stronger feeling if his administration funnels some money into the arts," Ira snapped. He knew it was an unnecessary comment, but it annoyed him the way his mother always looked for good in situations that were irreversible. Dad fumed and fretted.

"How're rehearsals going?"

"So far everything looks good." Actually, he'd been surprised by how totally involved he'd become in directing somebody else's play. In truth, a writer was a director and actor as well. When he wrote, he sat at the typewriter and mentally acted every role, directed every move. "Of course, with our category of Off-Broadway contract we have only three Equity members. The other five can walk off any time the grass looks greener someplace else."

"Have you got something else lined up?" she asked wearily. "I mean, if you're a little short on money, I could—"

"I'm all right, mom—" He hesitated. "Listen, can I call you back? I have eggs frying on the stove—"

"Darling, go eat your breakfast. We'll talk another time. And dress warm. When dad went down for the *Times* earlier, he said it was awfully cold out."

Ira hung up and rescued his eggs. The coffee was

perking, the bagel was being toasted in the broiler. As he sat at the table, he thought about the play. He had two substantial actors in the major roles. He was working like the devil to provide appealing bits of business for the weaker cast members. If the reviews were good, Tim O'Brien promised to put up money for an all-Equity Off-Broadway company. Another revival, he said. But producers changed their minds.

He wasn't sure why O'Brien fancied himself the coming Off-Broadway producer. Maybe because it was some kind of tax deal. No matter. O'Brien had plenty of spare cash, and he meant to sock it into Off-Broadway.

Ira got up to take out the bagel and pour himself a cup of coffee. Freshly ground coffee was one of the few luxury items he could afford.

He thought again about the dinner party. Obviously Diane had decided that he and Laura were after her to put up money for his play. Damn! Why did he continue to let that bug him? He'd probably never see her again.

He'd hold off on talking to O'Brien about doing his play until the reviews came in on this one. He felt a rush of exhilaration at the prospect of directing his own play Off-Broadway. He might not make a lot of money, but he would be proving something to himself.

Laura kept telling him he was wasting time writing social plays, that he ought to knock out a commercial comedy like *Two for the Seesaw* or *The Best Man*. But he thought of Russ breaking his ass down in Atlanta; and he felt guilty that he was indulging himself by writing. He ought to be out fighting for civil rights. It was up to their generation to shape the future of the world.

This showed signs of being a decade of crusades. Most of the time—even in the midst of a war, except for those who were themselves involved—people were all tied up in knots about their own personal problems. They didn't see beyond the fence they erected around themselves. But this last year was different. At least, among the young.

Today they were inaugurating a president who was forty-three years old. Statistics Ira had read recently jogged across his mind. Adenauer was eighty-four, Nehru seventy-one, De Gaulle seventy, Mao Tse-tung sixty-seven, Khrushchev sixty-six. Maybe Kennedy's New Frontier would be just that.

He put the dishes into the sink, ran water to soak, poured himself a second cup of coffee, and went into the living room to watch the TV reports of what was happening in Washington.

Diane frowned at the intrusion of brilliant sunlight as she drowsed in the square, high-ceilinged guest room assigned to her.

"Come on, Di. You can't sleep all day." Clay stood beside the bed with a cup of steaming hot coffee in one hand. He had opened the drapes to awaken her. "We have an inauguration to catch."

Diane pulled herself up against the headboard and reached for the cup of coffee.

"You think we'll be able to get downtown?" After last night's reports, she wondered.

"We'll get there." Clay was in high spirits. "Jack

Kennedy lives in Georgetown. They had to clear a road; it wouldn't do for him to miss his own inauguration. He may have trouble staying awake," Clay conceded. "A morning newscaster said his old man gave a party for him at Paul Young's that didn't begin until two A.M."

"When do we have to leave?" She fought to clear her head.

"As soon as you dress and have breakfast. We have two seats at the East Plaza, right in front of the capitol inaugural platform, but let's be there in time to claim them. Of course, a lot of people will stay in their comfortably warm houses and watch the whole scene on TV, which will ease the traffic problem."

"I'll wear my ski underwear," Diane said. "I brought it along in case it was freezing." She flinched at the sound of the wind whipping outside the house. "Maybe the cook can give us a thermos of coffee to take along."

"I'll go downstairs and ask. Don't waste time, darling. God knows how long it'll take us to drive into town."

Within forty minutes Diane sat beside Clay in the car and nursed the thermos of coffee and the lunch box prepared for them by the Parsons cook. She wore a gray cashmere slipover and cardigan with her gray wool slacks, the Maximillian mink she had bought for her twenty-first birthday, heavy socks on her feet, gray suede boots that reached under her slacks almost to her knees, and a gray-and-burgundy ski cap.

The Washington, D.C., sanitation crews had accomplished a miracle. Clay told her they had used army flamethrowers to hasten the snow removal. Last night, in the middle of the blizzard, policemen had fired pistols into the air near the Capitol to scare the starlings away.

In downtown Washington, Clay parked the car, first seeking advice from a snow-removal crew.

"I hope it's here when we come back," he said. "Come on, let's walk."

People had been arriving at the Capitol plaza for the past two hours, they discovered. But with the bitter wind and subfreezing temperature, despite the brilliant sun, the numbers were far less than anticipated. Diane and Clay took their seats, set up between mounds of snow, and wrapped themselves in a pair of car blankets.

The red, white, and blue bunting decorating the inaugural platform fluttered wildly in the northwest winds. The Capitol dome rose behind the platform against a cloudless blue sky. In spite of the weather, the mood was festive. Clay pointed out a ruddy-faced, white-haired man well into his seventies who had propped himself into a seat while encased in a sleeping bag. A woman wore a ski mask.

Others, too, had arrived with hot beverages. Already earlier arrivals were sipping warming drinks, eating sandwiches, or nibbling at fruit.

"It's only ten to noon," Clay said complacently. "We're here in time." The ceremonies were scheduled to commence at noon.

Already the inaugural platform was populated. There appeared to be a last-minute hassle to set up additional chairs. Eyes kept turning to watch for the arrival of the president-elect. At noon he had not yet arrived.

A man in his early forties with a neatly trimmed beard and smoking a pipe openly inspected Diane and Clay. For a moment Diane was afraid that he had recognized her.

"We're a motley crew here today," he said humorously. "All of us hopeful of witnessing a real turnaround in the country."

Clay laughed.

"We're all crazy to be sitting here freezing to death."

"I had to come." The man was serious. "I teach economics at a university in New York City. How could I face my students when the new term starts without having sat in on the most important inauguration in almost thirty years?" He looked around at the seats filling up. "We look prosperous enough here. There's a boom in the stock market. The five and a half million unemployed workers get kind of swept under the rugs. Nobody wants to know that business failures today are higher than at any time since the Depression. That in hundreds of communities throughout the country people are hurting. The men who meet in the Capitol seem to brush aside the need to feed all those hungry people out there. Maybe it'll work," he summed up quietly. "Maybe the New Frontier will get this country moving again."

"There's a special excitement in the air," Diane said. "I've never been to an inauguration before, but I have a feeling that today is different."

"The closest thing since the inauguration of FDR," Clay said. "My great-aunt still talks about that. She said the country was in such bad shape when Roosevelt took office that people were scared of a revolution. The country was almost suicidal."

Now a middle-aged couple who sat beside the university professor joined in the conversation. They had been Depression children, and they described the past so vividly that Diane began to feel slightly sick. She was relieved when the U.S. Marine Band swung into "Hail to the Chief." President Eisenhower was arriving. It would be the last time this would be played for him.

A few minutes later the new First Lady, Mrs. Eisenhower, Mrs. Nixon, and Mrs. Lyndon Johnson arrived and settled themselves in front-row seats. Cheers rang out when, about twenty minutes behind schedule, the president-elect appeared on the platform. Senator Sparkman, chairman of the Inaugural Committee, walked to the lectern and called upon the Marine Band to open the ceremonies with *America the Beautiful.*

Diane felt tears sting her eyes at the stirring music. She was not alone. Now she felt especially guilty that she hadn't voted. She thought again of Ira Ross. He had such a personal commitment to humanity. He cared about people. Jessica Parsons would like him.

Don't think about him, she told herself. He would fall in love with some bright, committed girl like himself. What room was there in his life for a Diane Dickenson—except as a backer for his play? *Concentrate on now.*

She gazed at the inaugural platform. President Truman was sitting there, along with the widows of two Democratic presidents, Wilson and Roosevelt. The president-elect's two children, Caroline and

John, Jr., were at the family home in Palm Beach. If *she* were the First Lady, she'd want her daughter to be here today.

The invocation by Francis Cardinal Spellman seemed unusually long. He continued even when wisps of smoke emerged from the lectern, to be put out by anxious Secret Service men at the cardinal's "amen." The crowd of twenty thousand rose as Marian Anderson began *The Star-Spangled Banner*.

There was a second prayer by the archbishop of the Greek Orthodox Diocese of North and South America, and then Lyndon Johnson was sworn in by House Speaker Sam Rayburn. After a third prayer read by Dr. John Barclay, pastor of the Central Christian Church of Austin, Texas, Robert Frost rose and walked to the lectern to read his famous "The Gift Outright."

Clay reached for Diane's hand.

"It was a touch of genius to bring Robert Frost here today," he whispered.

Ira would like that, too, Diane decided. *Damn.* Why did she keep thinking about him? She smiled faintly as she remembered that the first poem she had ever loved enough to memorize—at eleven—had been "Fire and Ice" by Robert Frost.

Now the sixty-eight-year-old poet struggled to read a dedication to the new president as a preface to the poem. Vice-President Johnson leapt forward with his high silk hat—*de rigueur* again at this inauguration after being supplanted by the Homburg at the Eisenhower inauguration—in a futile effort to shield the manuscript from the sharp wind.

"This was to be the preface to a poem that I can say

398

without reading," Frost told the crowd, then proceeded to recite the poem, amending the last line in honor of John Kennedy's New Frontier.

Diane was mesmerized by the ceremony. She sat at the edge of her seat when John Kennedy shed his overcoat and rose to be sworn in as the thirty-fifth president of the United States.

The atmosphere was electric as the new young president began his inaugural address. Diane listened expectantly, but a segment of her mind strayed. She felt a kind of personal vindication that one of the richest men in America—himself a millionaire via trust funds—had reached the highest office in the land. But in spite of his wealth John Kennedy was fighting to accomplish something in the world on his own. She remembered Laura's words: *"I have to know I've accomplished something on my own in this world."* Could *she* do that?

Kennedy's speech was shorter than the usual inaugural address, but it was powerful, eloquent.

"Short and to the point," Clay said as they applauded. "But not as short as George Washington's at his second inauguration—that was only 135 words."

Now the benediction was delivered by Rabbi Nelson Gluck of the Hebrew Union College of Cincinnati. The crowd rose to its feet again as the Marine Band played *The Star-Spangled Banner.* When the new president and his official party walked out, the band played *Hail to the Chief.*

Clay turned to Diane.

399

"Shall we hang around for the parade?"

"Oh yes!" Diane said. "How could we not?"

According to the local news, almost a million people had lined the parade route along broad Constitution and Pennsylvania avenues. No doubt the presidental luncheon would be cut short to try to keep as close as possible to the official one-thirty P.M. starting time. Diane and Clay joined those waiting at the starting point of the parade. At two P.M. the bubbletop presidential limousine carrying the president and the new First Lady appeared, signifying the beginning of the parade.

"Aunt Jessica told me there'll be 32,000 people in the parade," Clay said, holding fur-lined gloves against his cheeks. "It's the biggest parade in history."

Despite the weather and weakening moments Diane and Clay clung to their positions for more than an hour while the parade moved past them. Diane felt sorry for the young majorettes in their brief costumes, their legs turning blue, and the enthusiastic baton twirlers with frozen fingers. More than forty bands of 16,000 soldiers, sailors, airmen, and marines would march before the parade was over.

"The parade theme is 'World Peace through New Fronters,'" Clay remarked wryly, "but half the parade seems to be the military."

"Let's try to get back to the car," Diane said at last. Her feet, in wool socks and boots, were numb. "I'd like to defrost before the Inaugural Ball tonight."

* * *

At last they were back at the Georgetown house and welcomed into the music room, where Jessica was watching the parade on her new color television.

"What a marvelous age we live in!" she said as they came in. "I can sit here in absolute sybaritic comfort and see more than most of the people who're there in person can see. But I suspect that television will change the mode of our choosing not only presidents but all elected officials. Now they'll have to be performers as well as politicians."

Diane was content to sit in the cozy warmth of the Parsons music room and watch the rest of the parade on television. Dinner was to be served early so that Diane and Clay would have enough time to dress and get back to downtown Washington for the Inaugural Ball.

When Diane came downstairs, dressed in an exquisite short Mainbocher evening dress of pink brocade with satin slippers in pale avocado and a long cape of Aurora chinchilla over her arm, Jessica reminded her that above-the-elbow gloves were considered proper attire for guests at the five-part Inaugural Ball.

"Don't worry, my dear," she said. "You have small hands like mine. I'll send Marie upstairs to bring a pair down for you. Of course, these lovely slippers will be ruined in the snow. But so will those of all the other ladies."

Properly attired except for the unglamorous galoshes on her feet—at Jessica's inspiration—"Old, darling, so just toss them away in the ladies lounge at the Mayflower when you arrive"—Diane trooped beside Clay to the waiting car. The trip into town was slow and arduous despite the snow-removal efforts of the sanitation crews.

The glamorous Gold Ballroom at the Mayflower was the scene of the Inaugural Ball. When Diane and Clay arrived at nine-twenty—twenty-five minutes before the president was scheduled to arrive, the ballroom was already jammed with guests. The music was lively, the Presidential Box was draped with blue satin and red, white, and blue silk ropes and marked with the presidential and the vice-presidential seals. A glittering gold curtain was a backdrop before which had been placed a head-high, three-tiered arrangement of red carnations. The other thirty boxes about the room were adorned in white satin and festively decorated with tall arrangements of red and white carnations.

"My God, Di, I feel like I'm at another fancy debut," Clay said. "There's Lester Lanin on the bandstand." Lester was being spelled by Washington's own Roland Haas.

Suddenly the ballroom crowd became a stampede. President Kennedy and the First Lady had appeared in the Presidential Box. Guests were shoving their way into the best viewing positions, ignoring the expensive gowns of the ladies that would probably be unwearable after tonight. Nobody danced.

"Let's get over to the side." Clay put his arm around Diane and led her away from the crowd. "The presidential party must have come in through a special entrance straight to their box."

"Clay! Diane!" a female voice called out. "Isn't this smashing?"

Struggling against the crowd to their side came a

402

classmate from Miss Framingham's and her fiancé, who looked thoroughly bored.

"Isn't this ridiculous?" she squealed. "I mean, we saw Jack and Jackie at parties down in Palm Beach last month. They aren't any different now. I don't think she's all that gorgeous. She may have been the Debutante of the Year in 1947 or whenever it was, but some of the girls who went to school with her said she was a real iceberg."

Diane flinched. Chris's words coming back to her: *"You're as cold as an Arctic Circle iceberg. My super-rich beautiful bride. An iceberg."*

She tugged at Clay's arm.

"Clay, let's leave. I'm getting claustrophobic. We've seen enough."

They left the ballroom and made their way into the street. There was melting snow everywhere, and by the time they reached the car, Diane's slippers were ruined.

"You'll warm up in a few moments," Clay said. "I'll turn on the heater as soon as we're moving at a decent clip."

They listened to a woman reporter on the radio:

At last night's gala the First Lady wore an Oleg Cassini gown of heavy ribbed silk with a full skirt and a short train. The sleeves of the gown end just above the elbow, and its only trim is a white silk roseate at the bodice. For the Inaugural Ball she's wearing a gown created by the custom-design salon of Bergdorf Goodman in New York, a lovely floor-length sheath of white *peu d'ange* beneath white chiffon. Her bouffant hairstyle was arranged by Kenneth of Lilly Daché in New York, who traveled to Washington especially to style the new First Lady's coiffure.

"Enough." Diane switched stations, looking for one that would play some music—but tonight all the stations were covering the inaugural affairs.

She gave up. She was still glad that Clay had insisted on their coming here. Maybe her own life would change a little after these two days of momentous events. Of course, she wouldn't ever be president of the United States, but she *could* give her life a purpose. Clay and she would concentrate on classes in every subject that would be useful to them as interior decorators. And then they would open a shop: Diane and Clay, Incorporated.

Chapter Twenty-Three

Back in New York Diane and Clay signed up for classes at the Parsons School of Design, starting with courses on art history. Clay said it was important to learn period, color coordination, and design—and some general knowledge of architecture.

In addition to the extensive reading demanded by the classes, she made a point of reading all national and local news in the *New York Times* every day. She watched for the TV programs that dealt with timely topics. But Clay deflected all efforts on her part to draw him into discussions of world affairs, insisting that he was a hedonist. But he was seeing a psychiatrist three times a week.

In mid-February Deirdre phoned Diane.

"Darling, Lenny and I are going to spend a few weeks sailing around the Caribbean, and I want you and Clay to come down with us. How can you bear all that rotten weather in New York?"

"Dee, it sounds lovely, but we can't get away now," Diane said. "Clay and I have classes. We'll see you when you come home." She hesitated. "Dee, are you happy?"

"Deliriously." She laughed, a little nervously. "Dad and mother and the lawyers are having fits. Of course, they can't do anything. Only grandmother sent a wedding present. She sent it to mother. She forgot I moved into my own apartment. It's a set of Waterford crystal. When we get back to New York, I'll donate it to that thrift shop your aunt's involved in."

"Staying slim?" Diane asked. That was always a barometer of Deirdre's moods.

"I'm on the scale every day. I haven't gained a pound. We play tennis and swim and ride bikes. We won't be doing that on the yacht, but there's an exercise room, so I'll be okay. Di, you're sure you can't come down? Maybe for next weekend? You don't have classes then."

"I wish I could, Dee. But when I'm not in classes I'm tied up with the April in Paris Ball." It wasn't quite the truth, but she couldn't bear the thought of spending even a weekend in Lenny's company. "But you have fun, Dee."

Deirdre didn't return to New York until late March. She called Diane from the airport.

"Di, let's have lunch tomorrow, okay? Just the two of us—like old times. Between your classes and the April in Paris Ball routine."

"Okay. Tomorrow at one?"

"Great. Let's go down to that place where you took us to dinner. What was it called? La Petite Maison?"

"Fine. Shall I pick you up with the car?"

"No," Deirdre said. "I told Lenny I had to see my

gynecologist about a diaphragm."

"Dee, you're not pregnant!"

"No. I really do have an appointment with the gynecologist. I called him from Nassau. Lenny hates kids. But I thought we could have lunch first. Listen, I'll see you tomorrow, okay? At La Petite Maison. At one. Bye."

Before Diane even had a chance to say goodbye she heard the click of the receiver. Lenny must have interrupted them.

At one o'clock sharp the next day Diane arrived at La Petite Maison. A few minutes later, Deirdre tottered in on ridiculously high heels. Diane was instantly alarmed by her appearance—even in the muted light of the restaurant Deirdre looked gaunt.

"Dee, have you been on another one of those starvation diets?"

Deirdre sighed. "If I look awful, it's because we didn't get much sleep the last few days. Lenny met this character at the hotel in Palm Beach. He got Lenny all excited about investing in a chain of health clubs. The guy is coming up to New York next week to talk to Lenny about going into business with him."

"Let me guess: with Lenny putting up the money."

"Di, he keeps me up half the night talking about how they'll make a fortune. And how all he needs is an investment of three hundred thousand. I can't lay my hands on that kind of cash." She toyed with her bracelet. "I mean, not until I'm thirty."

"Did you tell him?"

"I'm scared to. Don't look at me like that. He's so excited about this. But even if I went into court, I couldn't get that much money. You know how strict the rules of my grandfather's will are."

"Di, Lenny's never even managed an ice-cream cart. What would he know about running a chain of health clubs?"

"If I had the money, I'd give it to him." Deirdre was staring hard at her. Suddenly Diane realized that Deirdre wanted *her* to lend Lenny the money. "I'll be able to pay it back in eight years, Di. What do you say?"

"You're asking me to loan you three hundred thousand dollars so Lenny can invest in this weird scheme? Lenny will lose every cent. What does he know about this man he met in Palm Beach anyway? He's probably some phony promoter."

Deirdre leaned forward, her face taut.

"Are you saying you won't lend me the money?"

"Dee, it would be insane. I mean—" But Deirdre was already on her feet.

"I thought we were so close we'd do anything for each other. Obviously I was wrong. I'll find another way."

"Deirdre, wait—" But she was already heading for the door and something stopped Diane from getting up and following her. She'd call her later and they would talk it out. She'd have to get Deirdre to see that she wouldn't be doing anyone a favor by lending Lenny the money.

She managed a smile when the waitress came to take her order, and explained self-consciously that her friend had remembered a pressing appointment. In all the years they'd known each other, she and Deirdre had never fought.

She went right home after she'd eaten. In the privacy of her upstiars sitting room she settled into a chair, reached for the phone, and dialed the line in Deirdre's bedroom that only she answered.

"Hello?" Deirdre, faintly breathless.

"Dee, we have to talk."

"You've changed your mind!"

"I can't, Dee—"

"You mean you don't want to."

"It would be wrong. I think we—"

"I don't care what you think!" Deirdre slammed the phone down.

Diane sat by the phone. Her instinct was to call Deirdre back and agree to lend the money—anything to make peace. But she couldn't give in to what she knew was wrong.

In the following weeks, Clay did his best to intervene and make peace between Diane and Deirdre, but Deirdre refused to talk to Diane and was quiet and withdrawn with Clay.

So Diane filled her time . . . with classes at the Parsons School of Design, her activities for the April in Paris Ball, and Clay's company. At the spring intercession Clay was scheduled to fly to Bermuda with his mother.

"I'd ask you to come along," he said, "but I know you'd hate me. Mother's decided—God knows why— to buy a house down in Bermuda, and she insists I have to help her choose one. It's been narrowed down to three."

Diane laughed. "Bermuda doesn't seem quite her cup of tea."

"There's this retired army colonel she met in Palm Beach who spends a lot of time down there. Can you imagine my mother in love?"

"Maybe she's just lonely. At least he's not somebody half her age." Her own mother was involved with some French beautician she'd met at Cannes. Catty acquaintances always managed to keep her abreast of her mother's latest adventures. They reported that the scandal sheets in Paris said the marquise de la Frontaine was buying a ski lodge at Montreaux for the two of them.

A few days after the close of school, Diane got a phone call from Laura.

"I have a pair of tickets for the Off-Broadway opening next Thursday of *The School for Scandal,* Diane. Would you like to go? Sheridan's not my favorite playwright. Actually, I'd never even heard of him until Ira began directing this company. But I've sat in on a rehearsal and he's done a terrific job—"

"Thanks for inviting me, Laura, but I'm leaving in two days for Southampton. My aunt hasn't been too well, so I'm going out to help her open up the house for the season. I'll be tied up out there for at least two weeks. But why don't we do something when I'm back in town? I'll call you."

They talked a few minutes longer, mostly about Laura's job. She'd recently been promoted to story editor.

"It's a major step career-wise. And I haven't forgotten that if it weren't for you, I wouldn't be there. I don't think you realize what a terrific favor you did me."

Off the phone, Diane thought about Ira. Well, even if she wasn't scheduled to go to Southampton with Aunt Claudia, she was *not* going to his opening. Of course, she *could* drive into town for the performance and then go back next morning . . . *No*. Ira would see her and start thinking again about her backing his play.

On the Friday after the opening of the Off-Broadway production of *The School for Scandal*, she read the brief review in the *Times* theater section.

"A young director with a fine touch for comedy," the review began, and wound up predicting a successful future for him. So, she thought, maybe Ira Ross would forget about playwriting and make a career for himself as a director. But something told her that Ira Ross was not the kind to abandon his chosen field without a struggle.

In early June—at her aunt's urging—Diane agreed to join Clay at the Bermuda house for a few days. It was not high season, but even in June the weather in Bermuda was delightful. They would be on hand for the finish of the multi-hull race from Newport to Bermuda and the Queen's Birthday parade.

Clay, almost finished with decorating the house, was eager to consult with her on the details. His mother was in Nice so there would be only Clay and a small staff.

She enjoyed their few days in Bermuda. The house was a stately, exquisitely restored colonial that sat in a hillside garden with a panoramic view of the ocean, and Clay had done a magnificent job of decorating. Diane suspected he was more in need of her approval than her help, but she enjoyed confirming his choice of fabrics for drapes and curtains, helping him make the final decision on several important pieces he had discovered at Trimingham's in Hamilton.

Over dinner, which Clay ordered served on the veranda overlooking the sea, their talk tended to resolve around Deirdre. Occasionally he picked up some gossip from mutual acquaintances, but Deirdre was uncharacteristically discreet about her marriage.

"I've never given her a wedding present," he said the night before they were to fly back to New York. "Let's run out tomorrow morning, and I'll buy something. I'll charge it to my mother's account for the house."

Philippe was at Idlewild with the car, waiting to drive her back to Southampton. Clay insisted he would taxi into New York. He promised to come out to the beach house in a week or two. Clay looked well, Diane thought as she watched him charge off behind a porter carting his luggage. He was staying off pills, drinking only a glass of wine with dinner.

She and Clay planned to open up a small interior decorating shop somewhere off Madison Avenue. Though excited by the prospect, Diane was filled with doubt. Maybe they were being presumptuous. They needed far more training. More experience. All right, she told herself, they'd take a heavy schedule of classes in the fall. They'd prepare themselves.

She was worried about her aunt's health. Though

Aunt Claudia never complained, it was obvious that she was often in pain, and she constantly fought with Diane and Mrs. Avery, the housekeeper, about taking her medication.

Again this season Diane planned to avoid much of the Southampton social scene except for when Clay came out to stay for two or three weeks. This summer Aunt Claudia stayed away from all activities, even her volunteer work.

One hot late June afternoon Diane returned to the house from a trip to the library and was told by Mrs. Avery that Deirdre had called. With Deirdre's pride, only an emergency would have pushed her into phoning her. Trembling, she dialed.

"Hello?" Deirdre sounded oddly subdued.

"Dee, are you all right?" Diane asked anxiously.

"No." Deirdre's voice cracked. "Di, you were right about Lenny. I never should have married him—"

"What's happened?"

"He beat me." Her voice broke. "It was awful. He's been on my back for months to put up the money for that string of health clubs. This morning I had to tell him I can't get the money until I'm thirty. He hit me! Like some pimp might beat a prostitute that was holding out on him. I hurt, Di. I hurt all over."

"I'll call Aunt Claudia's doctor and ask him to send someone over to you," Diane said. She turned cold at the thought of sweet, vulnerable Deirdre being beaten by that creep . . . but it didn't surprise her. "I'll drive right into town and—"

"No doctor. Just you. I don't want to see anybody but you."

"I'm coming, darling. But at least let me call

413

Clay." God knew how badly Deirdre was hurt. She might need hospitalization. "He's in New York right now."

"No," Deirdre rejected. "Maybe later. Hurry into town, Di. Please."

"I'll be there in two hours." Traffic into the city would be light. "Just lie down and rest. I'll be there soon." *She could kill Lenny for this.*

Diane swore under her breath every time Philippe had to slow down. Why hadn't she just loaned Deirdre the money? At last the car was moving across the Queensborough Bridge and into Manhattan.

Finally Philippe drew up at the curb before Deirdre's apartment building. She told him to garage the car and wait at the house until she phoned him. If Aunt Claudia needed a car, Mrs. Avery's was available.

Where were the servants, she wondered, as she approached the door to the apartment. Wasn't there a couple who came in five days a week to clean the apartment and prepare the meals? She rang the bell, and a moment later Deirdre opened the door, dressed in a caftan, one side of her face already discolored, one eye half-shut.

"Oh, Dee." Shocked, Diane pulled her friend into her arms and kicked the door closed behind them.

"I never thought he would hurt me," Deirdre said, sobbing. "He carried on a lot and yelled—but I never thought he'd beat me."

"You need a doctor."

414

"No. I don't want anybody to see me like this."

"Let's put you to bed, then." She considered an icepack for Deirdre's swollen face, but it was too late for that.

"Nothing's broken," Deirdre said. "I'm all bruised, but he didn't crack my jaw or any ribs or anything. Maybe for once being fat was good."

"When did this happen?"

"About five hours ago. He stalked out of the apartment right afterwards, calling me all kinds of names. I think he's off on a drinking binge or something. He does that when he gets sore at me. Di, I don't care how much he carries on, I'm divorcing him."

"Of course you are. Where are Jean and Helmut?"

"I sent them off on vacation for this week. I knew I would have to tell Lenny I couldn't raise the money for him. I didn't want them to hear him carry on. But I didn't expect this."

"I think we ought to have pictures of you looking this way," Diane said. Deirdre looked shocked. "For your lawyers, Dee. They'll have to make Lenny understand he has to agree to a divorce—without sharing your money—or you'll have him thrown in jail. That's why it's important for a doctor to see you."

Deirdre looked away. "We'll talk about it later. The doctor, I mean. How can we take photographs?" She moved gingerly against the pillows. "Lenny broke my camera last week in another temper tantrum."

"I'll call Clay," Diane said. Clay had a collection

of cameras. "You know how good he is at photography."

"All right. I guess Clay's close enough to know the truth."

"I'll call him on the other line." Diane stood up and walked out into the foyer. It would be easier to explain to Clay what had happened if Deirdre wasn't at her elbow.

Within half an hour Clay was at the apartment.

"That bastard won't dare fight your lawyer, sweetie," he said. "Not when he sees these photos, anyway. Be sure to check the Yellow Pages for a locksmith, Di. We have to change the locks on the doors. And I'll tell the doorman not to let Lenny up."

"I wish you'd let the doctor see you, Dee," Diane said. "You may need him for evidence in court."

Deirdre's hands fumbled with the border of the silk sheet. "But I feel so ashamed—"

"You're going to be all right." Diane took Deirdre's hands. "It's the three of us together. You're not alone."

A locksmith arrived to change the tumblers in the locks. Deirdre's lawyer—shocked and enraged—had been informed of what had happened and would be arriving later to discuss plans for Deirdre's divorce. Reluctantly Deirdre let Diane call her family doctor, and he was on his way.

"Where're Lenny's valises?" Clay asked when he returned to Deirdre's bedroom with iced coffee for the three of them.

"He keeps them in the bedroom across the hall," Deirdre said. "Why?"

416

"I'm packing one valise with his clothes," he said. "I'll leave it in the package room for Lenny the next time he shows up. Everything else goes to that children's clinic thrift shop your aunt sponsors, Diane. Looks like the party's over for Lenny Jackson."

Deirdre's lawyers made it clear to Lenny that either he agreed to a Mexican divorce—with no financial remuneration—or face a prison term for assault. Her mother would learn about the divorce when she checked out of Silver Hill and her father when he returned from a business trip to Hong Kong. Deirdre told Clay while he waited with Diane and her for their flight to Cuernavaca, Mexico, where she was to file for her divorce.

After a few days in Mexico, her divorce granted, Deirdre would fly to Maine Chance for four weeks. Diane would return to Southampton to be with her aunt. Clay would join his mother in Venice for a month.

A few hours before Diane and Deirdre were heading for the airport, Deirdre heard that bets were running high in jet-set circles on Olivia's marriage to a publicity-prone Greek shipping magnate. Diane knew better. Her mother was the beautiful little Jewish girl who had made it into the *Social Register*, European royalty, and the inner circle of the international jet set. She was the Marquis de la Frontaine; she valued her title far more than the shipping magnate's billions.

As the plane took off, Diane read *Time*. Deirdre flipped through *Vogue*, then put it aside and stared out the window.

"Di," she said wistfully, "what's the matter with us that we both picked the wrong men to love? Do you suppose it's a kind of curse because we have all that money?"

Chapter Twenty-Four

Diane was grateful for the arrival of autumn, because it meant the return of her class routine. Deirdre had returned from three weeks at Baden-Baden and what she referred to as a "pseudo-emotional reunion" with her mother, who seemed to consider her an equal now that she was a divorcée. Clay had played the dutiful son for two weeks at Newport and was waiting impatiently for his mother to leave New York for a month at White Sulphur Springs.

Deirdre was ecstatic at the prospect of being involved in the Diane & Clay Inc. shop. She signed up for exercise classes at Manya Kahn's, took a modern dance class twice a week, and started shopping for a chic new wardrobe.

With the approach of the Christmas holidays, Diane was aware that Clay had started taking pills again and cutting classes. But when she mentioned it to him, he shrugged her off.

"What are we learning in school that we can't

learn in the shop?"

"Clay, we learn something new every day." She was upset. She suspected that Clay was afraid the shop would fail. As a result, her own confidence sagged.

Four days before Christmas, when Clay was scheduled to meet his mother in Palm Beach, he called Diane shortly past six in the morning.

"Clay, are you all right?"

"I'm rotten." He sounded scared and defeated. "Will you come over here and drag me out of the house and up to Dr. Reeve's sanitarium? He's been after me for weeks to sign myself in. Bring Deirdre. She can drive and you can hold my hand. Di, I'm such a mess!" His voice cracked.

"Just sit down and wait for us." She'd known this would happen someday. It had to. "I'll be there in ten minutes. Deirdre will come over with her car." *Please God, don't let him hurt himself before we get there.*

She dialed Deirdre's bedside phone. Deirdre picked up on the fourth ring. Diane briefed her on what was happening. Instantly she was awake.

"I'm going right over to the house. Park out front," Diane said. "When I see the car, I'll come down with Clay."

In pajamas and robe, Clay was standing in the hall when Diane arrived. She remembered a similar scene . . . but then it was Deirdre, and Lenny had just beaten her. She had seen the same desperation and fear in Deirdre's eyes.

"Clay, you'll be all right." She pulled him close. "Did you pack some clothes?"

"No."

"We'll pack together." She took his hand and led him, as though he were a child, to the stairs.

"I couldn't face another two weeks at Palm Beach with mother," he said, his voice barely a whisper. "But I was forgetting what pills I'd taken and how many. All at once I was scared I'd O.D. My life isn't worth shit, but I'm not suicidal."

"Clay, you'll spend a month or two in the sanitarium. You'll come out and see Dr. Reeves regularly. And we'll open up our shop, Clay." She tried to sound cheerful. "Next fall or winter."

"Di, do you honestly think we can do something with our lives?"

"We will. Of course we will. Don't even think otherwise."

In Clay's room she alternated between helping him pack and looking out a window into the winter-dark morning to watch for Deirdre's car. There was a comfortable thought in all of this. She, Deirdre and Clay would never really be alone in the world: they had each other.

She saw Deirdre's car pull up.

"Clay, Deirdre's here."

She walked to the closet and pulled out his Burberry raincoat. Tenderly she draped it about his shoulders. "Let's go down to the car now. Aren't you glad we won't have to drive through a blizzard like the one when we went down to the inauguration?"

A brilliant sun was rising in the sky as they stood before the tall wrought iron gates of the Connecticut sanitarium.

"I'm not crazy," Clay said as they drove up the

wide veranda of the main house. "I just know I need help."

"A crazy guy doesn't ask for help," Diane said. "You get your act together in there, darling. We have a shop to open."

"My mother is going to be pissed off when she gets the bills from here," he giggled. "But with her luck she'll have an insurance policy that'll cover everything."

"We'll come to visit as soon as we're allowed," Diane said. "And you do exactly what the doctors say."

"Yes, mommy," he drawled, but his eyes were serious. "God, I love you two."

That Christmas Diane and her aunt remained in New York, with Deirdre as their houseguest. At the last minute, Diane called Laura and asked her to join them for Christmas dinner. She tried to tell herself it was because Laura was a special part of her life, that it had nothing to do with hearing news about Ira Ross.

On New Year's Day, four years after her Las Vegas marriage, Diane heard on a TV newscast that Chris Ames had married an Italian movie star new to American films and sixteen years his senior.

"He's looking for a mother figure," Deirdre declared, leaning forward to switch off the TV. Diane sat silently. Deirdre knew how much this hurt her—not only because of the failed marriage, but because of the child that might have been born of that marriage. "Hey, Di, let's go out and catch a movie, okay? I think *West Side Story* is at the Rivoli. Or maybe we should see *Exodus* at the RKO. I'm mad about Paul Newman.''

Late in January, Diane and Deirdre drove up to visit with Clay. He was optimistic about the future, full of plans for the shop and vowing a long-term commitment to therapy. His mother phoned regularly. She was scheduled to drive up for a visit the following week.

"Before she goes into a New York hospital for some minor surgery.'' There was a humorous glint in his eyes. "That probably means another facelift. She's acting like a sixteen-year-old about this retired army colonel, whom I'm supposed to call Uncle Henry if we ever meet. I'm nervous about some changes she said she's made in the Bermuda house. Why don't you two run down for a week while mother's in the hospital fighting gravity? She'd love to have the servants busy.''

"I can't,'' Deirdre said. "I promised to go to my grandmother's for ten days. All of a sudden she's anxious to see her only grandchild. The heart attack last month scared the hell out of her.''

He turned to Diane.

"Why don't you go down with your aunt? I'll make all the arrangements.''

"I'll talk to Aunt Claudia,'' Diane said, not expecting her aunt to agree. But Clay seemed so anxious for her to spend some time at the Bermuda house.

"Call me tonight or tomorrow so I'll catch mother

before she leaves for New York. And tell me every little change mother's made—even if it's only the placemats.''

Laura deliberately dallied at her desk until everyone except Bernie had left for the day. They were going out to dinner straight from the office. It was imperative, Bernie always reminded her, that nobody know about them. She slid a manuscript into her attaché case, reached for the smart black coat she had bought at Saks' after-Christmas sale for more than a week's salary, and headed for Bernie's office.

Bernie glanced up and gestured for her to sit down while he continued to listen to a voice at the other end of the phone.

''Great Tom. I'm looking forward to our get-together. Yes, I'm sure we can. Good. See you then.''

He put down the phone and leaned back in the leather swivel chair, his eyes narrowed in concentration.

''Problems?'' She knew her own position depended on Bernie's clout in the company.

''Nothing I can't handle. Listen, I want you to arrange to take four days on leave next week. Make some personal excuse. We're heading down to Bermuda on business.''

''If it's business, then why am I asking for leave?'' When she attended that convention with Bernie last October, it had been considered part of her regular work week.

''This isn't Menlow Films business.'' His smile was smug. ''This is a side deal. You'll go with me as

424

my associate. Go buy some gorgeous clothes at Saks and Bergdorf's. But remember, Bermuda isn't Florida. Think in terms of spring clothes this time of year." He reached into a drawer for his checkbook. "Look expensive. We have to convince a multi-millionaire Georgia industrialist that we're the hottest team in independent films."

"Is something going sour with Menlow?" For the past six months she had overheard bits of disturbing conversations about profit and loss statements.

"Clayton Enterprises may be dumping Menlow."

Laura was suddenly cold. If that happened, there'd be a frantic overhaul. Would Bernie be out? How safe would *her* job be in the new set-up? She knew she'd be in trouble without Bernie.

"The board figures one year is long enough to know whether they've got a hot property or a dog. They're trying to negotiate a sale. If Menlow leaves the Clayton umbrella—" He tore the check out and handed it to her "—I'm in the doghouse. I sold them on buying the company." His eyes were appraising. "But that doesn't mean I'm finished, baby. If the bomb drops, I'll set up as an independent producer. It's important to sell Tom Mason on bankrolling a film."

At that she brightened. If Bernie meant to be an independent producer, then she could be important to him. He might be a financial wizard, but he had no sense of what would make a commercial movie. That was a special talent. She had it; Bernie didn't. She would start off in his new company as his assistant. Then she would become an associate producer by making herself indispensable to him.

Laura arranged for a week's leave to rush to the bedside of her "dying grandmother," hoping that no one would connect her personal emergency with Bernie's winter vacation jaunt to Bermuda. It was understood that his wife was flying in from California to accompany him. He didn't have to worry about her calling him in New York. He'd given her the Bermuda number for any emergency.

Snow blanketed the city the night before Laura and Bernie were to leave. She worried their flight might be canceled. It was the first time she had ever flown, the first time, in fact, that she had ever been off American soil. The knowledge was intoxicating. She was awake and in the shower before six o'clock. Bernie liked early flights. He was picking her up in a limousine.

Fighting yawns, she was downstairs in the dingy foyer ten minutes before Bernie was due to show, confident that her neat-white suit with its smart beige-and-white silk surah striped blouse, tucked and sashed at the waist, was not only smart but flattering. Over the suit she wore a feather-light mohair-and-wool coat, beige streaked with rust in a subtle check. She carried a scaled-down calfskin bag. Purses were smaller than last year.

The Vuitton luggage at her feet was on loan from Bernie.

A limousine pulled up at the curb. Laura hurried out as the driver opened the door for her.

"You look good," Bernie approved. "I understand Mason has an eye for sexy-looking women."

Laura tensed.

"Am I supposed to be bait?" Her tone was wary.

Bernie laughed.

"He can look, that's all." His hand slid beneath her coat. "You're along on this trip as my very sharp associate. I told him you have an uncanny feeling for what's commercial in story lines." That much was true. Laura smiled, relieved. "We'll discuss four with Mason. You look through my notes on the plane. By the time we land in Bermuda, you'll know what to push." Bernie knew *she* would make the final decision.

"Where are we staying?" Laura had stopped by the Bermuda Tourist Bureau for brochures. She knew Bernie would choose a luxury hotel. She hoped it would be the Princess on the harbor near Hamilton.

"Mason is putting us up at his house. Didn't I tell you? He has a house in Georgetown, one in Bermuda, an estate in the Atlanta suburbs, a penthouse in Manhattan, and a pied-à-terre in London."

"Sounds exciting." She really *was* moving up in the world. Christmas dinner at Diane's house on Fifth Avenue . . . and now a guest at Tom Mason's house in Bermuda for four days and three nights! Even Ira had been impressed that she was traveling to Bermuda on business. She hadn't mentioned that it wasn't Menlow business.

At the airport they were delayed while a crew shoveled snow off the runway. When they took off, Bernie gave her his notes. She read with total absorption, ignoring the fantasy of fluffy white clouds and blue sky outside her window. The last forty minutes before the plane came down at the Bermuda airport, she argued with Bernie about the choice of material.

Now she understood why he had told her to hold back on the four sets of bound galleys she considered most commercial. Bernie Kramer, independent producer, meant to have first crack at what came into Menlow at this point. If they could make a deal with Mason, then Bernie would put in a bid for the material they chose. She would not pass it along to the executive story editor.

She was aware of an unexpected surge of excitement as the plane settled down on the runway at the small Bermuda airport. *She was in a foreign country*. Even the swift trip through Customs seemed an adventure. Now she was stepping out into the sun-washed Bermuda air.

As arranged, a limousine was waiting to whisk them away from the airport to Mason's house. Bernie had been in Bermuda only once before, on his honeymoon eleven years earlier. He was proud of the distance he had traveled career-wise since then.

From her window, Laura watched the parade of pastel-colored houses, surrounded by semitropical flowers. Sooner than she anticipated—though she remembered the island was only twenty-one miles long and one-half mile wide—they were turning off the road into the circling private driveway of a modern multilevel masterpiece of stucco and glass that hung over the incredibly blue ocean. A pair of smiling servants ambled over to the limousine to collect their luggage.

A tall, lean, athletic-appearing man in gray slacks and sweater waited to welcome them on the terrace that faced the road. Bernie placed a hand at her elbow in a gesture she knew was to indicate that their relationship was both professional and personal. Laura approached Tom Mason with a polite but reserved smile.

"Did you have a pleasant flight?" Tom asked when the introductions were over. His eyes rested admiringly on Laura.

"Beautiful." She smiled at him. "They were shoveling snow from the runway so we could take off, and here we find this." She gestured her pleasure in the warmth and sunshine.

"Ernestine will show you up to your rooms," he said as his elegantly groomed black housekeeper appeared. "We'll have lunch on the rear terrace whenever you're ready."

Laura's bedroom, decorated in white and gold, had a white Carrara marble parquet floor. The furniture was an eclectic blend of old and new. The bathroom was built around a sunken, round mosaic bathtub of white and gold. A small terrace was accessible from the bedroom.

At once thrilled and self-conscious in such lush surroundings, Laura changed from skirt and sweater into a Mary Quant dress that showed off her marvelous legs. Despite his age—around fifty, Laura guessed—Tom Mason was an attractive man. She was drawn to the aura of power he exuded. Rich and powerful men had a special kind of excitement. At the same time she reminded herself that she was here as Bernie's associate and romantic interest. *Nothing more.*

Trying to appear self-assured and casual, Laura went downstairs. As she arrived at the black-marble-floored foyer, Ernestine appeared to guide her to the sprawling first-level terrace that hung over the water. The luncheon table was set for three. Bernie and Tom were sitting at the far end of the terrace.

From the minute they sat down to a lunch of famous Bermuda lobster, Tom played the cordial southern host to perfection. He even insisted that his chauffeur drive Laura into Hamilton so that she might spend the afternoon shopping along colorful Front Street.

"No woman comes to Hamiltion without shopping for perfume and cashmeres. Hector will wait for you and bring you back at your leisure, though I must warn you that most of the shops close at five-thirty." While he glanced at his watch, Laura shot a questioning glance at Bernie, who gave a barely perceptible nod of approval. "Don't be polite," Tom said. "Have your lunch and run."

It never failed to give Laura pleasure to step inside a limousine, but today was special. Alone in the luxury of Tom Mason's Mercedes, she remembered the Newport years, when her poverty had been highlighted every summer by the arrival of the super-rich resort people. Who would have believed that Kathy Devlin's little girl would grow up to travel about Bermuda in such style? It was high season in Bermuda. How many of the Newport Old Guard were here now?

She recognized Front Street from the travel brochures, leaned forward for a clearer view of the bobby who directed traffic from the birdcage stand at the corner of Front and Queen streets. She was fascinated by the ships lined up at the water's edge right on Front Street; tourists from the cruise ships had only to walk across the street and into the shops.

Hector deposited her in front of Trimingham's with the promise that he would check regularly along Front Street until she was ready to return to the house. She'd already decided to limit her purchases to one bottle of French perfume, and one cashmere sweater from Scotland.

Before going into the store she inspected the Hamilton landmark bearing the legend "Est. 1844," admiring its quaint and colorful decor, its shop windows shaded by a storewide portico, with white shutters at the second-floor windows.

For a few minutes she was content to stroll through the aisles and browse. She smiled, remembering her awe of fine department stores like Saks—where she now had a charge account—when she first arrived in New York. It had been a year before she dared wander above the main floor of the Fifth Avenue department store. Now she looked for the perfume bar. When she found it, she stood before the display of French perfumes, already knowing which one she was going to choose but enjoying a moment of indecision.

"Laura?" an astonished feminine voice—a familiar voice—whirled her away from an atomizer of Diorissimo.

"Diane!" She stared. "Well, how wonderful to run into you! What are you doing here?"

"Just here for a few days. And you? Are you here on vacation?"

"Actually, it's business," Laura said. It *was* the

truth, she told herself. "I came down with my boss to sit in on a deal he's working on with Tom Mason. He's—"

"Tom Mason is involved in the movie business?" Diane looked astonished.

"Do you know him?"

"I met him very briefly in Washington during the inauguration. He has a home down there next door to Clay Brentwood's aunt." She hesitated. "Are you busy shopping, or could we go somewhere for tea? We *are* in a British colony—tea seems appropriate."

"I'd love it," Laura said. "Do you know a place around here? I only arrived this morning."

"I've been here three days. I came down with Aunt Claudia. I thought it might be good for her to sit in the sun for a week. Clay offered us his mother's house while she's away."

It pleased Laura that Diane seemed to be glad to see her. Her mother would have said, *"It was meant for you two to meet. God moves in mysterious ways."* Laura had the feeling that her life would forever be entwined with Diane's.

"After all that snow in New York the sun feels marvelous, doesn't it?" she said. "And the pace here seems so restful."

Diane smiled.

"It does. Listen, how about going to the Parliament Club here on Front Street? We can have tea on the terrace. Or we could go to the Princess Hotel—"

"The Princess," Laura said, telling herself that she would pick up the check. The Princess might be a plush resort hotel, but she had enough in her wallet to take care of tea for the two of them.

"The Brentwood car is waiting right down the street. The chauffeur will take us to the hotel. It's just a few minutes away. But first, if you don't mind, I'd like to drop by the Phoenix Drug Store to pick up a copy of the *Royal Gazette* for Aunt Claudia. She loves reading the local newspapers. I think she was fascinated when she learned that the *Gazette* was published from 1803 to 1816 by three women—the daughters of the owner who had died. They're probably the first women newspaper publishers in the world." Diane looked wistful. "It must have been wonderful to be a pioneer in a man's world."

"It's still a man's world," Laura said wryly. "There isn't one woman at the head of a film studio."

"But you plan to change all that, don't you?" Diane smiled, but Laura saw the respect in her eyes.

"Give me another fifteen years," Laura said. "I'm going to make it there."

When Laura returned to the Mason mansion-by-the-sea at close to six o'clock, she found Tom and Bernie having cocktails on a seaside deck.

"You didn't shop?" Topm lifted an eyebrow in mock disbelief.

"I got as far as the perfume bar at Trimingham's and ran into an old friend." She made a point of being casual. "Diane Dickenson. She's staying at the Brentwood house with her aunt." He remembered Diane, all right—she could see it in his eyes. "We went to the Princess for tea."

"Diane's here in Bermuda?" He leaned forward. "Did you tell her you're my guest?"

"Yes. She said she'd met you in Washington."

"Then why don't I ring her up and ask her to join us for dinner tonight?" He was already on his feet. Bernie was struggling to hide his exasperation. He was impatient to talk business. Clearly Tom was in no rush.

"Did you have to mention you'd met Diane Dickenson?" Bernie muttered when Tom was out of hearing.

"I knew *they'd* met."

"So what?"

"I have a hunch that having Diane here for dinner will be good for us."

"I hope so," he said grimly. "Because if I don't make a deal with Tom Mason, we'll have to do some fast hustling back in New York. Remember that phone call I made at the airport? It was to New York. Menlow's been sold. So get your fur coat ready, baby; we may both be out in the cold."

Chapter Twenty-Five

Pausing before the cheval mirror in her Early American bedroom, Diane inspected her short, tiered blue chiffon dinner dress with an air of uncertainty. Clay had told her that except on formal evenings at the hotels people in Bermuda usually dressed casually. The dress was right, she decided. Tom Mason would expect this for dinner at his home. She reached for the matching blue velvet coat and hurried downstairs and out onto the veranda where her aunt sat gazing at the approaching twilight—a delicate blend of charcoal and pink sky over dusk-mutted turquoise ocean.

Again she felt guilty that she was leaving her aunt alone for the evening. The invitation had included Aunt Claudia, but Diane knew she wouldn't accept.

"It's chilly out here, Aunt Claudia. Shouldn't you be inside?"

"Oh, I'll go indoors in another five minutes, dear," Claudia promised cheerfully. "It's just so beautiful out here."

Diane frowned as she tucked the lap robe more securely about her aunt.

"I shouldn't have let you talk me into going out tonight," she said. "But I think it's too late to call and say I can't make it."

"Don't be ridiculous. You'll have a lovely evening. I'm glad you're finding some diversion here."

"Tom Mason is sending his car for me." Diane sat down beside her aunt. "You do like the Brentwood house, don't you?" The stately old colonial seemed a perfect background for Aunt Claudia.

"Oh my, yes. Clay did a marvelous job of decorating. I adore those Tiffany windows he found for the library. He has a real flair for blending different periods, and a genuine feeling for what's right for a house."

Diane turned as a maid approached.

"Mr. Mason's car is waiting for you, Miss Dickenson."

"Thank you, Melinda. I'll be right there." She leaned forward to kiss her aunt. "Don't stay out here till you're chilled."

While the chauffeur drove her to the Mason house, Diane recalled her fleeting encounter with Tom Mason just over a year ago. She had sensed a kind of ruthlessness beneath his cool charm—a Rhett Butler quality that would be attractive to move women. Even at his age. Jessica said he had two married daughters in their late twenties. Apparently he and his wife had only the pretense of a marriage.

Diane was relieved to find that Laura and her business associate were downstairs when she arrived. She was glad she had dressed for dinner. Both men were in dinner jackets. Laura wore a long dress of pleated black crepe, cut in classic, narrow lines.

Diane responded to Tom Mason's warm welcome, and was again drawn to his aura of inner strength. She would never have suspected him to be interested in filmmaking. But Laura said the film business as she had known it was changing. Men like Mannie Coleman were being replaced by conglomerate-trained corporate executives.

Over a dinner of filet of sole almandine and fresh asparagus, Tom dominated the conversation, keeping conversation away from the movie world. He talked mainly about himself—with special pride in his rapid rise to the top.

"I'll be flying down to Cuernavaca in May or June for my divorce." His eyes rested on Diane for an instant before moving on to Laura and Bernie Kramer. "If you're in the mood for a few days in Mexico, I'd be delighted to have you as my guests."

She knew by the way he looked at her that he was soon to be free of marital ties, and wanted her to know it. She supposed she ought to be flattered. What had Clay once said about men like Tom Mason? *"Men in powerful positions have a special sexual attraction, darling. That's why beautiful women flock around them."*

"How long will you be in Bermuda?" Tom asked Diane while they seated themselves in his private parlor for after-dinner liqueurs.

"We'll be flying back to New York in four days." Diane was uncomfortably aware of Laura's eyes on them.

"Why don't we all go sailing tomorrow afternoon?" he said casually. "I keep a boat here on the bay. Don't worry, Bernie," he teased, "we'll have plenty of hours to talk business. Whenever I'm on the island, I like to be outdoors as much as possible." He must work at staying so trim and fit, Diane decided. And he had to know how attractive that deep tan was with his salt-and-pepper hair. "In Atlanta—or at the other mills around the state—I'm usually tied to a desk."

"Sailing sounds marvelous," Laura said. Diane noticed that she had waited for a nod of acquiescence from Bernie.

Diane was uncomfortable.

"I don't think I should leave my aunt alone tomorrow."

"Oh come on, Diane, we'll have you back within three hours," Tom said. "You said your aunt was here to rest. There's nothing more restful than lying on a chaise and gazing out at the water. We'll pick you up with the car at one. Have a picnic lunch aboard the sailboat. I'll have you back at your aunt's side no later than four. I promise."

"Diane, it'll be such fun," Laura said.

Diane wavered.

"All right. But—" she smiled at Tom. "I'm going to hold you to that four o'clock deadline."

When Diane returned to the Brentwood house, Aunt Claudia had already retired for the night. The next morning at the breakfast table, a maid told her that her aunt had ordered breakfast served in bed this morning. That wasn't like Aunt Claudia, she thought uneasily.

Immediately after breakfast she went up to her

aunt's bedroom. Claudia was lying on a chaise by the window. She looked pale and drawn.

"Aunt Claudia, you're not feeling well." Diane dropped to the edge of the chaise.

"I'm just a bit tired from the trip. I thought I'd rest up today. I'll stay up here in my room until dinnertime." Claudia's smile was gentle. "I'm glad you found your friend Laura in town. You two must go sightseeing together."

"We've been invited to go sailing on Tom Mason's boat this afternoon," she said. "But I—"

"You'll go, of course," Claudia turned to gaze out the window. "The color of the sea down here is exquisite. I enjoy just sitting here and looking at it."

"I don't like leaving you when you're not feeling well—"

"I'm simply tired, my dear. There's nothing you can do for me by staying here, Diane. Have a lovely sail this afternoon."

Bermuda weather this time of year was glorious—too cool for swimming in the sea, but with the caressing warmth of perfect spring days. Diane told herself she ought to be enjoying this parcel of time aboard Tom's "sailboat"—a three-masted schooner complete with engines and stabilizers, and capable of crossing an ocean—but she was worried about her aunt. The lunch packed in a wicker basket by the Mason cook was delicious—pâté, crusty French bread, and cheese. Diane tried to join in the merriment of the small party.

"You're concerned about your aunt, aren't you?"

Tom said, pouring coffee from a thermos.

"She's not well." Diane hadn't realized it was that obvious. "Aunt Claudia never complains—we never know how badly she's feeling."

"If you'd like to have a local doctor see her, call me," he said. "I know a top-grade physician here."

"Thank you. I'll remember."

Diane was relieved to return home and find her aunt on the veranda, reading the morning's *Royal Gazette*. Maybe she had just needed a rest. They were served tea trays on the veranda, and Diane reported on the afternoon's excursion.

"I've been invited to swim tomorrow morning in the indoor pool at Tom Mason's house," she reported. At Clay's insistence she had packed a swimsuit. "It's Laura's last full day on the island. She leaves for New York next morning"—a day earlier than she and Aunt Claudia were to return to New York.

Now Diane's thoughts focused on Clay, up in the Connecticut sanitarium. Did Clay know that his mother's army colonel was living here in the house much of the time? According to the servants, Colonel Williams had gone to New York with Mrs. Brentwood. His presence was apparent throughout the house. A pipe rack and a half-used container of a fine British tobacco in the library. A chess board and pieces set up at a small table near the fireplace in the living room. Diane knew that Mrs. Brentwood was not a chess player. The *Wall Street Journal*—addressed to Colonel Henry Williams—arrived every day by mail.

At dusk Diane and Claudia went indoors. A fire

had been lighted in the library, where they warmed themselves against the evening chill until dinner was announced. Immediately after dinner Claudia retired to her room. Diane read the copy of *Time* she had picked up yesterday at the Phoenix Drug Store until she found herself fighting yawns. All that sea air, she thought, and abandoned reading to go up to her room and to bed.

Again Claudia did not appear at the breakfast table. Immediately after breakfast Diane went up to her aunt's bedroom. Claudia was still in bed, sipping at a cup of tea, her breakfast tray otherwise untouched. This morning Diane could see the pain in her aunt's eyes.

"Aunt Claudia, Tom Mason knows a doctor in Hamilton—"

"No," Claudia snapped. "But I would like to return to New York today if we can get reservations on a flight. I can be ready in an hour."

"I'll go make calls." But she was frightened—she knew her aunt wouldn't make such a request unless she was feeling very ill. "I'll send up Melinda to pack for you."

At the phone Diane remembered that a car was coming to drive her to the Mason house. She hastily called Tom to explain that she and her aunt were returning to New York on the first available flight.

"You're returning because your aunt isn't well?" Tom asked.

"Yes. I'm sure she's in great pain if she's asked to go back to New York—"

"I'll call the airport immediately and order my flight crew to stand by." He was calm but brisk.

"We'll all fly to New York together on my plane. Laura and Bernie will come along with us—we've finished up our business. And I have to head for London myself in a few days. Your aunt will be far more comfortable on my plane than on a commercial airliner. There's a private cabin with a bed where she can rest during the trip."

"I don't know how to thank you," Diane stammered. She felt unable to cope with this emergency.

"It's frightening to be sick in a strange country," Tom said. "I'll call the hospital here and have an ambulance take your aunt from the house to the airport. Then I'll make arrangements for an ambulance to be waiting at Idlewild when we arrive. Can you both be ready within an hour?"

"Yes. It's wonderful of you to help this way, Tom—I really do appreciate it."

"Phone your aunt's doctor in New York right now," he said. "Let him talk to her if he's reachable. He may decide to hospitalize her on arrival in New York. We don't want to have her shunted around any more than necessary."

"I'll call him right away." *Thank God for Tom Mason.*

"She's going to be fine, Diane," Tom comforted. "We'll be back in New York in time for a late lunch."

Tom's private plane was as luxurious as his home. The fuselage interior was divided into two units: the forward section was furnished with leather banquette and matching lounge chairs, a marble-topped table that provided dining space, and a small desk jutting out from the wall.

Tom pushed open the door to the rear section, where there was a small bedroom, equipped with double bed and its own washroom. Claudia was immediately installed in the private cabin.

"What a kind man," she whispered, squeezing Diane's hand when they were alone in the cabin. "I've so dreaded the flight."

Diane smiled.

"Tom took charge of everything, Aunt Claudia. And Dr. Weinstein has arranged for you to go directly to the hospital for treatment. Not that he feels this is serious. But he wants to run some tests and it'll be easier for you to go straight to the hospital."

"When I first fought with your mother for custody of you, Diane, I never guessed how dear you would become to me." She managed a wisp of a smile. Diane understood how difficult it was for Claudia, always so reserved, to talk about this. "I only knew that I couldn't allow you to be brought up in the atmosphere she provided."

"I've always been glad you did," Diane said.

"I must confess, my dear, I was scared to death of you. What did I know about raising children? But now you're very precious to me. The child I never had."

Tears in her eyes, Diane kissed her aunt.

Throughout the flight, Laura and Tom came into the cabin to speak to Claudia, Tom bringing pots of fresh-brewed tea. Usually reserved with strangers, Claudia opened up to talk with Tom, who—like herself—was a connoisseur of teas and always traveled with a tin of his favorite blend. Privately

443

Laura confided to Diane that Bernie and she had secured a commitment from Tom that set them up as independent producers, and she was ecstatic.

At Idlewild an ambulance was waiting. Diane insisted on riding with Claudia to the hospital. Both Tom and Laura said they would phone to check on her aunt's condition in the evening. Diane stayed at the hospital until Claudia insisted she go home.

For the next three days Diane commuted between the Fifth Avenue house and the hospital. She talked with Deirdre, dallying longer than expected at her grandmother's house in California because "Grandma just hired this gorgeous private detective since a ghastly robbery last month." She talked to Clay, who was determined to remain at the sanitarium until he was confident he would not go back to pills and alcohol.

Laura called to ask about Claudia and to report that "All hell has broken loose at Menlow, both in California and New York." Both Laura and Bernie Kramer had been ousted, as anticipated; but they were preparing to take off momentarily for California to move into production on their first independent film.

"Diane, I'm moving ahead so fast I'm dizzy. But that's the movie business," Laura said, gloating.

On her third night back in New York Diane allowed Tom to persuade her to have dinner with him. They drove up to a secluded restaurant in Westchester County, where the food was superb and where they would be unrecognized. She marveled at the way she could relax in his company. She felt comforted and protected.

Back in the city by midnight, she invited him into the house for a drink. Tomorrow night he was leaving for business in England and flying from there to Egypt and then to Japan. She might not see him again for months. She was eager to express her gratitude.

Philippe responded to the doorbell. His face was grave.

"Mrs. Avery is waiting up for you, Miss Diane," he said. "She's in the library."

"Thank you, Philippe." Why was Mrs. Avery waiting up for her? She'd been with Aunt Claudia less than four hours ago. She was responding well to the new medication. "Mrs. Avery—?"

Mrs. Avery appeared at the library doorway.

"Dr. Weinstein called," she reported, trying to mask her anxiety. "He said to ring him at this number no matter what time you returned."

"Did he say anything else?" Diane took the slip of paper.

"No, but Mrs. Carstairs called." Mrs. Avery's voice wavered. "She said to tell you she's scheduled for surgery in the morning. She asked me to cancel all her appointments for the next four weeks."

"Aunt Claudia called and I wasn't here!" Diane turned to Tom in anguish.

"Diane, you were with her all day," Tom put her arm around her. "Phone Dr. Weinstein—"

"Good night, Miss Diane. Mr. Mason." Mrs. Avery seemed anxious to leave before she started crying.

Diane walked to the phone. *Why this sudden rush into surgery?* What had Aunt Claudia been keeping from her?

On the second ring Dr. Weinstein picked up the phone.

"Hello, Dr. Weinstein."

"It's Diane Dickenson."

"Diane, we've arrived at the proper medication to handle your aunt's arthritis." His matter-of-fact tone mollified her for an instant. "However, in the routine testing we discovered a tumor in her left breast. It's quite likely that it's benign, but of course we have to check it out. Immediately. I've scheduled her for surgery at nine o'clock tomorrow morning. Her surgeon, Dr. Roman, is one of the finest—"

"Breast cancer?" Diane interrupted, white with shock.

"We have to face that possibility," he said gently. "I've discussed this with Miss Carstairs. If the biopsy shows that the tumor is malignant, we'll do a mastectomy immediately. The statistics are most encouraging." Diane flinched. *Her Aunt Claudia was not a statistic.* "But," he added, "we don't even know that it's malignant yet, so let's not panic. Most tumors prove to be benign."

"There's no way of knowing through X-ray?"

"We can't be sure until we're in there. But the success rate in this kind of surgery improves every year."

This wasn't real—it was a nightmare. Four hours ago she had sat beside Aunt Claudia and talked about this year's April in Paris Ball. She'd tried to coax her into a trip to Phoenix or Palm Springs. And now Dr. Weinstein was talking about a mastectomy. The thought of her painfully modest aunt exposed to that kind of mutilation . . .

"Aunt Claudia understands what may happen?"

"She understands, Diane," he said softly. "I explained how up until a few years ago every surgeon did a radical mastectomy if he found a malignancy. That is, he would remove the entire breast plus the lymph nodes in the armpit and the pectoral muscles. But now the surgeons prefer the simple mastectomy—when it's possible. They remove only the breast."

"Dr. Weinstein," Diane forced herself to say it. To think it. "Could she die under surgery?"

"In any surgical procedure there is some element of risk," he said cautiously. "But I feel confident that Miss Carstairs will come through the surgery well— whether we simply remove a benign tumor or the entire breast."

"Will I be able to see her before she goes into the operating room?" Diane struggled to keep her voice even.

"You'll be able to see her in the morning, but she'll be sedated. Please stay only a few moments."

"Thank you, Dr. Weinstein."

Haltingly Diane repeated Dr. Weinstein's conversation to Tom. Why hadn't she stayed at the hospital tonight? Why had she gone rushing off to dinner with Tom?

Tom, of course, tried to be encouraging.

"She'll be all right. I'll drive by to pick you up at eight-thirty tomorrow morning. I'll stay with you while she's in surgery. Now go upstairs and try to sleep." He led her away from the phone and toward the door. "Your aunt will come through this with flying colors."

Chapter Twenty-Six

In bed, Diane lay wide awake. She could cope with her aunt's arthritis, but cancer . . . Sweet, gentle Aunt Claudia. *Why?*

Staring into the darkness, Diane remembered the one time Laura had spoken about her mother's illness, the horror of standing by and watching her die of cancer. She had to talk to Laura. *Now.* It was three hours earlier in California—she wouldn't be waking her.

She left the bed and hurried into the sitting room of her suite, where she'd left her address book. Cold despite the heat from the radiators, she returned to the bedroom clutching the small, leather-bound book, slipped into a robe, and sat at the edge of her bed to telephone Laura. Praying she would be home.

The phone rang a dozen times. Laura wasn't home, she decided in disappointment. But just as she was about to put down the receiver, Laura's voice came to her.

"Hello." Bright and reassuring. *But Laura didn't know.*

"Laura, it's Diane." She paused, bracing herself for what must be said.

"Are you all right?" Laura asked anxiously.

"I had to talk to you. I remembered how your mother died, and—" Diane took a deep breath. "It's Aunt Claudia. She's going in for surgery in the morning. The doctors found a tumor in her left breast—"

"Diane, a tumor doesn't always mean cancer."

"I remember what you said about your mother. Those awful long weeks in the hospital. The pipes and the machines—and the pain. Laura, why do these things happen?"

"Diane, even if it is cancer, your aunt has so much on her side. She'll have the finest care in the world. My mother was in the charity ward of a city hospital. The nurses came when they could." Diane could hear—even now—Laura's frustration and anger. "Your aunt will have private nurses around the clock. Everything that can be done to make her comfortable will be done. Women survive breast cancer,"

"Some of them die."

"Diane, she'll be all right. She's got the best surgeons, the finest nursing care. Don't torment yourself this way."

"I've never been through anything like this before. Only my grandmother's stroke. And I barely knew her—" She remembered visiting her other grandmother at the nursing home—and arriving there to find her gone. She remembered the desolation she had felt then.

"Diane, being sick-poor and being sick-rich is worlds apart. You know she'll have the best of everything."

"Being rich won't save her life—"

"It'll go a long way toward it. The odds are on your aunt's side, Diane. And you don't even know that it *is* cancer. It may be nothing serious."

"Thank you for listening to me, Laura."

"Call me." Laura's voice was gentle.

"I will," Diane whispered.

She put the phone down, suddenly feeling exhausted, and slid beneath the comforter again. It was close to dawn before she fell into dream-troubled sleep. The shrill intrusion of her alarm clock woke her at seven. She lay still, trying to prepare herself to face the day ahead.

She called down to the kitchen and asked for coffee. When Tom's limousine pulled up before the house, she was in the foyer, dressed and waiting. She opened the door and walked out into the cold, sunlit morning as Tom crossed the sidewalk to her side.

"Traffic's light this morning," he said, a hand at her elbow. "We'll be at the hospital in five minutes."

Tom held her small, cold hand in his while they drove through the city streets.

"Diane, this will most likely be minor surgery. Don't think the worst. We all spend so much time in life worrying about things that never happen. We should save ourselves for the real crises."

"We had no hint of it," she said. "Nothing."

"It'll probably turn out to be nothing serious," he said. "She could be home in three days."

Diane went to her aunt's suite. A nurse was with her. This morning, wearing a starkly utilitarian hospital gown rather than one of the fine silk, high-necked gowns she usually wore, her gray hair in a braid over her shoulder, she seemed so defenseless. She looked up when Diane came in.

"Don't look so worried, darling."

In the hall, Diane talked to Dr. Weinstein and the surgeon. With a cheerfulness obviously meant to reassure her, they explained the procedure briefly. She glanced at her watch. It was almost nine o'clock.

"How long will the operation take?" she asked.

"If it's benign, she'll be in the recovery room by eleven A.M.," the surgeon said.

"And if it isn't?" Diane forced herself to ask.

"It'll be well into the afternoon. Excuse us, Miss Dickenson. We'd like to go in to see your aunt now."

A few minutes later Claudia was wheeled into the operating room. Diane and Tom sat in her suite and waited. Twenty minutes later Tom's chauffeur arrived with a breakfast tray for two.

"I was sure you hadn't eaten," he said, dismissing the chauffeur.

"I'm trying to be optimistic." Her smile was awry. This morning the house had seemed empty and intimidating without her aunt. Aunt Claudia had been the one constant in her life since she was eleven. And now she might lose her . . .

She did her best to eat, only to please Tom, but all she could think about was the surgery. How would her aunt deal with the trauma of a mastectomy?

Tom talked, mostly about his childhood, and despite her anxiety she found herself caught up in the humorous, poignant stories of a nine-year-old Tom Mason picking cotton for three hours every morning before he set off for school, twelve-year-old Tom Mason working at odd menial jobs so that he could go to high school. He had been determined to become neither tenant farmer nor cotton-mill worker.

"Until I was twenty-two," he said, "I'd never been farther away from Atlanta than Columbus—which is about a hundred and twenty miles to the south. I've made up since. I've got business in every corner of the globe today. But my base of operations is Atlanta, and my permanent home is in Atlanta."

When eleven A.M. had come and gone and Claudia was still in the operating room, Diane suspected the worst.

"Why is it taking so long?" she asked. But they both knew the answer.

"I'll go out and rustle up some coffee for us. I won't be long."

Diane crossed to the window to look down upon the city. Thousands of people were going about their daily lives. It was hard to believe. She tried to focus on the fact that a mastectomy would save her aunt's life. Dr. Weinstein had said so, over and over again.

Diane closed her eyes. *Please God, let Aunt Claudia be all right.*

"Diane—" At Tom's voice, she turned away from the window. His face was serious. Dr. Weinstein stood beside him.

"How is she?"

"She came through the surgery well," Dr. Weinstein said. "She'll be in the recovery room for a while." He hesitated. "I'm afraid we had to do a radical mastectomy—"

Diane turned white.

"Oh my God—"

"But Dr. Roman is confident that the malignancy has been removed. It's fortunate that she was not responding to the arthritis medication. We might not have discovered the tumor for another six months. By then it could have spread further."

"Thank you, Dr. Weinstein." She forced herself to be polite. "And thank Dr. Roman for us."

She'd have to ask Aunt Claudia's priest to visit her. *That* bothered her. She and Aunt Claudia were Jewish—no matter that both of them had been baptized. A few words and a splash of water could not eradicate their Jewish heritage. But seeing her priest would bring comfort to Aunt Claudia. That was all that mattered now.

She wondered briefly if she should ask her mother to come home from Palm Beach and then decided against it. Mother and Aunt Claudia had not spoken for years, except in public, and Mother was still furious that she had not flown to Paris for Charles's funeral. How sad that two sisters could be estranged at a time like this.

Even before Claudia was brought to her suite from the recovery room, the wide window in the bedroom was a bower of spring flowers that Tom had ordered early in the morning. He waited in the reception room while Diane spent a few moments with

Claudia, still groggy from medication but lucid enough to know what had happened. She lay immobile, a massive white bandage around her chest, her left arm resting on a pillow, tubes inserted in one hand.

"Dr. Weinstein says you'll be fine now," Diane said tenderly. "In no time you'll be home again." Dr. Weinstein had told her that a therapist would help Aunt Claudia accept the surgery and at the proper time demonstrate the exercises that would be part of her recuperation. She knew that psychologically and physically it would be a painful process.

"I think she's drifting off to sleep again," the private duty nurse told Diane. "She's heavily sedated."

Tom postponed his trip to London for another four days. He coaxed Diane from her aunt's bedside for lunch each day, picked her up at the hospital each evening to take her out to dinner in quiet little restaurants where they would not be recognized. Every day there were fresh flowers from Tom. Thus far Claudia insisted that no other than the household staff know that she had undergone a mastectomy. She was not yet prepared to face well-wishers.

Claudia's recovery was slow, but Diane pushed everything aside to help her. Deirdre returned from California, and Diane was touched by how sweet and sympathetic she was with Claudia.

"Di, I want to cry every time I look there and know what's missing. Do you suppose she ever knew what it's like to have a man touch her breasts?"

At Claudia's urging, Deirdre took Diane to luncheons and nights at the theater. One afternoon, they drove up to the sanitarium to visit Clay.

On his return from Japan, the last point on his itinerary, Tom stayed in New York for three days at his Sutton Place penthouse. Once again he drove Diane to Westchester County for dinner. He talked animatedly about his travels, then about the problems with his mills in the South.

"I'll shut them down before I'll submit to unions, Diane. In a democracy, why does a man have to take orders from a union leader out for glory when *he's* taking all the gambles? I'm fair to my workers. No mill in the South gives more to its employees. But I refuse to be dictated to by some outsider."

She was relieved that Tom made no romantic overtures. She needed his friendship, his strength. For now, that was enough.

Tom Mason's white Rolls-Royce pulled up before the columned white Greek Revival mansion, flanked by towering magnolias amidst four acres of formal gardens in the lush Atlanta suburb of Buckhead. He smiled, remembering that a recent *Fortune* magazine article had referred to Buckhead as the "biggest encampment of top business executives in the Southeast."

Leaving the car and walking up the steps to the wide veranda of Magnolia Acres he could hear the television set droning on in the upstairs sitting room of his wife's personal wing. Tammy Lee Mason's favorite pastime was watching soap operas.

While his long-time houseman took his luggage to his own rooms, Tom headed down the long hall to his wife's suite. He paused, one hand on the door. For a moment his mind shot back thirty-five years to high school graduation, when Tammy Lee had been seventeen and the prettiest sight he had ever seen.

The youngest in a family of five children, he was the only one to graduate from high school. He had known even then that he would not spend his life working on a farm or at a loom in the cotton mill. He was mad about Tammy Lee Watson and he was going to make a fortune for the two of them.

Well, he made the fortune, but he lost his wife. Tammy Lee knew way back there was no place for her in the new life he was creating. Dammit, it was her fault! She'd refused to grow with him.

She spent a fortune on clothes but always looked like an obese farm wife. She'd never learned to be comfortable with anybody who earned over five thousand a year. And she had refused any kind of professional counseling.

They hadn't shared a bed in nineteen years. Not since the doctors made it clear she'd never give him another child. A son to inherit his dynasty. Tammy Lee was glad he didn't "bother her" anymore. Even in his early years she never seemed to enjoy their sex life—she merely made herself available.

He opened the door and walked inside. Tammy Lee was too caught up in the problems of the Hughes and the Stewarts on "As the World Turns" to notice. Wearing an embroidered kimona, she lay sprawled, barefoot, on a mauve satin lounge chair, her eyes on the TV screen, a box of chocolate-covered cherries

457

on the table beside her.

"Tammy Lee, I'm back," he said brusquely. Surely she wouldn't be too surprised by what he had to say. He'd been hinting about a divorce for years.

"Wait, Tom—please wait for the commercial, okay?"

He crossed to the window to gaze down at the ducks swimming among the blossoms in the water-lily pond. They reminded him of his wife, who seldom moved beyond her own lily pond. Her life revolved around the house and their two spoiled, arrogant daughters and their husbands.

Betsy's husband Clint was planning on running for the state legislature next time around. At least then Tammy Lee might get off her butt to go out to campaign for Clint. The way she did when he ran—unsuccessfully—for district attorney. She would take herself off to that fat farm out in California and dump forty pounds, letting the makeup people and hairstylists give her some temporary polish, all to play the political scene. In maudlin moments she admitted to dreaming of having a son-in-law in the White House.

He'd had more than his share of women who would have been ecstatic to replace Tammy Lee, but it was only during the last year that he had been serious about a divorce. Since he had walked into Jessica Parsons's house in Georgetown and come face to face with Diane Dickenson.

In her own right Diane was as rich as he, so he didn't have to worry about her being after his money. She had style and breeding. Her family was in the *Social Register*. All this was important to him. It never failed to irk him that even with his enormous wealth there were houses in his native Georgia where he was not received socially. In every major city in the world he was welcomed in the finest—and wealthiest—homes, but the watered-down blue-bloods in his hometown would never forget that he came from generations of tenant farmers.

Diane was young and beautiful. At fifty-two he didn't get aroused as easily as he did at twenty-two. But Diane could make him passionate. He could still get it up—maybe not two or three times a night, but often enough to give a young wife a child. With Diane he could have the son Tammy Lee had never given him.

"Tom, have a chocolate cherry—"

"Tammy Lee, we have to talk." He swung away from the window to face her.

"What about?" She reached for a bottle of magenta nail polish and began to apply it to one long nail.

"About a divorce."

She was still for a moment, then sat up with such suddenness her kimono parted to reveal pendulous blue-veined breasts.

"Now Tom, every time you get mad at me you talk like that. What did I do this time?"

"I mean it, Tammy Lee. I want a divorce. You'll be well provided for—you'll never have to worry about money."

"What's the matter?" Her voice was shrill. "That skinny little thing you been keeping all these years getting greedy, honey? Well, you just tell her Tammy Lee is not about to let you off the hook."

"I'm not planning to remarry."

"Then why do you want a divorce? Oh, I know. You think you'll do better with the women if they figure you're a bachelor. 'The richest, most eligible bachelor in America.' Honey, you're fifty-two years old. Haven't you had enough by now?"

"Tammy Lee, you will agree to a divorce because if you don't, I'll make sure Clint never gets elected to any public office. He may have graduated *magna cum laude* from Emory Law School, but he did a disgustingly dumb thing his first year as a practicing attorney. It cost me a bundle to bail him out. The newspapers would have a field day if they got word of it."

"You wouldn't do that to Clint and Betsy," she said with shaky bravado. "You wouldn't dare disgrace your own child."

"I'll do it if you push me." And he meant it. He loved his two spoiled daughters, but they were a painful disappointment. He had no respect for their husbands, either—two weaklings who had married them for their money. "Tammy Lee, you know me. I'm a man who lets nothing stand in the way of what I want. I'll go to Mexico for the divorce. You'll agree. The lawyers will draw up the financial settlement. It won't change your life one bit." Except that he meant for Tammy Lee to move out of this house. He would tell her about that later. The Atlanta house was another symbol of his success. The former plantation mansion, restored far beyond its original glory, was part of his image. "When the papers are ready, you'll sign them. For Betsy."

And without another word he returned to his room, where he placed a telephone call to a New

460

York City florist. His file-cabinet mind reminded him that Diane had once confessed that red roses carried unhappy memories for her.

Nothing must go wrong in this campaign. He'd laid his groundwork well. Within six months, Diane Dickenson would be Mrs. Tom Mason.

Chapter Twenty-Seven

Twice a month Tom Mason was in New York. Either he flew up from Atlanta in his private jet for a weekend, or stopped over between business jaunts to London, Rome, Hong Kong or Tokyo—wherever his vast industrial empire took him. Every time he was in town he arranged to take Diane out to dinner. When he mentioned a flight to Cuernavaca, she assumed his Mexican divorce had gone through. Now that he was "free," they dined at the Colony or Le Pavillon, where a choice table was always available for Tom Mason and Diane Dickenson.

Flowers arrived on her doorstep regularly—masses of tulips, hyacinths, dogwood, or lilacs, and small bouquets of forget-me-nots. Diane knew she should make it clear to Tom that she cherished him as a friend more than as a suitor, but she couldn't bring herself to say it. He had earned a special place in her life. How lost she would have been without him during that awful time with Aunt Claudia!

Early in June, Diane prepared for the move to

Southampton for the summer, handling all the details herself since Aunt Claudia was still recovering from surgery. She wrote Tom a brief note telling him that she and Claudia would be staying at the Southampton house, then on impulse invited him to stay with them when he next flew up to New York.

She had expected Deirdre to be at Southampton with her at the same time Tom was scheduled to arrive for a weekend. Instead, Deirdre flew out to California again to visit her grandmother. Diane worried that it was the private detective Deirdre had met out there who was the real attraction.

Now Diane worried about how to entertain Tom. She'd already turned down invitations to all the Southampton parties. But she could always take him to the Beach Club and the Meadow Club, where Aunt Claudia had kept up their memberships. The problem was, she was never truly comfortable at either the Beach or the Meadow Club because she couldn't forget that Jews were not acceptable. It struck her as ironic that, while Aunt Claudia had buried her Jewish origins, she became increasingly conscious of hers with each passing year.

She and Tom would swim, play tennis, walk along the beach. They would drive to the summer theater for a performance one evening.

On a Friday morning in mid-June Diane saw Tom's Rolls-Royce pull into the driveway. She hurried to the door.

"You brought wonderful weather with you," she said. "It's rained for the past two days." She was surprised how glad she was to see him.

He kissed her on the cheek.

"It wouldn't dare rain when I was coming." He took in the slim length of her, in white linen shorts and tailored turquoise blouse. "Your tan becomes you."

"Thank you." The intensity of his gaze unnerved her. "Flora," she called to the maid who had appeared at the door, "please show Mr. Mason's chauffeur where to take his luggage—" She stopped as she saw the chauffeur's holstered revolver.

Tom caught her look.

"Don't let that worry you. My board of directors insisted on a bodyguard—only temporarily. Because of some stupid trouble at the mills. There've been some threats." He smiled. "I humored them by bringing David up here with me."

"I went through that when I was growing up," Diane said. "Because of some stupid kidnapping threat."

Tom stopped, took her arm.

"I would personally kill anybody who touched you."

She managed a shaky smile. She was moving into a relationship that she wasn't sure she was ready for. But she felt powerless to stop it.

"Have you had breakfast?"

"We stopped on the road," he said. "You know what I'd really like to do? Take a dip."

Twenty minutes later she and Tom walked from the house to her private stretch of beach. The sky was a vivid blue, unmarred by a single cloud.

"Nobody loves the ocean as much as a land-lubber," Tom said. "I grew up seeing nothing wetter than the Chattahoochee River—which in summer

465

was so dry we could walk from one side to the other. There's something about a stretch of sea that's challenging."

"I've always loved the ocean," Diane said. "To walk beside it or just to sit and stare." In swimming trunks, Tom Mason looked years longer than fifty-two. His shoulders were broad, his waist slim, his stomach firm and flat.

He reached for her hand.

"Come on, let's see how cold the water is."

Diane and Aunt Claudia appreciated Tom's courtliness over dinner, though Diane suspected that the southern-gentleman was just one of the many roles Tom Mason played—to perfection.

After dinner, Claudia excused herself to go up to her room and rest. Tom suggested that he and Diane go for a walk on the beach.

"But send up for a jacket, Diane. It'll be cool by the water."

With a blue flannel jacket over her apricot silk blouse, Diane walked hand in hand with Tom in comfortable silence. She never felt forced to make conversation with him, the way she did with younger men. In the days of her debut she had agonized over every silence. Even now, she never truly relaxed with strangers.

"Diane, I don't want you to give me an answer yet," Tom said softly, "but I'm in love with you. I can think of nothing that would give me more pleasure than to be married to you."

She stopped dead, her heart pounding.

"Tom, I don't know—"

"Take your time, my love. But for now—to show you how I feel—I'd like to give you this." He reached into his pocket and pulled out a small velvet box. "My heart, Diane. It's all yours."

She opened it, knowing she shouldn't. The prospect of life without Tom Mason was disconcerting. And yet the prospect of living with him . . . She lifted the heart-shaped ruby dangling from a platinum chain and gazed at it, tears welling in her eyes. How sweet Tom could be despite his sophistication, his powerful position in the international business world. Tonight he seemed like a boy in love, unsure but earnest.

"Tom, it's beautiful."

"Wear it." He took it from her and fastened it around her throat.

When he lifted her face to kiss her, Chris's words came back to her. *Oh no, she wasn't cold.*

That night, Tom made no effort to come to her room. He was Old South, Diane told herself, more disappointed than she cared to admit. But this weekend had meant a great deal to her. When Tom left on Sunday, she would tell him that yes, she would marry him.

She gave her aunt casual hints during the summer that her interest in Tom Mason went beyond friendship. She sensed that her aunt was troubled despite her admiration for Tom. What did it matter that Tom was older than she? He made her feel loved and cherished and protected.

Late in September, Clay left the sanitarium and in the same week Deirdre returned from yet another trip to California. Diane gave a small dinner party for Clay at El Morocco, after which they all went to the Peppermint Lounge.

"It's that new little gin mill near Broadway," he said to Deirdre and Diane. "They've brought *le twist* to New York. Remember, I told you about seeing Régine do *le twist* in Paris?" He grinned at Diane's expression. "Don't look so appalled, darling—I drink straight ginger ale these days."

"After the Peppermint Lounge let's go straight down to the East Village," Deirdre said. "I hear there are really jazzy places down there now—"

"No," Diane said. "After the Peppermint Lounge, we go home."

She didn't want to go to the East Village. According to Off-Broadway reviews in the *Times*, Ira Ross had directed the season's first major hit downtown. Thinking about him still disturbed her.

But why was she thinking about Ira when she was going to marry Tom? She would tell Tom the next time he came up to New York. They would set a date for the wedding.

From the Peppermint Lounge Clay insisted on driving them to Serendipity for cappuccino.

"What about you?" he turned to Diane, stirring his cappuccino with a cinnamon stick. "Is Sheilah Graham right about you being in love with Tom Mason?"

"Maybe." She hadn't realized the columnists had picked up their appearances around town together.

"You're going after a father," Clay said calmly.

"The daddy you never had. But that's all right—it might work."

She rolled her eyes.

"I wish you would forget all that shrink nonsense! When I'm with Tom, I don't look at the calendar. He's somebody very special."

"Clay, you are being obnoxious again," Deirdre said.

"Not really," he sniffed. "Just candid. But if it works for you, Di, then I'm all for it."

"Well, I'm glad, Clay. Because Tom's asked me to marry him."

He stared at her.

"Are you going to?"

"Maybe." She knew that that was as good as an admission. "But Clay, I want you to open up the shop anyway. I'll be a consultant."

"You'll be living in Atlanta and chasing all over the world with your husband. You won't have time to be a consultant."

"I'll make time." She folded her arms around her chest. "You'll see."

In mid-October, Tom flew up to New York to spend a weekend with Diane. He had suggested that on the night of his arrival they have dinner at his Manhattan apartment because he had "something special" to show her.

This was nothing new. Tom was constantly bringing gifts. Each time she was amazed that a man so involved in his business would take time out to search for a gift for her. And, she admitted to Deirdre,

469

she loved the way he paid so much attention to her.

Tonight, even though they were dining in his Sutton Place penthouse, she dressed for dinner in a long, sleeveless white silk crepe, the neckline scooped to a depth that displayed just a hint of high, full breasts. Tonight she wore the ruby heart that had been his first gift to her.

Tonight she would tell Tom she would marry him. Maybe tonight she would stay with him at his apartment.

Clay's words kept coming back to her. *"You're going after a father. The daddy you never had."* It wasn't like that at all. Tom excited her.

Tom opened the door and kissed her before she even had a chance to step inside.

"Diane, you look lovely. You don't mind that we're having dinner here?"

"Don't be silly." She let his hands linger for a moment at her shoulders as he took her white mink cape. "I love this apartment."

"Come into the library and look at what I've bought for you." He reached for her hand.

In the wood and leather-accented library Tom opened the top drawer of the sleek modern desk and brought out a box from Van Cleef and Arpels. His eyes steady on hers, he opened it. A dazzling twelve-carat marquis-cut diamond ring reflected the light.

"Tom, it's—it's magnificent," she said. "You read my mind. You knew that tonight you'd have my answer. And you knew it would be yes."

"When?" he said quietly.

"New Year's Day." Maybe that would erase forever the memory of her marriage to Chris in Las Vegas on that New Year's Day long ago. "Is that all right?"

"Honey, any day is all right." He put the jewelry box on the desk and pulled her into his arms. "Let's keep it a secret until the wedding. That way we'll avoid some of the nonsense in the scandal sheets."

"I'll wear my ring only when we're alone. It'll be our secret."

Dinner was superb, served graciously by Greta and Frederik, a Swedish couple who came during the day to take care of the house. After dinner Tom led Diane into the drawing room, its window walls looking out upon the East River on one exposure and upon the United Nations on another. A chilled bottle of Dom Perignon sat in a silver bucket near the television set.

"Kennedy's talking on TV in a few minutes," he said. "Would you mind if we watched?"

"I'd like that." She was never quite sure about Tom's politics. He had warned her that he was a maverick.

"I like to know which way the wind is blowing." He popped the cork, poured champagne into a pair of glasses. "I have to know how to play the game. That's why I run up to Washington two or three times a year when my bills are coming up." Diane remembered Jessica had told them that Tom had made his congressmen.

"You enjoy running the mills, don't you?"

He smiled. "That and all the other manipulations. I've become diversified through the years. With taxes what they are, it's a must." He paused to adjust the color television set. "Joe Kennedy fascinates me. Whenever I hear any of the Kennedys talk, I know it's that canny old man who's pulling the strings."

Tom gave her a glass of champagne and sat down beside her.

"To us. To New Year's Day, 1962."

Together they listened to President Kennedy talk about conditions at home and abroad. Tom was silent, intent only on absorbing what the president had to say. When the address was over, he shut off the TV set.

"Jack Kennedy knows how to evoke commitment—especially in the young." Diane was interested, but something bothered her about Tom's tone. She sensed a coldness in him, a ruthlessness. But then she told herself she was being silly. "I'll tell you this," Tom said, "for a president who was considered pro-business he sure is acting strangely." His face tightened. "He made a lot of enemies in big business by the way he handled the steel strike settlement."

Diane touched his cheek.

"Is he causing problems for you?"

Tom chuckled.

"Darling, nobody causes problems for me."

"Excuse me, Mr. Mason—" Frederik, the houseman, stood in the doorway. "If there's nothing else you need, Greta and I will leave now."

"Go right ahead." Tom waved his hand. "And tell Greta that dinner was perfect."

"Thank you, sir. Goodnight, Miss Dickenson. Goodnight, Mr. Mason."

Tom stood up and refilled his champagne glass, offering her some. She held her glass out, conscious that for the first time she and Tom were alone in his

472

apartment. She had told him she would marry him. Her girlish reticence was no longer appropriate.

She watched Tom refill his glass and walk back toward her. She had slept with only two men in her lifetime—Chris and Amid. She wanted Tom to make love to her, but what if she couldn't make him happy? How was she supposed to know what he liked and didn't like?

"Do you have to go home tonight?" he asked, sitting down next to her.

"No."

"I've waited a long time for you, Diane." His hand crept onto her knee. "But it will be worth it, I know it will."

He finished his champagne, took the still-half-filled glass from her and drew her to her feet. She felt unnaturally stiff, tense. He kissed her, gently at first and then with more passion, and walked with her into the dimly lit master bedroom. A king-sized bed, already turned down for the night, sat on a dais.

He drew her into his arms.

"I feel as though I were eighteen and making love for the first time," he said.

She let him undress her, enjoying the tenderness and care with which he removed each article of clothing. When she was naked, he turned off the lights. In the dark she stood absolutely still, watching the outline of his figure as he undressed. This was new for her; Chris had always wanted the lights on when they made love.

Her arms closed tightly around his shoulders as he lifted her up and carried her over to the bed. At the first touch of his hand on her breast, she knew he would be a wonderful lover. This was their wedding night.

Deirdre and Clay were sworn to secrecy about Diane and Tom's imminent marriage. Claudia, while not enthusiastic, seemed to accept the idea though Diane sensed that the age difference disturbed her.

Diane flew to Paris to assemble a trousseau with Deirdre and Clay.

They sat together in the lush but uncluttered Louis XIV salon of Givenchy, and chose four daytime dresses, two suits, three dinner dresses, and a ballgown. Feeling uncharacteristically daring, Diane splurged at the last minute on a full-length sable. For evenings out, she told a shocked but approving Deirdre.

The trio roamed Paris's narrow, winding streets for nightgowns and negligées. It was a thrilling, carefree time for Diane . . . except for the day she drove out to the country to see Miss Jeanne, who lived in a small house beside a brook with her aging mother. She was touched to discover that Miss Jeanne kept a group of photographs of her on the dining room sideboard. She wondered briefly why Miss Jeanne had been so cool to her these last few years.

Tom had said that because of his Mexican divorce, they would have to be married in Connecticut. He seemed to assume that she would prefer a very private wedding, and in fact she did. So it was arranged that a judge who owed Tom a favor would marry them on New Year's Day. Diane wanted Aunt Claudia to be present at the wedding ceremony, but since her mastectomy Claudia had been more reclusive than ever.

Late in December Diane bumped into her mother at the International Debutantes' Ball. It was a chilly encounter. They exchanged perfunctory kisses. Diane introduced Tom to "my mother, the Marquise de la Frontaine," and then her mother darted off in search of her escort, a talented and very young new French designer.

"Let's have lunch tomorrow, darling," she called over her shoulder. "One o'clock at the Colony. I'll make reservations."

"She doesn't know about us, does she, Di?" Tom said. He laughed. "I must admit, I feel deflated. She doesn't remember meeting me at a party Barbara Hutton gave at her house in Tangier several years ago. She was rather distracted then, too," he recalled. "There was a young matador who seemed to fascinate her."

"That sounds like mother," Diane sighed. "We see each other about twice a year. It's never a happy experience."

"But you are going to have lunch with her tomorrow, aren't you?"

"I guess so. But I can read you the script: she'll rattle on about where she's been for the last six months and what new man is absolutely mad about her. Of course, she'll never remarry unless it'll get her another title. I'll tell her about us after the ceremony."

The next day, promptly at one o'clock, Diane was seated in the gold-and-white main dining room of the Colony. Late as always, her mother arrived in a Mary Quant dress that was entirely too youthful for her. Not that Olivia admitted to her age. She still spoke of "dreading hitting forty."

"I'm taking a house at Palm Beach for two months, Diane, darling." She sipped her Kir Royale. "Why don't you come down for a week or two? And by the way . . . who was that man with you last night? I forget his name. Is he one of the partners with Mr. Lewisohn?"

"He's Tom Mason." Diane suppressed a smile. "No, he's not an attorney."

Olivia squinted.

"I think I've met him somewhere—"

"At a party at Barbara Hutton's house in Tangier, mother. He remembered you. Of course, Tom says he never forgets a name or a face."

"That's it!" Olivia·looked triumphant. "He's that terribly rich man from Atlanta. But socially, darling, he's nobody. Where did you meet him?"

"When Aunt Claudia got sick in Bermuda, he flew us home in his jet."

"And of course he presumed upon that to try to pursue the social contact." Olivia shrugged. "Barbara really should start screening her guests. You meet the oddest people at her parties. Darling, what about coming down to Palm Beach? You might find it amusing for a few days."

"I think not, mother," Diane smiled. "Palm Beach is not one of my favorite places."

*　　　*　　　*

476

Early in the afternoon on New Year's Day, Tom and Diane, with Deirdre and Clay as their witnesses, drove up to the judge's staid colonial home for the brief ceremony.

Tom said that Atlanta would be their base, but they would spend much of their time traveling. In New York they would stay at the Fifth Avenue house. They decided to keep his Sutton Place apartment for entertaining. Living in the house where Tom had lived for so many years with Tammy Lee wasn't Diane's first choice, but he *had* told her she would have a free hand in redecorating it. "It won't be the same house when you've redone it, Diane."

For her wedding day, Diane wore a Givenchy suit in the glorious new apricot beneath the Russian sable coat by Ben Kahn that was Tom's wedding gift. For their honeymoon they were to fly to the house in Bermuda for a three-week stay. The dozen valises containing her trousseau were already installed on his private jet, just rechristened *The Diane*.

With Chris, she had felt more like a performer in a movie fantasy than a bride. Today, standing with Tom before the judge who was about to marry them, she was a bride. She clutched a tiny bouquet of forget-me-nots as they listened to the judge's words, Clay and Deirdre standing at one side. At the proper time, tears in her eyes, Deirdre took the bouquet from Diane. Clay handed Tom the platinum band encrusted with diamonds.

"I now pronounce you man and wife." Tom took her in his arms and kissed her warmly, then kissed Deirdre while Diane and Clay exchanged kisses.

The judge's wife signaled to a servant hovering at the door, and a moment later an impressive wedding cake and a bucket of champagne were wheeled into the room on a teacart.

"May you be as happy as the judge and I have been for thirty-two years," the judge's wife murmured, gazing fondly at her own wedding band. "And I must confess that you're the prettiest bride the judge has ever married."

"And the richest," Deirdre giggled. "Maybe Mike and I will come up here to be married." Her eyes were dreamy. "I got my divorce in Mexico, too."

"Deirdre," Diane said, "are you going to marry Mike? This is the first I've heard of it—"

"I might." She shrugged. "It may be the only way I can get him into bed. He's such a prude. He won't even sleep with me unless I marry him. We've done everything else—"

"Dee, don't rush into marriage again. Be sure first."

"I'm trying." Deirdre sighed. "Maybe I'll buy a house out in Aspen—he's mad about skiing."

"It's time for the bride to cut the cake," the judge's wife called out. "Remember, the groom gets the first piece."

Tom was in no mood to prolong the festivities. He rushed their party to the waiting limousine, and they headed for the Fifth Avenue house and the wedding dinner catered by Le Pavillon. When Tom instructed the chauffeur to switch on the car radio so that they might hear the six o'clock news, the announcer was giving a report on the marriage of Diane Dickenson to Tom Mason in Connecticut. The judge and his wife had been sworn to secrecy, but there had been a leak.

At the wedding dinner, Tom gave lavish gifts to all: an emerald-and-diamond necklace for Deirdre, a priceless antique cameo set in a pearl-and-diamond frame for Claudia, and for Clay a pair of ruby-and-diamond cuff links. The servants at the Fifth Avenue house received Cartier watches. Ordinarily, Diane would have disapproved of these extravagant gestures. But she was beginning to understand that this was Tom's way of showing how happy he was to be marrying her. Back at the Fifth Avenue house, Aunt Claudia insisted that Diane phone her mother at the Palm Beach house with the news. It was the right thing to do, she said, and what if Olivia had already heard the news about it on TV or radio? That was no way for a mother to hear about her daughter's marriage, she clucked. No matter how serious the rift between them was.

Remembering her mother's reaction to her first marriage—*"But darling, it would have been more chic to be married Episcopalian"*—she picked up the phone and dialed.

Would it bother Tom to know that she was Jewish? No. Nobody could ever accuse Tom of being bigoted.

"Marquise de la Frontaine's residence," a melodic southern voice at last responded to the ringing phone.

"May I speak to her, please? This is her daughter in New York."

In a minute, Olivia was on the phone.

"Darling, let's make this quick. I'm just about to leave for a party at Concha Marina. Are you coming down?"

"I'll make it quick, mother. I was married this

479

afternoon to Tom Mason."

"To that man you were with at the International Debutantes' Ball?" Olivia's voice soared. "Why, he must be sixty years old!"

"Mother, Tom's fifty-two."

"Have you lost your mind, Diane? He's years older than I am!" He was a year younger. "You'll make me a laughingstock! How will it look to our friends that my son-in-law is older than I am?"

"Not as bad as my mother sleeping with men young enough to be her sons!" She heard a gasp at the other end.

"You bitch!" Her mother's voice was low, threatening. "You forget what I went through to bring you into this world! How dare you talk to me like that!"

"Go on to your party at Concha Marine." Diane hung up. *Why had she even bothered to call her mother?*

Shortly before eleven A.M., Diane and Tom left his New York apartment for the airport. There, each member of the crew of *The Diane* received a crisp thousand-dollar bill. At noon *The Diane* lifted off the runway for the flight to Bermuda. Tom warned her there might be brief intrusions of business associates, but for most of those three weeks they would be alone. At his orders the architect had designed the house so that even the servants were out of sight most of the time. The Bermuda house was his personal hideaway.

With his arm around Diane, Tom led her to their private cabin. Diane couldn't help but feel embarrassed as the crew watched from barely a dozen feet away.

"Have you ever made love in the sky?" he whispered, drawing her into his arms.

"No."

He smiled.

"There are a lot of things you haven't done, my sweet. Let me teach you."

Chapter Twenty-Eight

Ira walked slowly down Second Avenue, wary of patches of ice beneath the snow, his shoulders hunched against the early January gusts. He was exhausted, drained by the tension of this final, crucial week of rehearsals, even though he was pleased with the results.

This was the most expensive production he'd ever directed. It was good for his ego to be directing—even Off-Broadway—a former Broadway star. Good for his career, too. If this play made it big, he would be able to land a commitment uptown—not bad, considering he was still in his twenties.

Twenty-nine in September. When he was a kid, he'd assumed that by the time he was thirty he would accomplish something that would change the face of the world forever. But now thirty was right around the corner. And what had he accomplished?

Mom and dad were mildly impressed by his Off-Broadway success, though he knew they'd be happier if he had gone into law or medicine. Or even teaching. Anything but this crazy theater world. His sister Kathy, however, was delighted. She'd brought a party down from Westchester to see the last play, boasting throughout the evening about her "baby brother."

'Truth was that though he enjoyed directing, it wasn't what he wanted to do with his life. His real love was writing. Writing about things that mattered. But was there an audience for that?

Between directing stints he'd write another play, he promised himself as he swung on to East Fifth Street. Just to keep his hand in. Theoretically he should have plenty of time to write, but directing took so much out of him. Some writers wrote from five until eight in the morning before heading for their regular jobs. He was a night person. But too many nights he was so exhausted from hassling all day with his cast that it was all he could do just to take his clothes off and fall into bed.

As he walked into the building, he felt as if he were noticing for the first time just how drab the building was. At twenty-two it had been enough to have a pad of his own in the East Village, the hotbed of theater. In those days he'd been able to ignore the squalor— he'd even romanticized it enough to see it as America's version of the expatriate Paris of the twenties. But now things were different. He was different.

He was earning enough to move into a better building. So why did he stay on? For one thing, he loved being so close to all the playhouses. Once he landed a Broadway commitment, maybe he'd move into one of the new luxury apartment houses springing up along Second and Third avenues, ten or twenty blocks north.

Was that his phone ringing? He took the stairs two at a time, fumbling with the keys, and threw open the door. He got it on the fourth ring.

"Hello?"

"Hi!" It was Laura. "I'd just about given up on reaching you."

"I'm in rehearsal. Wait a sec. Let me catch my breath. You calling from California?"

"No, I'm here in New York—just for four days, on business. I have to talk to the distributors. Bernie's down with the flu. Are you free for dinner tonight?"

"Yeah. Sure. Just give me time to shower and change. Where do you want to eat?"

"Somewhere in the Village. Let me think a minute—what was that place we went to with Diane? That was fun."

"La Petite Maison." It wasn't his first choice; in fact, he'd made a point of avoiding it ever since. But he didn't feel like making an issue of it. "Shall I pick you up or meet you there?"

"I'm all the way uptown, at the Pierre. This is expense-account time, darling. I'll grab a cab and meet you there in an hour. Where is it exactly?"

"Hold on—I'll check it in the phone book."

After giving Laura the address, Ira hung up and took a quick shower. Why did Laura have to pick La Petite Maison? He still felt uncomfortable thinking about that dinner. Diane had been so sure that he and Laura were after her money—and it *had* looked that way.

Forty minutes later, he pulled his London-bought

sheepskin coat over a Shetland sweater and corduroy slacks and hurried from the house. At Second Avenue he signaled a cruising cab and settled back for the short ride across town. It had been two years since he had seen Diane. He'd probably never see her again. The super-rich girl he had known briefly, he mocked himself. So why the hell was he reacting this way?

Laura was stepping out of a cab as his pulled to a stop.

"Laura!" He charged toward her, just managing to keep his balance as he slipped on an ice ptch.

"Ira!" She threw herself into his arms.

"God, you look great." He pulled back for a moment to inspect her. "Successful. What's this you've got here?" He fingered the lapels of her mink coat.

"Like it?" she twirled before him. "I bought it myself. My Christmas bonus. C'mon." She took his hand. "Let's get inside. Even with my new mink I'm cold. God, I love that California weather!"

After they were settled with their drinks—two scotches and sodas—at their table in a small, elegant side room, a fire crackling in the fireplace, the conversation became more serious.

"So," Ira said, "tell me about picture-making."

"I'm working my tail off. We're already into our second production. The problem is, Bernie won't give me screen credit—not even as production assistant. It's driving me nuts. I'm making marvelous contacts. You know, if you ever decide to come out to the Coast, I can introduce you to some important people."

"That's not my scene." He pushed his drink away. "I'm hoping for a Broadway assignment if this play brings in good reviews. And on the side, I'm working on a play."

Laura leaned forward. "You should start thinking commercial, Ira. Think Neil Simon. What's the use of writing a play if you can't get a production?"

"I'll direct whatever they give me. I'll write what I want to write. What about you? Like what you're doing?" He was striving for a lighter mood.

"It's fabulous. The first production didn't make box-office records, but it showed a respectable profit. Bernie and I pulled in some nice salaries." She smiled. "And Tom Mason is setting up a corporation with enough capital for us to make a real splash with the next film."

"Tom Mason?" Ira frowned. "Isn't he that bastard with all the cotton mills down south where the workers are always fighting for a union?"

"I told you about Tom when he came up with the first financing. You made the same crack then. But I don't give a shit where his money comes from. I'm just happy he's investing with us."

"It's probably some kind of a tax dodge."

"I nearly dropped dead of shock when I heard about Tom and Diane—"

Their waitress arrived and handed them menus.

"What about Tom and Diane?"

"Don't you know? Oh, I forgot," she giggled. "You don't read the *News* and *Mirror*. But it was on the TV and radio news. They were married on New Year's Day."

Slowly, Ira put the menu down.

"Diane married that son of a bitch?"

"She sent me this just before the wedding." Laura held up an alligator bag. "She said she bought it in Paris when she was shopping for her trousseau to thank me for bringing her and Tom together. She'd met him briefly in Washington, D.C., during Inauguration weekend when—"

"He's more than twice her age!" Ira looked pale, distracted. "Why did she marry him? God knows she doesn't need his money."

"Tom Mason may be over fifty, but he's an attractive man. Of course, I wouldn't expect a man to understand that," Laura gibed. "After Diane's crazy marriage to Chris, I imagine Tom Mason seems solid and substantial."

"Tom Mason is a power-grabbing egomaniac," Ira snapped. "He manipulates and connives and buys what he wants. How could she marry a creep like that?"

"I hope it works—for her sake. I always remember that lonely little girl back in Newport. I don't think Diane has ever been terribly happy. Even with all that money."

"Laura, my dear, I know this may sound terribly old-fashioned and dull, but money can't buy everything."

"But it goes so far. I don't care what you say, Ira. I never want to be poor again. And I don't care what I have to do. Maybe I won't ever be as rich as Diane, but by the time I'm forty I'm going to be rich enough to buy whatever I want in this world." She brushed a hand over the mink coat draped over the back of her chair. "This was the first payment from the world to me."

Dressed in lightweight olive wool slacks and a raspberry sweater-jacket, Diane lounged on a chaise on the deck off her decorator-designed pink-and-white bedroom, its cool contemporary furniture warmed by antique Far East accessories Tom had collected during his travels. Clay would have to see this house. It was a masterpiece.

Every morning she phoned Aunt Claudia, who seemed at last to have accepted her loss.

Tom was in his office sitting room at the far end of the wing. Apparently the meeting with the two men who had come down from Atlanta was not going to his liking. He was yelling, swearing. This was a side of Tom she had never seen, and it unnerved her.

In another three days they would fly to Atlanta. She dreaded meeting Tom's daughters. He wasn't a man who talked about his children, and she hadn't the faintest notion of what they were like. So far she hadn't even seen any family photographs—either at the New York apartment or the Bermuda house.

She hoped—knowing it was unrealistic—that she would never have to come face-to-face with Tom's first wife. It wasn't jealousy—Tom made it clear that his marriage to Tammy Lee had been over for years. But she hated the thought of his family making her feel guilty for breaking up the marriage.

Diane dozed, awaking to the touch of Tom's lips on hers.

"They've gone." He was sitting at the edge of the

chaise. "I'm sorry for these business intrusions, my love."

"Tom, I understand."

And she did.

She loved these idle days; she felt tucked away from the world. She *had* been a little surprised that they did not share a bedroom—she'd been looking forward to waking up in Tom's arms. But he explained that he had a set routine, and he never let anyone disrupt that routine. He rose early, swam for twenty minutes in the indoor pool, exercised in the adjoining gym for another twenty minutes—or in the case of the New York apartment, swam and exercised in the rooftop health club. Then, over breakfast, he did some business on the phone. Even on their honeymoon, he didn't waver from this schedule. He took it for granted that she would sleep late, breakfast in her bedroom or on her deck, and meet him at the luncheon table about one o'clock.

"There was a call this morning from Clay's mother," he said. "She's just arrived from Palm Beach. She invited us for dinner, but I explained we were leaving for Atlanta in three days. She made it sound rather urgent that we see her before we leave. Something about Clay. I know how close you and Clay are, so I agreed that we'd drop over for cocktails tomorrow afternoon. Is that okay?"

"She's an awful bore. Why on earth does she want to talk to me about Clay?"

"Whatever it is, you'll know tomorrow." He smiled. "Would you like to have dinner aboard the boat? We'll watch the sunset, then eat on deck."

"That sounds marvelous."

490

"And darling," he took her in his arms, "if you look at me like that another moment I'll pick you up and carry you off to the bedroom."

"Wonderful. Yours or mine?"

Tom was a thoughtful and tender and passionate lover. She'd almost forgotten Chris's word—*iceberg*. Almost.

Diane prepared herself to face Mrs. Brentwood as the limousine pulled up in front of the beautiful old house.

"Don't worry, my love," Tom said, helping her out of the car, "we won't stay long. I'll remember an important business call."

Diane was relieved to see that the house remained virtually unchanged. She was surprised, too, by the new softness she encountered in Mrs. Brentwood, still plump, but stylishly gowned by the House of Dior. Maybe Clay was right about her being in love . . .

Colonel Williams was gallant. Thirty years ago, he would have been dashing. Now in his late sixties, his hair white, his military bearing slightly hindered by a pot belly not completely hidden under the finest British tailoring, he seemed to fit perfectly into his elegant, old-world surroundings. It was clear that he was the host here.

Over their second cocktail, Mrs. Brentwood revealed with a surprising girlish coyness that she and the colonel were getting married in three weeks. She wondered if Diane could suggest the best way to tell Clay about it.

"I know how close you and Clay are." She turned to Tom. "Like brother and sister. If you would drop a hint to him, so it doesn't come as such a shock." She turned to the colonel. "Clay will always be my baby, of course. I adore him."

Diane thought this approach rather silly, but she didn't want to make waves. And, knowing Clay, it probably would be better if he had some advance warning. "Okay, Mrs. Brentwood. I'll try. I'll phone him tonight to say I've seen you."

"Good. Tell him that I think he's right—it's time he made a home of his own."

Back home, Tom made it clear that he wasn't impressed with Colonel Williams.

"I know the type. He'll take her for every dollar he can squeeze out of her. And he's a lush."

"How do you know?" Diane was shocked by the venom in his tone.

"Are you kidding? That whiskey belly, the whiskey flush—that sure ain't Bermuda sun. Besides, I know about these things—I watched my ex-father-in-law drink himself to death."

"I don't think Clay will be particularly upset. He rarely sees his mother."

"I hope the colonel doesn't hoodwink him out of his inheritance," Tom said. "If Mrs. Brentwood is smart—and I doubt she is—she'd arrange for a premarital settlement that would protect Clay."

Diane thought for a minute. He had a point. "I'll talk to Clay about it. It was always understood that Clay would inherit the Brentwood fortune. His mother was considered sort of a trustee."

"Whatever. But I'll tell you this—if anything

happens to me, my daughters will be two wealthy women." He put his arm around her. "But they'll be far less rich if you and I have a child. What do you say, darling?"

All at once Diane was trembling.

"Tom, I'd love to have your baby."

"Then why do you look so startled?" He was smiling. "Did you think I was too old?"

"Oh, no. It's not that. It's just that—"

He pulled her to her feet, his hand at her breast. "Let's go into the bedroom, my darling," he whispered. "Maybe we'll make a baby."

After dinner, Tom excused himself to make a phone call to Bernie Kramer in California.

As she sat in the dining room sipping her coffee, Diane thought about Laura. Though they didn't see each other often—they made tentative lunch dates for whenever they were both in the city—she felt that Laura played an important part in her life. And she was glad that one of Tom's investments had brought them all together.

She put her coffee cup down. Aunt Claudia had been thrilled when she said that she would be at the Southampton house for the summer. From the very beginning, Tom had reassured her that they would spend a lot of time in New York. He knew she worried about being away from Aunt Claudia for long stretches of time.

When he learned about the Newport house, Tom thought it might be fun to open it up for the yachting season. In the spring of next year—when she'd be twenty-five—she would be free, according to the will, to sell the house. According to Tom, the old Newport "cottages" were selling for nothing these days. He suggested donating it to a charitable foundation for a tax credit.

She glanced at the Piaget watch that had been a surprise gift hidden in her breakfast napkin this morning. Eight-thirty. She had planned to phone Clay later, but now she couldn't wait. She went to put a call through on his private line.

He answered on the second ring.

"You'll never guess who I saw today," she said.

"My mother. Let me guess—you're both in Bermuda. Goddamn. Even when you're on your honeymoon, she's dreaming about marrying you off to me. Where did you meet her? Trimingham's? She shops there every morning."

"She phoned to invite Tom and me over for cocktails," Diane said. "We met the colonel." She took a deep breath. "Clay, your mother plans on marrying him."

There was a long silence. Finally, "I was only joking when I talked about her adolescent romance."

"She's not, Clay. She's scared to death to tell you. She asked me to drop a hint."

"That's my mother." He laughed. "Delegating bad news."

"Tom thinks you ought to talk to her about making a premarital arrangement with Colonel Williams. She'll probably live to be a hundred, but just in case . . ."

"I can't do that," he said flatly. "That would be admitting she has complete control over me. I can't

494

live like that, Di."

"Oh." She was a little puzzled by his abrupt tone, but she decided to let it drop.

"So," he said, "how long before he knocks her off for the money?"

"Clay, don't talk like that!"

He paused.

"When are you coming home?"

"We're leaving for Atlanta day after tomorrow. We'll stay there about six weeks and then return to New York. Clay, I'll call you from Atlanta. Maybe you'll want to fly down for a few days."

"I don't know, doll. All this honeymooning is getting on my nerves. First Tom and you, now mother and the Colonel."

"Clay, I think you should start looking for an apartment for yourself." She was beginning to learn how to deflect his moods. "We'll have a marvelous time furnishing it when I get back. Try for something with a view. A place you can really make a life for yourself in."

"Sure." He laughed. "Now the old lady can't complain about how much I spend. She wants me out of the house."

Diane looked out the window of *The Diane* at the endless tracts of forest below.

"We're almost there," Tom said, squeezing her hand.

"Really?" She looked again. "It doesn't look like we're anywhere near a city."

"Well, we are. You'll love Atlanta, Di. Almost

everyone does. Some people say it's the only real city in the whole Southeast. It's more than a city—it's a way of life. People in Atlanta remember and cherish their heritage; they've kept southern gallantry alive. But they're no fools either. They're shrewd business-men. Atlanta's got everything—gracious living, galloping industry, culture, and superhighways."

"I don't know, Tom. My only experience in the South is Palm Beach in season and vacations at White Sulphur Springs." She stopped. What about the sit-ins at lunch counters in Atlanta and Martin Luther King's arrest for "trespassing" in the Mag-nolia Room at Rich's Department Store? Tom had talked a lot about Atlanta's half-hearted efforts to achieve even token integration in its schools. How could Buckhead—the suburb they'd live in—be the casual, low-pressure oasis Tom claimed?

"Don't worry, darling. You'll fit in like you were born there." *The Diane*'s Fasten Seat Belt sign flashed on. "In six months you'll be a native."

But as the plane touched down on the runway, Diane realized how nervous she was.

She managed a smile as Tom helped her down from the plane and to a white Rolls-Royce where David—Tom's chauffeur from New York—waited to whisk them to Magnolia Acres. When he turned to greet her, she noticed that he still wore a holstered gun. Her smile froze. Could Tom's life still be in danger?

The late morning sky was blue, the sun high.

"You can never be sure about late January in Atlanta," Tom said, settling in the back seat of the car. "I remember times we've had snow and others when I've played golf. It's beautiful country, Diane. Wait till you see it in dogwood and magnolia season."

As David eased the limousine onto the four-lane expressway, Diane was startled by the way drivers changed lanes, ignoring directional signals, all traveling at high speed.

"California drivers," she laughed, faintly uneasy.

"At a cocktail party in Buckhead a psychiatrist said that Atlanta drivers all have a castration complex," Tom said. "But don't worry, darling. David can handle anything."

"Let's hope," Diane thought.

At last they left the expressway for the lush, rolling countryside. Hilly stretches of tall Georgia pines, deep valleys, and winding roads were lined with handsome houses. Even before Tom told her, Diane knew they were in Buckhead.

"See that white-columned Georgian mansion there—" Tom pointed to a magnificent house sitting in a private enclave. "That's Robert Woodruff's house. The Coca-Cola man. It's *the* tourist attraction around here."

But Diane couldn't concentrate on the scenery anymore.

"Tom, I'm a little nervous about meeting your daughters. Maybe it sounds silly . . . I just hope they're not upset that you've remarried."

"Diane, you married *me.*" His voice was soft. "Not Betsy. Not Jill. I love my girls, but they don't dictate my life. They're bright enough to know that, at least. Of course, other times I think they were short-changed in the brain department. Betsy's husband is a lawyer. He has political ambitions. Jill's husband is an executive at the Atlanta mill. While he appreciates the high salary I pay him and all the perks of being my son-in-law, I have a hunch he thinks he married beneath him socially. The women in his family are all DAR and UDC. The women in *my* family did their own cooking and cleaning and worked in the fields.''

Now that she thought about it, she realized that she did know a few things about her new family: of the five Mason children, three had survived. Tom's oldest brother had died in World War I, a sister in childbirth. His widowed older brother and maiden sister lived in South Georgia on a farm managed by a nephew. Other nephews and husbands of his nieces had been absorbed in his various business enterprises in Texas. Once a year, Tom said, there was a little family reunion at Magnolia Acres. Beyond that, Tom saw little of his family. Except for Betsy and Jill.

"The property begins right at the next turn in the road." He turned back to Diane. "I'm sure you'll want to make changes in the furnishing." She had surmised from his remarks at irregular intervals that while Tom loved the house and property of Magnolia Acres, he detested the interior decor. "I don't care if you throw out everything, as long as we have a bed. Maybe you'd like to bring down an interior decorator from New York—"

"Clay—" Her face lit up. What a perfect idea! He'd love the challenge. "His taste is exquisite."

Tom looked surprised.

"Clay's a decorator?"

"He's planning on opening a shop. Oh Tom, let's

be his first clients. He did over the Brentwood house in Bermuda. Before you and I saw it, it was Victorian. Awful. Old and dark and clunky. But after Clay redid it . . . Remember how much you liked it?"

He nodded.

"Yes, I did."

"And Clay will let me work with him," she pursued, trying to ignore the fact that Tom was unaware of her own interest in interior decorating. It was her own fault—she hadn't felt like telling him about it. And most of their time together, it seemed, Tom talked and she listened. "He called me down to Bermuda to help with his mother's house."

"David, what the hell's going on down there?" Tom leaned forward suddenly. "Were those people there when you left the house this morning?"

"No, sir." David took one hand from the wheel and and pulled out the revolver.

"Tom, what is it?" Then she saw the line-up of people at one side of the road just ahead of them. Mostly young people. They were carrying banners.

"Goddammit." His face was taut with anger. "Strikers from the mill. Who the hell told them we were coming home this morning?"

Diane was thoroughly confused.

"Why are they picketing the house?"

"To embarrass my new wife," he snapped. "These people never stop with their stupid unionizing. I've warned them. Well, they're fighting a losing battle. I'll close the mills before I let a union come in. David, let them know we're moving straight ahead."

Diane watched in horror as David put the gun beside him and stepped on the accelerator, one hand

499

on the horn. The strikers, in a tight formation, stayed where they were. *What if somebody was killed?*

David made a wide sweep and turned into the long private road. But not before Diane had read the signs. "$100,000 FOR A RUSSIAN SABLE FOR HIS BRIDE; $10 FOR HEALTH CARE FOR HIS WORKERS."

"Those ignorant bastards!" Tom stared through the rear window of the car. "They'll pay for this!"

Diane sat still, her eyes straight ahead. She tried to smile as Tom's hand reached for hers.

"I've built a clinic right in the mill village here in Atlanta. I set up health stations at the other mills. They've got health care!" A vein throbbed at his temple.

"Tom," she said quietly, "are *they* the reason David wears a holstered gun?"

"Yes." He sighed. "There's always some rabble-rouser, some fanatic who goes berserk. My board of directors insists on caution. Don't look so stricken, darling. Nobody's going to kill me."

She wished they were back in New York. She wouldn't feel safe here. And how could she bring herself to wear the sable coat again?

"Did I exaggerate about the house?" Tom intruded on her thoughts as the car swung left and pulled to a stop.

She followed his eyes to the elegant, double-galleried white colonial. That much was certain: he hadn't exaggerated.

"Tom, it's lovely." She looked around the grounds visualizing the gardens in spring and summer. "Really."

"Tammy Lee spent a fortune and went through half a dozen decorators." David opened the rear door and Tom stepped out, reached a hand to Diane. "I'm sure she drove them crazy with her demands. You'll make it live up to its exterior."

Tom's hand at her elbow, she walked up the steps and across the wide veranda. A cluster of immaculately uniformed servants, smiling in welcome, had been assembled in the huge marble foyer—self-consciously adorned with Grecian statuary—to meet their new mistress. She had forgotten the velvety softness of southern speech. The years of traveling to American and English locales had lent a different cadence to Tom's speech.

"Miss Betsy and Miss Jill are waiting in the sunroom," the housekeeper said. "When should I serve lunch, sir?"

"Give us an hour to settle in, Samantha—" He winked. "And there'd just better be a pecan pie for dessert. I've been looking forward to it for weeks."

"Oh yes, sir!" Samantha glowed.

Tom put a hand at Diane's elbow and led her down the cluttered hallway to the sunroom at the rear of the house. They paused at the entrance. Two expensively dressed, stiffly coiffed young women sat in white wicker lounge chairs, apparently absorbed in current issues of *Vogue* and *Harper's Bazaar*. It had to be Betsy and Jill. Both tall, blonde, pencil-slim. Except for what Diane suspected were perpetual pouts, they would have been very pretty.

"Don't I get any welcome around here?" Tom said. The girls leapt to their feet to fling themselves into his arms.

"Daddy, did you see those awful people down below? Can't you do something about them?" Betsy had a whiny little-girl voice in jarring contrast to her sophisticated appearance.

"Don't worry about it. I'll be on the phone with the sheriff's office in a little bit." He reached for Diane. "Girls, this is Diane. Betsy—" he indicated one, obviously older, in a Mary Quant dress, "and Jill."

"Oh, goodness, daddy," Jill said, oozing southern charm, "you didn't do Diane justice. Daddy didn't tell us you were so beautiful and so elegant." Her eyes lingered on the sable coat over Diane's arm.

"I just adore your suit," Betsy bubbled. "I think I saw it in Paris last spring. It's a Marc Bohan, isn't it?"

"Yes, it is." Actually it was part of the winter collection, but she decided not to say anything.

"Daddy, we've arranged a welcome-home dinner at our house tonight," Jill said. Diane saw a fleeting look of irritation touch his face. "Just family. So we can get to know your bride."

Clearly Tom's daughters weren't exactly thrilled to be sharing their father with a new wife. Were they afraid there would be a loss of an inheritance for them? Were they afraid she would give their father yet another child to share in the Mason fortune?

"Daddy, you won't mind if mother comes to dinner, too?" Betsy asked. Diane froze. "I mean, since she's living with Jill until her new house is finished. You two had such a civilized divorce." She smiled sweetly. "And mother's just dying to meet you, Diane."

"I'll bet she is." Tom's expression was enigmatic, but Diane knew he was furious. "But let's not confine such an occasion to your house, Jill. Call the Creek Club and make arrangements for dinner there. I want to share my beautiful bride with everybody."

For a split second Jill looked disconcerted; then she was all gracious charm again.

"Of course, daddy. Whatever you say. I'll call the club right now."

Diane knew now that her stepdaughters could be as charming as they liked—for the three of them, it was war.

Chapter Twenty-Nine

Diane tried to ignore the stiflingly fussy Victorian decor of her huge, high-ceilinged bedroom as she dressed for dinner. She was relieved to know this had not been Tammy Lee's bedroom. Tom had made it clear that her bedroom would be in his wing of the house. The second floor of Magnolia Acres had been divided into Tom's wing and Tammy Lee's wing.

She tried not to think about meeting Tammy Lee. In a moment of panic she had considered pretending she was sick, but she knew that was ridiculous. Someday she'd have to meet Tammy Lee; it might as well be now.

Rosetta, the maid who had been assigned to her, was warm and eager to please. In earlier years Rosetta had been the girls' nursemaid. Diane had noted that most of the servants had been with the family for at least twenty years, which meant they were treated well. But she couldn't forget those mill strikers.

"You sure you don't want a Coca-Cola before you go downstairs, Miz Mason?" Rosetta asked for the third time.

"No, thank you, Rosetta."

As Rosetta opened the door to leave, Tom appeared. He walked inside and closed the door behind him.

"You're wearing the ruby necklace," he said. "My heart at your throat."

"What do you think, Tom?" She twirled. "Am I overdressed?" The neckline of the full-skirted and low-cut long black crepe set off the ruby necklace nicely.

"On Friday evenings at the club the women tend to dress formally," he said, obviously pleased with her appearance. "Betsy and Jill will be in long dresses. Honey, you're not fretting about Tammy Lee being at dinner tonight? Don't worry—she wouldn't dare face up to the competition. That's why I insisted we have dinner at the club. I knew she wouldn't dare show up there. At home with the girls is one situation. On public view is another."

"No, I'm not worried." What was one lie? "I'm afraid Rosetta considers me a foreigner." She reached for her jacket. "I kept turning down offers of a Coca-Cola."

Tom laughed.

"May I remind you that you're in Coca-Cola country? Half the fortunes in this city were made on Coca-Cola. The day Asa Candler spent something like eighteen hundred dollars to buy the recipe from Doc Pemberton is etched in Atlanta's history. When Coca-Cola dividends rise, all of Buckhead celebrates. When they fall, everybody starts talking about petty economics." He held her jacket out to her. "The greatest things that ever happened to Atlanta are Coca-Cola and *Gone with the Wind.*"

She laughed.

"It's too warm for my sable, isn't it?"

"Wear the chinchilla cape," he said. "That's a show-stopper."

As she and Tom were led to their table in the lushly modern country-club dining room, Diane felt the long and curious scrutiny of the other guests. They stopped at four tables for brief introductions before they were seated at their own.

"When a man's a Big Mule like daddy, it takes him a while to get across the dining room floor," Jill said after Diane had been introduced to Clint and Bruce, the two sons-in-law.

Diane turned to Tom.

"What's a Big Mule?"

"They're the movers and shakers in Atlanta—the men who've had the good sense to become rich." He looked around the room with pride. "Atlanta's first millionaires began to surface not much more than fifty years ago. Most of them making it on Coca-Cola, or in real estate. I moved into the cotton mills on what I scratched out of real estate."

"Up until ten years ago," Betsy said, "Buckhead was home to nobody but Big Mules. But now, with the city exploding the way it is, other people—most of them scatter-bred, have been moving in all around us. In those ranch houses that don't cost a cent more than a hundred thousand."

Tom caught Diane's puzzled expression.

507

"Scatter-bred means they were not Georgia-born, darling. We have two definite groups of businessmen in Atlanta now. The Big Mules are the top executives of the important companies. Then there are the Nomads—the representatives of all those corporations flocking to the city to share in the boom. They live well—but not as well as the Big Mules."

Clint was frowning. "They're transients," he said.

"They don't take a real interest in what happens to the city," Tom said. "They steer away from anything controversial."

Jill shot Tom a warning look.

"Now, Clint, we're not going to talk politics." She smiled coquettishly. "There are ladies present."

Further conversation in this vein was automatically blocked by the arrival of their waiter. Diane was impressed by the cosmopolitan menu. They might have been dining at the Colony. But Tom had boasted about how cosmopolitan Atlanta was.

Over dinner, the talk revolved around the Atlanta Symphony, Rich's new suburban store, and the plans Jill and Bruce were making for a new swimming pool. As in California, everybody seemed to consider a swimming pool one of life's necessities. Tom's two girls seemed intent on making Diane appreciate Atlanta—particularly Buckhead.

"I don't know how people live in big cities like New York," Betsy said. "Rushing all the time. Down here we lead real civilized lives. Clint always has breakfast at home with me, and we swim or play tennis before he leaves for the office if weather permits—and he's almost always home before six. We have a cocktail or two until Loretta is ready to

508

serve dinner."

"We do a lot of entertaining," Clint said self-consciously. Because of his political ambitions, Diane thought to herself. "Either at home or at the club."

Diane could tell that Tom was proud of her and of the relaxing, low-pressure atmosphere of the club dining room. But over dessert and coffee the conversation became tense when he voiced some of his concerns with the Kennedy administration's plans.

"Only trouble with Jack Kennedy," Bruce said, "is that little brother of his. Bobby."

"No more politics," Jill said, turning to Diane. "I can't wait for April and Opera Week. Did daddy tell you that for the past fifty years the Metropolitan Opera has been coming here to Atlanta for a one-week season? It's just one round of parties then."

"We almost didn't have a season last year." Betsy's mouth was a hard thin line. "Mr. Bing started that business about not allowing the company to perform in Atlanta before a segregated audience. I guess because they had that Negro soprano in the company—I think her name is Dobbs."

"That brilliant Negro soprano happens to be Atlanta-born," Tom said with reproof. "I'm glad it was worked out for the company to sing before a nonsegregated audience." Diane glowed at his support of the soprano. Nobody could ever accuse Tom of bigotry.

"It's all moving too fast," Bruce said. "For a long time we've had an integrated police force and bus and trolley lines—"

"Even the golf course," Jill said. "Why did *they* suddenly have to rush everything? All that business with the schools and the lunch counters came at the same time."

"We've had good government in Atlanta for a full generation," Tom said. "The city has had the best race relations in the South. But we have to be realistic. We have a big middle-class Negro community, and it's making demands. Of course we've acquired several hundred thousand more rednecks in the past few years. They're white, poor, illiterate—and they hate the 'niggers' because they're fighting in the same job market."

"That's been a pattern through history, hasn't it?" Diane said. "The waves of immigrants that poured into this country—the Irish, the Italians, the Jews—all met the same kind of hostility."

"It's different when they're black," Betsy said delicately.

Tom turned to her. "Honey, you have to understand one thing. We're Atlantans. That makes us a little different from all other southerners. During Reconstruction, when other southern business leaders were crying in their cups, we were chasing up North to persuade eastern insurance companies to open in Atlanta and make it the insurance center of the Southeast. They talked New England mill owners into relocating down here. To us they weren't 'damn Yankees'—they were eastern capitalists investing in our city."

"My roommate at the University of Georgia said his father always claimed that Atlantans were really resettled New Yorkers," Bruce said with a smile.

Diane remembered that Bruce's family had arrived in Savannah in 1733, more than a hundred years before the railroad terminus that was to become Atlanta even existed.

Tom looked annoyed. "Men like myself are not typical southerners. We're businessmen first. Our main concern is Atlanta, and we see the integration crisis as a *business* problem. Believe me, when we handled that situation with the Negro community on the lunch-counter sit-ins, it had nothing to do with morality. It was necessary for business reasons. We have to compete with other major cities. Suppose some dark-skinned South American billionaire arrives in Atlanta to invest? Are we supposed to tell him he can't stay at a posh 'For Whites Only' hotel and ship him off to the local Negro YMCA?"

Jill, who had been looking bored, perked up at that. "Wasn't it just awful when that Arab prince was visiting Atlanta on his way to Palm Beach a few years ago and some people tried to throw him out of the Piedmont Driving Club because they thought he was a mulatto?"

"You see, Diane," Clint turned to her, "this is a club city. Almost everybody important belongs to the Piedmont Driving Club and the Capital City Club."

"Except for Dick Rich and three or four other Jewish Big Mules." Tom was amused that both Betsy and Jill seemed pained at this turn in conversation. "They belong to the Standard Town and Country Club. The story around town is that Dick was invited to join the Piedmont Driving Club, but turned it down when he was told that the rule hadn't changed but an exception was being made in his case."

511

Diane knew that anti-Semitism existed, but since she had never felt its impact in her own life, it was difficult for her to accept. Yet she knew that even now, Jews were excluded from clubs around the country: in New York's Racquet and Tennis Club, the Knickerbocker, the Links, or the River Club; in Washington's Chevy Chase Club; and in Atlanta's Piedmont Driving Club and Capital City Club.

"Diane, you're dreaming—" Tom's voice brought her back to the table. "Jill just asked you if we plan to attend the Atlanta Symphony concerts."

While she waited for Clay to fly down from New York, Diane let herself be swept up into Atlanta's social scene. She knew that Betsy and Jill were under orders from Tom to include her in all the activities. Two or three times a week she and Tom entertained at the club. Another two or three nights they attended parties at various clubs around the city. More often than she liked, Betsy and Jill swept her off to the Lenox Square Shopping Center for shopping sprees and long ladies' lunches.

At the end of her third week in Atlanta, Clay arrived, full of stories about his mother's wedding in Bermuda.

"I expected sixty West Point cadets to lift their swords and form a canopy for the bride and groom to walk under. It was enough to make me throw up. Thank God they've gone off on a world tour for five months."

Diane sensed his anger and, as always, tried to divert him.

"Clay, you should *see* the house. It's beautiful. But it does need a lot of work; the interior is a disaster. Tom says he doesn't care if we throw out every stick of furniture as long as we leave beds to sleep in." It felt so good to have Clay here. Only now did she realize how lonely she had been.

"Good. I need a challenge. Listen, have you talked to Deirdre recently?"

"No." She tensed. "Why? Is anything wrong?"

"She took off for Aspen two days ago. Some broker called her about a small house out there. She says she's going to buy the house and learn to ski. You-know-who is mad about skiing."

"Sounds like he's letting Dee do all the chasing, Clay. What do you think?"

He laughed.

"Maybe. But he can't get married for a while yet. Dee told me he's sitting out a California divorce. He was married briefly to some Las Vegas showgirl. I gather he's a small-town boy at heart—Dee says he was devastated when he found out he was sharing his bride with a long line of high rollers. He's thirty-six now. He didn't get married until he was thirty-one."

"Oh well," she smiled. "Guess there's nothing we can do about it, is there, pal? Why don't you tell me about *your* apartment."

As Diane had expected, Clay turned on his charm and won over everyone he met in Atlanta, even Betsy and Jill. They spent one hectic week choosing wallpapers, wood paneling, and drapery materials. Clay insisted on bringing in an architect to advise on structural changes before they made any decisions about the furniture.

At the end of the week Clay and Tom returned to New York on *The Diane*.

"No point in your trying to catch up with me, Di," Tom said as he hurriedly packed. "I'll be in New York for twenty-four hours, stop over for an appointment in Washington, and then I'll be back on the plane to Atlanta. We'll go up together late in April."

Diane tried to hide it, but she wasn't happy about their six weeks at the Atlanta house being extended. She missed New York. She spent hours on the telephone with Aunt Claudia, Clay, and Deirdre. Sometimes the days seemed interminable as she waited for Tom to come home. And more often than she liked, their evenings together were spent with business associates and their wives.

As time passed she realized that Tom expected her to be beautiful and gay, the perfect wife who expressed no serious thoughts of her own. The other wives were like that. Pampered, expensive toys. She thought about a book she had bought a few days earlier at the Lenox Square Shopping Center—she'd sat up half the night reading *The Feminine Mystique*, by Betty Friedan. It had given her a whole new perspective on men's attitudes toward women.

At the end of April Tom and Diane flew up to New York. He stayed in the city for three days then left on a business trip to Shanghai and Hong Kong. He made it clear that he understood Diane's need to spend time with Aunt Claudia, run around the New York stores with Clay, and choose furniture for the house. He told her he would be back in mid-May, and they'd fly "home"—by which he meant Atlanta—together.

Deirdre returned from Aspen slim and radiant—and bearing the news that Diane already suspected: she was marrying Mike in late September.

"Darling, I know you worry about me," she said, watching Diane as she dressed for dinner. "But Mike's wonderful. He's sweet and gentle and he thinks I'm terrific. He even laughs at my stupid jokes. And you know what? He *respects* me. We haven't even slept together yet. I think it's a reaction to what happened with his first wife. He says he found out right away she was an awful little tramp."

"Dee, do your parents know?"

She smiled mischievously. "Why tell them now? After the wedding I'll let them know they have a new son-in-law. Di, I want to be married by that same judge who married you and Tom. Do you suppose Tom can set it up for us? Just any time late in September. We'll go to the Homestead on our honeymoon. Virginia's so beautiful in the autumn."

Diane thought back to the autumn of six years ago, when she first met Chris at the Greenbriar. Had it really been only six years ago?

Impossible.

When Tom returned from Shanghai, he and Diane flew back to Atlanta. He was again in trouble with the would-be unionizers. Diane read newspaper articles reporting on the threatened strike, relieved yet guilty when it became clear that for now he had won. She still couldn't forget those picketers marching before the entrance to Magnolia Acres when she'd first arrived. All they wanted was health insurance for the workers. But Tom had accommodated them—he'd financed a free clinic—open three evenings a week. Apparently that wasn't enough. Just the other day, while sitting in the Ferrari at a traffic light, she heard two women in a dilapidated pickup truck talking with contempt about "Tom Mason's clinic."

For the next few weeks, the city was a steaming cauldron. Just walking outside was like stepping into an inferno. Diane couldn't wait to return to the Southampton house and its cool ocean breezes, even though she felt guilty about leaving Tom behind.

"Honey, don't worry about me," he said as they waited for *The Diane* at the airport. "I'll come up on weekends. This should be a pretty easy summer for me, business-wise."

"I'll miss you."

He hugged her. Smiled. "If you find out you're pregnant, you call me, you hear?" He reached into his jacket pocket and pulled out a small box. "Don't open it till you're on the plane. It's just a little trinket to remind you of me."

The "trinket" was a sapphire-and-diamond bracelet made by Asprey's on New Bond Street in London.

The summer sped past. Deirdre commuted between Southampton and her place in Aspen. Occasionally she and Diane drove into New York to shop for Deirdre's trousseau. Once every couple of weeks, Diane went into the city to meet Clay and pick out furniture.

Tom was much busier than he had expected to be, and ended up spending only three weekends in

Southampton. Diane flew to Atlanta for a few weekends, most of which she spent by the pool. One weekend, they invited people over for an oyster fry beside the pool.

"You didn't know I could cook when you married me, did you?" he said, busy at the barbecue pit.

Diane laughed.

"Never guessed it."

"You see this pit?" he said. "It was a trench where some of General Sherman's men did their damndest fighting. The fighting in Atlanta wasn't just something Margaret Mitchell dreamt up for *Gone with the Wind*."

"I don't like to think about war, Tom. Any war." Recently she'd been reading about the American soldiers dying in Vietnam. None of it made any sense to her. Why were they there?

"I know what you mean, darling. I'm kind of glad about that treaty prohibiting nuclear testing 'in the atmosphere, in space, and under water' that the United States, Great Britain, and Russia signed last week. Did you read about that? Especially since Five Points, 'the Wall Street of the South,' is marked on Russia's map as number three target for a nuclear bomb."

Diane shuddered. "Enough, my love. Can we talk about something a little more cheerful?"

"Sure." He speared an oyster. "How about dinner?"

Deirdre and Mike were scheduled to be married by the judge who had married Diane and Tom. Tom would be in Iraq, but Diane and Clay would drive up to Connecticut for the ceremony. Deirdre's parents and grandmother would be informed of the marriage afterwards, once she and Mike were on their way to the Homestead.

"Grandmother will be furious for five minutes," Deirdre said. "She really adores Mike. Because he likes her poodles. She doesn't understand that Mike loves any dog."

Deirdre was thrilled to hear that Diane had decided she liked Mike.

"Di, that's the sweetest wedding present you could give me!" She flung her arms about Diane. "Thank you!"

"Hurry up and dress," Diane scolded. "Mike will think you're walking out on him."

"Never. Mike is the best thing that happened to me in my whole life. Lenny was a nightmare. Mike will be heaven."

Diane hugged her. "Be happy, Dee."

"I'm going to be. Oh God, I hope I've packed everything! But no diaphragm. I hope to hell I get pregnant the first night."

That was something Diane had been trying not to think about. She and Tom had been married almost nine months. He pretended it didn't bother him, but she knew he was worried that she had not become pregnant yet. She knew it was silly, but she couldn't help wondering if it had anything to do with the abortion. The doctor had told her afterwards that she was fine.

Tears wet Deirdre's cheeks as Mike slid the simple wedding band on her finger. She barely heard the judge's final words. *She was Mrs. Michael Thomas. Good-bye, Deirdre Swift.*

Mike kissed her as though she were a fragile piece of porcelain. It would be different in a few hours, she rejoiced. They were spending the night at her apartment before flying down to the Homestead.

"Deirdre, you were a beautiful bride," Diane whispered, holding her close. "Mike's lucky."

Deirdre kissed her on the cheek. *"I'm* lucky."

Deirdre couldn't wait to be back in New York and in the apartment alone with Mike. He had no idea how horny his bride was. But first there was the very small dinner party at Diane's New York house arranged by Claudia Carstairs.

Except for distant relatives out in Arizona, Mike had no family. His father had died when Mike was a toddler, his mother when he was nine, and he'd been raised in foster homes. Maybe that was why he was so crazy about the little house in Aspen. At first he'd thought of living there, until a detective agency in New York offered him a job. Then he'd decided to keep her apartment in New York and buy a house out at Southampton, where they could spend a lot of time.

Deirdre knew that Mike was uncomfortable about spending her money, but she was confident that he'd get over it. Why should they honeymoon in Atlantic City for three days when they could have two weeks at the Homestead? He'd love that big, rambling red-brick house, with its tall white columns and all the little cottages.

"Clay, I want to redo my apartment," Deirdre said as they sat down to dinner in Diane's Fifth Avenue house. "Mike hates all that art nouveau stuff I was into for a while."

"But Dee, *I* don't hate it," he said.

"You do, too," she insisted. "It's going to be our home, and it has to be right for both of us." She turned to Clay. "It's a professional assignment. I want you to start as soon as you can."

"Great."

At last Deirdre and Mike were in a taxi on their way to her apartment. She dropped her head on his shoulder. Her life was going to be normal now. Maybe she'd even learn to cook . . .

The apartment was empty. The servants were on vacation. Deirdre went into the bar for the bottle of champagne being chilled since morning. She knew Mike never drank, but his wedding day was an exception.

"Pour a couple of drinks and bring them into the bedroom," she said. "I'm going to have a fast shower."

She carried a black lace-trimmed nightie and a pair of high-heeled black satin slippers into the bathroom. Standing under the hot stinging shower, she inspected her slimness with satisfaction. It was great to be thin. She was never going to let herself get fat again. Five pounds beyond what she was right now and zingo, out to Maine Chance to take it off.

She left the shower in a sudden surge of arousal, wrapped herself for a moment in one of the superlush towels that traveled everywhere with her now, then pulled the diaphonous nightie over her head. This was one bride who didn't have to worry about whether she was passionate enough to please her husband. She was ready to jump Mike this minute.

Mike was sitting up naked in bed. The two glasses of champagne sat on the night table. His weekender lay across a chair. The rest of his luggage, along with her own, was already at the airport.

"Well, now that you've seen this I might as well take it off." She slid the slender straps from her shoulders and allowed the nightie to fall to the floor.

"Dee, you're sensational," Mike said, his eyes sweeping the length of her.

"Oh Mike, I couldn't have survived another night without you." She tossed aside the sheet and settled herself beside him. "This is one marriage that's going to last forever. I'm breaking ground in my family."

Pausing to fondle her breasts for a moment, Mike reached for the two glasses.

"I never thought I'd ever marry again. Nobody but you could have changed my mind."

"Mike, I love you."

"I love you, too."

"Enough drinking," she laughed, her voice uneven. She took his glass and put it, along with hers, on the night table. "I don't want my husband smashed on our wedding night."

She closed her eyes as Mike began to kiss her. His mouth traveled from her throat to her breasts.

"Mike I want to be a wonderful wife," she whispered. "I don't want you to have any reason to go chasing after other women."

Her hands tightened on his shoulders as she felt his own probing between her thighs.

"Mike, now—" She was ready for him. Her hand

reached lower. *He wasn't ready.* A coldness swept through her. What was the matter? "Mike?"

"Just wait a minute," he snapped, "it'll be all right."

But it wasn't.

"Don't worry." She tightened her arms around him. "It happens to lots of guys. So we don't do it tonight. We'll do it tomorrow night. At the Homestead. Won't that be classy?"

"No." He looked pale, tense. "Tonight I'll make you happy." He leapt from the bed and began looking through his suitcase. "Here," he stood up smiling, "now everything will be okay."

Deirdre stared.

"Mike, you brought a vibrator on our honeymoon?"

Chapter Thirty

Autumn was magnificent in Buckhead, the foliage an unending procession of glorious color. Clay and Diane finished redecorating Magnolia Acres and were both pleased with the results of their eight months' work. Cluttered Victorian and self-conscious colonial—Tammy Lee's taste—had been replaced by an eclectic blend of European and Oriental antiques.

Delighted by the transformation, Tom decided to launch into lavish entertaining. He loved showing off his new young wife and his new house. Diane worked earnestly at the role of being Tom Mason's beautiful and gay young wife, letting Betsy and Jill involve her in local social activities and volunteer work. Now she and Tom entertained at a series of dinners, mainly for his business associates. On the surface, the atmosphere was always casual and relaxed, but Diane began to realize that business was also conducted—subtly—during the evening. It pleased her that their invitation list included several prominent Jewish families.

Diane gathered that the ugliness at the mills had subsided. Tom always brushed aside her questions with a brusque, "Don't worry about it." But she did worry—and was always aware of David's holstered gun.

As always, she talked regularly on the phone with her aunt and with Deirdre and Clay, constantly extending invitations to the three of them to visit Magnolia Acres. Early in November Tom decided they would go to New York to have Thanksgiving dinner with Clay, Deirdre, Mike, and Claudia at the Fifth Avenue house.

From Betsy, Diane understood that Tom had decided to have Thanksgiving in New York to avoid an encounter with Tammy Lee. For the past six years it had been traditional for the family to gather at Betsy's home for Thanksgiving dinner. Tammy Lee would, of course, be with her daughters for the holiday dinner.

Shortly before two o'clock on November twenty-second, Diane was dressing for a charity fashion show at the Capital Club when the private phone in her bedroom rang. Aside from Tom, only her aunt, Deirdre, and Clay used this number.

"Hello—"

"Di, have you been watching TV?" It was Deirdre.

"No. Why? What's happened?" She could hear the sound of an overwrought newscaster in the background.

"President Kennedy was shot in Dallas! Word just came through that he's dead! Turn on your TV. I'll hold on—"

Stunned, Diane put down the phone and switched on her bedroom television set. While a newscaster's voice, shaking with emotion, reported on the assassination, she returned to the phone.

"Miss Diane!" a weeping maid burst into the bedroom without remembering to knock. "Did you hear what happened to the president?"

All activity in every city and town in the country came to a halt as the terrible news traveled around the world. Shortly before three P.M., Tom phoned and told Diane to have their valises packed. *The Diane* was being readied for takeoff. They would attend the funeral in Washington, D.C., on Monday. He had notified the housekeeper at the Washington house that they would arrive in time for dinner tonight.

"Tom, it's so awful," Diane said, still in shock. The assassination held a special terror for her because she knew that Tom, too, walked in danger. The gun that David carried was a constant reminder. "With all the Secret Service men around him, still he was killed." Tom traveled around the world with only David to protect him.

"Johnson's already been sworn in," Tom said. "I've been on the phone with Washington. We'll be staying in Washington until after the funeral. Meet me at Hartsfield no later than four o'clock."

Within forty minutes Diane was at Hartsfield.

On the short flight to Washington, Diane huddled against Tom. For the first time in the life of most living Americans a president had been assassinated. It seemed unreal. She remembered watching the inauguration with Clay less than three years ago. And now for John Kennedy it was all over.

As they were driven from the airport to the Georgetown house, they listened on the car radio to the somber news that dominated every station, every TV channel in the country. Diane saw people pouring into the churches they passed. In cars on either side of them, motorists listened to their radios, unable to believe what had happened in Dallas.

After dinner Diane suggested that she and Tom call on Jessica Parsons. They found her seated before her TV set, watching accounts of the assassination.

"It's too much to ask of any American to live through two assassinations," she said. "I remember when McKinley was assassinated in 1901. That was enough for one lifetime."

They sat together over coffee, the TV set muted but recounting the events in Dallas and now in Washington, where Air Force One had arrived at Andrews Air Force Base with the body of JFK in its aft cabin and the new president, Lyndon Johnson, in the forward cabin.

Jessica asked about Clay.

"How's Clay really taking his mother's marriage?" she probed. Diane knew she was sincere in her concern. "Edward tells me he isn't upset, but then Edward sees him about twice a year."

"Clay wasn't entirely surprised." Diane hesitated. "Tom thought Clay ought to talk to her about providing for a premarital arrangement. There was no 'in trust' clause in his grandfather's will, though he knows he's supposed to inherit. But Clay refuses to discuss it with his mother."

"Stubborn little twerp," Jessica snapped. "My brother meant for that money to go to Clay when he came of age, but Louise keeps stalling. Edward says she put Clay out of the house and raised his allowance. Personally I think it's time he got away from her apron strings."

"Clay's delighted to have his own apartment," Diane said.

But as she spoke, she couldn't help wondering how they could sit here and talk about such things when the president had been assassinated a few hours ago.

On Monday night Diane and Tom returned to Atlanta. Despite the tragedy that rocked the nation, he'd decided they would still have Thanksgiving dinner at the Fifth Avenue house, as scheduled.

"Diane, it might be a good idea for you to see Dr. Edwards when we return from New York," he said, pausing beside the queen-sized bed. "There may be some physical problem that's preventing you from conceiving."

Diane was afraid to look at him.

"All right—" *Was* there something wrong with her?

"I'll see him, too," Tom said hastily, and grinned. "Let's get this show on the road."

Though the tragedy in Dallas hung over this Thanksgiving Day, Diane felt a warm sense of peace as the traditional dinner was served in the formal dining room of the Carstairs house rather than in the family dining room. Instinctively she had known that Tom would appreciate the grandeur of the room with its dazzling crystal chandeliers, fine old furniture, and exquisite drapes. There was a sense of family here today.

She was delighted when Tom brought up the idea of Clay's remodeling the Georgetown house, but she was worried that Clay had done nothing about opening up an interior decorating service in New York, as they had so often talked about. He'd made several vague references to a job as a consultant to one of the fine department stores, but intuitively she knew he wouldn't follow through. Maybe after this second assignment he would be more confident. She hoped so.

After dinner, Tom, Mike, and Clay settled themselves—and Claudia—in the library to watch TV while Diane and Deirdre went upstairs to Diane's bedroom for private talk.

"Are you pregnant?" Deirdre asked the minute they were behind closed doors.

"Not yet," Diane said. "I have a doctor's appointment next week. Tom thought I should have a checkup."

"What about Tom?" Deirdre said. "He's—what? Fifty-three years old? Not exactly prime time for fatherhood."

"He's seeing a doctor, too. Oh, Dee, I worry that maybe something happened to me that time in California." Even now she couldn't bring herself to say "when I had the abortion."

"Don't be ridiculous," Deirdre said. "There's no need to get phobic about this. And anyway, so what if you don't get pregnant? Is that the end of the world?"

Diane smiled.

"What about you and Mike? Are you happy, Dee?" Why did she have the feeling that Deirdre's marriage was in trouble?

"I'm deliriously happy," Deirdre said heartily. But Diane recognized a forced quality to her gaiety. "Did I tell you I've signed up for a cooking course? And Mike and I are looking for a house out in Southampton—nothing lavish, because I can't touch my capital for another four and a half years, and Mike's against taking out big loans with high interest rates."

Later in the evening, alone with Clay, Diane questioned him about Deirdre's marriage. He sighed.

"Maybe Deirdre just can't cope with marriage. Mike's a hell of a nice guy. If there's anybody Deirdre can make a go of marriage with, I'd think it would be with Mike."

Both Diane and Tom received clean bills of health from their doctor. Diane prayed that on their first wedding anniversary she would be able to tell Tom she was pregnant. But Christmas and New Year's rolled past with no indication that she was pregnant.

In late January they went to the Bermuda house for ten days. He persuaded Diane to invite Deirdre and Clay—winding up a temporary residency in the Georgetown house while he was redecorating it—to come down to Bermuda to stay with her for another three weeks. He was heading for South America on business. Diane was surprised when Deirdre showed no reluctance about leaving Mike for three weeks. Clay, too, was delighted with the invitation since his mother and her new husband would be in the south of France until March, when they were scheduled to return to Bermuda.

Diane saw Tom off at the airport. Deirdre and Clay would be arriving on a New York-to-Bermuda flight within an hour. She was amused by the pair of giggling thirteen-year-old twins—Hyacinth and Tulip, nieces of the Bermuda housekeeper—who were accompanying Tom on the flight to Atlanta. The housekeeper had persuaded him to give them jobs as maids in the Atlanta house. Diane was faintly concerned about how the pretty black teenagers with their Bermuda background and accent would fit in with the Georgia-bred staff.

Accustomed as she was to large household staffs, Diane was nevertheless astonished by the number of servants in their Atlanta house. Tom explained that most servants preferred these days to live away from the house of their employment, which necessitated hiring more servants than ordinary.

"But servants come cheap in the South," he said. "A fine cook, able to turn out chicken Kiev or veal Cordon Blue, can be had for forty dollars a week." What about the girls' schooling, Diane wondered. She determined to discuss it with Tom when he returned from South America.

As always she was happy to have Deirdre and Clay in her life. They swam in the indoor pool, rented motor bikes to sightsee about the island, attended the soccer games and hotel entertainments. The days and nights were a relaxing respite from reality.

Calling her aunt in New York, Diane learned that Mr. Lewisohn had died four days earlier and had been buried immediately, as required by the Jewish faith. His son Arthur was now in charge of her estate and would be in touch when she returned to Atlanta,

Claudia reported.

Though she hadn't seen much of Mr. Lewisohn in her daily life, Diane felt a tremendous sense of loss upon hearing the news. He had been the link to her family, to her Jewishness.

On their last night in Bermuda Deirdre admitted that there were problems in her marriage. She was scheduled to begin seeing Clay's psychiatrist on her return to New York.

"I know Mike is sweet and considerate and always trying to please me," she said, "but Di, I need sex more than once in six weeks! I'm not one of those wives who thinks she's doing her husband a favor every time she lets him sleep with her. I feel angry and guilty at the same time. Angry at Mike because he can't do anything, then guilty that I'm angry. Damn it, why didn't he tell me before we got married?"

"He was probably afraid of losing you," Diane said.

"Either this shrink tells me how to cope, or I'll be out there chasing after other guys," Deirdre said bluntly. "I'm not thinking about a divorce. I don't want to wind up like Barbara Hutton. What's her score now? Husband number six or seven?"

"Dee, what about Mike going to a shrink?"

"I tried to talk to him about it. He gets the shakes at the thought of it. And we're fighting all the time now. I've tried everything to make him passionate. He keeps telling me he's mad about me, but the message doesn't reach down there. I'm twenty-five years old and hot. I can't wait five or six weeks for him to get it up."

*   *   *

531

When Tom arrived in Atlanta he told Diane that for the next three months she was to accompany him on all his business trips. A doctor he had met at a party had explained to him that there was only a forty-eight-hour period each month when a woman could conceive.

"Why didn't that bastard Gaskin tell us this?" he demanded.

She laughed.

"Tom, it's not exactly a secret."

"All right," he said, "then we'll make love every other night—no matter where we are. In three months you'll be pregnant."

Early in April Betsy announced that she was pregnant. The news further eroded Diane's confidence. Why couldn't *she* get pregnant?

Tom made love to her around the world . . . in luxurious suites at the Mandarin in Hong Kong, the Plaza-Athénée in Paris, the Mamounia in Marrakech, the Palace in Milan. But their lovemaking had begun to seem to her like a plotted campaign. Lovemaking should be spontaneous, she thought, motivated only by a need to share a wonderful experience.

Sometimes, too, when Tom made love to her, she sensed that his body was with her but his mind was involved in the next day's business appointments. Each month when it became clear that she was not pregnant, she grew tense. Tom did not accept failure.

Was he regretting their marriage? She had been convinced that he had married her because he loved her. That he needed her to make his life complete. Now she was obsessed by doubts. He was flying to

Hong Kong late in May. He'd indicated that he expected her to open up the Southampton house early in June. The campaign to make her conceive was over.

Had Tom lost hope of her ever becoming pregnant? Was that all she meant to him—a woman to give him another child? A son to inherit his dynasty?

Two days before her scheduled departure for Southampton Diane was to attend a baby shower for Betsy—to be given by Tammy Lee.

She dressed with special care that afternoon. Usually punctual, she waited until the latest possible moment to be driven to Tammy Lee's modified Greek Revival house, which boasted a solarium with tropical orchids—Tammy Lee's latest diversion. Wearing a printed chiffon by Galanos, a narrow, body-skimming dress that was particularly flattering to her slim figure, Diane approached the door. Other guests had arrived.

"Diane, you look marvelous!" Jill hurried into the marble foyer to greet her as a maid ushered her inside. "You know just about everybody here, I think—except mother."

Diane tried her best to be polite to Tammy Lee, who also wore a printed chiffon, but one twenty years too youthful for her matronly figure. She was relieved when at last it looked as though the shower was coming to an end. Both Betsy and Jill insisted she stay for the champagne toast "to celebrate daddy's first grandchild."

"Isn't it silly?" Jill giggled. "Imagine, Diane,

you're going to be a step-grandmother."

"I'll bet Clint's bursting his britches with pride," Tammy Lee drawled. "You know men. They think women are made just to have kids." She gulped her champagne. "Of course, Tom is a little different. He thinks women are playthings. Born to provide him with—what's the word. *Kinky.* That's it, kinky sex. I told him, with his money he could have all the kinky sex he wanted. Only don't bother me with it."

White and shaking, Diane rose to her feet.

"It's late. I really must be getting home now. It's been a lovely party."

Chapter Thirty-One

The alarm clock on the night table sounded especially loud this morning. Without opening her eyes, Laura groped and shut it off, burrowing her face in a pillow.

The party last night at Bernie's new Bel Air house—with the customary boasting about box-office grosses and complaints about stars' salaries—would have been a huge success, except for Fran Kramer's nasty habit of referring to her as "Bernie's wonderful secretary." Everybody in the business knew that she and Bernie were partners—in fact, if not in name. Bernie might be a whiz at finances, but he knew nothing about the creative side of producing. That was her department.

It was time Bernie gave her screen credit as associate producer. She worked twelve hours a day, five days a week, took home scripts to read around the swimming pool over the weekend. Every production problem landed in her lap. The money she collected every week—plus the bonuses—was sensational.

Now she wanted recognition.

By 6:45 she had showered, dressed, had her grapefruit juice and coffee, and was about to leave for the studio. The phone rang.

"Hello?"

"I figured you'd be awake by now." It was Ira. "Guess where I am?"

"Sardi's." Damn, she'd totally forgotten that Ira's newest production had opened last night on Broadway. "You sound happy."

"The reviews were great. One extravagant character refers to me as the 'Boy Wonder of Theater.' That should up my money on the next go-round."

"Ira, that's marvelous!"

"It would be marvelous if they were talking about Ira Ross, playwright, instead of Ira Ross, director."

"Ira, you're a big success. Enjoy it."

"I'm trying. I guess I'm scared I'll get to like it too much. Anyway, I'm keeping my promise to call you after the reviews came in. Of course, working with Aurora Madison took five years off my life. Why can't you keep your Hollywood creations out there?"

"Why don't you come out here and loaf for a few weeks? I can introduce you to some important people."

He hesitated.

"No, I'm not the Hollywood type. I'll head out to Montauk. Russ's father has a fishing cabin out there I'm inheriting for two weeks."

"Isn't that where you took me for dinner once? Three hours to get there and three hours to get back, if I recall correctly. I *will* admit that it was the best fish dinner I ever had."

536

Ira lughed. "When we drove through Southampton, you wanted to settle for that."

"I always had rich ideas." Diane had a house in Southampton.

"You're doing all right. Enjoying it?"

"You bet I am. Enjoy your success, Ira." Laura glanced at her watch. She made a habit of being the first person in the studio office every day. "Stop thinking you have to go out and change the world."

"How's your sex life?" Okay, so he wanted to change the subject.

"Fair." She always told him the truth. "It would be a hell of a lot better if you were out here. I'm in a weird position—a woman moving up where only men have ruled so far, I've got to be so damn careful about whom I'm seen with. You wouldn't believe the gossip out here—all the way up to the top. I can't even have dinner with a big wheel from a rival studio. The men do it all the time. I can't. I'm a 'conniving bitch' if I do. Hey—am I keeping you awake?" Ira seemed to be fighting a series of yawns.

"Know what, babe? Tonight I could be in bed with you, and I'd be asleep before anything could happen."

She laughed. "Go home, Ira. You need some sleep."

She hurried from her apartment and out to the parking area to her car. Learning to drive had been a necessity for California living and a special triumph. Her current-model Corvette was a symbol of how far she had come since Newport.

Driving to the studio she tried to figure out exactly what to say to Bernie. Damn it, she deserved screen credit. He would have to stop with the lame excuses. He knew she could move on to other larger and far more important studios any time she liked. Unfortunately he also knew that she appreciated the free hand she had at TDM Productions. She was learning more here than she could anywhere else. But Bernie needed her. Right now *she* determined what films TDM would make, who would star in them, who would direct. Bernie worked out the budgets, fought over contracts, and usually handled distribution.

At the studio, Laura settled herself at the huge executive desk in her oversized office. She liked being alone in the building. This was her quiet time, when she worked without interruption, when she felt like the studio was hers. *Her baby.* Her lover. Her husband. Everything she needed in her life.

She heard the voices of the first arrivals, then her secretary came into her office with her morning coffee. Another small satisfaction: now someone brought *her* coffee.

A few minutes later she heard Bernie's voice. He was always the last to arrive. To him, that was a status symbol.

She waited until Bernie was settled at his desk and then left her own office to charge across the hall into his, closing the door behind her.

"Bernie, you've got to do something about your wife," she said. "Make her understand that I'm not your secretary." She could see from the look in his eyes that for a moment he thought that she meant for him to divorce his wife. Well, Fran was welcome to him. Bernie was fine for a roll in the hay; he filled a basic need in her life conveniently. But marriage wasn't a part of her plans.

"Laura, you know she doesn't mean anything," he said. "To Fran, women in the movie business are either actresses or secretaries."

"That's exactly what I want to talk to you about. There are other places in films for women—and we know that, darling. When we make up the credits for this new movie, I want to see 'Laura Devlin, Associate Producer.' It's time, Bernie."

"Baby, I know you deserve it." His deceptive softness put her on her guard. "But not yet. We can't afford to antagonize Tom. You know how he feels about women in business."

"How *does* Tom feel about women in business?"

"He's Old South. He believes women in business operate on emotion. But soon I'll be able to say to Tom, 'Go fuck yourself.' It's coming. You can afford to wait." He reached across the desk for her hand. "What about four days in Paris in July? We can set it up as a business trip. We'll have a ball. We won't think about business for four whole days. We won't even go to a movie. Now get back to work before I forget I have a ten-thirty appointment with the lawyers and jump you instead."

On the drive to Southampton from the airport, where Philippe had met her with the limousine, Diane tried to concentrate on the *New York Times*. Last night Tom had called her from Rio to tell her that he'd bought a painting for her. She sensed he was trying to show her that he still loved her. But she could feel the wall between them. Once she became pregnant, that wall would vanish.

She flipped through the pages of the newspaper, lingered over the theatrical section. Ira Ross's name leaped out at her. He had directed another hit play. The critic praised Ira for getting a superb performance out of a Hollywood sex goddess who until now had been considered a meager talent.

Frowning, Diane folded the newspaper and dropped it on the seat beside her. She wondered if Ira was still writing plays. If not, it must be awful to give up on one's first dream.

A few days after her arrival, after she had sworn that she would pull all such thoughts out of her mind, Diane became suspicious that she was pregnant. Her aunt had not yet come out for the summer. Deirdre was due momentarily for the closing on the house she was buying. But she wouldn't tell Tom until she was *sure*.

Over dinner with Deirdre, she couldn't keep her secret. Deirdre was thrilled.

"How do you feel?"

"Excited," Diane said. "Scared I may be wrong."

"Call Tom."

"But he's in Hong Kong—"

"They don't have phones in Hong Kong?"

"I'll wait until I'm two weeks late. Then I'll be sure."

"Come on, Di, you've got all the signs. Every time I turn around, you're rushing to the bathroom. You're falling asleep half a dozen times a day. Are you queasy?"

"No."

"So you're not having morning sickness. You're

always peeing, you're always sleepy, and you're almost two weeks late. Three out of four is good enough. You're pregnant, baby!"

And two weeks later, the tests confirmed it.

Tom was thrilled at the prospect of being a father. They decided that she would have the baby in Atlanta, at the private hospital where Betsy would give birth only a few weeks earlier.

He flew with Diane back to Atlanta for an appointment with the obstetrician he had chosen. He would fly up each month to accompany her for her monthly visit until she closed the Southampton house for the season and returned to Atlanta.

Tom was convinced that it would be a boy.

"Suppose it's a girl?" Deirdre demanded when Tom had left for Atlanta again. "Are you going to send it back?" She looked wistful. "You can always give it to me."

Apparently, her situation remained unchanged. Mike was warm and sweet and ever apologetic about his problem, and while Deirdre tried to joke about their efforts, Diane could feel her frustration. Still, Deirdre never talked about divorcing Mike.

Diane became totally involved in her pregnancy. Both Deirdre and Claudia fussed over her as if she were the first woman on earth to become pregnant. Tom phoned every night, whether he was in Atlanta or Rio or Los Angeles.

Almost as excited as Tom about the pregnancy, Clay found a fine French dressmaker who came out to Southampton to plan Diane's maternity wardrobe. The three of them shopped for the baby's layette. Diane decreed that Deirdre and Clay would be the baby's godmother and godfather. It was a beautiful period in Diane's life. She had never felt so loved, so cherished.

Late in September, Tom arrived in New York to accompany Diane back to Atlanta.

"You look so damn pregnant," he gloated. "He's going to be a big boy."

Diane used her pregnancy to avoid being caught up in Atlanta's social whirl. But it *was* difficult to avoid the football season. Tom would go to any lengths to be in Atlanta when Georgia Tech was playing on home ground.

Football in Atlanta was an all-day affair. Before the game, Tom and Diane had people over for brunch. Then limousines transported Tom, Diane, and their guests to their country club, where a bus provided by the club carried them to Grant Field. After the game the bus took them back to the club, where everyone had a drink before going home. If Tech won the game, parties went on at the clubs and in the Tara-like houses at Buckhead until far into the night.

As Diane moved into her sixth month, she was plagued by queasiness and began having trouble sleeping. As a precaution, her obstetrician told her to stop lovemaking until after delivery.

To amuse her, Tom had the *New York Times* delivered daily, left orders at her favorite bookstore to have a half-dozen new novels delivered three times a month. He cut his traveling to a minimum and encouraged her to invite Deirdre and Clay for visits. He offered to fly Claudia down on *The Diane*, but— as Diane had expected—her aunt could not bring herself to face new surroundings. Instead, they talked on the phone almost every day.

On Thanksgiving Day Betsy gave birth to a son. Tom was happy to become a grandparent, but all he really wanted was to become a father again.

In her eighth month, Diane moved—at Tom's insistence—into an improvised first-floor bedroom. He was terrified that she would trip on the stairs and lose the baby. The teenage twins Tom had brought from Bermuda to help around the house slept in a small bedroom off the kitchen. A bell was installed that would summon them at Diane's call.

No matter how busy his schedule, Tom never missed their visit to the obstetrician. He stood beside her in the examining room and held her hand, peppering Dr. Gaskin with questions.

Late one night, unable to sleep in the midst of a winter storm, Diane went to the kitchen to make herself a cup of tea. With the tea in hand, walking carefully, she left the kitchen and headed back toward the bedroom. She paused for a moment at the sound of faint, girlish giggling. The twins, she guessed. But why were they up at this hour?

She glanced up the wide carpeted staircase. Tulip was lovingly fondling Hyacinth's breasts. Tom sat beside them.

"You be quiet," he whispered. "I'll skin you alive if you wake my wife."

Diane swung around, almost tripping. A few drops of hot tea spilled over and stung her hand. Tammy Lee's voice came back to her: *"Tom likes kinky sex. I told him, with his money he could have all the kinky sex he wanted."*

So Tom had brought these two from Bermuda for his . . . needs, whatever they were. She felt sick. How could he, even if he had no wife to consider? They were children!

Her child had been fathered by this man. How could she have been so blind? Her hands closed protectively about her swollen stomach. She would protect her poor, sweet baby from the ugliness in his father.

She heard the high childish prattle of the twins become whispers as they disappeared into their room behind the kitchen. She forced herself to sit at the edge of her bed and sip the hot tea. Her instinct was to fly home to New York in the morning, but she knew Dr. Gaskin wouldn't want her to travel this late in her pregnancy.

Nothing mattered now, except the baby. She had to stay calm. She had to forget tonight ever happened. Somehow she must endure these next few weeks until her delivery.

When Diane moved into her ninth month, Tom told her over dinner that Dr. Gaskin had brought him into his office for a consultation.

"Why?" Diane was instantly alarmed. "Is something wrong?"

"No, Di," Tom said quickly. "It's just that he feels it's advisable that the baby be delivered by Caesarean section. For both your sakes."

"Why?" She was trembling. "What's wrong with me?"

"You're both fine, and Dr. Gaskin wants to make sure it stays that way. So I think that if he advises a C-section, then we should go along with it."

She hesitated.

"When?"

"He wants to have you in the hospital in two weeks. The following morning he'll schedule the section. Honey, you'll miss all that rotten business with labor. The baby will be beautiful—he won't have to go through all the battling." *He*, Diane thought. What if it was a girl? "Gaskin says that babies delivered by Caesarean section have perfectly molded heads."

But Diane didn't want to have major surgery. *Why couldn't she have a normal delivery?*

She and Deirdre discussed it over the phone. She dismissed Deirdre's suggestion that they ask for a consultation with another obstetrician, knowing Dr. Gaskin would consider it an insult—and Tom would be furious. It was decided that Deirdre would fly down three days before Diane was to go into the hospital. No one was to tell Aunt Claudia until after the baby was born—to spare her any undue concern. Tom phoned two or three times every day. He waited impatiently for the turquoise, amethyst, and diamond necklace he had ordered from Van Cleef and Arpels, to be presented on the arrival of their first child.

Tom and Deirdre took Diane to the hospital the afternoon before the Caesarean section was to be performed. Tom had arranged for round-the-clock private nurses for Diane and special nurses for the baby, who was to have his own private adjoining suite. While Deirdre hung up the fine silk nightgowns and the array of designer robes Tom had personally ordered by phone from Neiman-Marcus in Dallas, Diane changed in the bathroom into a burgundy velvet hostess gown. Tom came forward to help her with the zipper.

"You never looked more beautiful," he whispered.

"I can't really believe it," she said, "by tomorrow this time the baby will have been born."

"I can't wait." He caressed her swollen stomach for a moment, then looked at his watch. "I have to put a call through to Switzerland. I'll use the phone in the baby's suite."

Deirdre came over and hugged her.

"I'm so excited, you'd think it was me."

After Tom and Deirdre left, Diane changed into a nightgown and climbed into bed. Tonight her thoughts were with Zelda and those Friday evenings they attended services together.

She remembered the one occasion when Zelda had taken her to a *bris*. She felt an odd sense of loss that, should her baby be a boy, he would be denied this beautiful ceremony. But he would still be a Jew. Zelda had told her that any child born of a Jewish mother was considered a Jew.

Especially since her pregnancy, Diane wondered why she continued to deny her faith. It wasn't Tom— he wouldn't be shocked to discover his wife was Jewish. And yet . . . he hadn't been exactly displeased that the Carstairs family was in the *Social Register*. That she had been a top debutante of the year. Would she ever be honest about her origins?

Though she'd been sure that she wouldn't be able to sleep, she drifted off easily into light slumber.

She was awakened by a sharp pain in her belly that was more than the kicking of her restless child. The sheets were wet. Her heart pounded. She was going into labor. *She'd be able to have this baby through regular labor.*

She waited for the next pain, her eyes on the clock. Four minutes apart. She reached for the bell and summoned a nurse.

The nurse changed her quickly into a hospital gown and hurried off to phone Dr. Gaskins.

"Call my husband, too," Diane said. "He'll want to be here."

All at once the pains were coming one right after another. She tried not to cry out. A nurse came in to lift the gates on either side of the bed, stayed with her, murmuring comfort whenever she cried out. An intern stroked her hair.

She tried to stay in control between pains. This baby was impatient. Dr. Gaskin was leaning over her, barking orders to nurses and interns. Then she heard Tom's voice in the sitting room of her suite.

"She's gone into labor?" He sounded furious. "What's the matter with you? I told you. My son is to be delivered without a blemish. Now you get her into the operating room right now!"

"Tom, we don't like to do a C-section unless it's necessary."

"Listen, Gaskin, my wife is a great lay and I want it to stay that way. I don't want her stretched out like a cow."

"She can have this baby within the next hour or two the way she's going."

"No," he snapped. "Do it my way. You owe me,

547

Gaskin—don't ever forget that.''

As she held her son Jeffrey in her arms, Diane told herself that he would be her whole life. Her marriage was over, but she had her child. She would devote herself to being the kind of mother she had always wanted. Jeffrey would never doubt that he was loved. She would always be there when he needed her.

Chapter Thirty-Two

While Diane grappled with a slow and uncomfortable recovery, Tom reveled in fatherhood, boasting to everyone about his handsome son. He set up a ten-million-dollar trust fund for him, keeping it a secret from his daughters and Tammy Lee. He gloated that not only the *Atlanta Constitution* but the *New York Times* carried an announcement of the birth of the child who would inherit the Carstairs fortune and the Tom Mason empire.

Every night Tom rushed home from the office to go straight to the nursery, set up in quarters next to Diane's bedroom rather than in the separate wing he had wished. A new bathroom, designed for the comfort of one of the richest infants in the country, and including heated towel racks lest tiny Jeffrey be chilled, had been installed weeks earlier. An English-trained baby nurse had been hired.

Diane had been disappointed when Dr. Gaskin and the pediatrician decided Jeffrey should go on formula; she had planned on nursing him. But he was a hungry baby and her milk didn't seem to satisfy him. She cherished those moments in the early morning hours, his tiny body nuzzled against hers while he sucked at the bottle in noisy pleasure.

Gifts poured in from all over the world. Zelda sent a white mink carriage blanket and a heartwarming letter of congratulation. Laura sent a sterling silver porringer and mug. Diane was especially touched by the small, delicate tapestry sent from Chris with a note suggesting she hang it in Jeffrey's nursery.

In the hospital he had been circumcised. She wished again that this had been performed at a traditional Jewish *bris*, as had her own father's. Once, in her ramblings, her Seligman grandmother had talked about his *bris* as though it were the high point in her life.

Diane was amazed when her mother arrived in Atlanta. They had not spoken since Diane called to report her marriage to Tom. Wearing a suit by Courrèges and very tall, high-heeled boots, Olivia was accompanied by twenty-two pieces of luggage and a handsome twenty-four-year-old actor.

"We're on our way from Palm Beach to New York," she announced. "Peter has some acting auditions. Darling, I can't *believe* I'm a grandmother!"

For four days the Marquise Olivia de la Frontaine was feted by local society. It amused Tom that his daughters were impressed by the title and the fact that their new half-brother had a grandmother who was a marquise. Olivia paid scant attention either to her grandchild or her son-in-law, but she enjoyed the parties. When at last Olivia and Peter flew off to New

York, peace again reigned at Magnolia Acres.

Diane was grateful that Dr. Gaskin had told her and Tom not to resume lovemaking for a while. She knew that for her sanity she had to leave Tom. It was just a matter of time.

Late in March, Tom left Atlanta for a five-week jaunt across Europe. *Now*, Diane told herself. But she made no move. Everyday she talked to Claudia, who was eager for every word about her only grandnephew and waiting impatiently for June, when she would see him at the Southampton house. Tom called nightly from wherever he might be to inquire about the baby.

For Jeffrey's sake she wondered if she should try to hold their marriage together. She dreaded facing the world with yet another divorce behind her.

She'd grown up with no remembrance of her father—only a string of uncaring stepfathers. For Jeffrey it would be different. Maybe, if she could send the twins back to Bermuda, she could stay with Tom. What he did outside her sight she would ignore.

She telephoned the twins' aunt, their Bermuda housekeeper, and after implying that the girls were homesick, offered to supply funds each month to pay for their room and board and tuition at a private girls' school in Bermuda until they were graduated from high school.

Diane stressed that Mr. Mason was not to know about this. The housekeeper was overcome with gratitude. She would write Hyacinth and Tulip immediately and explain she had second thoughts about their being so far from home. She would send the airline tickets as soon as Diane arranged for the transfer of funds. Diane assured her that Tom would not cause any problems. *He wouldn't dare.*

By the time Tom returned, Diane was already preparing for the summer at the Southampton house. For several weeks Clay had been supervising the installation of a nursery, which he jubilantly reported would be ready well ahead of their arrival.

Only once before Diane left for Southampton with Jeffrey and Mrs. Evans did Tom come to her bed. The urgency in their lovemaking had evaporated. Diane sensed his mind was on other matters.

In Southampton, at Deirdre's prompting, she started painting again. Now without a decorating assignment, Clay came out to Southampton to stay with Deirdre, who confessed to being nervous alone in the house on the midweek nights when Mike had to be in New York at work. Mike refused Deirdre's pleas to forget about his job for the summer.

With Jeffrey and her painting, Diane felt that she had all she needed in her life. And she was thrilled that he was growing up in an atmosphere of love. Aunt Claudia adored him, and Deirdre kept a diary of his progress. At the first hint of a tooth, Clay bought him a sterling silver teething ring from Tiffany's.

Tom flew up twice in the course of the summer, each time arriving with gifts for Jeffrey and Diane.

Diane was astonished by Tom's interest in her painting. He insisted on taking two landscapes back with him to contribute to an Atlanta charity bazaar. Deirdre hung one in her beach house, and was asking for another for the Manhattan apartment.

As always avoiding family occasions that would include his first wife, Tom decided that they would spend Thanksgiving and Christmas-to-New Year's period in New York. He explained he would be involved in business meetings in the city.

For Jeffrey's first birthday, Tom and Diane flew to Bermuda. Tom had to leave after three days for a business trip, but *The Diane*—taking him to New York for a flight to Cairo—would bring Claudia, Deirdre, and Clay for a three-week visit to Bermuda. Only the news that Jeffrey had recently taken his first steps had persuaded Claudia to make the trip.

The night before he left the Bermuda house, Tom talked to Diane about a gallery showing of her work in New York, possibly in early autumn. Of course she was convinced that she wasn't good enough.

"I say you are. While I'm in New York, I'll make the arrangements. I'll even arrange for a publicist. We have to do this thing right. One of these days," he winked, "I may be known as Diane Mason's husband."

Laura sat across the desk from Bernie, her eyes blazing.

"Bernie, you've got to be crazy! We can't cut the budget! We can't come in ahead of schedule!" She waved a sheaf of papers under his nose. "We can't make do with this slashed promotion allotment. No picture takes off by itself—we have to sell!"

"I think we can," Bernie said coldly. "That's where I shine, Laura. In cutting costs."

"But we have the money. We went over the whole budget item by item. There's no need to come in ahead of time. No need to throw out advertising."

"Laura, listen: we do it my way or we don't do it at all. Talk to Weinstein about spending so much time coddling the cast. We're not a Method studio. He doesn't have to shoot every scene twenty-two times. We're running a business here—not a school for actors." He reached for his attaché case, shoved in a mass of papers. "I have to go. Fran's father is coming for dinner."

As usual, Laura lingered at her desk until everyone else in the studio offices had left for the night. But tonight she had a special motive. She wanted to find out why the new picture—the first one on which she was to receive screen credit—was being short-changed.

Knowing only the night watchman was on duty, she went into Bernie's office. None of Bernie's files was ever locked. She searched them thoroughly for a clue to this sudden budget slashing. Nothing.

But then she noticed a scrap of paper on the floor, bent down to pick it up. On it were two columns of penciled figures, one marked with Bernie's initials, the other marked "Company Net." Her thoughts were racing. Was Bernie stashing away money for himself?

I owe Bernie nothing, she thought. *He took me out of Menlow for his own good—not mine. He knew I'd be an asset. I can't afford to let our personal relationship stand in the way of business. Bernie is cutting my throat when he skims money off a production. The first time I get screen credit!*

She knew now what she had to do. But not until the film was finished. During the editing she could leave for New York. That gave her two days to think the whole situation out clearly and figure out how to handle it. She spoke to Tom Mason on the phone, saying only that it was imperative that she meet with him in New York within a few days. They arranged a time that would fit in with his travel plans. He didn't ask any questions; he knew it had something to do with Bernie.

Laura arrived in New York on a sunny day awash with the scent of spring flowers. As soon as she was settled in her expense-account suite at the Pierre, overlooking spring-green Central Park, she phoned Ira. The last time they'd talked, he'd told her he was working on a new play. He'd be at home, pounding away on his IBM.

"Hello—" He sounded irritated.

"I'm sorry—I must be interrupting you."

"For you I'll take time off. How's my favorite lady producer?"

"I'm here in New York for four days," she said. "On business. Could we have dinner tonight?"

"Let's have dinner at my place—my culinary repertoire has expanded," he chuckled. "This time you won't get spaghetti."

"Seven-ish?"

"Great."

Laura unpacked, hung up her clothes, and left the hotel to stroll down to Bergdorf's to shop a bottle of Detchema because she had forgotten to pack perfume.

Tomorrow was her lunch with Tom Mason at Le Pavillon. Either she would push her way very close to the top—or she would be out on her fanny. She was gambling that Tom would buy what she had to sell—and she'd always been a pretty good gambler.

At a few minutes to seven, wearing a Mary Quant minidress, Laura waited while the doorman of Ira's building announced her arrival. Though his new apartment was not in the fashionable East Sixties, he had progressed to a luxury building in the Gramercy Park area.

Ira waited for her in the doorway of his apartment. It was incredible, she thought, the way he could turn her on. Yet she knew there was no room in her life for Ira Ross—except for these occasional meetings.

"Let me show you the apartment," he said, an arm around her. "I've finally got enough space. The second bedroom is my office—the second bathroom a standby." He laughed. "When I took this place, mom got all excited. She figured I was about to announce that I was getting married."

"How is your love life?"

Ira shrugged.

"Comme çi, comme ça."

"Not worth mentioning, eh? Well, tell me about the new play, then."

"Not until I get dinner on the table," Ira said, bringing out a bottle of chilled wine. "What shall we drink to?"

"To us." She smiled. "We sure have come a long way from East Fifth Street, haven't we?"

Ira served vichyssoise, scallops poached in wine, saffron rice, and a tossed salad. There was pastry from a fine bakery on Third Avenue. While they ate, he talked about the new play.

"Of course, I'll have to lay off in a few weeks. I have to do all the groundwork for a new play I'm directing in September." He paused. "By the way, what's with your friend Diane?"

"Well, let's see . . . you know she had a baby over a year ago?"

"That would have been hard to miss. The week he was born Jeffrey Dickenson Mason got more newspaper coverage than Jackie Kennedy." He plopped a scallop into his mouth. "Is she happy?"

"From her letters I'd say she's mad about Jeffrey. She doesn't mention Tom." She could tell Ira still had a thing for Diane. "How's your family?"

"Mom just retired from the school system. Dad says he'll retire in another five years, but I can't see it happening. He's too fascinated by his business. Kathy and Craig have moved back into the city—they live a few blocks from my parents. That makes two kids for Mom to spoil: Janis and Karen."

Laura smiled. "I'm glad I don't have parents waiting breathlessly for me to get married. I'd be a bitch of a wife. And I'm not the type to have children." She leaned across the table, covering Ira's hand with hers. "But whenever I'm with you, I have this hankering to hop into bed."

"So let's hop," Ira said. "Forget the dishes."

As he took her in his arms, she realized that if she could marry anybody, it would be Ira. But there was no room in her life for a husband. Only for the top spot in a Hollywood studio. *She mustn't ever forget that.*

*　　　*　　　*

Shortly past one the following day Laura sat across the table from Tom at Le Pavillon. They had ordered luncheon and were sipping their martinis. Without going into detail, she told Tom she suspected Bernie was skimming money off the production budget for his personal use.

"I can't come up with any proof that Bernie's stashing it away," she said, "but it's not in the till. We needed every dollar allotted for the new picture. We needed the money set aside for promotion. It's not there."

"I'll look into it," Tom said carefully. "He could be feeding a Swiss bank account. I appreciate your telling me this, Laura—" All at once he was staring across the room. "Excuse me a moment, please. There's someone at a table over there that I should talk to for a moment."

"Of course."

Her eyes followed him as he crossed the room and paused at a table where two women had just arrived. One woman was about thirty and strikingly attractive, the other considerably older. The younger woman was introducing Tom to her companion. Even at this distance Laura could sense an intimacy between Tom and the younger woman.

She pretended to be admiring the costume of a celebrated stage star just arriving in the restaurant when Tom sat down across the table with a faint conspiratorial smile.

"I had to talk to the publicity woman who's handling Diane's gallery showing in late September," he said. "It's terribly important to Diane, but she's naive about the arrangements of things."

"I think it's a great idea! I just hope I'll be in town then. How's Jeffrey?"

"Handsome little devil," Tom said, beaming. "Running all over the house already. I wish I didn't have to be out of town so much. He's being smothered by all those women around him."

And his father, Laura thought with sympathy for Diane, was screwing every good-looking woman who came his way. But not me, Laura thought. At least, not yet.

During that summer Tom appeared at the Southampton house only once—for four days in mid-August. There was trouble again at the mills. If the workers decided to strike, he vowed, he'd replace every one of them. He would not be dictated to by his employees.

He admired the paintings Diane had completed for the gallery showing. Everything was arranged. They would fly up to New York the day before and give a dinner part at the Rainbow Room after the opening.

"Tom, I shouldn't be having a show," she said. "We could call it off."

"Don't be absurd, Diane. Everything is scheduled. Of course we'll have the show."

Diane was relieved when Tom left Southampton. She had expected him to be a warm, attentive father, but after those first few months Jeffrey became just another toy for him, another jewel in the emperor's crown. He was power-mad, always looking for fresh fields to conquer. Not that he ever discussed his business ventures with her. Except—once in a while—he'd mention a new project at TDM Productions. Because he knew that Laura was her friend.

Shortly after Labor Day, Diane returned to Atlanta with Jeffrey. To her distress, there was much talk among the Buckhead set about her New York show. Why did Tom arrange a show in New York? Why not some local show with the proceeds going to charity? *That* she could have carried off.

Deirdre phoned from New York with the news that the New York newspaper columns were carrying items about the show. That had to be the work of Tom's publicist. She was afraid people would come to the show just to see Diane Dickenson Mason.

Tom made arrangements to fly a dozen people—mostly business associates and their wives—up from Atlanta for the occasion. They would make the appropriate comments while they wandered about the gallery. A few would be pressured into buying. Diane couldn't forget René LeClerque's words: *"You are a talented amateur, my dear. Paint for your own pleasure."*

Her natural instinct when they arrived in New York on a late September morning that hinted at a glorious autumn was to go directly to the gallery to supervise the hanging of her paintings, but Tom insisted that everything was being handled. Tomorrow afternoon, before the opening, they would go over together.

"You'll have dinner with Claudia," he said. "I have to drive up to Connecticut for a meeting. I probably won't be back until all hours so don't expect me downstairs for breakfast."

She and Claudia had lunch together while Mrs. Evans fed Jeffrey in the nursery that had been set up by Clay in the Fifth Avenue house at Tom's orders when Jeffrey was only a few weeks old. While Diane and Claudia dawdled over coffee, Deirdre arrived.

"I'll have coffee in a little while. I'm here to see my nephew," Deirdre bubbled from the entrance to the family dining room, and then disappeared down the hall.

Deirdre returned downstairs when Mrs. Evans insisted it was time for Jeffrey's nap. Diane loved the way conversation centered on the baby. Later in the afternoon, when Mrs. Evans took Jeffrey out to the park, Deirdre talked about a new boutique she had discovered on Madison Avenue, and Claudia sent them off to shop.

Slim again after two weeks at Maine Chance, Deirdre bought practically everything in the store. The owner agreed to send all Deirdre's purchases by taxi that same afternoon so that Diane and Deirdre could go for tea at the Plaza's Palm Court unencumbered by parcels.

"I feel like I'm eighteen again," Deirdre confided as they strolled arm in arm down Madison Avenue. "Like we've just made a grand escape from *everything*."

Diane inspected the building numbers along Madison Avenue.

"I think the gallery is on the next block. Let's take a peek."

At the next corner, Diane stiffened. Wasn't that Tom walking across the street? But he was supposed to be in Connecticut by now. And that was David, getting out of the car to open the rear door for him. *Who was that girl with Tom?* He had his arm around her waist.

Deirdre saw Tom too.

"Let's cross over to Fifth Avenue, Di—"

Diane let Deirdre move her to the side street.

"He told me he would be in Connecticut all this afternoon and well into the evening," Diane said. *She would not cry.* It was humiliating enough without that. "I don't suppose you have any idea who she is?"

Deirdre hesitated.

"Her name is Amy Anderson, Di. She's in publicity. I was working up the guts to tell you. Tom's name has been linked with hers on and off for several months now. You'd think he was smart enough to stay out of places where they'd be recognized."

"I'm leaving him." That was it. She should have left Tom the night she saw the twins come from his room. She'd only stayed with him because she had convinced herself Jeffrey needed a father. But what kind of a father was he proving to be? For a few hours a week he fussed over Jeffrey, then dashed off to a life that didn't include a wife or son. She couldn't stay with a man who took two young teenagers for his pleasure, who flaunted his affairs. "I don't want to be in New York when Tom returns to the house."

"Where will you go?" Deirdre said unhappily.

"I'm getting on the phone to find a place that will give us immediate reservations. I'll fly there tonight with Mrs. Evans and Jeffrey. When Tom comes down to lunch tomorrow—after his late night in Connecticut—he'll receive my note to call my attorneys. Our marriage is over."

Another failed marriage.

Like her mother.

Chapter Thirty-Three

Deirdre and Diane went to the Palm Court for tea anyway. Diane needed time to absorb everything that had happened before she faced her aunt and attorney. She knew Aunt Claudia would be devastated by the news.

"Di, call the Homestead," Deirdre said. That was where she and Mike had spent their honeymoon. "They may have a last-minute cancellation. You'll unwind at the spa, and the food—mmm! From April through October the Grille Room serves tournedos Rossini and roast baby pheasant *au madère* with wild rice and grapes. I'll call," she said. "If they have a room, I'll go with you."

"Will Mike be angry?" Diane said. Deirdre was constantly taking off—to Maine Chance or to be with her.

"Fuck Mike," Deirdre said under her breath. "Pardon me, he's incapacitated. You've got a husband with overactive balls, and mine can't get going at all. Why the hell can't we pick the right guys?"

"Call the Homestead," Diane said. Deirdre left the table to find a phone.

Deirdre returned in ten minutes to report that they had a cottage at the Homestead and a chartered flight to the private airport nearby at ten-thirty P.M. She'd rush home, explain what was happening to Mike, and pick up Diane, Jeffrey, and Mrs. Evans in a rented limousine at nine o'clock.

"That leaves us plenty of time in case there's a traffic tie-up."

"God, you're organized," Diane said.

"I think I've learned that from Mike, Di. I wish to hell he'd go into therapy. He's got so much going for him—except for sex. And he's so damn stubborn," she flared in frustration. "It's not the shame of the century that he needs help. Sometimes he's so humble I could kill him."

Deirdre dropped Diane at her house and continued on her own. Watching the taxi swing off Fifth Avenue while she waited for the door to be opened, Diane tried to figure out a way to tell her aunt that she was divorcing Tom. No playing games. She'd tell Aunt Claudia everything.

Philippe appeared in the doorway.

"Miss Diane, Mr. Lewisohn called an hour ago. He said he'd wait in the office until you returned," Philippe told her.

"Thank you, Philippe." Arthur Lewisohn had taken over his late father's practice. She hurried upstairs to her rooms, grateful for the brief respite before she had to confront her aunt. Sitting on the edge of the bed she dialed Arthur Lewisohn.

"Diane, I'm sorry to bother you," he said. "I called

Atlanta, and the housekeeper told me you were up here. Your mother's facing a problem right now." He hesitated. "You're in no way obligated to see her through this, but she phoned me from Cannes and she was hysterical. She's borrowed against her capital as much as she can. The hotel is insisting on payment of her bill and local shops are up in arms. Some Swedish physician is suing her." Yet another face lift—or whatever—Diane figured. "Of course, she's out of line in threatening to sue to upset your grandmother's will but—"

"Arthur, please—just pay the bills." She didn't want to hear any more. "Work out an allowance for her that'll be practical without letting her squander a fortune on those greedy young boys she runs with. Make her understand she has to live within her allowance. No more Ferraris or polo ponies or Saville Row wardrobes for her love of the moment."

"You're very generous," Arthur said quietly.

"Her consolation prize for my making her a grandmother," Diane said wryly. "That must have been quite a blow to her."

Now Diane turned to the divorce. She told Arthur everything: her husband was unfaithful, and she wanted a divorce. Tomorrow, she was quite certain, Tom would be calling the law firm. There would be no financial decisions to be worked out. She had no need for child support from Jeffrey's father. She was willing to let Tom see Jeffrey whenever he liked.

"That's not apt to be often," Diane told Arthur. "Tom's away from home more than he's there. I'd like a quick Reno divorce—" For a painful moment she remembered her last trip to Reno. "But if that's

567

impractical, then whatever you feel is best. I'll be at the Homestead in White Sulphur Springs for the next two or three weeks. No one—Tom especially—is to know. If you need to talk to me, please call me there."

Shortly before midnight Diane and Deirdre, followed by Mrs. Evans carrying a sleeping Jeffrey, were taken to their cottage at the Homestead. A kind of peace settled over Diane when she was alone with Deirdre. She had long ago cut her ties to Tom, but she would not deprive Jeffrey of a father; she would be mother *and* father.

At eleven the next morning Arthur Lewisohn called.

"I'm afraid your husband is fighting the divorce," he said unhappily. "Mr. Mason denies any improprieties." He paused. "I know you won't like this, but I think it may be necessary to hire a private detective."

"Arthur, hold on please." Her heart pounding, Diane turned to Deirdre. "Mike handles divorce cases, doesn't he?"

"That's a lot of what he does," Deirdre said. "He says it's cheap and shoddy, but he's great at it."

"Arthur, a private detective named Mike Thomas will contact you. Please put him on the case. Tell him. I don't care what he has to do."

Diane sat in silence for a few moments after she hung up the phone.

"So Tom's going to be a bastard," Deirdre finally said. "Mike's good. He'll get the dirt on him. You'll

568

be headed for Reno before Christmas." Diane winced. Deirdre made it sound like a vacation.

Early in November, Mike returned from a trip to Atlanta with enough documentation of Tom's extramarital activities to ensure a fast, smooth divorce. Mike had photographs of Tom cavorting with several other important businessmen and two young women, all in the nude, at a lush and very private porno club. Tom cherished his image in Atlanta. He'd trade for the negatives.

A few days later Arthur Lewisohn called Diane to report that Tom was willing to withdraw his objection to a divorce provided he could see his son whenever he wanted.

"I'll go to Reno as soon as you make contact with a lawyer out there," Diane said. "And Arthur, I'd like you to send a check for $100,000 to the Mason Mill Strike Fund in Atlanta. You'll know how to keep my name out of it."

"Diane, that's a lot of money."

"That's what Tom paid for my sable coat," she said softly. "Send the check to the strike fund."

Laura sat in her office and listened to the slamming of file drawers in Bernie's office. It had taken almost eight months for Tom to pin down Bernie's operation at TDM. It was already February, 1965. As of a week ago, Bernie was out on his ass. The whole town buzzed with the news. He had come back today to clear out his desk—after having been locked out of his office for a week.

The auditors discovered that Bernie had skimmed a million and a quarter from the company. It would be a long, involved court case. But Bernie's father-in-law had a lot of contacts; Bernie would never go to jail.

Laura tensed at her desk. Bernie came out of his office, attaché case gripped in one hand.

"You had to go crying to Tom, didn't you?" he said, his face contorted. "You couldn't wait to get me out."

"You'll be okay, Bernie. You're a survivor." Both of them knew it would have been absurd for her to deny that she'd talked to Tom.

"Ungrateful little bitch!" He headed for the door. "Someday you'll pay for this."

Tom was replacing Bernie with a man from one of his Manhattan enterprises. She was now head of production. Tom Mason was her immediate superior. Tomorrow morning she would be on a plane bound for New York for a conference with Tom and Roger Holmes, the new financial head of TDM Productions. Tom was stopping over in New York on his way to Saudi Arabia.

Given the fact that it was she who had brought Tom and Diane together, their divorce had made Laura nervous. But from her coast-to-coast phone conversation with Tom, it seemed that he didn't hold it against her.

In the master bedroom of the new house she had rented recently in Bel Air—with an option to buy at the end of a year's rental—Laura packed for her trip to New York. She couldn't wait to be back in

Manhattan and feel the freedom of the city where she'd had her start.

She kept a low profile during the fireworks, refusing all interviews. The newspaper and magazine people seemed absolutely fascinated by the rise of a woman—a *young* woman—to production head of a film studio. For five days in New York she would unwind from the insane tensions and suspicions that made up the movie world.

Tomorrow night she was having dinner with Tom and Roger Holmes at Le Pavillon. The night after that she'd be seeing Ira. In fact, she would probably see Ira *every* night until she flew back to California.

She was unpacking in her room at the Pierre in New York when Tom phoned to talk about Roger Holmes before their joint meeting.

"If Roger gets carried away about money and you feel it's necessary, just say 'Let's go to Tom for arbitration.' I'll be on your side, honey."

"Thanks, Tom."

"Wear something sensational tonight," he said. "I like to walk into a restaurant with a gorgeous woman on my arm."

Laura chose a dramatic black crepe by Saint Laurent—narrow and boldly outlining her figure. She inspected herself in the full-length mirror before going downstairs. She looked chic and sexy—just the right combination. Tom would approve.

Dinner table conversation revolved around business. As usually happened at important business lunches or dinners, Laura was scarcely aware of the food—caviar, petite marmite Pavillon, and chateaubriand—as they discussed the future of TDM Productions. Before dinner Laura had wondered if Tom might change the company name since Diane was no longer his wife. Apparently not.

Roger Holmes excused himself from the meeting —and Laura suspected this had been prearranged— while she and Tom awaited their crepes suzettes, cognac, and coffee. Tom was his most charming tonight. When they left Le Pavillon, he suggested that she come to his apartment for a nightcap. Tom Mason might be—probably was—a bastard when it came to women, Laura thought; but there was something about his ruthlessness that excited her.

"We're a lot alike, you know," he said, helping her out of her black mink in the foyer of his penthouse apartment. "We both came from nothing."

"But you've come a lot further." She laughed.

"You're smart and you're beautiful and I'd lay odds you're passionate as hell." He placed a hand on her breast. "The trouble with Diane was that she was a lady, even in bed. I'll bet you're a hellcat."

"That's what you brought me up here to find out, isn't it?"

"It sure is. So why waste time?"

Hand in hand, they walked into his bedroom. The bed was already turned down, the servants gone for the night. Perfume filled the air. He pulled her against him, his hand fumbling for her zipper. Her Saint Laurent dress fell to the floor. Underneath, Laura wore only the flimsiest of black lace bras and the sheerest of black pantyhose.

"I'm a man who likes to take my time," he said, unhooking the bra and letting it fall to the floor.

"We have all night," she whispered as he peeled

away the black pantyhose. But before tonight was over, she had to make Tom Mason as hot as a teenager. "Why rush?"

She reached to fondle him as he tossed aside her pantyhose. He cupped her breasts in his hands. To her amazement, she became aroused.

"You always fascinated me," she said. "From that first time we met down in Bermuda."

"Show me how much I fascinate you," he said. "You be good to Tom, and Tom will be good to you."

At seven the following night, Laura sat across the table from Ira at La Petite Maison, which he confided had become one of his favorite Greenwich Village hangouts. He was excited about the new play he'd written.

"It pleases me," he admitted. "That's rare. And Larry Kaufman—that's the first producer I worked with Off-Broadway; Chris Ames went to Hollywood from one of his productions—has a potential backer, provided we can bring in a Hollywood name. Actually, Chris would be great for the part." He sighed. "Larry can't get through to him. That Italian movie-star wife of his wears the pants in the family—nobody talks to Chris unless she approves. I gather she doesn't approve of Larry."

"I never thought of Chris Ames as a terrific actor." Laura's smile was skeptical.

"That's where you're wrong. Despite all the crap he does, he *is* a good actor. Better than good. Larry saw it years ago in his crummy non-Equity Off-

Broadway production. But every time Larry calls, Chris's wife comes to the phone and says he's too busy to talk. Larry says he's sure she's even intercepting his letters."

"What makes you think Chris would want to come back to the stage?" Laura said. "Especially Off-Broadway, which pays so little."

"Chris asked Larry to send him any play that came along that Larry thought was right for him. He's dying to do a play. Larry would take off a few days and fly out but he's afraid to let this backer off the leash. It's his first show-business investment—Larry's holding his hand every night with promises of coming up with a star." Ira smiled. "The investor's wife is just mad about Chris Ames."

"I think I can get the script to Chris," Laura said. "But even if he reads it I can't guarantee he'll like it."

"You're serious?" Ira leaned forward, obviously excited.

"Sure am. Send me home tonight with the script. Chris will have it within twenty-four hours after I land in California. He owes me one."

"I'll give it to you when I put you on the plane," Ira said. "Let's have dinner and go back to my place. You still have the same effect on me, Laura."

"I know," she laughed. "It's a good thing I don't get to New York too often. You'd be an old man before your time."

Early in April, Deirdre told Diane that Chris had signed up to appear in an Off-Broadway play in the fall.

"The play was written by Ira Ross," she added while Diane reached for the newspaper clipping. "That's your old flame."

"Deirdre, I hardly know Ira Ross," Diane protested. "Anyhow, that was long ago." Deirdre knew she had developed a crush on Ira after the divorce from Chris. Actually she had thought a lot about him even before she left Chris. She'd been so young and vulnerable then.

"Isn't it weird that Chris is coming back to the theater in a play by Ira? It's going to be directed by Ira, too. Doesn't that give you a creepy feeling?"

"No," Diane said firmly. "Let's walk over to the park and see Jeffrey."

Her son was a constant source of joy. At a few months past two he was astonishingly handsome, a bright and happy little boy.

Once every three or four months Tom showed up to see his son—only when it tied in conveniently with his business ventures. Jeffrey was friendly but guarded; he didn't recognize his father.

Their lives fell into a comfortable pattern. Diane told herself that she didn't need anyone else. She had Deirdre, Clay, and Aunt Claudia. That was enough of a family for Jeffrey. Mike was "Uncle Mike"— warm and always available, though Diane was worried about his and Deirdre's marriage.

Diane was grateful that Mike allowed Deirdre such free rein. Deirdre—and often Clay when he wasn't on the occasional decorating assignments that came his way through friends—traveled with her, along with Jeffrey and the cherished Mrs. Evans, when she went for a month to the Homestead each autumn, to the

Bahamas for the month of February, to Southampton for the summer. Maybe it was these separations that kept Deirdre's marriage alive, Diane told herself. Maybe.

As usual, that year Diane moved her entourage to Southampton early in June. Clay was her escort at whatever social activities she attended. Often Clay was an escort for both Deirdre and Diane. Mike stubbornly insisted he had a job in the city—he refused to live off Deirdre's money any more than was absolutely necessary.

In late August Deirdre came over for breakfast before they were to leave for the club to play tennis.

"Did you see this morning's *Times?*"

"Not yet. What's happening?" She led Deirdre to the deck, where they could have breakfast overlooking the ocean.

"Chris is in rehearsal in Ira's play. They're opening Off-Broadway in four weeks. Ira's directed half a dozen Broadway hits." Deirdre was respectful. "He must be really good. At least, as a director. Why don't we go to the opening?"

"No."

Deirdre looked at her sharply.

"I thought you'd gotten over him."

"I have. I'm not angry at him anymore. I hope he's happy. I know he wanted to do a stage play for a long time—"

Both girls were silent as a maid served them juice, herb omelets, and coffee.

"It's Ira," Deirdre said gently when they were alone again. "You've always had a thing for him."

"Dee, you sound like a B-movie. The only man in

my life is Jeffrey. That's the way it's going to stay."

"Diane, you're twenty-eight years old. That's too young to give up men."

"Twenty-eight and with two divorces behind me. I feel like you, Dee. I don't want to wind up like Barbara Hutton, with half a dozen ex-husbands."

"Honey, even in baseball you're not out before three strikes."

"Deirdre, don't try to throw Ira Ross at me," Diane warned. "That never had a chance. Now eat your breakfast and let's go play tennis."

"Okay." Deirdre sighed. "But tennis is no substitute for sex."

A few days after her return to the Fifth Avenue house, Diane received a hand-delivered envelope. In it were four tickets to the opening night performance of *Second Chance*, Chris's play, along with a brief note from Chris.

> *Dear Di,*
>
> *I've finally taken time off to do a play—though Mannie almost had a heart attack. I hope you'll come—and to the party afterwards. Laura's going to try to come to New York too, but so far she's not sure she can get away.*
>
> *Please come. I want you to see I can do something besides the garbage they throw at me in pictures.*
>
> *Love,*
> *Chris*

Diane said nothing to Deirdre about having received the tickets, mainly because she wasn't even sure she was going. If she didn't, she knew she would feel guilty about disappointing Chris; but if she did she'd have to stay for the party and come face-to-face with Ira.

Two days before the opening, she decided to go. Clay was intrigued by the prospect of meeting Chris. He had total recall of Diane's small dinner party at La Petite Maison, when Ira had been among the guests.

"Sure I remember Ira Ross," he grinned. "He's the guy I told you looked at you like he'd died and gone to heaven. I made a real ass of myself at that dinner, didn't I? You know I'm always jealous of every man who looks at you. You're my little sister, and nobody's good enough for you."

Diane invited Clay, Deirdre, and Mike for an early dinner at the house before the performance. She changed her dress four times before she was satisfied. It was an opening night with a big Hollywood star, but it was Off-Broadway. Then Deirdre arrived in a gold brocade caftan—her evening uniform when the pounds were once again accumulating—and chided her about dressing as though they were going to a neighborhood movie.

"Chris is a big star, Di. He's been nominated for two Academy Awards. People will dress for opening night. Clay and I even managed to push Mike into wearing a tux." She sighed. "I wonder if Chris knows what I'm giving up for him tonight."

"Deirdre, you promised me you'd stay out of Friday's," Diane said. Occasionally Deirdre—in disguise—took off for the singles bars and whatever one night stand appeared interesting.

"Di, every once in a while I've got to have more than Mike's silly games. I know the singles bars are a zoo scene, but most of the time I leave with somebody—and sometimes it's good. Not always," she conceded. "But the odds are good enough to make me have an orgasm just thinking about it."

"What about this?" Diane pulled a dress from her closet.

"Fine." Deirdre glanced nervously at her watch. "You know your aunt won't let us out of here without eating. Aunt Claudia is the perfect Jewish mother."

It was absurd to make such a fuss about seeing a play, Diane thought as she changed. She tried to tell herself it was because she was seeing Chris again. But it was really Ira Ross who made her heart pound this way.

Diane took a final hasty glance at her reflection in the mirror. The simple black crepe with her pearls was understated and elegant.

Diane looked in on Jeffrey, then let Deirdre rush her down to the family dining room. Dinner was served with record swiftness, and the four hurried out to the waiting limousine. Diane fretted at the surge of downtown traffic that threatened to make them late for the performance while Clay and Mike talked about the way the East Village had become hippie heaven.

"It's gotten almost as wild as Haight-Ashbury," Mike said. "I was out in San Francisco on a case and figured I'd do some sightseeing as long as I was there. I ran into a guy who'd been a stockbroker in L.A. a couple of years earlier. Now he wore his hair in a ponytail, a straggly beard, and boots with bells on them and carried on about how all you have to do is 'love.' Everywhere you looked you saw crazy outfits and everywhere you walked you smelled marijuana and heard acid rock."

"What's the matter, baby," Deirdre cooed, "you don't like acid rock? It's so sexy."

Night had not yet fully descended on the city as Philippe pulled up before the Off-Broadway playhouse. The playgoers who had been milling about on the busy Greenwich Village sidewalk moments earlier were hurrying inside.

"It's almost curtain time," Deirdre guessed. "Let's go!"

In the cozy playhouse a smiling usherette, admiring their festive attire, led them to fourth-row-center seats. Clay lingered in the aisle, talking to various acquaintances who passed by.

"Clay, come on, sit down," Deirdre said. "The curtain's going up."

For the first few minutes Diane tried to cope with her emotions at seeing Chris after all these years, but soon she was caught up in the play. *Chris was good.*

Poor tormented Chris. But it meant so much to him to earn recognition in the theater. She was happy for him.

The play *was* powerful. From what little she knew of Ira she should have expected this. He was a man of strong opinions and strong commitments. She remembered when she had thought Tom was strong. She had mistaken ruthlessness and a desire for power for strength.

The producer had been right in choosing to

present Ira's play Off-Broadway. An audience out for a big night on the town would not be drawn to a play like *Second Chance*.

At the end of the first act Clay, Deirdre, and Mike said they wanted to go out into the lobby.

"You three go on," Diane said. "I'd just like to sit here."

"You all right, Di?"

"I'm fine," she smiled. "I've always hated act breaks. When I'm enjoying a play, I loathe intermissions."

When the curtain fell, the audience was wildly enthusiastic. Chris refused to take an individual curtain call until the other nine cast members, in silent conspiracy, withdrew, leaving him alone. Diane knew it was his moment of triumph, and she was genuinely pleased for him.

"Author!" someone shouted.

Diane watched as Ira—clearly reluctant—was hauled out on the stage to murmur his thanks to the cast and audience. Finally the audience was content to leave the theater. A few people, like Diane's group, moved down the aisle to the stage, which would shortly play host to a party. The conversations all revolved around the play.

"I don't see Chris's wife here," Deirdre whispered.

"She's probably backstage," Clay said.

"Isn't Chris married to an Italian movie star or something?" Mike asked.

"They've separated," a woman standing by said. "I read about it in a column last week. She was furious that he came back east to do the play."

Tense and insecure, Diane waited for the stage to

be cleared and the party to begin. It had been years since she last saw Chris; they had both matured since then. He had written a beautiful letter when Jeffrey was born, and she'd written back with genuine affection. She was sorry his second marriage was on the rocks. But she wasn't surprised.

"Maybe we ought to go backstage to see Chris," Deirdre said.

"Forget it—he's probably being mobbed." Clay made a face. "Give the guy a break."

Then the curtains opened again. The stagehands had pushed the set's furniture against the flats, leaving an open area where a caterer's crew was setting up the buffet. Shouts of congratulations went up from the guests as Chris—the first of the cast to appear—came out.

"Diane!" he called, pushing through the crowd. "I'm so glad you came."

Instantly she relaxed.

"Chris, you were so good!"

"For six weeks I'll know I'm an actor," he said. "I think more than anybody else you know what this means to me."

"Chris! Hey, man, you were great!" Someone slapped Chris on the back. In a moment he was surrounded by others eager to congratulate him.

"Let's talk more later, Di," he whispered. "Don't run off."

Clay pulled Diane aside.

"Introduce me when you get a chance, okay? I'm not leaving this playhouse until I've met the magnificent Chris Ames."

Was there a little hostility in his tone? Diane

searched his face.

"There's plenty of time for that, Clay."

"Darling, don't worry," he crooned, "I wouldn't dare make a pass at him."

Now the other cast members, some out of costume but still in makeup, joined the guests. Diane looked for Ira, pretending to be fascinated, along with Deirdre and Mike, in Clay's reminiscences about his brief experience in the theater.

A buxom, heavily bleached blonde of about sixty, dressed like thirty, came toward them. "You're Diane Dickenson, aren't you? I'm Gloria Watson, the company's publicity woman. What do you say to a few TV shots of you and Chris—"

"No," Diane said firmly.

"Gloria, I think Ted Miller from Mannie Coleman's office is looking for you," a familiar voice intruded. Diane swung around. *Ira.*

"Please excuse me." Gloria turned and hurried away.

"Ted isn't really looking for her," Ira said, smiling, "but you looked like you needed rescuing. Laura phoned me this morning to say she couldn't make it tonight. She said to tell you to give Jeffrey a hug and a kiss for her."

She smiled. "I will. Thanks. It's a wonderful play, Ira. I'm sure the reviews will be great."

"Let's hope. But this is a crazy business. Who knows? With Chris, we'll run six weeks. But without him, we're not guaranteed anything."

"Come on, Ira, it's a damn good play. Why shouldn't it run without Chris?"

"Because it's out of its time. There's no way I can

compete with Edward Albee or Neil Simon."

"Ira, hi!" It was Deirdre, with Clay and Mike trailing behind.

"We loved the play. Don't you remember me?"

"You're Deirdre, right?" Ira, smiling, came toward them. "And you're Clay."

"This is Mike," Deirdre said. "My husband."

While Mike and Ira shook hands, Deirdre winked at Diane.

"Ira, I'm having a small dinner party next Friday. Can you come?"

For an instant Ira's eyes met Diane's.

"I'd like that very much, Deirdre," he said slowly. "When and where?"

"Ira," Chris called. "Come over here and convince Ted Miller to let me stay with the play another month!"

"Excuse me, ladies," Ira said apologetically, "I'll be back in a minute."

Diane turned on Deirdre.

"Dee, what are you up to? Not that it's too hard to figure out. This is the first I've heard about a dinner party next Friday."

"Me too." Deirdre laughed. "But one thing's for sure. You still have a thing for Ira Ross."

Chapter Thirty-Four

Diane hovered over Jeffrey's bed, watching for a sign that the vaporizer was relieving his labored breathing as he slept. She knew it was absurd to panic every time he came down with a cold, but heart inevitably ruled over mind. The pediatrician teased her for being overly protective, but how could she not be? Jeffrey was the most important thing in her life.

"He's doing fine," Mrs. Evans said. "He'll sleep right through the night." Last night Diane had sat by his bed for hours. "You go on to the party."

"All right—" Diane said. "But be sure to call me if he wakes up and wants me. I can be home in five minutes."

She dressed quickly, aware that in a little while she would be sitting beside Ira at the dinner table. Deirdre had seated her between Ira and Clay. She hurried downstairs and into the waiting limousine.

"Someone will drive me home, Philippe," she said. "I won't be calling you." Deirdre had insisted she come early, before the others arrived, to see the new outfits her mother had air-mailed her from Paris.

"Di, do I look too far out?" Deirdre asked, pirouetting before her in her new Bonnie Cashin hostess pants and top. She had sworn off caftans.

Diane laughed.

"You look great."

"Great like 'wonderful' or 'great with child?'"

"Great like wonderful. Now show me what your mother sent." Deirdre's mother never wrote, rarely called, but frequently sent clothes in what Deirdre called her attacks of maternal guilt.

"I can't wear them yet," Deirdre said, "but they're smashing. This year mother loves the Paris boutiques. Ever since she heard that the duchess of Windsor shopped at Dorothée Bis. If you shop at Biba in London—that's where Brigitte Bardot and Julie Christie are always buying—or at Laura or Dorothée Bis in Paris, then you're a swinger."

Diane and Deirdre admired the clothes spread across the king-sized bed in the newly decorated master bedroom until the doorbell rang. At the sound, Deirdre ran down the hall to answer it.

"Mike's going to be late," she called over her shoulder. "I don't know why the hell he has to hang on to that crummy job when we don't need the money."

The new arrivals were Clay and a girl—someone he'd met at a fabric shop, Diane remembered.

Patricia Kelly was two years out of a midwestern college, pretty, chic, and thrilled to be immersed in the world of the super-rich. Clay introduced her to Deirdre and Diane.

"I want Pat to meet Ira Ross," he confided. "She's dying to get into stage designing—and she'll be great at it."

When Deirdre's new houseman arrived with cocktails, Clay asked for Vichy water.

"I had dinner with my mother and the colonel last night." He smiled. "She's drinking too much—to keep up with the old bastard. Thank God, they're leaving in a week for a houseparty in Tangier."

The doorbell rang and Deirdre hurried on her high-heeled sandals to welcome the latest arrival. Pretending to be listening while Clay and Pat argued about the merits of two Broadway set designers, Diane heard Ira's voice in the hallway. Deirdre came in with a bouquet of chrysanthemums, Ira behind her.

"Ira, I believe you know everybody except Pat. Pat Kelly, Ira Ross."

Immediately, Clay began hinting that Ira introduce Pat to some Broadway producers, which seemed to make Pat extremely uncomfortable. Diane was reminded of the night at La Petite Maison when Laura had tried to manipulate her into backing Ira's play. Maybe Ira had been surprised, too; the thought had never occurred to her before.

The houseman appeared in the doorway and gave the signal that dinner was ready to be served.

"Okay, everyone, let's go in to dinner." Deirdre smiled and whispered to Diane, "I'll kill Mike for this."

As they headed for the dining room—walls hung with champagne moiré and the furniture a modern symphony of glass and tubular steel—Mike arrived, apologizing for being late.

"We'll never be able to keep servants if you can't be on time for dinner," Deirdre said, loudly enough for their guests to hear. "Don't bother changing for dinner."

"I hadn't planned on it," Mike said, turning to the others. "Excuse me while I wash up."

Clay held center court throughout dinner, talking mostly about show business. Diane heard Ira promise to introduce Pat to several people.

"Pat reminds me of Laura when I first knew her," Ira said quietly to Diane while the others discussed the merits of the new Ira Levin novel, *Rosemary's Baby*. "She's done well for herself."

"Marvelously," Diane said. "And so have you."

He seemed uncomfortable with her flattery.

"You have a son. How old is he now?"

"He'll be three in February. He's wonderful."

"Let's have coffee in the living room, where we can kick off our shoes and be comfortable," Deirdre said.

When they settled themselves in the starkly modern black-and-white living room, conversation became more serious. Ira talked about the long, hot summer behind them, when some of the worst race riots in the country's history had taken place. Clay brought up the subject of Vietnam and American involvement in the war.

"How can young American kids let themselves be shipped off to a place where we have no business being and go out and kill?" Clay protested.

"Many of them have been brought up in God-fearing blue-collar homes," Mike said seriously. "They grew up believing patriotism is an all-important virtue and that it's their duty to do whatever the country demands without asking any questions. I'll bet a lot of them think differently now that they're over there. Patriotism is necessary, but let's ask questions."

"Come you, you great intellectuals," Deirdre said, "let's not get morbid. This is a party." She hesitated. "I've got some joints, if anybody's interested."

Diane was startled. How could Dee bring up the subject of drugs—even something as minor as pot—after what Clay had been through? But she understood: Deirdre was eager to appear hip. Diane knew that Mike occasionally smoked pot to unwind.

"No joints," Clay said. "Deirdre, remember Régine in Paris? Can you still twist?"

At the end of the evening Ira offered to see Diane home. In the cab he asked her to have dinner with him and see a revival of Shaw's *Heartbreak House* on Sunday night.

"I remember Laura complaining about all the revivals on Off-Broadway," Diane said, laughing. She was dying to see Ira—but afraid of what would happen.

"It doesn't often happen on Broadway," he said. "Off-Broadway gives us a chance to see the great playwrights we'd otherwise miss. You'll like this production of *Hearbreak House*. It's excellent." The taxi pulled to a stop at a traffic signal, and in the street light, Diane saw the urgency in his eyes.

"I'd like to see it with you," she said softly.

Ira took her to dinner and to the stage revival, and

afterwards they went out for coffee. He was surprisingly open and forthright with her, and when he asked her to go out with him again two nights later, she didn't refuse. There were periods in her life when she felt as though she had no will. This was one of those periods.

She and Ira began seeing each other three or four nights a week. He took her to the Lower East Side. they ate at Ratner's and Katz's Delicatessen, and Diane bought a Judith Leiber handbag at Fine and Klein on Orchard Street.

They went to museums and foreign films and had dinner at small ethnic restaurants. They ice-skated at Rockefeller Plaza and haunted the Strand Bookstore on Broadway.

Together they took Jeffrey to see children's theater, and on a cold crisp sunny afternoon when the snow was piled high in Central Park, Ira came over with a sled and insisted they take Jeffrey sledding. Watching Ira and Jeffrey together, she knew that Ira would be more of a father to Jeffrey than Tom ever had.

Ira kissed her passionately in taxis and whenever he said goodnight at her house. She knew the day was coming when he would invite her to his apartment for dinner. She knew they would sleep together. She told herself—recklessly—that she wanted to spend the rest of her life with him. But she was grateful that he was careful not to rush her, even while she wished he would.

Though they tried to avoid places where Diane would be recognized, Deirdre told her that the columnists were beginning to talk about her and Ira. The "Boy Wonder of Theater" was himself highly visible. Diane knew her aunt worried that she was seeing so much of Ira. He was invited to Jeffrey's third birthday party and brought the present Jeffrey most adored: a tiny red baseball jacket.

On an unseasonably warm early March day Ira brought his car out of the garage, and they drove to Southampton for a picnic on the deck of Deirdre's closed-up house. Afterwards they walked hand-in-hand along the deserted beach.

"I used to envy normal people," she said, "you know, people with families who loved them and worried about them—who had *time* for them." Ira's kind of family. "For a while I adopted the Barbour family on radio—remember 'One Man's Family?'"

"Sure," he said. "My mother never missed an episode."

"I hardly knew I had a mother," she said. "I was brought out when she wanted to parade as 'the beautiful young mother.'"

Diane told him about her succession of stepfathers, including the marquis. Ira was shocked, holding Diane's hand as she talked about her loneliness, at how difficult it was for her to believe that people liked her for herself and not her money.

"Thank God for Deirdre," she said. "Poor Dee. Every time she became attached to a nursemaid or governess, her mother would become incensed and fire her. Ira, you can't imagine how Dee and I longed to be part of a real family!"

Diane came home from the Southampton outing with Ira to hear that Deirdre had been calling her constantly. Alarmed, she dialed Deirdre's number.

"Di, I'm such a shit," Deirdre sobbed. "I threw

Mike out of the house. I told him I never want to see him again. I'm going to Mexico for a divorce."

"I'll be right over."

"At this hour? Philippe must be asleep by now."

"I'll phone a taxi. Put up a pot of coffee."

Within half an hour she was in Deirdre's kitchen, Deirdre pouring them strong black coffee into mugs.

"Dee, are you sure you want to divorce Mike?"

"Don't tell me how good Mike is—maybe that's part of our trouble." Her voice soared into shrillness. "I feel terrible when I go out on a one-night stand. I know Mike guesses—and it kills him. But I can't play his games anymore. He won't do anything to help himself. He won't go to a shrink. He went just once to that doctor who told him that physically he was fine. Mike makes me feel so rotten guilty all the time. I can't live like this anymore. Look at me—I'm forty pounds overweight. I have trouble at even the lousiest singles bars now."

"Dee, before you go to Mexico, go back to Maine Chance."

"That's getting to be my home away from home." Deirdre's laugh was shaky. "But no, darling. First, I get rid of Mike. Then I lose the pounds." She dabbed at her eyes with a tissue. "My mascara's running like hell. It's supposed to be waterproof. Di, will you go with me to Mexico?" Now her voice broke. "I know how you feel about leaving Jeffrey, but it'll be just for a few days."

"Of course I will." Aunt Claudia and Mrs. Evans would be with Jeffrey, and she'd phone every night.

They talked for a long time. Diane knew she would stay overnight. She'd make sure she saw Jeffrey before Mrs. Evans took him out for his morning airing, she promised herself. Not until she was in a borrowed nightie from one of Deirdre's slim periods and preparing for bed did she broach the subject of a marriage settlement. Not that she expected Mike to be demanding.

"Mike said he didn't want anything from me. He just said he would appreciate a twenty-thousand-dollar loan so he could quit his job and set himself up in business. Of course, he can have that." Her voice cracked. "Next year I come into all the inheritance."

"Dee, this is crazy; you're still in love with him."

"So what? I can't live with him. I torment the two of us. I can't do that to me—and I can't do it to Mike."

"When would you like to leave for Mexico?"

"As soon as I've talked to the lawyers and the arrangements are made. They do it fast—by the end of the week. I knew I could count on you, Di."

After four days in Mexico, Deirdre flew directly to Maine Chance for two weeks and Diane returned to New York. Diane had been at the Fifth Avenue house less than an hour when Clay phoned. He was down in Palm Beach redoing a house for a friend of his mother's.

"I will never again take on an assignment for a friend of my mother's," he said. "Though that's being damned independent for a decorator who's not exactly in great demand. But this woman is an absolute bitch. She doesn't know what the hell she wants. Anyway, forget me. How's Dee?"

"Depressed."

"You sound depressed, too, Di. Come down here for two or three weeks. For that little time Palm Beach can be fun."

"I don't like to uproot Jeffrey," she said. "He's just started nursery school and adores it."

"I know." He laughed. "It's so important that Jeffrey's social life be properly organized. The right nursery school gets him invited to the best birthday parties and the afternoon visits at the best houses. Soon he'll be accepted at the right dancing schools and before you know it—"

Diane laughed, too.

"Clay, shut up. How much longer are you going to be stuck on that job?"

"Another couple of weeks, then I'll be home. Keep a light in the window for me."

They talked for another twenty minutes, Clay gossiping about the Palm Beach set. He was hoping to be invited to do a resort house in Monte Carlo.

"They want it ready for August because by then everybody who's anybody congregates there. But I don't know if I'll get it. They're talking about Billy Baldwin."

"Clay, I wish you'd stop just playing and open up a shop."

"Only if you'll come in on it with me. You know I'm a social butterfly at heart."

"You're a dedicated, talented interior decorator. And I'll help all I can. You know that. But Jeffrey has to come first. I can't go dashing off on assignments at the drop of a hat anymore."

"Darling, you're the perfect Jewish mother. Who would have thought it of you?"

"When you talk to Jessica, give her my love," Diane said self-consciously. Clay would laugh if he knew how true his joke was.

Feeling oddly at loose ends, she phoned Ira. He was working at home on the script he would start directing in ten days. Though he was thoroughly disciplined and always busy, he told her that he could take a coffee break any time she called.

"You sound depressed," he said after they had talked for a few minutes. "Deirdre's divorce must have upset you."

"Yes, it did. She still loves Mike. I wish there was something I could do to straighten them out."

"Sometimes all you can do is hold a hand and commiserate. What about dinner tonight? My place. I don't think I've ever cooked for you, have I?"

"No, but you've bragged enough about it." Her heart was pounding. She had never gone to Ira's apartment alone.

"I'll make you my famous scallops poached in wine," he said. "You can enjoy my view of the Brooklyn Bridge while I make culinary history."

"Okay, I'll bring dessert." She remembered that his favorite was Black Forest cake. "Around seven?"

Diane decided to go shopping for a new outfit. Tonight, looking chic wouldn't be enough. She had to wear something ultrafeminine. Romantic. Something he had never seen her wear before.

At last, in a small boutique on Madison Avenue she found a low-cut light blue silk dress. Feeling like nineteen instead of almost twenty-nine, Diane hurried home. Ira would be the fourth man she had ever slept with—not much in an era when girls talked about their lovers in dozens.

At a few minutes to seven Philippe dropped her off in front of Ira's building. Clutching the bakery box containing dessert, she walked across the sidewalk into the ornate lobby. She waited for an elevator while the doorman—no longer impressed by the presence of Diane Dickenson at his pseudo-luxurious apartment house—announced her arrival.

She would not think about where her relationship with Ira would go after tonight. She knew only that she had never felt for any man what she felt for him. Ira was thirty-three. He had known a lot of women. But she felt as though they had been waiting for each other. She remembered a quotation from the Bible that was a favorite of her aunt's: *"To everything there is a season . . ."* This was her season to be loved—by Ira.

Emerging from the elevator at the nineteenth floor, she could hear the muted sounds of Aaron Copland's *Appalachian Spring* filtering through the door of his apartment.

The apartment door opened. Ira must have heard the elevator.

"You look beautiful," he said. "Sorry, but I'm fresh out of chef's hats."

"Something smells marvelous." She lifted her lips to his for a kiss.

He kissed her lightly, and with his arm around her, led her into the apartment.

"Have a glass of the white wine I picked up this afternoon. I'm not a connoisseur," he said, "but the man at the liquor store insists it's a French national treasure." He took the bakery box from her. "Let me guess. Black Forest cake."

She giggled.

"How'd you know?"

"Because you'd remember what I like best and bring it," he said. "You're a very special lady, Diane."

It felt strange and wonderful to be alone in the apartment with Ira. She stood in the kitchen doorway while he tended to the contents of a skillet.

"What can I do to help?" she said.

"Take out the salad bowl. The scallops will be ready in one minute. The rice and broccoli can go on the table right now."

They both tried to keep dinnertime conversation light. Then, over Black Forest cake and coffee, Ira suggested they drive out to Hershey, Pennsylvania, some time in May to show Jeffrey the Hershey factory. Diane felt her throat tightening. Ira talked as though they were a family. *Was she ready for this kind of commitment?*

"Di—" Ira seemed to sense her mood. "I want to marry you, but I know this isn't the time to ask you. Will you give me a hint when the right time arrives?"

"Ira, I've made such a mess of marriage. But yes, I'll give you a hint."

"Let's let the dishes sit." He pushed back his chair and rose to his feet. "Di?" He held out his arms to her.

"Oh Ira, I've loved you such a long time." She closed her eyes as he pulled her to him. "Why am I such a coward about marrying again?"

"Forget about it for now," he whispered. "I don't think I can survive another night without making love to you—"

Chapter Thirty-Five

Back from Maine Chance pounds lighter, Deirdre met Diane to shop for what she called her "interim wardrobe." Afterwards, they had lunch at her apartment.

The table in the smoky blue and mauve breakfast room, where Deirdre preferred to have lunch, was set for two.

"You don't have to tell me—you're sleeping with Ira," Deirdre said, spearing a grape from her fruit salad. "You've got that look."

Diane blushed.

"I didn't know it showed." In truth, she didn't know that she could be so happy.

"When are you marrying him?"

"I don't know." Only Deirdre would understand how she felt. "I'm scared to death of losing what we have now if we marry. Dee, I really do think this one will last forever; but I've married and divorced two men. I must have thought the same about them."

"Diane, you've always had a special feeling about

Ira," Deirdre said. "And it feels funny without a man around once you've been married. Not just the bed part. Some women are complete in themselves—they don't need anybody else. I think Laura is like that. We're not."

Diane hesitated. "Dee, Mike called me twice while you were away to ask how you were. He's working very hard at setting up the new agency."

Deirdre pretended disinterest. "How's he doing?"

"He said things are slow, but he's optimistic. He misses you like crazy."

"I won't go back to him," she said flatly. "So he might as well stop using you as an intermediary. Is Clay still down in Palm Beach?"

"He's due back any day. He's addicted to the April in Paris Ball. He and a decorator friend are taking us."

"That will be a night without sex," she said. "But anyhow, the ball is always for a good cause."

"Would you like to go to a play tonight? Ira has a dinner meeting with some producer."

"I'll call daddy's broker and see what he can get for us."

"Great." Diane stood up. "I think I'll go home and entertain my son. Why don't you come over for an early dinner?"

As Diane knew she would, Deirdre came up with tickets for a play. Afterwards, they went to the Stage Delicatessen for a posttheater supper. Ira had said he would be there if his meeting broke up early. Ira was not in the bustling restaurant; he was still involved with business.

Diane was in her bedroom, getting ready to change

into a nightie, when Ira called.

"Di, have you heard the news?"

"No—"

"Martin Luther King, Jr. was just killed."

"Oh my God. Where? How?"

"In Memphis. I should be down south with Russ. I feel rotten that I'm not working beside him. I talk a lot, but I'm doing nothing. What the hell is the matter with me? All I worry about is my own hide."

"Ira, are you home?"

"Yes."

"I'll be there in twenty minutes." Tonight he needed her.

Diane knew the best way to comfort Ira was by their making love. Afterwards, they lay back against the pillows and watched the news on TV. The repercussions of the assassination—the second in the United States in less than five years—were being felt around the nation. New York was calm, but rioting and arson were breaking out in many other urban areas.

Rioting continued for days. Martin Luther King, Jr.'s body was taken to Atlanta for burial on April ninth. That day the attention of the world was centered on Atlanta: mourners included Vice-President Hubert Humphrey, Governor Nelson Rockefeller, high officials from every branch of government, and the ordinary people who understood the loss the nation had suffered. Seventy-five thousand marchers paid homage to a man of peace.

Less than three weeks after the assassination, students at Columbia University began a sit-in to protest the university's plans to build a gym for the use of the students because the gym would usurp land needed by the neighboring black community. On April twenty-sixth the school was closed. Ira applauded the students' concern for those less fortunate than themselves.

The night after the closing of Ira's alma mater his parents were to celebrate their fortieth wedding anniversary at a small family dinner. Ira had persuaded Diane to go with him despite her recurrent misgivings. She knew his parents were eager for him to marry—and she knew how they would interpret Ira's bringing her to a special family dinner.

Did his parents read the gossip columns? The columnists were already predicting that she and Ira would marry. By the time Ira arrived at the house to pick her up for the dinner party, she was fighting panic.

"Diane, relax," Ira scolded as they waited for a taxi. "We're going to a party."

"Do your parents know you're bringing me?" she asked for the third time.

"They know," he said tiredly. "I brought Laura to my sister's wedding. She survived." He squeezed Diane's hand in reassurance.

"Ira, I want them to like me."

He hugged her.

"They'll love you. For the last ten years mom's been worried because I don't have a steady girl. Now I do."

A taxi pulled to a stop at the curb and Ira helped her inside. The taxi swung off Fifth Avenue to travel through night-darkening Central Park. Ira kept Diane's hand in his.

"Mom and Aunt Marcia have probably been cooking all day," he confided indulgently. "Kathy told them to cater the dinner. Mom might have gone along, but not Aunt Marcia."

"Ira, remember 'The Rise of the Goldbergs?'" Diane said. "When I was about twelve, I used to pray every night that I'd go to sleep and wake up Rosalie's little sister."

"Diane, don't expect my mother to look like Molly Goldberg." He sounded amused, but she could tell he was irritated. It *did* sound patronizing.

"I'm sorry, Ira, I didn't mean that. It's just that my concept of a family is wrapped around 'One Man's Family' and 'The Rise of the Goldbergs.' They were terribly important to me when I was a child."

"I'm sorry. I guess I'm uptight about tonight, too. I was talking to Russ the other night about what being a member of a minority can do to somebody. Either he takes pride in his background or he's bitter and resentful. There doesn't seem to be much in between."

"Gertrude Berg put Jews on the map when she played Molly Goldberg," the taxi driver said. "Everybody wanted to be part of the family. Me, I'm Jewish. Like I tell my kids, there comes a time in every Jew's life when he realizes he's different from a lot of people in the world. Maybe because somebody in school makes a crack. Or he reads somethin' in a newspaper. Of course, along came Hitler in the forties—and we all knew being Jewish was different."

"When I was a little kid, I thought I'd grow up in a world where there was no anti-Semitism," Ira said.

"Listen, it'll always be there." The taxi driver nearly sideswiped a truck. "There'll always be people who'll hate Jews and blacks and Catholics and Italians and Poles. Any minority, somebody's gonna hate 'em."

"For all that," Ira said quietly, "I'm proud of my Jewish heritage."

"You should be," Diane said.

The taxi emerged from the park and slithered through westbound traffic to West End Avenue and north. The driver, now immersed in cutting through heavy traffic, cursing to himself, withdrew from the conversation.

She was ashamed of her family's pretense, Diane confessed to herself. *Tell Ira now.* Let there be only honesty between them. But at that moment the cab pulled to a stop before what she realized was their destination. The moment was lost.

Ira hurried her across the sidewalk into the tiny lobby. The rotund, elderly doorman greeted Ira with the warmth he might have accorded a favorite grandson.

"Kathy's already here with the kids," he reported. "And your Aunt Marcia has been here all day. It ain't every day a couple celebrates a fortieth wedding anniversary."

In the elevator Ira explained that they had lived in the building since he was four, and that Henry had been the night doorman as long as he could remember.

"When Kathy gave birth, mom ordered dad to go phone Henry and let him know," Ira recalled. "Before Kathy married Craig, Henry rushed to tell mom about any 'young professional' who moved into the building."

As they stood before the apartment door, they heard the sound of laughter inside. Savory aromas of spices and fresh baking filtered out into the hallway.

The door was opened by a small, dark-haired woman. Instantly Diane knew it was Ira's mother.

"Mom, this is Diane."

"We're so pleased Ira brought you tonight, Diane. But Ira, doesn't she have another name?" *She's wondering if I'm Jewish,* Diane thought.

"I'm hoping to change it to Ross," Ira said. His mother beamed. Diane was startled by his candor. "But I don't push her, mom. All in good time."

In minutes Diane was surrounded by Ira's father, his sister Kathy, and eight-year-old Janis. Though they didn't know who she was, apparently it was enough that she was Ira's girlfriend.

"You're pretty," Janis decided, elated at this decision. "You're beautiful!"

"Thank you." Impulsively Diane reached to hug her.

"Henry said Aunt Marcia was here," Ira looked around.

"Where would Marcia be but in the kitchen?" his mother laughed. "With Karen supervising the icing of the cake. Karen is four," she explained to Diane. "No cake is ever iced in this family without Karen's supervision."

"Ira, now that you're a famous director, you can't come kiss your aunt?" Ira moved forward to kiss a taller, slightly younger edition of his mother. She squinted nearsightedly at Diane when Ira released her. "Aren't you Diane Dickenson?" Marcia asked.

"Yes."

"You're prettier than your pictures," Marcia said. "Do you like chocolate icing?"

"I'm a chocolate freak," Diane said, astonished and relieved that they thought nothing of who she was. "Like Ira."

Karen—a pretty four-year-old bundle of energy—darted out of the kitchen to announce that *she* had printed the words on the cake. With a little help from Aunt Marcia.

"We love you," she said and giggled infectiously as her grandfather scooped her up in his arms.

In a few minutes Kathy's husband Craig arrived, and Marcia ordered everybody to the table. To Diane the affection that richocheted about the dining room was infinitely precious. Under the table Ira reached for her hand.

"So mom, tell us how you did it." Craig asked. "How did you put up with dad for forty years?"

"It's like any marriage that lasts," his mother-in-law shrugged. "You learn to compromise. You learn to listen. You don't read into words what isn't there. You fight, and then it's over." Her eyes met her husband's. "I tell you the truth, when I married I wasn't sure it would last so long."

"I'm glad you both have the good sense to stay here in New York instead of running off to retirement in Florida," Marcia said, ladling more vegetables onto Diane's plate. "Eat, darling. Young girls today always worry about looking like Twiggy. A man wants something to hold besides bones."

606

"Forget about retiring," Mr. Ross chuckled. "That's like announcing you're standing by to die."

"I've been a widow seven years," Marcia told Diane. "My husband, may he rest in peace, wanted to be the richest man in the cemetery. I told him, 'Joe, how many fur coats can I wear at a time?' He worked himself into an early grave." She looked serious. "Now when I look at a good-looking man on the street, in a restaurant, on a subway, I ask myself, 'Is he single? Divorced? Widowed?'"

"Aunt Marcia, you wouldn't marry again if the best-looking, richest man in America asked you," Craig teased. He turned to Diane. "She's got children and grandchildren all over the United States, Diane. She does more traveling than an airline stewardess. What man would put up with that?"

By the time they left his parents' apartment, Diane was euphoric. She felt embraced by Ira's loving family.

"Stay over with me tonight?" he asked.

"All right." *She would marry Ira.* She would tell him tonight. "As long as you promise to be sure I'm awake by eight. I always see Jeffrey for a little bit before he goes off to nursery school."

When she and Ira walked into his apartment, she told herself that she would leave here tomorrow a different woman. Promised to Ira Ross, whom she would love for the rest of her life.

"My family likes you," he said while he helped her out of her coat. "Janis and Karen will disown me if I don't make you their aunt."

"In September," she said slowly. "Late in the month when the worst heat is over."

"You're saying you'll marry me in late September—"

"You asked for a hint." She laughed shakily. "Shall we go back and rewrite this scene?"

Normally she fell asleep in Ira's arms after lovemaking, but tonight Diane was wide awake.

"You're not sleepy," he said, fighting yawns.

"I'm too excited," she confessed. "And a little scared, too. This will be my last marriage ever."

"I'll make some coffee for us." He threw aside the comforter and reached for his robe on the nearby chair. "Unless you'd rather have champagne."

"I'm drunk already." A wonderful drunk. "Ira, you're sure your parents aren't going to be upset?"

"They may be faintly disturbed that I'm marrying a *goy*," he conceded. "But so long as you don't try to convert me they'll be happy." He stood beside the bed, enjoying the sight of her. "We can't have a church ceremony. It'll have to be a civil wedding."

She sat upright in bed, pulling the comforter around her because the heat had gone down and the bedroom was chilly.

"I want a Jewish ceremony," she said softly. "I want to be married by a rabbi in your parents' apartment."

"You're willing to convert?" His face lit up. "For mom and dad you'll do that?"

"I want a Jewish wedding," she said. "I want to carry the bible my grandmother carried at her wedding. I want you to wear my grandfather's *tallis*. Ira, there's no need for me to convert. My Carstairs grandfather was born Cohen. My mother married David Seligman, who changed his name to Dickenson. It's all been a pretense, Ira. I was born a Jew and I'll die a Jew."

Diane knew her aunt would be upset that she was marrying again. She knew, also, that her being married by a rabbi would be a traumatic experience for Claudia. As she had anticipated, Deirdre and Clay were amazed by her revelation about her Jewish heritage. Later she would write her mother and tell her she was married again.

Everyone concerned was sworn to secrecy about the marriage, though hints were flying wildly about the gossip columns. Diane decided that two floors of the Fifth Avenue house were to be redesigned as a private apartment for Ira, herself, and Jeffrey. When the structural changes were finished, Clay would redecorate.

The summer was flying past. Ira managed to be out at Southampton often, and Diane made frequent trips into the city to consult with Clay about the work at the Fifth Avenue house and to spend nights with Ira in his apartment. Out of respect for Claudia, they did not share a bedroom at the Southampton house. Ira was scheduled to start rehearsals on another play in mid-October. This would allow Diane and Ira a three-week honeymoon in a rented house in Montauk while Jeffrey and Mrs. Evans would stay at nearby Gurney's Inn.

On the last Sunday in September, with only Ira's immediate family and Deirdre and Ira in attendance,

Diane was married to Ira beneath an improvised white velvet *chupah*. Jeffrey, not really sure what was happening but happy to be part of the occasion, was their ring-bearer.

Only for the first few minutes did Jeffrey seem intimidated by strange faces, Diane thought happily. He loved "Uncle Ira"—and Ira's mother won him over instantly. To her, Jeffrey was another grandchild.

Diane wore a short turquoise silk Galanos dress and carried the ivory-covered bible that her maternal grandmother had carried at her own wedding plus a single red rose in memory of her Seligman grandmother. Ira stood beside her under the *chupah* with her grandfather's silk *tallis* about his shoulders. This was her first real marriage, Diane told herself in jubilation. A marriage that would last forever. Her only regret was that her aunt could not bring herself to be here today.

After the wedding dinner, Diane and Ira drove to their rental house in Montauk with Jeffrey and Mrs. Evans, who were staying at nearby Gurney's Inn. In the morning Diane and Ira would have breakfast there with Jeffrey and Mrs. Evans.

The house was a small modern masterpiece sitting high on a bluff overlooking the Atlantic with a wall of glass facing the ocean. With the drapes of the bedroom open to the night sea, Ira made love to his wife.

"Feel any different now that the rabbi has said the proper words?" he murmured, holding her in his arms. The night was silent except for the sound of the waves caressing the shore.

"I feel like the heroine of a forties movie," she laughed, tears in her eyes. "Good things are worth waiting for."

To Diane's relief, they had been able to keep their marriage out of the press. Eventually the newspapers would find out, but for now they were just any other couple, newly married and deeply in love.

On the first morning in Montauk they walked along the deserted stretch of white beach, arm in arm, to the attractive complex that was Gurney's Inn. They had breakfast with Jeffrey and Mrs. Evans in the Admiral's Room and after breakfast took Jeffrey for playtime on the still summer-warm sand.

As the days passed, Diane learned the charm of the little town that Carl Fisher had vowed—back in 1926—to make "the Miami Beach of the North." She was grateful that because of financial problems he had failed. Ira showed her the seven-story office building Fisher had built on Great Plain, in the center of the modest business district—seven stories high so that he might see all of Montauk from his top-floor offices. Diane admired the low Tudor stores and the Tudor Professional Building that Fisher commissioned at that same period.

Shopping for groceries so that they might have supplies if they were in the mood to dine at home, they talked with an elderly lifelong resident who enjoyed reminiscing about Montauk's past, when such notables as Stanford White and Frederick Law Olmstead, who designed New York's Central Park, were involved in the building of "summer cottages."

"A lot of important people stayed here in town," he said with pride. "President Hoover and President

Franklin Roosevelt fished here. Marconi, the wireless man, and Dr. Felix Adler, the educator, John and Lionel Barrymore, Alla Nazimova, Theda Bara, A. Conan Doyle all visited."

"It's a lovely town," Diane said. "My husband has been coming here for years." She felt a small thrill to be calling Ira *my husband.*

"Let's go over to White's and pick up the New York newspapers," he said, his arm around her.

While Ira went to buy newspapers, Diane lingered over a display of postcards.

"Di," he said somberly, as he returned to her side, "don't be upset, but the word is out." He showed her the headline on the *Daily News:* DI'S THIRD B'WAY STAGE DIRECTOR.

"How did they find out?" she asked, ashen. "We were so careful."

"Di, it had to come out sooner or later," he said. "It doesn't change anything. Hey—let's have dinner at home tonight. We'll eat on the deck at sunset, then come inside for coffee before the fireplace." Nights were cool in late September.

Diane was relieved that nobody in New York knew where they were honeymooning, and that the local people were unconcerned and friendly. She enjoyed their beautiful oasis of privacy. They spent their days watching the sunrise, spending mornings with Jeffrey, taking long walks on the beach, having dinner at Gurney's Inn or at Bill's if they preferred to dine away from the house. And having perfect nights alone.

*　　　*　　　*

Three days before Diane and Ira were to return to New York, they were awakened by a midnight phone call.

"I'll get it," Diane said, instantly awake, her heart pounding. *Something had happened to Jeffrey.* "Hello—"

"Why in hell didn't you tell me you were marrying again?" It was Tom, furious.

"I didn't see that it concerned you," Diane shot back.

"It does concern me," he said through clenched teeth. "I won't have my son raised by a New York Jewish radical! I'll be in New York for three days next week. I want custody of my son!"

"You can't have him!" Panic caught at her throat. "You agreed at the time of the divorce. Tom, the situation hasn't changed," she reminded with a show of bravado. "Arthur Lewisohn has those negatives in a bank vault."

"For a divorce I could be blackmailed." Tom was blunt. *"But this is my son we're talking about now!"*

"Your son, whom you haven't seen in months!" But Diane was scared. She knew how devious Tom could be.

"I'll call Lewisohn in the morning and arrange a meeting in New York," he said. "You'll be there with Jeffrey. I'll have a court order."

Chapter Thirty-Six

Cold and trembling, Diane repeated her conversation with Tom, grateful for Ira's comforting presence.

"You have nothing to worry about," he said. "You won't appear at that meeting. Arthur Lewisohn will handle everything. No judge will award Tom custody just because you've married again. Not even when your new husband is a New York Jewish radical."

"Ira, I remember my own childhood," Diane whispered. "I remember when mother and Aunt Claudia fought over my custody. I was so terrified about what would happen to me. I don't want Jeffrey ever to go through that."

"It won't happen," Ira said.

"I'm not like my mother—" Her eyes sought his. "Ira, tell me I'm not like her."

"Darling, you could never be like your mother." He pulled her into his arms. "No judge will give Tom a court order to get custody of Jeffrey—no matter how many arms he tries to twist. Tom will bluster a lot. Arthur Lewisohn will straighten him out. We'll see this through, Di. Nobody's taking Jeffrey from you."

Ira had said, *We'll see this through*. What a beautiful word *we* could be.

"Until it's all settled, I don't want to be where Tom can reach me."

"We're not running away, Di," Ira said. "We're here on our honeymoon. We won't allow Tom or anybody to spoil this time for us. Tom called up in a moment of fury. He's too shrewd to believe he can take Jeffrey from you."

"I'm calling Mike right now," she said. "I'll ask him to arrange for a bodyguard for Jeffrey until this is cleared up. I remember how I grew up with a bodyguard always at my heels. Hating it. I didn't want Jeffrey to grow up that way."

Diane was grateful that Ira's rehearsals would not begin until the day after Tom's scheduled meeting with Arthur Lewisohn; Ira would be with her. But this morning she sent Jeffrey off to nursery school in the chauffeur-driven limousine and in the company of Mrs. Evans and the bodyguard Mike had hired rather than on the school bus. Yet except in a crisis situation she was determined that Jeffrey would live a normal child's life.

"I know it's ridiculous to think that Tom might try to kidnap Jeffrey," she said wryly, watching from their living room while Jeffrey climbed into the limousine, "but I'll feel better this way."

She and Ira sat in the sun-filled living room overlooking the park and drank coffee while they waited to hear from Arthur Lewisohn.

"Di, everything is going to be fine," Ira said.

"Well, what's taking so long?" she snapped. "How much have they got to say to each other?"

"Tom probably showed up late. Then there's the sparring period—"

The phone rang. Diane ran to pick it up.

"Hello—"

"Everything's fine, Diane." It was Arthur Lewisohn. Relief swept through her. "We've had to make some minor concessions so Tom could save face—"

"What kind of concessions?" *She didn't trust Tom.*

"Tom wants to be consulted on Jeffrey's schooling. He has some specific ideas, for example, on boarding schools—"

"Jeffrey won't be going to boarding school. He has a home where he's loved and wanted."

"And he expects to be consulted on Jeffrey's religious affiliations."

"Arthur, Tom goes to church only when it's good for business. Jeffrey will be raised in his mother's faith. My son will be raised a Jew."

Reporters assumed that she had converted to Ira's religion. Ever since Liz Taylor converted for Mike Todd, the press could accept this without astonishment, as did those in the show biz and jet set worlds—though she would probably be dropped from the *Social Register*. She hadn't bothered to explain the truth to anyone other than Ira's family, Deirdre, and Clay; For Aunt Claudia's sake she'd let people believe what they liked. In three weeks, Aunt Claudia would be celebrating her eightieth birthday, and Diane didn't want anything to spoil her surprise birthday party.

"Tom won't bother checking on Jeffrey's religion." Arthur's voice intruded on her introspection, his contempt for her ex-husband obvious. "Everything's all right, Diane."

Even though she knew that Arthur was satisfied that Tom would make no trouble for her, Diane was tense for weeks. Gradually she began to relax and enjoy her marriage. She was delighted that Jeffrey and Ira were so warm and loving toward each other.

And she was getting to know her husband. When he was moody or depressed he wandered into the music room and played the *Moonlight* Sonata. When he was feeling romantic he played Cole Porter's "Night and Day." Both by ear. She ordered studio pianos for the apartment and the beach house.

Ira's new play took him on the road for several weeks, but she joined him for two or three days of each week in whatever city the play was appearing. She enjoyed being with him during the intense days and nights of the play's tryouts. Too exhausted to sleep some nights, Ira would talk to her till dawn. And when he wasn't talking, they made love. She felt gloriously involved in his life.

The play opened to rave reviews. Ira's direction was singled out for high praise. She reveled in his success.

By early spring Ira was negotiating for another directing assignment after having rejected several plays he considered destined for failure. Diane pleaded with him to take time out to write. There was no question now about her backing one of his productions. But to her astonishment, Ira rejected the offer.

"I have to do it on my own," he said. "Not on your money." Diane knew it would be useless to argue with him.

Soon Ira was caught up in plans for the new play. Casting began. The producer was haggling with a Hollywood star. Diane, Jeffrey, and Claudia went out to the Southampton house. Ira came out for long weekends. Clay appeared for brief stays, escaping from either the heat of a New York summer or the boredom of his mother's house at Newport. He was upset by his mother's heavy drinking and suspicious that the colonel was beating her. Twice she had appeared at breakfast at the Newport house with black eyes.

Deirdre came out to Southampton with her newly enlarged domestic staff—Simone and her husband had been fired for telling Tom's private detective that Diane and Ira were honeymooning in Montauk. Deirdre had hired another couple and a sleep-in maid. She hated being alone in the apartment overnight.

"Look, all the money is in my control now," Deirdre pointed out ebulliently while she and Diane sat over lunch on the deck of her beach house. "Why shouldn't I spend it any way I like? Daddy's outraged that he can't manipulate it anymore."

"I'm sorry the summer's almost over," Diane confided. "It's so peaceful out here."

"As long as you stay out of the summer social

circuit it is," Deirdre said. "Sure you don't want to go to that supper dance tomorrow night? I can rustle up a pair of escorts. And I don't mean Tex and his buddy," she giggled. "A couple of oldish stock-brokers from our crowd."

"Dee, don't get involved with Tex," Diane said. She knew Deirdre spent hours every day sprawled on a chaise beside the pool—hiding again under a caftan and waiting for the lifeguard.

Deirdre shrugged.

"Why not? It's just for the summer. So I give him a few presents." Including a brand new Thunderbird. "Tex gives me some gorgeous nights. What about the supper dance tomorrow night, Di? It's for a good cause."

"I don't think so. Ira'll be here, and I know he'd hate it."

"Mike sent me a check for four thousand dollars against his loan," Deirdre said with brittle laughter. "He can't bear being in debt to me. Hey, I've got an idea—let's drive into New York. Tex is off today. He went home for his mother's birthday. What do you say?"

"Now?" Diane was startled. "It'll be past four when we arrive, even if we leave right away."

"If I call the furrier, they'll stay open. Come on Di, let's go. Maybe we can drive Ira back with us tonight."

Diane let herself be persuaded to drive into the steaming-hot city. Traffic was light. By a little past four they were sitting in the deliciously cool quarters of Deirdre's new furrier. The owner assured Deirdre that they would stay open until she had finished her shopping.

"May we have Celia, please?" Deirdre asked.

The owner smiled. "But of course, Miss Swift."

"Celia is the salesgirl who sold me my darling blue sable," she whispered while they sat down in a pair of petit point chairs. "She knows exactly what I like."

While Diane sipped iced tea, Deirdre concentrated on the parade of furs being modeled for her.

"Celia, let me try the white fox greatcoat," she decided. "Is white fox fashionable?"

"A white fox greatcoat like this is always fashionable," Celia said, stroking the fur lovingly. "It's a glorious coat."

"It would look sensational on you. With your black hair and that marvelous tan." Deirdre called to the owner. "Mischa, I want this one. On second thought, I want two of them. One for me and one for Celia. My advance Christmas present," she told the startled saleswoman. "For being so nice to me."

Diane just gaped at her friend. But she didn't say a word until they were back out on the street.

"Deirdre, you've got to be out of your mind! How can you give a gift like that to a saleswoman?"

"Celia's darling to me. I want to give it to her." But Deirdre wouldn't look Diane in the eyes.

"You can't give expensive presents to everybody who's nice to you."

"All right, so I got carried away. But Mike sent back that four thousand. I didn't really ever expect to see it again. And Celia was so thrilled."

"Deirdre, you go to your lawyers and have them

put you on a monthly allowance. Even *your* money isn't endless if you start giving fur coats away to salespeople."

"Darling, there's more money there than I can ever spend." Deirdre refused to be ruffled. "If I have fun, why shouldn't I spend?"

"Let's go over to the house and see if Ira's there. Maybe he can have dinner with us." Diane understood Deirdre's need to feel loved. Even by a saleswoman in a furrier's shop.

When Diane got home, she found Ira on the telephone in the study. Deirdre went to the kitchen; she'd decided to cook dinner for them.

"I've got good news," Ira said after a welcoming kiss. "We can stay out at the beach house for all of September. Rehearsals won't begin until the first Monday in October. I can work out there as well as in the city."

"Ira, that's marvelous!" They would celebrate their first wedding anniversary at the beach house. They'd go to Gurney's Inn for dinner. "September's a perfect month. Most people are already heading back for the city."

While she and Ira were out there alone, she would find the right moment to talk to him. Jeffrey would be five next February. She'd love to have him grow up with a younger sister or brother. She couldn't wait to have Ira's child.

Diane persuaded Ira's parents to come out for a week early in the month when Claudia returned to the city. Earlier in the summer Kathy and Craig and their two little girls had spent a week with them. For Diane it was a special pleasure to be a part of this family.

On the eve of their first wedding anniversary, with a hint of autumn in the air, Diane and Ira drove to Gurney's Inn for dinner. They came home from Montauk, changed into warm slacks, sweaters, and sneakers, and went to walk at the water's edge. Moonlight spilled over the beach and washed the sea with silver.

They were content to walk hand-in-hand in silence until Ira paused to point out the lights of a fishing vessel far out at sea.

"Russ used to say the only real peace in the world is out on a fishing boat in the middle of the night." She could feel the tension gripping him.

"Ira, don't think about Vietnam now."

"I don't want to think that someday Jeffrey might have to go fight in another Vietnam," he said quietly.

"Please. No talk of Vietnam." She kissed him. "Tonight's a happy time."

"Darling, I'm sorry. I didn't mean to be morbid and insensitive."

"Ira, you're wonderful with Jeffrey. I'm so grateful for that."

"Jeffrey's very special to me," he said softly. "Like his mother."

"He'll be five in February. Wouldn't it be wonderful for him to have a brother or sister?"

"You want another child?" He stared at her. "Di, you'd be happy bringing another baby into this insane world?"

"Our baby—" She stared up at him in bewilderment. "I thought you'd want that—"

"Not in the world we live in." His face was taut in the moonlight. "We have Jeffrey. We're a family. We don't need more children." He reached for her hand again, his eyes shutting her out. "Let's walk back to the house. It's getting cold."

At the house, Ira tried to restore their earlier mood. He started a fire in their bedroom fireplace, went downstairs again to bring up the bottle of chilled champagne. Diane changed into a nightgown and robe and sat staring into the pine-scented blaze with a fixed little smile while Ira poured champagne into a pair of long-stemmed glasses.

Ira gave her a glass and pulled up a chair close to hers.

"Happy anniversary, Di."

Diane tried to accept the fact that she and Ira were never going to have children. She understood his concern for humanity. Vietnam, the battle for civil rights, the state of the environment caused him deep-seated anxiety, as they did millions of others. But she had never once suspected that he would deny them the joy of bringing a child into the world because of it.

She tried to focus her attention on the logistics of closing up the house for the season. Ira was moody and unfamiliarly unapproachable during these last days at the beach house. Diane told herself it was his normal habit of tensing up before going into rehearsal with a new play.

On their final day at the house, when Mrs. Evans

had taken Jeffrey off to bed, Ira suggested a walk on the beach at sunset.

"Put on a sweater, Di. It'll be cool with the sun down."

"I'll be just a minute."

They left the house to watch the glorious Hampton sunset, but Diane was only vaguely aware of the sun's orange-red splendor. She knew Ira was upset. They walked in silence. When he was ready, he would talk.

"Di, I wasn't honest with you when I asked you to marry me. I know I've been behaving like a bastard these last three days—" He stopped to gaze at the waves coming in to shore. "I guess I didn't tell you because I was afraid of losing you."

"Darling, please tell me. Whatever it is, we can talk about it."

"I had the mumps when I was nineteen. Isn't that the damnedest thing for a college kid to come down with?" His chuckle was synthetic. "Nobody knows— not even mom and dad. Di, I can't give you a child. I'm sterile." He took a deep breath. "If you want a divorce—maybe in the circumstances you're entitled to an annulment—I won't fight—"

"Ira, shut up," she said tenderly. "I would have married you, sterile or not. I love you, Ira. If we can't have children I won't stop loving you."

"I ought to tell the family." He pulled her close, and she felt the tremor that shot through him. "It isn't fair to let mom and dad go on hoping for grandchildren from us."

"Ira, it won't change how they feel about you. And we *have* a child. Jeffrey is yours, too. We'll raise him

625

together." Later she would talk to Ira about adopting a second child.

Despite her insistence that Ira's sterility in no way changed her love for him, Diane felt an indefinable frustrating barrier rise between them in the following months. She wished she'd never brought up the subject of children.

Professionally, too, Ira was living through a rough period. He directed two financial flops in a row. He was moody and impatient, dismissing Diane's constant reminders that he had received fine reviews on both plays.

"I can't go to the bank with reviews!" he lashed out at her on a late May afternoon as they got ready to go to his parents' apartment for dinner.

"Ira, if you need money, we have plenty."

"I don't want my wife's money." He paused at the sight of her stricken expression. "Di, I didn't mean that the way it sounded. I just don't feel like a man unless I'm earning money."

"Another play will come along," she said. "Every director has a bad streak."

"I don't know. Maybe I've lost my judgment."

"Ira, that's ridiculous!"

"Remember when we had dinner with Laura the last time she was in New York? She said any time I was in the mood to direct a film she could work out something for me—"

"You don't want to be part of the movie business," Diane said. "You love theater. It's where you belong. Maybe this is the time when you should settle down to finish your play—"

"Larry has a new script and a prospective backer," Ira said. "It has a fairly large cast, so the net will be rough. Larry may have to bring in additional money. He's sending over a script for me to read." He glanced at his watch. "Go rustle up Jeffrey. We'll be late for dinner if we don't leave right away."

At ten o'clock the next morning a messenger arrived with the script. Ira settled down to read. Over lunch with Diane, he was enthusiastic.

"Then you'll do it?" Diane was relieved that he had a new assignment.

"I'll do it. I hope I'm choosing right." Apprehension crept into his voice. "I can't afford three flops in a row."

He threw himself into plotting out directions, even before the money was up and a theater set. Diane was nervous because Larry Kaufman was having problems raising capital in addition to what had been pledged. On impulse she offered to arrange for backers' auditions at the Fifth Avenue house; Clay and Deirdre would be delighted to help:

Diane loved being so closely involved with Ira's work. She played hostess to prospective backers, her enthusiasm for the project dissipating her natural shyness. When the money was at last raised, both Ira and Larry considered Diane instrumental in the accomplishment, and she reveled in their approval.

The play was scheduled to open on Broadway in late October of the 1970–71 theater season. Diane went along when the company left for the out-of-town tryouts, arranging to spend half of each of those tryout weeks with Ira, sitting beside him during performances and in the strenuous daytime sessions when rewrites were being rehearsed. It was a hectic and anxious period.

Four days before the company was to come into New York, an actress in a bit part was injured in a traffic accident on her way to the theater. Diane was terrified when Larry and Ira insisted she fill in until they found a replacement.

"What about Equity?"

"Di, we have a performance in two hours," he said. "You look right for the part. You have wardrobe."

"But I'm not an actress."

"For three lines you can be an actress," Larry said. "We'll make an announcement at curtain time. 'For tonight's performance the role of Candy will be played by Diane Dickenson.'"

She turned pale.

"Larry, no. Diane Ross." *This was insane.*

"Diane Ross won't bring us publicity. Forgive me, Ira," he said, "but for column breaks let your wife be Diane Dickenson tonight."

Ira stayed at her side backstage until her entrance. He had coached her, and knowing he was there in the wings, she felt confident. After the performance the other cast members congratulated her on her performance.

"Honey, you were fine," Ira said, glowing. "With three lines you got a hand."

"It was what I had to say," she said. "And you told me exactly how to say it."

In New York Diane joined Equity and stayed with

the company. The reviews were mixed and Larry pointed out that her presence in the cast was a wedge to acquire column items. The play ran for nine weeks—until the leading lady exercised her contractual right to withdraw and go out to accept a film commitment.

Now Diane tried to push Ira into completing his own play, and with some reluctance he agreed. He knew that a play protesting the proliferation of nuclear weapons and warning that the world was on a course for self-destruction was not exactly the stuff that packed theaters.

It was understood Ira would not permit Diane to finance a production. He was willing for her to set up backers' auditions to try to raise the necessary capital when the play was finished, even though Larry warned it would be a rough deal.

Early in February he drove out to Montauk with Diane to talk to a real estate broker about renting a house for a few weeks. He was uptight and anxious, but he was confident that in a house beside the sea he would be able to relax and finish the play. A tiny house devoid of servants—large enough only for Diane and himself. Diane would commute between New York and Montauk.

It was a special time for Diane. Sometimes Ira could talk of nothing else but the play; other times he disappeared for long solitary walks along the foggy beach and returned to the typewriter without a word. It was enough for him to have Diane there when he needed her.

In April the play was finished. Diane enlisted the help of Deirdre and Clay again in arranging for the backers' auditions. Larry persuaded a major Hollywood star to accept the lead, which helped to bring in the necessary money. A theater was signed for an early fall opening.

Diane was stunned when early in the summer a producer friend of Ira's invited her to appear in a new play being cast. The part was small but showy—obviously the producer wanted Diane Dickenson in his production. She didn't understand Ira's insistence that she accept.

"Di, I'll work with you," he promised. "You'll be fine. It'll be an exciting experience for you."

"You won't have time." What was she doing? She wasn't an actress. "And how can I go out of town with a play and leave Jeffrey?" Why was Ira so eager for her to be an actress? But then she understood: he needed to be alone during the period of his own rehearsals, she surmised. That way he could be totally immersed in the play during those weeks. He'd feel guilty if he thought he was neglecting her.

"The play will only be out of town for three weeks," he reminded. "Jeffrey and Mrs. Evans can travel with you. It'll be a sightseeing tour for Jeffrey," he encouraged. "My play will have one week of previews and open here in town. I've checked with all the schedules. You'll be opening in New York the same week as my play."

"All right, Ira." She accepted with much trepidation. Even with three lines she had been a nervous wreck before each performance. But if this would give Ira some peace of mind, then she'd do it.

*　　*　　*

Diane was amazed to find herself caught up in the excitement of rehearsals. As he had promised, Ira worked with her at every free moment. Deirdre acted as though it were *she* who was opening on Broadway. Clay teased her, but she knew he was impressed. And now she understood why Ira had insisted that she do the play: the theater was to be a substitute for the child he couldn't give her.

While Diane was in Philadelphia, Ira called with shattering news. The major film star appearing in the lead in the play had suffered a stroke. Fortunately it was a mild stroke, but it would keep him away from acting for at least six months. They'd rushed in a replacement—a competent Broadway actor—but Ira was dubious about the play surviving without a movie name.

"Ira, the play is terrific," she encouraged. "It won't need a film name to make it."

The opening of the play was postponed for one week to allow the replacement rehearsal time. That meant it would open cold, without previews. Diane returned to the city to find Ira taciturn and moody. He was anxious about personality problems within the cast of his play.

"Everybody's on edge because of the replacement," Ira confided while he accompanied her to the theater for her own opening. "God knows he's good; but a Hollywood star guarantees an advance sale. Larry says we've had a lot of concellations among the theater parties."

"It's a wonderful play, Ira. Whatever happens, you can be proud of it."

"Nervous?" He reached for her hand.

"Scared to death. I have this horror of walking on stage and going completely blank. I've never worked so hard at anything in my life." The out-of-town reviews had been generally excellent. A couple of critics had even singled her out for praise.

Diane went through opening night exhilarated but terrified. Afterwards, she and Ira joined the company in going to Sardi's to wait for the reviews. Diane kept warning herself that a play could do marvelously on the road and fail in New York. She sat with her hand in Ira's when the first editions of the morning newspapers were brought into Sardi's.

"It's a hit!" their producer announced jubilantly. "We're in for a long run, kids!"

The newspaper reviews were handed about among the company members. Diane's own reviews were tepid, though two critics remarked on her sincerity and charm.

"You were good," Ira insisted. "If it was some girl nobody knew, they'd be talking about a terrific future in the theater for her."

"Ira, let's leave," she whispered, trying to conceal her hurt. "You have to be at the theater tomorrow at ten."

Four nights later, Diane sat with Ira at the back of the theater for the opening of *his* play. He was worried that the previews had to be canceled. He would have liked four weeks out of town.

Diane was absorbed in the play. The audience seemed to be engrossed. She was convinced she was seeing fine theater, the kind of theater Ira respected.

She prayed the reception would be good; Ira had waited so long for tonight.

Most of the reviews were poor. Only one critic called it "stupendous, urgent theater." The closing notices went up the second night. Ira was quiet and withdrawn.

When Diane suggested that she withdraw from her own play Ira was not only angry, but he pushed her into a role in a television drama. The new medium was bewildering, the director intimidating. Ira was called in to direct when the original director declared he couldn't get a performance out of Diane.

Ira managed to elicit a mediocre performance from her, and Diane vowed she wanted no more of acting. One night, after a few drinks, Ira admitted to Diane that she was a poor actress.

"Great for an amateur. But not for Broadway or TV."

Diane wanted to remind him that she had only gone into the play to please him. *Everything she did was to please him.* But she held her tongue; he wouldn't have talked to her this way if he hadn't been drinking. Even if it was the truth.

Diane gave the required notice and withdrew from the play. She knew her absence would cause no real problem. Her acting career was finished forever. One more failure.

In the weeks that followed Diane tried to help Ira through this difficult period. He hated his failure as a playwright, resented his success as a director. She talked to his mother about it.

"Give him time, darling," she said. "Ira does everything the hard way."

She decided it was time to approach Ira about adopting a child.

As they dressed for the Passover seder at her in-laws' apartment while Jeffrey watched TV in the living room, she said, "Ira, remember my telling you about that adorable little girl that Jeffrey plays with almost every afternoon?"

"His first love, right?" he said, looking for a tie.

"Yes. Why?"

"Her mother told me today that she's adopted." She paused. "Ira, why don't we adopt a baby? A newborn—it'll be almost like our own—"

He glared at her.

"No! Every time I looked at it, I'd remember I'm not enough of a man to give you a child of my own!"

"Millions of couples adopt, Ira. They don't look at it like that."

"Well, I do," he snapped. "I don't want to hear another word about adoption. If you have to have another baby, divorce me and marry somebody who can give you one!"

"Ira, don't be ridiculous!" Tears filled her eyes.

"Tell mom some business meeting came up. I can't make the seder tonight. You go with Jeffrey."

When Ira came home, cold and uncommunicative, it was six-thirty in the morning. She saw Jeffrey off to school and returned to their apartment to find Ira fast asleep.

Not until two days later did Diane know where Ira had spent his night away from home. A gossip columnist reported that Ira and a Eurasian model known only as Odalie had circulated around the nightclub circuit and afterwards had to be forcibly restrained from nude bathing in the fountain at Lincoln Center. Ira was quoted as saying that he would make Odalie a Broadway star.

Diane knew her third marriage was finished. Trembling, she telephoned Deirdre.

"Hello?"

"I'm sorry, Dee, I woke you, didn't I?"

"Don't worry about it. We had a crazy party last night. I think the last person left at seven. What's up that couldn't wait until later?"

"Come with me to Mexico, Dee. I'm divorcing Ira."

Chapter Thirty-Seven

Diane and Deirdre stayed in Mexico for a week. On the flight back to Palm Springs—where Jeffrey, Mrs. Evans, and a tutor were established in a house rented for a month—Diane thought how sad and ironic it was that she and Deirdre had both divorced the men they still loved.

"My mother was in Palm Springs two years ago," Deirdre said. "When she phoned me from there, she sounded like a transplanted Hollywood tourist guide. She told me about the house Debbie Reynolds and Eddie Fisher honeymooned in, and the one where Liz Taylor and Eddie spent theirs. Then there was Alice Faye's house, and Conrad Hilton's, and the golf cart that Eisenhower rode in—"

"I must confess, I rented the Palm Springs house hoping Aunt Claudia would come out," Diane said. "She used to say the desert was the best place for arthritis."

"She's upset about the divorce, Di. You should have expected that."

"Dee, I didn't divorce Ira to make her unhappy."

Deirdre smiled.

"I don't think it's made you particularly happy, either, my friend."

"Dee, shut up. Who expects to be happy all the time?"

At the airport they were met by a chauffeur in a rented limousine.

"I'm going on a starvation diet," Deirdre said, as they drove toward the house. "I'm absolutely going to lose weight. Do you suppose Maine Chance has a Palm Springs branch?"

But Diane wasn't listening.

"Dee, what did I do wrong? What's wrong with me that I couldn't hold Ira?"

Deirdre shrugged.

"So he got drunk and made an ass of himself with that kooky model. Don't you think you overreacted?"

"You think I was wrong? But how could I live with him after that?"

"Sweetie, do you know how many women close their eyes to that same scene every day? How many *men?* Mike knew all the crazy things I was doing. But he loved me so much he looked the other way."

"Are you saying I didn't love Ira?"

Deirdre hesitated.

"I think you let pride get in the way. You know, you could call Ira and say it was just an awful nightmare. You could take him back."

"No." Diane lifted her head defiantly. "Not after the way he behaved. What could there be for us?"

"A lot more than there'll be for you alone," Deirdre said. "You two had something great."

"It's over. She'd always be between us."

"Whatever you say, baby." Deirdre hugged her. "So what are we going to do with ourselves in Palm Springs for a month if we don't play golf? I hear by nine o'clock everybody's yawning." Then she brightened. "But mother says there're some wonderful boutiques on Palm Canyon Drive."

Within a week Diane's resolve was weakening. She knew Deirdre was waiting for her to contact Ira. He wouldn't be at the apartment. He wasn't likely to go back home to his parents.

"I think I'll call mom," she said self-consciously after dinner on their seventh night in Palm Springs. Mrs. Evans had taken Jeffrey off to bed. "She must be terribly upset about the divorce."

"Good. Ask her where you can reach Ira," Deirdre said.

Mrs. Ross was pleased to hear from Diane, but she was upset about the divorce.

"Ira wouldn't tell me a thing, except that your marriage wasn't working out."

"Mom, where is Ira staying?"

"He left for California this morning," Mrs. Ross said. "He's seeing Laura Devlin about a possible screenwriting assignment. He's staying at the Beverly Wilshire in Beverly Hills. Wait, I'll get the phone number for you."

Twenty minutes later, under Deirdre's gleeful surveillance, Diane was packing for a flight to Los Angeles. A phone call to the Beverly Wilshire had elicited the information that, yes, Ira Ross was registered at the Beverly Wilshire but that he was not in his suite. Diane decided not to leave a message; she would show up in person. Contrite and loving.

"I can't believe it!" Diane glowed. "Ira's only a hundred miles away. How could I have been so insane? I'll spend the rest of my life loving him."

"Miss Swift," Mrs. Evans called from down the hall. Her voice oddly tensed. "May I talk to you for a moment?"

Diane reached into a drawer for a particularly lovely nightgown and brought it over to her valise for packing. Only for Ira could she bring herself to go to Los Angeles again. She couldn't wait to see his face when he saw her at the door of his hotel suite.

"Di—" Ashen, Deirdre stood in the bedroom doorway. "Unpack, darling. Mrs. Evans just heard it on the news. Ira married that model, Odalie."

Diane told herself that her life would center around Jeffrey. She made every effort to provide an aura of family around him. How could she explain divorce to a seven-year-old? She just told him that "Uncle Ira went to California to work." After a few weeks he stopped asking wistfully for Ira. When Ira's mother called to invite them to dinner, she invented excuses not to go. Finally Ira's parents understood that she couldn't bear to continue the relationship. She told Jeffrey that "Grandma and grandpa moved to Florida—we'll go down to visit them some time." But she felt guilty at depriving Jeffrey of the warmth of their love.

Claudia lavished love on Jeffrey. She declared he

was the joy of her old age. Deirdre and Clay played the loving aunt and uncle. On Jeffrey's eighth birthday a lavish gift arrived from Ira.

Diane was relieved that Tom showed up only occasionally to spend an hour or two with his son. When Jill and Betsy were in New York, they made no effort to see their young half-brother. For Tom's other family Jeffrey seemed not to exist.

By winter the Hollywood columnists were hinting that there was trouble between Ira and Odalie. In New York on business early in March, Laura met Diane for lunch at La Caravelle.

"I give Ira's marriage six months," Laura said as they sipped at preluncheon martinis. "Odalie is an overambitious little bitch who will dump Ira for the first important film producer who makes an offer."

"Is he happy?" Diane asked softly.

"He's miserable. He went on a drinking spree when you left him. He doesn't even remember marrying Odalie in Las Vegas."

"I hope he's not blaming his marriage on me—"

"No," Laura said quickly. "He blames nobody but himself. He said he just wasn't capable of being the man you expected him to be."

"I expected him to be faithful. Obviously I expected too much." *She couldn't talk about Ira.* "From what I read, you're doing fabulously in pictures, Laura. You've staked out fresh territory for women in the field."

"I'm doing great," Laura agreed, her eyes serious. "But I know that I'm only as good as my last picture. Either the films I produce bring in long lines at the box office, or I'm out. I never get off the griddle, Di."

"But you love it. You're right up there where you wanted to be—and well ahead of schedule."

"But I never forget that six months later I could be out on my rear. I don't know why Ira is staying out there—it's not his scene. He keeps talking about sitting down with me to work out a directing deal or settling down to write a screenplay. He's had offers from several people, but he's not really doing anything." The concern in Laura's eyes refuted the casualness of her voice. "Just partying and trying to push Odalie ahead. She's developed a reputation for being hard to handle. You can't get away with that today unless you're a superstar—and I hear the two films she's made so far don't show that kind of potential."

"Ira's too busy playing Pygmalion to write." Bitterness crept into Diane's voice. "I disappointed him, too. He thought he'd make a Broadway star of me."

"He's still in love with you."

"Did he say that?"

"He doesn't have to. I see it in his eyes any time your name is mentioned."

"He didn't try to stop me when I told him I wanted a divorce. He told me to go ahead."

"Because he thought that was what you wanted. Why don't people open up and talk honestly when their whole lives are at stake? I wonder how many divorces would never have happened if husbands and wives didn't leap into wrong guesses?"

"I've made three mistakes. I'll never marry again."

"What shall I tell Ira when I go back to the Coast? He'll know I've seen you."

"Tell him I hope he'll be very happy. Tell him I'll watch for his name on the screen credits."

Diane was relieved when lunch was over and Laura rushed to her next appointment. She wished she could sit down for a long talk with Deirdre, but Deirdre would be at Maine Chance for another three weeks.

Around ten the next morning, while Diane was dressing for a committee meeting for a charity ball, Clay phoned.

"Clay, calm down," she said. "I can't understand you."

"I'm at my mother's house—" His voice was shrill. "Di, I think my mother's dead. I think that bastard killed her."

"Did you call a doctor?"

"He's on the way. Di, can you come over? The colonel is dead drunk in his bedroom. Mattie's hysterical. She took mother her breakfast tray and couldn't wake her. She's got a black eye and bruises. Di, it's awful!"

"I'll be there in five minutes."

By the time Diane arrived, the doctor was with Mrs. Brentwood. Clay sat at an edge of a chair in the living room, his face ashen.

"Dr. Gorton threw me out," he told Diane. "I know she's dead. He probably killed her hours ago."

"Clay, you don't know that," Diane said. "Wait till Dr. Gorton comes out."

"And that fucking bastard is lying naked and dead drunk in the next room! He probably doesn't even

643

remember what happened!"

Clay leapt to his feet at the sound of Dr. Gorton's voice in the hall.

"This is Diane Dickenson, my closest friend," Clay introduced her. "Dr. Gorton, Diane."

"I'm sorry, Clay," Dr. Gorton said gently. "Your mother's dead."

He paused, swallowed hard.

"You saw the bruises on her face and jaw? And Mattie says she had a bad bruise on her chest. That son of a bitch killed her!" Clay's voice soared again.

"Clay, get hold of yourself," Dr. Gorton said sharply. "This is a difficult situation. We know your mother was drinking heavily. She's suffered two bad falls in the last six months—"

"Dr. Gorton, that black eye," Clay interrupted, a tic in his right eye betraying his agitation. "She didn't get that in a fall."

"It could have happened earlier." Dr. Gorton seemed to be fighting to arrive at some decision. "Clay, we could ask for an inquest, but do you understand the implications of that?"

"Damn it, yes! I'm implying that my stepfather is guilty of murder."

"The evidence against him is inconclusive. Furthermore, would you want your mother involved in a murder scandal?"

"You think I should just let him go scot-free?" Clay was outraged. "I was afraid of something like this from the day they got married."

"Your great-aunt Jessica is getting on in years. She's a proud old lady. Clay, could you put her through that kind of ugly situation? Do you suppose your mother would want her name dragged through a murder trial? Provided, of course, we could even get an indictment.''

Clay stood still, his hands clenched at his side.

"No," he said quietly. "You're right. Mother would hate it. It would kill Aunt Jessica to see the Brentwood name spread across the tabloids and scandal sheets. Do whatever you have to do, Dr. Gorton. My mother died in her sleep.''

Diane saw Clay through a hastily arranged funeral with a closed casket. He accepted the sympathy of his mother's friends with stoic politeness while the colonel hovered nervously in the background. Diane suspected that the closed casket was causing a stir among Mrs. Brentwood's circle, though no one said anything. They probably suspected that she had fallen while drunk.

Diane sat beside Clay and held his hand while the will was read in the offices of the Brentwood family attorney. The entire income from the Brentwood estate went to the colonel. At his death Clay would inherit the estate. The attorney made it clear that it would be futile to contest the will.

"The old bastard will outlive me," he muttered to Diane. The colonel had remained with the attorneys to discuss his financial status—and to avoid a confrontation with Clay, Diane surmised. "If he had gone up for murder, the estate would have come straight to me. Like my father planned," Clay said in the elevator.

"Clay, you don't need to worry about money,"

Diane comforted. "You must know that."

"Di, we had awful scenes between us. But she was my mother. I can't believe she died like that. Please come home with me. I don't want to be alone."

Except for brief trips home to see Jeffrey each day, Diane stayed with Clay at his apartment for a week. Alone with her, and freed of the necessity of keeping up a pretense of acceptance, Clay fell apart. He blamed himself for not interceding earlier, hated himself for not demanding an inquest. He had been off drugs for years, but Diane feared that now he might start again.

"Clay, you'll open up a consulting service as interior designer," Diane said. "I'll be your silent partner. You're very good at it. And it's a terrific investment for me."

"It was great when I was doing houses for Deirdre and you and some of my mother's crazy friends. But Di, I don't know if I can handle it as a business."

"You can," she said confidently. "You have a real flair. And I'll work with you whenever I can. You should have done it years ago."

She was astonished to see tears in his eyes.

"I love you, Di. I bless the day Dee brought us together."

When she was sure that Clay was back in control, she left him and returned to her own house. Mrs. Evans had left a note for her to call Jill in Atlanta—she had phoned three times that day.

Trying to convince herself that it was nothing serious, she dialed Jill's home.

"Hello, Diane." Jill was cool.

"I found a message that you'd called."

"Yes. Daddy had a heart attack last night."

Diane was silent for a moment, stunned.

"Is he all right?"

"Oh, he's fine. It was a very minor attack. But daddy thought Jeffrey ought to be told."

"Jill, he's an eight-year-old child—"

"He's daddy's child, and daddy wants him to be told."

"I'll explain it to Jeffrey," Diane agreed. She would *not* tell Jeffrey that the man he saw two or three times a year for an hour or two had suffered a heart attack. What was the point?

Deirdre returned from Maine Chance, thinner again and vowing to stay on her diet. Diane swept her up into the plans to open Clay's shop.

Three weeks after the death of Clay's mother, Diane signed a lease for a shop for the new consultation service: Clay Brentwood, Interior Designer. Deirdre insisted they celebrate with lunch at La Caravelle.

"Today," Clay said, "we have luxury dining in New York. Gourmet dining is dead."

"After lunch I'll drop by Arthur Lewisohn's office," Diane told them. "He's having the incorporation papers drawn up for the business."

In happy camaraderie, Deirdre and Clay accompanied Diane to the lawyer's offices.

"Miss Dickenson. Mr. Lewisohn has been trying to reach you for the last two hours," the firm's receptionist greeted her. "I think it's something important." She was already buzzing the attorney.

Diane was ushered immediately into Arthur Lewisohn's private office. He rose to his feet and crossed the room to greet her, closing the door behind them. His expression grave.

"Diane, we're facing some problems with Tom Mason," he said without preliminaries. "I was on the phone with his attorneys this morning. He's demanding full custody of Jeffrey." Diane stared at him in disbelief. "I gather his recent heart attack made him very conscious of the existence of his son."

"Arthur, he's out of his mind!"

"He's playing a dirty game," Arthur said apologetically. "I've set up an appointment to talk with him and his attorneys tomorrow morning at ten. He's claiming that Jeffrey is being raised in an unhealthy atmosphere." Arthur was uncomfortable in what he had to say. "His attorney is citing your three marriages and three divorces. They're claiming that you left your home for an entire week to take up residence with Clay Brentwood."

"Clay was in a terrible emotional state after his mother's funeral. And Tom knows Clay's gay." But terror turned her to ice. How did Tom know about that? Did money buy any information?

"They have photographs and affidavits. Tom made it clear he's willing to splash this all over the newspapers if that's what's necessary to gain custody," Arthur said. "He could resort to the kind of claims you couldn't even imagine. He's a vicious man."

"You said Tom will be here in the morning?"

"That's right."

"Jeffrey and I won't be," Diane decided grimly. "We won't be anywhere in the country. I had my passport renewed two years ago, and Jeffrey's on it."

"Diane, how long can you stay out of the country?" Arthur was anxious.

"As long as it's necessary. Till Jeffrey's eighteen, if need be. I won't allow Tom to take Jeffrey from me. I'll be in Canada tonight. Tomorrow I'll fly with Jeffrey to Paris. Let Tom try and find us!"

Chapter Thirty-Eight

The Montreal-to-Paris flight landed at Orly. Diane marshalled her small entourage, which included Jeffrey, Mrs. Evans, Deirdre, and Deirdre's maid Elise through Customs and to a limousine waiting to transport them to the suite reserved for them at the Crillon. They were traveling with a minimum of luggage. Clay would arrange for later shipments.

"Di, do you realize this is the first time Jeffrey's seen Paris?" Deirdre said once they were settled in the limousine and traveling through morning traffic toward the city.

"I don't think he's seeing much this morning," Diane laughed, cradling him against her.

"Mommy, you're sure I won't be in trouble for missing school?" he asked between yawns.

"Uncle Clay will explain to the principal," Diane soothed. She smiled but her eyes were somber. There was no way of knowing how long they would stay in Paris. She remembered her own early years in the city, when French was more her native language than English. After all those years, she now wondered about Nanette, her classmate at the Paris school.

"I was in Paris for four days eighteen years ago," Mrs. Evans recalled, seeming nervous now about this sudden trip out of the country.

"I've never been further from New York than Atlantic City," Elise confessed. "It's so exciting."

"We'll stay at the Crillon until I can find a house or an apartment," Diane said. She knew that rentals were difficult to come by in Paris; it had become a city of condominiums. If necessary, she would buy.

Four days later, Diane and Deirdre were shown a charming house on the tree-shaded Quai d'Orsay, with tall balconied windows that looked out on the Seine. It was furnished and available for lease for a minimum of six months. Faced with a six-month commitment, Diane hesitated.

"Di, take it," Deirdre urged. "It's perfect for us."

The four women and Jeffrey settled themselves comfortably in the spacious, high-ceilinged rooms, furnished in a dramatic blend of periods and cultures. A tutor was found for Jeffrey, who was launched on a crash course in French. From what Mr. Lewisohn told them, it seemed as though they might have to stay in Paris indefinitely.

Diane tried to tell herself this was just another European vacation. She spoke on the phone regularly with Claudia. Jeffrey—always a child with a zest for living—was fitting well into his new life, with only occasional bouts of homesickness.

When the summer heat descended in full force on Paris, Diane took her entourage to a house in the country for six weeks. Early in August Clay joined them for a month to hunt for antiques for a Manhattan townhouse he was redecorating. He made every effort to involve Diane, promising to air-mail swatches to her.

Diane continued to hope for word that it would be safe to return to New York. But so far Arthur Lewisohn had made it clear she would be brought into court the moment she was back on American soil. Apparently Tom Mason was furious at being thwarted.

Though she struggled to convince herself that Jeffrey was safe as long as he was away from America, she worried about what action Tom might take if his detectives tracked her down. She knew he wouldn't hesitate to kidnap Jeffrey if he could.

Now she hired around-the-clock bodyguards to watch over Jeffrey. Knowing that it was a matter of time before Jeffrey—so bright and outgoing—realized that he was being protected from some such action. She remembered the gun-toting chauffeur who had been her shadow when she was Jeffrey's age and how she had hated it all.

In the autumn Diane reconciled herself to sending Jeffrey to a private Paris school. She extended the lease on the house. She joined a modest Left Bank temple and took Jeffrey with her to Saturday morning services. She joined as Diane Seligman. In October she saw Deirdre off for New York.

"I'll stay just a month," Deirdre promised. "You know by now that I'm addicted to those shops on the Rue du Faubourg St. Honoré."

Diane had breakfast alone every morning in her

bedroom at a table overlooking the Seine. She spent much of the morning reading the *International Herald Tribune*, nostalgic for home, hoping for some news about Ira.

Tom was in the news again because of strikes at the Atlanta mills; he was still refusing to accept a union despite several violent outbreaks. Tom wasn't that concerned about the financial demands, she surmised. He couldn't bear to give up complete control of his mill empire. He was in Washington frequently now, fighting for tariffs on cotton imports.

Laura wrote in a recent letter—forwarded from the Fifth Avenue house because the Paris address was being kept secret—that at last Ira was working on a screenplay, and that it was likely that she would buy it for TDM. It was ironic, she thought, that one ex-husband was writing a screenplay to be filmed by a company controlled by another ex-husband.

Diane was ever-conscious of the need to keep herself out of the Parisian social whirl, to avoid being seen by American jet-setters who might report her whereabouts to Tom. It was a lonely, secluded existence. She sought diversion in visits to the Louvre, walks about colorful Montmartre, shopping at the markets at Les Halles. But all this merely kept her busy; it didn't fill the void in her life.

She was delighted when Clay commissioned her to shop for specific antiques for his various clients. Soon she was buying rare fabrics, wallpapers, planning whole rooms with Clay as though she were working side by side with him. The days lost some of their emptiness.

Claudia wrote that she would conquer her distaste

for travel to come to Paris in December. Mrs. Avery would be accompanying her.

"I can't bear not seeing Jeffrey and you for such a long stretch of time," she wrote. *"You two are the dearest things in my life."*

Diane waited impatiently for Claudia's arrival in Paris. Deirdre, now back from New York, planned interesting excursions for Claudia, who had not been to Paris for thirty years.

"Nothing too strenuous," Diane said. "She tires easily."

On the morning of New Year's Eve, Ira stood in the doorway of the master bedroom of the country ranch house he had rented four months ago for Odalie and himself and watched while she methodically locked the last four of seventeen pieces of luggage. He stepped aside while a chauffeur returned to collect the last of the luggage to be stashed away in a waiting white limousine.

Odalie straightened up and reached for the lynx coat thrown across the foot of the king-size bed.

"You have done nothing for me!" she said coldly. "I married you to become a star! I hate this house. I hate you. Rodney is flying me to Cuernavaca for a divorce." Rodney was the oft-married billionaire owner of a luxury hotel chain. "We'll be married immediately afterwards. He'll make me a star if he has to buy a film studio to do it!"

Ira stood still until he heard the front door slam. Then he closed the door of the master bedroom, where the air was permeated by Odalie's expensive and exotic perfumes. Thank God it was over. He had known all along that it would only be a matter of time before Odalie divorced him.

He walked down the hall into the huge beamed living room and dropped onto a comfortable leather lounge chair. He loved this house on a cul-de-sac looking down on Coldwater Canyon. The privacy it provided. The superb views. He had thought that here he could come to grips with his life. He thought that here he would write.

He had finished his screenplay. He had not shown it yet to Laura. She would know if it would work. But he'd had little joy in the writing. It was a product.

On a sudden impulse he left his chair and crossed to the phone. There would be partying at the studio today and an early dismissal, but Laura would be at her desk. He'd never known a woman who worked as hard as she.

"Hello," she answered warily, though this was the private line used only by her closest associates.

"I wrapped up the screenplay last night," he said. "And, not coincidentally, Odalie packed up and left this morning. Rodney is flying her down to Cuernavaca for a divorce." Most of Hollywood knew Odalie was sleeping with Rodney.

"Congratulations on both scores," Laura said. "What are you doing tonight?"

"Nothing. The Hollywood party scene doesn't turn me on."

"I'll be over around five. You can cook dinner while I read the screenplay. It's been a while since we've seen a New Year's Eve together."

"I'm warning you, my culinary repertoire is

limited. Would you like spaghetti or scallops in wine?"

"Let's live dangerously," she laughed. "Let's have both. I'll bring the champagne."

The huge wood-paneled, beamed kitchen was filled with the savory aromas of cooking. Ira set the round maple table at one side of the kitchen for two, sauntered out behind the house to pick a handful of camellias to add a festive touch. Laura was comfortable in a club chair in the living room, shoes kicked off while she concentrated on the screenplay.

Ira checked the spaghetti and the sauce. Both would be ready in two minutes. Time to poach the scallops, the first course. With the scallops simmering in the wine, he pulled the garlic bread out of the oven, the salad bowl from the refrigerator. Odalie had walked out of his life and all was right with the world. Well, comparatively right. Who expected perfection?

"Ira, I have to warn you of one thing—" Laura's voice swung him about; he had not heard her come into the kitchen. "When you get a nomination for an Academy Award for this thing—" She held the manuscript aloft. "You can't show up in a turtleneck with your tux."

"You like it?"

"I'm buying it," Laura told him. "It'll sell movie tickets like crazy."

"Come sit down," he said. "Dinner's almost ready."

"Ira, it'll be a major movie. How can you be so

blasé about it?" Laura stared at him in frustration. "You've got a sensational career ahead of you."

"Laura, I'm thirty-eight years old. So far all I've done is make a mess of my life. Forgive me if I can't get excited about a shitty screenplay."

"You are one of the most respected directors on Broadway, Ira. You're a terrific writing talent. At thirty you were the Boy Wonder of Broadway. At forty," she predicted, "you'll be the hottest screenwriter in Hollywood."

"Sit down and eat, Laura. There won't be any more screenplays. When this one is wrapped up—after the producer demands his changes and the director comes up with his—I'm going back to New York."

"Ira, that's crazy!"

"I'll rent a little house out at Montauk and settle down to write a novel." He refrained from mentioning that the first draft of the novel was two-thirds written. It had been his escape from Odalie. "I know what will happen if I stay out here. I'll be a *product*. Don't tell me otherwise—"

"But Ira, you can make so damn much money," Laura said softly.

"I've got enough stashed away to keep me comfortable for quite a while. I don't want to be part of the Hollywood circus. You gobble it up. I hate it. And damn it, I want some control over what I write. In the theater the playwright's at the mercy of the producer, the director, every actor in the cast. Everyone wants to rewrite. In Hollywood it's the same situation. Publishing is still more civilized. At least, in some instances. I've heard the publishing horror stories too—but they're not the norm. You write your novel. You work with one editor."

"What are you going to write about in this novel?" Laura pursued, settling herself at the table while Ira opened the bottle of vintage champagne she had brought.

"It's my first try," he said slowly. "So let's say it's like a school exercise. I'll write about Hollywood. I've had a crash course in the movie business in the close-to-two years I've been out here. I'll cut my teeth on that."

"It'll be a smashing best-seller," Laura said. "People love to read about Hollywood."

Ira smiled.

"The only thing I'll miss in Hollywood will be you."

"If I could ever be faithful to one guy, it'd be you," Laura mused. "But I'll never be faithful to anything but my career."

"How about being unfaithful with me sometime before 1974 rolls in?" he asked. Sometimes he didn't see Laura for years at a time, but in bed it was always as though they were back in that sleazy flat on East Fifth Street: sensational sex, no commitments.

"Why do you think I brought along the champagne?" Laura said. "To get you zonked so I can take advantage of you. But not too zonked. I expect plenty of action before the new year rolls around."

On Jeffrey's ninth birthday he received gifts from Ira and Ira's parents—forwarded, as usual, from the Fifth Avenue House. At Hanukkah and on his birthday gifts always arrived. His father never remembered until weeks later. This year, of course, Tom had a good excuse.

Devoted as always to the Broadway and Hollywood gossip columns—even in Paris, Deirdre learned that Odalie had divorced Ira and remarried, and that Ira was writing a screenplay. Diane knew that meant he was really depressed, and she was troubled that he had succumbed to Hollywood.

A week after Jeffrey's birthday she received a phone call from Clay.

"Di, has anybody called you about Tom?"

"What about Tom?" Alarm turned her cold.

"He was shot this morning by a fanatic mill worker. It's been on all the newscasts." He paused. "He was killed, Di."

"Oh, God." *Tom dead.* It didn't seem possible.

"You can come home now," Clay said gently.

"I suppose I should take Jeffrey to the funeral—" Jeffrey no longer had a father. But then, Tom had never been a real father.

"It's the right thing to do, Di. Call Atlanta and find out what the plans are. And Di, it'll be great to have you home again."

"I hadn't thought it would be this way—"

"We don't control fate, darling. I won't be a hypocrite and say I'm sorry."

They talked another few minutes. When Diane hung up, she was trembling. *They had been married. Tom was Jeffrey's father.* While she sat trying to gather herself together, the phone rang again. It was Arthur Lewisohn with the news.

"Jeffrey will be an heir," he reminded. "I'll be in touch with Tom's lawyers."

"Thank you, Arthur. I'm calling Atlanta to talk to his daughters about the funeral. I don't think there'll be any problem about airline reservations at this time of year. I expect to leave for New York tomorrow morning."

Diane phoned Tom's daughter Betsy first. The servant who replied reported—when Diane identified herself—that Betsy was at Jill's house with their mother.

Diane placed a call to Jill's Atlanta house. She sat tense and shaken while she waited for the call to be put through. Then Jill's voice, cold and imperious, came on the line.

"Yes, what is it?"

"Jill, it's Diane. I was so shocked to hear about your father—"

"Hold on." Diane heard her voice from a distance. "It's Diane, mom."

"I don't want her at the funeral!" Tammy Lee shrieked. "You tell her not to come, you hear?"

"Diane, if you're calling about the funeral, don't bother to come," Jill said. "We don't want you there. And don't think about bringing Jeffrey. Nobody ever believed he was daddy's child."

For a moment, Diane was too shocked to speak.

"How dare you talk like that!"

"She only wanted a child with Tom so she could get to his money!" Tammy Lee said.

"Jill," Diane forced herself to sound calm, "tell your mother Jeffrey doesn't need his father's money. He'll do very well without the Mason family."

Diane and Deirdre decided to end their exile as

soon as possible. A week after the news of Tom's death, they were at Orly Airport awaiting their New York-bound flight. By midnight New York time they were circling JFK.

Emerging through Customs, Diane was besieged by reporters. In dark glasses and a black wig, Deirdre went unrecognized. Mrs. Evans spirited Jeffrey—bewildered by the reporters and cameramen—away from the tumult while Diane and Deirdre tried to cope with the press.

When at last they reached the waiting limousine, Diane was grateful to discover that Jeffrey was dozing against Mrs. Evans's shoulder.

"I'd forgotten about the press," Diane said bitterly. "How did they know we'd be on this flight?"

"Somebody always tips them off," Deirdre said. "Reporters have to earn a living, too."

The following morning Diane called Arthur Lewisohn.

"I went to Atlanta for the reading of the will," he said. "Tom left the entire mill complex to Jeffrey. Everything else goes to his daughters. They've learned about the trust fund and are furious. They're threatening to sue to overturn the will because of the trust fund, but I'm sure their lawyers will explain that would be futile."

"Arthur, if they want the mills so badly, let them have them." Diane recoiled from even the threat of litigation.

"His father meant for the mills to go to Jeffrey," Arthur said. "Until he's twenty-one you'll act on his behalf. Actually, the mills are under capable management—there will be little required of you. I looked into the matter thoroughly while I was in Atlanta."

"You're absolutely right," Diane said. "Jeffrey should inherit the mills. And since I'll be acting in his behalf, let the mill workers know that the new owner approves of a union for the Mason mills. Will you inform the management of this, please?"

Arthur chuckled.

"With pleasure, Diane. You've won the everlasting gratitude of a lot of people."

Laura sat at her desk at TDM surrounded by a cluster of high-priced lawyers.

"All right," she said tersely. "You've read all the legal documents. You've talked to Tom's attorneys. Where do I stand?"

"The executors have orders to sell out. His family wants no part of the film business," Korman, the senior member of the law firm, said. "They've already had an offer from Kelsey Productions."

Laura made no effort to hide her astonishment. "That's a major studio. Why do they want to swallow up a mini-major?"

"The bottom line, Laura," Alan Goldberg, the youngest member of the firm, said. "TDM has made a lot of money since it went into operation."

"The deal should go through," Korman said. "There won't be any major changes. They'll retain the regular staff. Instead of reporting to Tom Mason, you'll report to Clifford Watson."

"Clifford Watson has been pretty firm in his dislike of women in the boardrooms of films," Laura shot back. "If he keeps me on, it'll simply be to show the world how open-minded he's become." *Everything she had worked for all these years now hung in the balance.* "And he figures all the publicity he'll get for keeping a woman in a top studio spot will in some way cover his gaffe of letting Bobby Blair get away." Bobby Blair had been responsible for half a dozen top box-office hits. The stockholders were teed off that Watson let him move on to independent producing.

"Laura, you'll have to play it by ear," Alan Goldberg said. "Expect to hear from Clifford Watson within the next six weeks."

"I'll stand by," Laura said. "For now, anyway."

Who the hell would have expected Tom Mason to be murdered? She didn't trust Clifford Watson. He'd use her until he figured his image in the film business had improved. Then he'd dump her. To Clifford Watson—like to many others in Hollywood—women in pictures were either actresses or secretaries.

Chapter Thirty-Nine

Diane immersed herself in the interior design shop. While Clay had enormous talent, he found it difficult to schedule himself in a practical fashion, so Diane handled business details and dealt with prospective clients. She and Clay worked together along creative lines as though they were two parts of a whole. Deirdre, slim again after six weeks at Maine Chance, called herself their "go-for."

Within six months they had expanded the shop to the point where it was necessary to hire outside help. Diane convinced Clay that they should open a branch in Palm Beach. Though they knew their names attracted clients, they also knew they were offering a highly respected service. The knowledge was intoxicating.

In December Clay went down to Palm Beach to set up the branch shop. With her entourage Diane flew down to work with him for a month. Clay would remain until April, when the shop would be turned over to the local assistants. Both Diane and Clay emphasized that their own ideas would be in every assignment they accepted.

Caught up in the excitement of their success, Clay insisted they hire a promotion woman. Their clients proliferated. They planned to open up a branch in Southampton. With summer breathing down their necks, Diane and Clay searched for an available shop.

By the first of June, the Southampton shop on fashionable Job's Lane was ready for its official opening. Diane was already in residence at the beach house. Deirdre, too, had opened up her small house. Jeffrey would attend a local day camp rather than go to a "sleepaway." Diane remembered Mrs. Ross's admonition that for some young children the separation could be devastating, and she felt guilty for having avoided contact with Ira's family since the divorce. She had cherished that relationship.

Now Diane moved around the shop in a last-minute inspection as Deirdre flipped through a collection of New York newspapers.

"Here's an item in Liz Smith's column about Ira!" Deirdre leaped to her feet. "He's written a novel and it's already been sold for a major movie!"

"Let me see—" Diane reached for the folded-back newspaper. She was thirty-five years old; when was she going to stop reacting like a lovesick sixteen-year-old every time she heard something about Ira?

"Liz Smith says it's supposed to be a *roman à clef.* Oh Di, do you think it's about *you?*"

"Dee, no. Ira wouldn't do anything like that." *Would he?* The Ira she had known would not have married an exhibitionist like Odalie, either, wouldn't have allowed himself to become part of the

666

"in" Hollywood scene.

"I can't wait to read it," Deirdre said. "I wonder if it's in the stores yet? Let's go over to Bookhampton South and see if they have it!"

A pyramid of *Reach for the Top* by Ira Ross was featured in a window display. Mindful that everybody in Southampton was aware that she had once been married to Ira, Diane sent Deirdre in alone to buy a copy of the book. According to the clerk, *Reach for the Top,* officially not yet published, was already reaching for the best-seller lists.

Deirdre said she would stay up all night if necessary to read the novel.

"I'll give it to you in the morning, Di. Before Elise gets her hands on it. She'll probably love it."

In the morning Deirdre reported that Ira had not written one word that could be construed as being about Diane.

"But Odalie is there," she announced with relish. "Oh, wow, did Ira get his revenge on her!"

Despite her conviction that she would hate *Reach for the Top,* Diane read every blistering page. It *was* a page turner, she had to admit. But it was disturbing, too; not at all like Ira. Still, she was sure it would be a huge commercial success.

In the coming weeks Diane and Deirdre saw Ira on various talk shows, read interviews, were aware of the avalanche of TV and radio commercials for the book. It rose from number ten to number one on the best-seller charts.

Diane threw all her energies into the Southampton shop, which was a success almost from the first day. When the shop closed for the season in October, Clay took off for Europe to buy antiques.

One day Diane read in a *New York Times* ad that Ira would appear for an autograph session at Barnes and Noble the following day. Deirdre went in to buy a book and rushed to tell Diane that Ira had asked about Jeffrey and her.

"He looks marvelous with that Hollywood tan," Deirdre bubbled. "Better looking than ten years ago."

"Dee, you are man-crazy," Diane said.

"So I chase around to single bars." Deirdre shrugged. "Sex is a natural instinct."

"The singles bars are dangerous," Diane objected. "You might pick up some psycho—he could kill you."

"Did I tell you Mike's paid off his whole loan? There was a note with the check. He claims he's been in therapy for almost two years. He says he's okay now."

"Well?" Diane demanded.

"Well what?" Deirdre gazed back ingenuously.

"Dee, you divorced him because he couldn't do anything in bed. You've never stopped loving him—"

"He just said he was okay, Di. He didn't say, let's give it a whirl again. Maybe he found somebody great on a test run. So who cares?"

When Clay returned from his European buying jaunt, he persuaded Deirdre to accompany him to Hong Kong, Singapore, and Tokyo in late April. Diane was pleased. She'd been nervous about

Deirdre's addiction to single bars, where she went in her inevitable dark-glasses-and-black-wig disguise and was never recognized.

While Deirdre was throwing herself into frenzied shopping prior to the Far East jaunt, Diane received a phone call from Mrs. Ross. She sounded nervous but determined.

"Darling, we haven't seen you and Jeffrey in such a long time—and Jeffrey's still my third grandchild." She was talking with unfamiliar speed, as though to forestall Diane's cutting her off. "Ira's out on another promotion tour—for the paperback edition of *Reach for the Top*," she said pointedly, "and Marcia's in Israel for six weeks. We'd love to have Jeffrey and you for the first seder next week. A Jewish child should know about a seder."

"We'll be there, mom," Diane said. "Thanks for inviting us."

Throughout the evening, Diane was conscious of Ira's absence. But Jeffrey was delighted with the reunion.

Diane knew that Ira's parents yearned to bring Ira and her together again. But Ira was caught up in success. There was no room in his new life for her. *The Ira she had loved was dead.*

A few days after the seder Diane joined a nearby Reform temple. She enrolled Jeffrey in Sunday school. He would know his Jerish heritage. At thirteen he would celebrate his bar mitzvah.

Only ten days before Clay and Deirdre were scheduled to leave for Hong Kong, Deirdre decided not to go. There was nothing Clay could say to change her mind.

"Find out what's bugging Deirdre," he asked Diane. "She's acting weird."

Clay's flight was an hour late in taking off. It was past midnight by the time Diane and Deirdre were driving over the Queensborough Bridge back into Manhattan.

"Stay over at my apartment tonight?" Deirdre asked. "Elise is still away on vacation. God, Con Ed stock must go up every time Elise takes off for a week—I leave on every light in the apartment."

"Stay at my place, Dee," Diane said.

"Of course, I could go to a singles bar," Deirdre said casually.

"Dee, you told me you were cutting out of that scene," Diane said. "You said you'd gotten the message."

Deirdre's expression changed.

"I got a different message from a singles bar."

"Dee, you didn't pick up something from one of those creeps?"

"We'll talk up in the apartment. Mine."

After Deirdre unlocked the door to her apartment, Diane pounced.

"Dee, what's happening?"

"I picked up this really nice guy about two weeks ago. He's a doctor—just through a bad divorce. I went up to his place. We went to bed and it wasn't bad. Not great, but not bad."

"Dee, stop stalling."

"He said—he said when he was feeling my breasts, he found a lump in the right one. He told me I ought to have a doctor look at it."

"Did you?" *Aunt Claudia.*

"No." Deirdre's eyes were frightened. "Not yet."

"You're seeing a doctor tomorrow," Diane said firmly. "I'll go with you. It's probably nothing, but you have to check it out."

At eleven A.M. the next morning, Diane and Deirdre, along with four other women of assorted ages, sat in Dr. Weinstein's pleasantly furnished reception room.

Diane was grateful that Dr. Weinstein had agreed to see Deirdre immediately. Pale and with dark crescents beneath her eyes, her face devoid of makeup this morning, Deirdre reached for a copy of *Town and Country*. Her hands were trembling.

Twenty minutes later, as though approaching the electric chair, Deirdre walked into Dr. Weinstein's office. Diane had almost convinced herself that Deirdre had nothing more than a benign lump, that it might not even need to be removed. After all, Deirdre was only thirty-seven. Aunt Claudia had been in her seventies when her lump was discovered.

It couldn't be the same thing.

It seemed like hours before Deirdre came out of Dr. Weinstein's office. She looked relaxed, Diane decided. The news must be good.

"Let's go out for coffee, Di. Dr. Weinstein's having the pictures developed right away. His technician said they'd be ready in an hour."

"He doesn't think it's anything, does he?"

"That's his guess," Deirdre said, "but we'll both

671

feel better when he sees the pictures." Deirdre smiled. "What cancer would have the guts to push itself on me? I mean, at my age?"

The receptionist was preparing to leave as Diane and Deirdre returned.

"Dr. Weinstein is waiting for you in his office," she said with a professional smile. "Please go right in."

"Come with me," Deirdre whispered and Diane followed.

Looking serious but calm, Dr. Weinstein explained that there was a growth in Deirdre's breast. There was a possibility it was malignant.

"You mean I have cancer?" Deirdre said quietly.

"We won't know until the surgeon gets in there. But we have to be prepared for that," Dr. Weinstein explained gently.

Diane and Deirdre listened while he explained the different types of mastectomies—and Deirdre remembered Claudia's surgery. Dr. Weinstein wanted Deirdre to see Dr. Roman—Claudia's surgeon—the following morning. He had already phoned to schedule an emergency appointment.

Three afternoons later Deirdre entered the hospital. Diane remained with her in her suite until visiting hours were over.

"I'm thirty-seven years old," Deirdre said defiantly as Diane leaned over to kiss her goodnight. "I can't have cancer."

"I'll be here tomorrow morning," Diane said. "I'm sure we'll be laughing about having been so scared."

*　　　*　　　*

Diane felt herself reliving a nightmare as she waited for Deirdre to emerge from the operating room. Remembering that if Deirdre was moved into the recovery room within two hours, the mass in her breast was benign. If she remained in surgery until well into the afternoon, Deirdre would have lost the breast.

It was almost three when Dr. Roman told Diane that Deirdre was in the recovery room. She had been given a "simple" mastectomy. Only the breast itself had been removed.

Diane went directly to Deirdre's suite, along with the private nurse, when Deirdre was wheeled into the bedroom.

Deirdre was heavily sedated. She seemed unaware of the presence of anyone in her suite when she was brought to her bed. Diane lingered for half an hour, then went home. Earlier she had ordered flowers to fill every corner of the room. She remembered how Tom had sent flowers to her aunt. Even now it was difficult to believe that Tom was dead.

Each morning Diane went to the hospital to sit beside Deirdre, saying little, holding her hand while Deirdre stared at the ceiling. When Deirdre was ready to talk, she would.

On the fourth day Diane arrived in the morning after a brief visit to Saks. She brought a dozen silk nightgowns of the kind Deirdre adored and an assortment of designer robes. Deirdre watched the unwrapping ceremony and burst into sobs.

"What man will ever want me like this? I'm not a woman. I'm a *thing*. I don't want to live anymore! Why didn't I die in surgery?"

"That's selfish," Diane scolded. "I need you. Clay needs you." She was frightened by Deirdre's expression. *What was she plotting?* She had to warn the nurses. "Millions of women have mastectomies. They go on to lead normal lives. This is not the end of the world, Deirdre."

"It's the end of my world," Deirdre said bitterly. "I've had all I want of this life." Deirdre turned her face away from Diane. "Go home, Di."

Diane stood immobile for an instant. Deirdre had never rejected her with such finality. Only that brief period during her marriage to Lenny. They were as close as two friends could be. In rejecting her, Deirdre was rejecting life.

In a sudden burst of emotion, Diane left the suite and hurried downstairs to a public telephone. She called information, scribbled down the requested number in a shaky scrawl, and began to dial.

The only person in this world to bring Deirdre back to the living was Mike. She prayed that he was in the city and not off on a case.

"Thomas Investigations," a blithe young voice greeted her.

"May I talk to Mike? Tell him it's Diane Dickenson."

The miracle Diane prayed for happened. Mike came back into Deirdre's life. He was stubborn, refusing to be rejected, grateful that he was needed. He was at her bedside every day. Warm and loving.

"And I'm all right now, honey," he boasted. "You were right all the time. I needed help."

"Can you stand there and tell me you want to do it with me now?" Deirdre challenged. "When I'm butchered this way?"

"Shall I climb into bed with you right now and prove it?"

"I think the two of you had better wait," Diane laughed.

"It doesn't disgust you that I have only one breast?"

"Honey, one's enough for any man." He turned to Diane. "I love you like a sister, Di; but would you please get the hell out of here so I can make my wife understand how much I want her? Before the nurse gets back?" He reached for Deirdre's hand. "You're still my wife. A few words in Mexico didn't change that."

Chapter Forty

Six weeks after Deirdre's surgery Diane was helping her zip up her Halston wedding dress. Deirdre had insisted on delaying her remarriage until Clay was back home, though Mike had returned to her bed. She proclaimed him "sensational."

"I'll stay thin forever," she said, turning in front of the mirror. "But even if I don't, Mike will love me." She gazed happily at her reflection in the mirror, touched a silken strand of newly auburn hair. "What do you think? Mike loves the new color." Now she squinted hard at Diane. "Darling, do I see gray in that gorgeous black hair?"

Diane laughed.

"It *has* been sneaking in."

"Make an appointment at Jon Guenter's tomorrow," she ordered. "Ask for Pam. She's great."

"Dee, I'm not concerned about a few gray hairs—" But it *had* unnerved her to see those reminders that *in three years she would be forty.*

"Di, I insist you make an appointment with Pam.

How much longer are you staying out of circulation? Do you plan to wait until Jeffrey's in college to go out with somebody besides Clay?"

"We have to leave." Diane checked her watch. "It's bad luck to be late for your own wedding."

Diane had not realized how painful it would be to stand again in the living room of the judge who had married Tom and her as well as Deirdre and Mike. Her mind charged back to the day that Ira and she had been married in his parents' apartment. Her only real wedding.

She still wondered if she had been too quick to push Ira out of her life. *No.* She didn't need Ira—she didn't need any man. She had been a failure at marriage. A three-time failure. At last she was successful at something. Everybody needed a sense of self-worth. She had that now.

She was touched by Deirdre and Mike's obvious happiness as the judge read the marriage ceremony. She would never feel that kind of happiness again. For a little while she had shared it with Ira. But that Ira was long gone. *She* had changed, too. They were two different people now.

Early in June, Ira's second novel was published and even before the official publication date it had already hit the best-seller charts.

This summer she and Clay were busy redoing a Southampton house for a New York publisher, Joshua Paul. It would be a jewel of a house, Clay declared. A magazine spread was already planned. There would be a lavish open house early in July when she and Clay would turn the house over to Joshua and Shira Paul.

Clay and she were guests of honor at the open house, both elated by the praise being heaped upon them as the interior designers.

"I have a marvelous idea for you two," Joshua Paul said, his arm around Diane as he herded her and Clay away from the conviviality in the drawing room and onto the terrace. "Why don't you put your heads together on a decorating book? I'll assign an editor to work with you from the beginning."

"But we're not writers," Diane said. "We couldn't possibly—"

"Of course we can," Clay said. "It's not like writing a novel. It'll be on a subject that we live and breathe every day." He turned to Paul. "Diane has this terrifically organized mind. She'll organize and I'll contribute ideas."

"Let's see . . . I'll assign Eleanor French to work with you. She'll be an enormous help. She's worked on several nonfiction books for us."

Clay was genuinely excited.

"Josh, I can't wait to get started! It'll be a hell of a lot more fun than showing up in the Grill Room of the Crillon in drag." Today it was all right to be candid about his homosexuality. At least, in sophisticated circles.

Contracts were drawn up in a few days and signed. Diane and Clay met for a business luncheon at the Four Seasons with Joshua Paul and Eleanor French. Over pâté with pistachio nuts followed by red snapper in vermouth with raw mushrooms and Malabra dressing, they worked out a rough outline of what the book would cover. Diane promised herself that this new venture would fill the void in her life created by Ira's absence.

Over chocolate velvet and coffee, Paul brought up advertising and publicity.

"You're both promotable, so we'll be sending you on an extensive book tour—"

"We can't take long periods of time away from the business," Diane broke in, alarmed at this prospect of the venture.

"We'll take turns," Clay said. "Of course the public will prefer seeing glamorous Diane Dickenson, but in some cities they'll just have to make do with me."

"You've been an actress," Eleanor French added. "That's a plus, too."

Diane focused on her chocolate velvet while the other three talked. It seemed strange to be moving into a field in which Ira had been so successful. But in her mind she could *see* the book taking shape. She was excited about putting their design ideas on paper.

"It'll be an expensive project because of all the color plates required, but that means less text for you two," Joshua was saying. "You'll be able to bring the book in around January. We'll start work now on the illustrations. Let's plan tentatively for a publication date in early fall of 1977."

To Diane's amazement, the book began to monopolize their lives. She and Clay worked every night and every weekend, driven to bring together the material that Eleanor would shape into a book. There was time in her life only for the business, the book, and, as always, Jeffrey. That was another obsession: not to cheat Jeffrey out of time with his mother.

In December Ira's mother called to invite Jeffrey to a Hanukkah party at Kathy's house. When Diane explained that she was too tied up to take him and Mrs. Evans was off for the day, Mrs. Ross insisted she would pick up Jeffrey, take him to the party, and bring him home.

"I'm still his adopted grandmother, Diane. Let him come. He'll enjoy the party."

After the party Jeffrey gave an exuberant report of the happenings.

"Guess who was there near the end?" His face was incandescent. "Uncle Ira! He didn't think I'd remember him, but I did."

For a moment Diane was angry. How dare mom try to use Jeffrey to bring Ira and her together? Couldn't she understand that what they had was dead?

Late in December, Eleanor French proclaimed the book complete. They scheduled a publication date in late September. A special publicist would be brought in to set up a promotion tour. Eleanor approved of Clay's suggestion that he and Diane appear in a TV commercial for the book.

With the book out of the way, Diane was able to see more of Deirdre, who was now eager to become pregnant. *"Before I'm forty, please God."* Mike insisted she check with the doctor. When she did, he warned that there was a faint possibility that

681

pregnancy would reactivate any cancer cells left in her body. Mike ruled out any pregnancy. They would adopt.

After luncheon with Deirdre on a springlike day early in April, Diane returned to the shop to receive a call from her mother. She was unnerved to hear that Olivia was recuperating in a Swiss hospital after a suicide attempt.

"Diane, Leon told me I was *old*. I just lost my mind for a few minutes."

"Mother, would you like to come home?"

"Lord, no." Diane heard the shudder in her voice. "I loathe New York. I'm having some tucks done here. I'll be in Palm Beach in February. Diane—" Her voice was almost coquettish. "You don't think I'm old, do you?"

"Of course not, mother."

"How's little Jeffrey?"

"He's fine." No point in going into the details. "He's doing very well in school."

"Darling, I have to go now. The hairdresser just arrived."

By August a few major reviews came in on the book. They were good, not great, but Joshua Paul was pleased. He was confident that Diane Dickenson and Clay Brentwood were strong enough names to shoot the book up onto the best-seller lists.

"It's just a matter of getting the proper TV and radio exposure. We're lining up every important talk show across the country. And a lot of unimportant ones, too. We want to reach every reader out there. This is not going to be just another coffee-table book. You've got something to sell that the public wants.

That little bride out in Duluth can do her house with Diane and Clay.''

A coach was brought in to work with Diane and Clay to help them radiate charm and charisma. A voice coach was provided. They were taught to handle their own TV makeup in the event a makeup person wasn't available. Eleanor French staged fake interviews so they would be accustomed to the kind of questions that would be thrown at them.

Though their publication date was officially September twentieth, Joshua explained that books would be shipped to the dealers in mid-August. As early as July column items had appeared on *Decorate With Di and Clay*. In August Clay set off for a five-week tour.

He called Diane regularly, usually in a state of exhaustion and exhilaration. He enjoyed the frenetic pace of TV and radio interviews, ladies' luncheons, and autograph sessions in bookstores.

Diane was tense when he returned to New York, and it was her turn to go out to plug the book. Joshua sent her out in the company of an enterprising and enthusiastic publicist, Andrea Gaines, who arranged for limousines, registered her at hotels, and found the best dining spots.

A day usually included six-to-eight TV or radio interviews and, frequently, lunch with a newspaper interviewer. Diane requested only that they cover no more than one city per day. Still, she was exhausted by the time they arrived in San Francisco.

Andrea registered them at the elegant Fairmont Hotel on Nob Hill. Diane insisted they have dinner in their suite rather than go downstairs to the opulent Venetian Room. Immediately after dinner they retired to their bedrooms. Diane had issued strict orders for Andrea, who had a bad cold, to ignore the wake-up call in the morning and stay in bed for the day.

At 5:30 A.M. sharp the switchboard operator called. Diane was already out of the shower. She phoned room service for breakfast. The limousine would pick her up at 6:30 to take her to the first TV interview.

Over breakfast she went over her day's schedule. In addition to the TV and radio shots she would be lunching at Trader Vic's with a newspaper reporter. No time, she thought, to shop at Gump's for a present for Deirdre.

The day went smoothly. When the limousine returned her to the Fairmont shortly past seven P.M., Diane sauntered into the hotel with a pleasant sense of accomplishment. Crossing to the elevator, she stopped dead. No more than forty feet away was Ira. He was dressed in an elegant three-piece suit, and was immersed in conversation with an attractive young woman—at least ten years younger than I, Diane thought with a pang. They were probably going to the Venetian Room. She knew that Ira, too, was on the book-promotion circuit. How odd that they should cross paths this way . . .

Later that night, unable to sleep, she called the Fifth Avenue house to talk to Claudia and Jeffrey, and then phoned Deirdre. She felt inexplicably home-sick. She didn't tell Deirdre about the near-encounter with Ira; thrilled with her own happy marriage, Deirdre seemed to want everybody happily married.

She wasn't up to Deirdre's well-intentioned efforts, not tonight.

The girl with Ira was probably a reporter or someone from his publisher's office traveling with him to ease the strain of the tour, she reasoned. For a moment she thought of calling his room. *No.* She turned off the bedside lamp. What was dead could not be resurrected.

Chapter Forty-One

Laura sat across the table at La Scala and tried to appear enthusiastic about this evening conference with Clifford Watson, chairman of the board of Kelsey Productions. She knew he was dying to throw her out of the studio. Every woman in a top position in the film world—and they were only a handful—was a personal affront to him.

She was president of production for the TDM division of Kelsey Productions. She earned two hundred thousand dollars a year, plus perks and bonuses. She was quite possibly the most powerful woman in Hollywood, answering only to Cliff. But if Cliff latched on to an excuse to push her out, he'd be ecstatic. There was no one to help her in this situation. She was completely on her own.

"We need to tie up a hot property," Clifford said smoothly. "Something that's bankable." His smile was bland. "I'm counting on you to come up with something, Laura."

Here it was. Either she produced something so big

that Cliff wouldn't dare fire her—or there'd be one less red Ferrari in the studio parking lot.

"Ira Ross is finishing up his new novel," Laura tossed into the ring. "It hasn't been put up for grabs yet."

"You got an inside track with Ross?" Cliff straightened up like a hound nearing the kill.

"Something like that." *Play it cool.* "Also, I bought his screenplay for TDM four years ago. Before an agent even saw it." Before Cliff's company took over. "I could fly out and make a pitch. He's holed up at his house in Montauk trying to polish off the last draft. I talked to him on the phone last week."

"Leave tomorrow, Laura." He leaned back in his chair. "I'll cover for you at the studio for a couple of days. I'll go up to half a million for the movie rights. That's a bundle, even to Ira Ross. But read the manuscript first. Even Ross can come up with a dog."

"I'll call and tell him to expect me."

Within three hours, Laura had reservations for a New York flight the following morning. She'd phoned Ira to say she'd be out to visit for a few hours the next day, then called a New York limousine service to reserve a car to drive her back into New York the same night. She'd catch a couple of hours sleep at the hotel at JFK before flight time. She didn't want to be away from the studio a day longer than necessary when Cliff was out for her hide.

By two the following afternoon, she was in the hired limousine and on her way to Montauk. She'd brought along a manuscript to read, but it was hard to concentrate. A lot was at stake here; she had to do

688

this right.

Traffic was light on a weekday in October. Laura had forgotten how beautiful autumn could be in New York.

She knew she'd have to read the manuscript first. Cliff was right: the most commercial of novelists could have a spectacular flop. Then she'd make the pitch.

Ira had come a long way in the past four years. Would he be as malleable as he had been with the screenplay? He had accepted her offer without quibbling, signed a contract—without an agent—that had brought approval from the legal department. He had an agent now, but knowing Ira she was confident *he* would have the final say about any negotiations. It was only because of their friendship that he had gone along with the screenplay sale without asking questions.

By four P.M. the limousine was gliding into Montauk. The driver stopped at a filling station for gas and to ask directions. Laura smelled the sea. An ocean breeze lent a brisk chill to the air, and she was glad she had worn a suit. After years in California, she was quick to feel the cold.

The driver slid behind the wheel.

"It's a couple of miles out on Old Montauk Highway. We'll be there in a few minutes."

"Drop me at the house and go off for some sightseeing," she said. "Have dinner somewhere. Try Gosman's. It's great for seafood. And it's pretty close. Just be back by ten."

Laura remembered that Ira said there was a chain across the driveway and a small sign bearing his name stuck into the grass.

"There's the house—" Laura pointed toward the ocean side of the road.

The driver left her at the entrance to the property and moved off. As she walked up the pebbled driveway toward the house, she saw Ira appear on the wrap-around deck. He'd heard the car.

"Hi!" He was charging from the deck and toward her.

"Ira, you look terrific," she said when they had kissed. "I thought you'd be beat from the tour and the rewriting."

"I recuperate out here," he said, an arm around her waist as they walked togther toward the house. "I sit out there on the front deck and stare down at the ocean, and all the tensions melt away. Until I go inside and look at the manuscript again."

"You're not happy with it?" She was instantly alert.

"The publisher's happy with it. My editor's happy with it. I asked for another six weeks to do more rewrites."

"Oh, Ira the perfectionist," she laughed. "Stop trying to be Faulkner or Steinbeck. You're doing commercial fiction. And you're sensational at it."

"First I spent years directing plays when I wanted to write them. Now I'm writing novels for which I have no taste—" He shook his head slowly. "There's no time—or place—to be Ira Ross."

"For God's sake, Ira, enjoy your success." She gazed at the sprawling redwood contemporary with masses of glass to take advantage of its spectacular locale. It must have cost at least four hundred thousand. "The books bought you this gorgeous house."

"How long will you be in the city?" Ira opened the side door to the house for her.

"I leave on an early-bird flight in the morning. I flew out to see you, because I want to read the new book. I'd like to make an offer."

"Laura, the book's still rough."

"May I read it?"

"Nobody but you and the publishing people. If it'll work as a movie, you'll know."

"Lead me to a comfortable chair, bring me the manuscript, and put up coffee. But first, could you point me in the direction of the powder room?"

Emerging from the guest bathroom and heading back to the living room, Laura paused at a collection of framed snapshots on one wall. Family, Laura realized—photographs of Diane and Jeffrey, among others.

"While you're reading, I'll run into town for a couple of steaks," Ira said casually, handing her the manuscript. "I'll grill them out on the deck later. You *will* take a dinner break?"

"Promise." She settled into a chair and kicked off her high-heeled Charles Jourdan pumps.

Ira brought her the manuscript, kissed her on the forehead, and walked out onto the front deck. Laura pulled out her reading glasses—a reluctant concession to the specter of her fortieth birthday—and began to read. Immediately, she was caught up in the story. After twenty pages, she knew it would be a great film. She had to persuade Ira to sell her the film rights *before* there was an auction. Cliff wouldn't dare fire her if she brought this in—it was sure to be a blockbuster.

"Take a break?" Ira said, two hours later. She had been vaguely aware of the aroma of charcoal-broiled steaks blending with the scent of the sea.

"Sure." She pulled off her glasses and put them with the manuscript on a side table. "Ira, the book's sensational. I don't have to read the rest to know. But I will. Thank God I'm a speedreader. This one's a biggie."

Ira smiled.

"Book buyers like long reads. Come out on the deck and have dinner."

Over steaks, baked potatoes, and salad, Laura plied Ira with questions about his book tours, wondering all the while how much to offer him for the film rights. If she brought the book in for less than the half-million Cliff was willing to go, she'd be in solid. What the hell, Ira had raked in enough already.

The major problem was to sew up a deal before Ira consulted with his agent.

"I hear the book Diane did with Clay is going great," Ira said.

"They had plenty of help." Laura smiled. "You know how it is with celebrity books."

"Do you ever see her?"

"Now and then." Laura stared hard at him. "Clay and she are doing marvelously with the shops, I understand. Of course, being Diane Dickenson and Clay Brentwood has been a great boost."

"Is she happy, Laura?" he said quietly.

"As much as anyone is, I suppose. What about you, Ira? Why can't you enjoy your success?"

"I don't like what I'm doing." He spread his hands in a gesture of futility. His eyes were troubled. "I'm forty-two years old and I haven't done a damn thing I set out to do. Maybe this is the mid-life crisis everybody's always talking about. It's especially tough when you're a bachelor with no family to prop you up. Sometimes I can't believe it." He shook his head. "Where did the years go?"

She took his hand.

"We're a long way from East Fifth Street, Ira."

He smiled, sadness in his eyes.

"What about you, Laura? Are you happy up there at the top?"

"I wouldn't give it up for anything in the world. I've got exactly what I want from life." She couldn't let herself believe otherwise. There was no room in her life for anything else. Not even Ira. Love was a luxury she couldn't afford. "Of course," she added, "I'm only there at the top as long as I can deliver. Ira, I want this new book."

"But you haven't finished reading it. Maybe it falls apart in the second half."

"All right, let me go inside and finish it." She stood up, looked at her watch. "I have time. My driver won't pick me up until ten." She saw the look of surprise in his eyes. He'd thought they would end up in bed. Not this time. She was here on business.

Close to ten o'clock Laura put down the manuscript.

"I still want to buy it, Ira. It's got a few minor plot problems, but overall it's solid. And it'll make a great movie."

"Okay." He looked pleased. "Talk to Morrie. I'll

tell him I want you to have it." His agent was a shrewd top-drawer manipulator who would be sure to milk her for every cent.

"Let's make the deal ourselves. Now. It's important to me, Ira."

He was silent for a moment.

"How much can you offer?"

"A quarter of a million. And the usual percentage of the net." A percentage of the net meant nothing because the company could finagle. Morrie would have demanded a percentage of the gross.

Ira paused. Thinking. Watching her.

"It's a deal. Call Morrie in the morning. I'll be in touch with him tonight."

While Laura slid her feet into her pumps and Ira came forward with her jacket, they heard the discreet honk of the limousine's horn at the foot of the driveway.

"Take care of yourself, darling." Laura lifted her face for a kiss.

Halfway into Manhattan Laura told the driver to take her into New York rather than to JFK. She'd find a hotel for the night and take a later flight out tomorrow, the better to talk to Morrie and sew up the deal first thing in the morning. She'd fly back to California with the knowledge that she had saved the company a quarter of a million. That ought to earn her a fat bonus. And while she was in the city, she'd have lunch with Diane. She owed Ira one.

Laura carried her weekender along with her from the Regency to the Four Seasons and checked it there before going into the Grill for lunch with Diane. Morrie was furious that Ira had made a deal without him, but there was nothing he could do about it—Ira made that clear. Laura had awakened Cliff at six o'clock California time to tell him to rush the contracts to Morrie. She smiled, remembering how impressed he'd been that she'd bought the book for one-half of what he was prepared to pay.

She had felt occasional pangs of guilt at cutting her offer to a quarter of a million. Still, she had to protect her own interests. Nobody else would.

Diane was already at their table. They greeted each other warmly and settled down to talk over glasses of white wine.

"I just came in from Montauk," Laura said. Instantly Diane looked uncomfortable. "I went out to spend a few hours with Ira. He has this gorgeous house on Old Montauk Highway. I went out to talk to him about his new book."

"For a movie?"

"Right. We're buying it. He asked about you and Jeffrey—"

"Oh?"

"He's still in love with you, Di," she said softly. "He has snapshots of Jeffrey and you on a wall in the house along with family."

"Ira can be very sentimental at times," Diane said carefully. "But he hasn't been in love with me for a long time." She sipped her wine. "How's the new book?"

"It'll be a best-seller. But you know Ira. He's never wanted to write anything that didn't have a message for humanity."

"Then why doesn't he?" Color touched the high ridges of Diane's cheekbones. "He certainly can afford to take time out to do anything he likes now."

"I think he's scared to gamble," Laura said. "He's at a crossroads in his life. He's lonely and unsure about his future. He said, 'I'm forty-two years old, and I haven't done a damn thing I set out to do. Maybe this is my mid-life crisis.' And he mentioned how hard it is to cope with when you have no family."

Diane wouldn't look her in the eye. "Ira has devoted parents. And a sister and brother-in-law who're very close."

"That wasn't what he meant. You know that. You and Jeffrey are his own family."

Diane shrugged.

"So he's having misgivings. Well, it's too late. He'll get over it."

For the rest of the day, Diane couldn't concentrate. That night, she couldn't sleep. Being around Deirdre and Mike highlighted her own loneliness, her feelings for Ira that had never changed. *Was there a chance that they could make it work again?*

She had been hurt and humiliated when Ira had walked out on her for Odalie. Now she forced herself to reexamine the situation. Ira had been so vulnerable then—and bringing up the notion of their adopting a child had only heightened that vulnerability. She had been insensitive to that. He had gone out, gotten drunk, and had the misfortune to run into Odalie. Maybe that was all there was to it.

She loved Ira. He'd loved her. Why had she let pride destroy their marriage?

As the darkness of night gave way to gray, she made her decision. Tomorrow morning she would drive out to Montauk to Ira's house. She had to find out the truth. Once and for all.

The next morning, she saw Jeffrey off to school and had Philippe bring the small Mercedes to the house. If traffic was reasonable, she would be in Montauk by noon.

By eleven-thirty she was on sun-washed Old Montauk Highway with Laura's directions, searching for Ira's house. *There it was.*

Her heart pounding, she pulled the Mercedes to a stop in front of a low gate, got out to remove the chain, then slid behind the wheel again and drove up to the house. Leaving the car in the driveway she heard the strains of the *Moonlight* Sonata. So Laura was right; Ira was depressed. She walked up the stairs to the deck and to the side door. Through the expanse of glass she saw Ira, in a gray turtleneck and jeans, sitting at the piano.

She knocked. Ira didn't seem to hear. She tried the door. It was open. She walked inside and crossed to Ira, hunched over the piano as he played.

"Ira—" He looked up. "I knocked but you didn't hear."

"Diane—" Stunned, he looked at her, looked around the room.

"I had lunch with Laura yesterday. She told me she'd bought the film rights to your new book." She

697

knew she sounded nervous. "I saw you last month in the lobby of the Fairmont Hotel. You were with someone. I didn't want to intrude."

"She was a newspaper reporter there to interview me over dinner."

"I figured." Her smile was wan.

"How's Jeffrey?"

"Fine. He's growing so fast all at once. He'll be thirteen in February."

"I know." His eyes met hers. "I miss him, Di. I miss you."

"We both miss you, Ira."

All at once he was holding her in his arms.

"Di, it's been so rotten without you."

"Make love to me, Ira," she whispered. "It's been so long."

Diane lay in Ira's arms, remembering their honeymoon.

"We'll be married again out here," Ira said. "On the beach at dusk, with the ocean as our symphony." He laughed. "Do you suppose it'll be a problem to erect a *chupah* on the sand?"

She smiled, her heart full.

"Knowing your mother, somehow she'll find a way."

"I'll never let you go again," he whispered. "We belong together. Jeffrey, you, and I."

"Jeffrey needs a father. I need a husband. We both need you." She hesitated. "Ira, you won't be upset if I continue with the shops? They won't come between us. I'm strong enough now not to let that happen."

"You'll keep on with your career and I'll redirect mine."

"Back to the theater? I think that's wonderful. Did I tell you how much I loved your play?"

"Several times, my love. I'm trying to turn it into a novel. The subject's more timely today than it was when the play hit Broadway. And I'll have more scope in a novel—"

Diane listened, sharing his excitement. She knew there would be rough times, but they would see them through together.

She had spent a lifetime of rootlessness. With Ira she would have stability.

Epilogue

The February Saturday morning was crisp and cold, the sky a brilliant blue when the sleek gray limousine drew to a stop before the temple. This morning was not only a celebration for the living, Diane told herself. With them this morning was her grandmother, who had lived a secret life behind a Coromandel screen, and her grandmother Seligman, whom she had sought out in a Westchester nursing home. Today, their great-grandson—Jeffrey Mason—was to celebrate his *bar mitzvah*.

Jeffrey jumped forward to open the door of the limousine without waiting for Philippe to perform this routine chore. Ira emerged, appearing endearingly solemn. He held out a hand to Diane. His eyes tender because he knew what this occasion meant to his wife.

"It's a beautiful day," Diane said. "God is pleased with you, Jeffrey," she teased. Radiant in her happiness.

They crossed the sidewalk to the wrought-iron

fence surrounding the temple property, the gates open wide in welcome. Diane reached for a hand of each of her two men while she paused at the bulletin board that had an announcement of the bar mitzvah.

Inside, Ira's parents sat in the first row. Jeffrey came forward to be embraced by his proud adopted grandparents.

Congregation members began to fill the seats. Soon Deirdre and Mike arrived, and moments later, Clay. Diane smiled. Almost all her family was here, except for Aunt Claudia. She couldn't expect her aunt—a fragile ninety now—to admit to herself, after all those years, that she was Jewish.

The services were about to commence. Through tears of pride Diane watched Jeffrey take his place on the *bimah*, the rabbi at the lectern on the left, the cantor at the lectern on the right. The cantor began to sing. "How lovely are your tents, O Jacob, your dwelling places, O Israel . . ."

Then the rabbi began the morning prayers. As the rabbi finished reading, Deirdre nudged Diane and pointed toward the rear of the temple. Walking slowly and proudly was Aunt Claudia, with Mrs. Avery at her side. She had come to terms with her own faith. Ira leaped to his feet to lead her to a seat beside Diane.

Tears of happiness filled Diane's eyes. Her entire family was here as one. When the time came for Jeffrey to take his place at the lectern, they listened as he began to recite the *Ve-ahavta*, the ancient adjuration:

And you shall love the Lord your God with all

your mind, with all your strength, with all your being. Set these words, which I command you this day, upon your heart. Teach them faithfully to your children; speak of them in your home and on your way, when you lie down and when you rise up . . .

Diane reached for Ira's hand. At last they'd come home. Together.